MW01222696

Choices: Victim or Victory

Rose's Legacy

MARSHA HOOD

Wishing you joy
+ success,
Marsha Hood

Rose's Legacy

By Marsha Hood

First Edition eBook: 2020
First Edition Paperback: 2020
ISBN (Paperback): 979-8561245343

Published in the United States of America

Dedication

For my parents, Carl and Ruth.

Thank you for your limitless love and faithful
guidance.

Part 1

In the world ye shall have tribulation: but be of good cheer; I have overcome the world.
John 16:33

Prologue

1963

Rose's hands trembled; her horrifying memories intensified. Perspiration beaded on her forehead and ran down her face and neck, her cotton dress sticking to her back and chest. Held captive by her terrifying past and devastating emotions, Rose sat motionless in her dark blue armchair. *I can't live like this anymore. My whole life I've been held in the grip of bitterness, hatred, and guilt. It won't let go...I can't shake it.*

Taking a deep breath, Rose forced herself to relax.

The house creaked in the sweltering summer heat. A small air conditioner in the front room window moaned as it worked hard to stir and cool the stifling air. The heavy drapes were drawn together against the glare of the sun.

Determination slowly set in. Rose took another deep breath and exhaled. It was time; she had to deal with this once and for all. The telephone sat on the end table beside her chair, daring her to make the call. As she glared at the phone, her breathing grew shallow and quick. Her heart rate increased. The walls seemed to be pressing in around her. The muggy air was hard to breathe. Rose opened and closed her hand as she reached for the telephone hand piece.

Lifting the receiver from the cradle of the phone, she fought the trembling in her arms and hands. Suddenly, the handpiece slipped from her fingers, bounced on the floor, and dangled by its coiled black cord.

Rose's doubts started to return as she watched the receiver swing back and forth just above the floor. *Who am I to tell someone—anyone—about what had happened? After all, am I not the one to blame? Wasn't it my fault?*

Staring at the phone's handpiece, she spoke into the still, hot air. "I don't need to do this. I've survived all these years without talking about it. Why should I now?"

She turned her face away from the phone, its receiver still dangling from the end of the cord, the dial tone sounding an angry buzz into the room. As she turned away, a picture on the wall caught her attention.

Above the couch hung her family's portrait. The bright eyes and smiling faces of her husband and children looked back at her. But even in the photograph, there was a familiar shadow of darkness in her eyes. Seeing the picture of herself with her family brought back her resolve. *After all these years, I'm tired of battling my emotions. I need to deal with this. I have to face these issues and talk to someone.* She looked down at the floor, now refusing to meet the smiling faces of her family.

She closed her eyes and let her shoulders droop. I want to live a normal life. Gradually releasing her breath, Rose slowly raised her head, pulled her shoulders back, and once more found her resolve. Reaching out, she grasped the dangling handpiece and put it up to her ear. I have to make the call. Now.

She dialed the phone number and watched as the wheel clicked noisily after each number.

A male voice answered, "Hello, this is Pastor Dave speaking."

She glanced back up at the family photo for reassurance.

With a quivering voice she addressed him, "Hi Pastor? This is R-Rose. I need to make an appointment to talk with you."

"Of course, Rose. When would be a good time?" he asked.

She knew she needed to do it now or she would change her mind. "Would right now work? If this isn't a good time, as soon as possible."

"Now would be fine." Pastor Dave immediately sensed the tension, the near panic in her voice. "Come on over to my office. I'll be expecting you."

"I'm on my way now."

Ten minutes later, Rose sat on the couch across from Pastor Dave, tears streaming down her cheeks. "Pastor, I n-need your help. I-I can't do this anymore." Rose sobbed. "I'm t-tired of reliving the past, and I need someone to talk to. You're the only person I could think of to call, the only one I felt I could trust." Her body shook with every sob. Fear to speak of the past and worry of judgment filled her being.

Pastor Dave got up from behind his desk and rolled his chair over in front of her. He sat down and leaned forward, putting his elbows on his knees and clasping his hands. She had his attention.

Looking compassionately into her eyes, he could see her pain and turmoil. His heart ached for her. Before Pastor Dave said anything, he sent up a silent prayer: *Lord, please give me Your wisdom and Your words to help Rose. Make Your presence known to her and give her a peace only You can give.*

Dave sat silently for a few minutes, waiting for Rose to calm down. Then quietly and gently he spoke. "Rose, I can see that you're hurting; your heart is broken. How can I help you?"

Rose tried to suppress her sobs. "Pastor, I-I can't let go of the past. I need to talk to someone." She paused, choking back another sob. "It keeps haunting me even though I give it to God over and over again. Instead of getting better, it keeps festering inside of me. I have tried to talk about it with my husband. He knows all about it, but he gets angry when I try to discuss it with him. He doesn't want to hear it, and I can't blame him."

The pastor sat quietly and continued to listen closely. Rose hesitated. "Pastor, I need to face the past and deal with it once and forever. Would you help me, listen to me, council me? I can't handle this hatred and bitterness anymore. It's tearing me up inside." Her eyes were begging him.

"Rose, I don't know anything about your past, but it sounds like it won't be easy to confront the issues, and it will probably take time," he warned. "But it looks to me like you might be ready and you being here suggests you're willing. I'm here for you. Would you like to tell me about it now?"

She took a deep breath, and with a shaky smile, she replied, "Thank you, Pastor. You have no idea how much this means to me."

Pastor Dave gave her a gentle smile and waited quietly.

Rose paused to think. Taking a handkerchief from her purse, she wiped her tears, blew her nose, and stuffed the cloth back into her purse. "M-my mother told me stories of things that happened before I was born and when I was a young child, I guess I'll start there…"

Rose stopped, took another deep breath, and began as she looked down to the floor to avoid the pastor's compassionate eyes. "I was born in the small rural town of

Emmett, Idaho. Even before I was born, chances that I
would survive were very slim…"

ONE

1927

The old Model T Ford skidded into the driveway, followed by a large cloud of dust. Doty shuddered; Fred was home. Her peaceful rest was over. She knew what was coming. Fred, whom she called Father, staggered into the one-room shanty with a half empty bottle of whiskey in his hand. Last night he had gone to get the midwife, but Doty hadn't seen him since.

He grabbed the door to steady himself and then walked over and took his first look at his newborn child. He shook his head and took a swig of whiskey. When he looked at the newborn, he didn't see a baby; he saw more responsibility. Doty knew his thoughts because they were hers too; *This was another mouth to feed, and he couldn't feed the mouths he already had.*

For a moment, Doty saw a look of helplessness come over Fred's face. Then his expression quickly changed to anger and then to despair. He stumbled back out of the house, onto the front porch, and slumped down into the old rocker, drinking till he passed out.

Fred spent the rest of the day and night sleeping it off.

Doty rested quietly on the worn mattress which lay on the floor in the corner of the one-room shanty. Covered by a grimy, handmade quilt, she cuddled her newborn daughter in her arms as she gazed at the infant. *At least Father notified the midwife. I'm glad she came and delivered my baby.*

Embracing her daughter, Doty kissed the child's forehead. Rose was the perfect name for this little girl; a beautiful flower born in the midst of a harsh land. *I think I'll call her Rosy.*

Rosy was the sixth child born to Doty and Fred. However, the first baby had been stillborn and the next two starved to death. Rose was the third surviving child. There were two older siblings, both sisters, Annabel, four years old and Carolyn, two.

April was a wonderful time of year to give birth; everything was fresh and new. Mother Nature seemed to be giving them a renewed start. The spring rains were beginning, and there would soon be plenty of fresh, much needed water. The semi-arid desert was coming to life. The grasses were greening and the bushes and flowers blooming. Birds nested wherever they could find a safe place; their songs were a pleasure to hear. The birth of her daughter made it feel even more like spring, more like a new beginning for her and her family. Doty lay back, relaxed, and gazed intently at her daughter with a mother's love in her heart.

Because of the warm early spring, there were already a few wild rose bushes starting to bloom outside their shanty. Annabel came running in the door. Handing her mother a scrunched handful of the wild yellow roses, she grinned and whispered, "This is for you and baby Rose." Stopping to look at her new sister, a smile spread across Annabel's face as she wiggled and squirmed with excitement. Giggling, she gave the baby a hug and ran outside to play with her younger sister.

Doty smiled. She raised the roses to her nose and inhaled the delicate scent. The beauty and fragrance of the wild rose held a special place in her heart. It was the one thing, except for her children, that brought her pleasure in this desolate land.

Living in this dry country was a hard life. The food was running short, and it would be a few months before the crops and the garden would yield its bounty. Money was gone, so Fred worked odd jobs around town in addition to farming his own land. During the day when he was working, Doty would finish her work and then relax and enjoy her girls.

Doty lay in bed holding her newborn daughter, her mind whirling. There was so much that needed to be done. She needed to bake bread, fetch water, do laundry, and scrub the house that was dusty from the ever-present dry winds. The list seemed endless. But all that would have to wait for a while. She was exhausted, her body drained of energy from giving birth.

Doty plucked off a petal of one of the roses that Annabel had given to her and put the tidbit in her mouth. Slowly, she rolled it over and over with her tongue. Then ever so gently she bit down on the fragile morsel. The sweet flavor flooded her mouth, and she savored every bit of it. Rose petals were the only delicacy that she had tasted in years. Placing another petal in her mouth, she relaxed and closed her eyes.

As the laughter of her young girls drifted in through the broken window and the baby slept peacefully in her arms, Doty slowly surrendered to the sleep she so desperately needed.

When Doty opened her eyes, everything was quiet. Rose was still sleeping peacefully in her arms. The angle of the light streaming through the window told her that the sun was going down. The air seemed a few degrees cooler than it was a couple of hours ago when she fell asleep.

On the splintered floor beside Doty's mattress, Annabel and Carolyn slept, lying in a pile, exhausted from playing outside all day. As she watched them sleep, Doty noticed their grimy clothes. The girls' skin, darkened by the sun, was covered with dirt, and their black hair was matted and thick with dust and lack of care. Their small calloused bare feet twitched as their chests rose with every breath.

The girls needed a bath. But since water was scarce in this country, baths were a privilege. However, the rain was here now, and water would soon be more plentiful. Doty, herself, was definitely looking forward to the opportunity of being clean again. Having water beyond the immediate necessity was a luxury that would, for a short time, improve their quality of life. With the spring rains here, there would soon be plenty of fresh, clean water.

Rose stretched and yawned as she slept in her mother's arms. Doty, filled with love for the infant, tenderly gazed down at her new daughter.

Suddenly the feelings of love were overcome by fear, and she tightened her embrace. As she gazed at her child, fear for her baby's future weighed heavy on her.

With a sigh, born of exhaustion and dread, Doty dropped her head back on the soiled pillow. Thoughts of the past tore through her mind, bringing back with them the remnants of the bad and the good. Like one of the flashfloods that were so common in spring, the thoughts careened through her, depositing debris from a tormented past and uprooting her hopes for the future. These issues—

her issues—had worked in her and created the essence of the girl she once was and the woman she had become...

TWO

1900s

Born in 1902, Doty spent her early childhood years growing up in Burns, Oregon. As a young child, she had lived a wonderful life that was filled with all the things a little girl needed—loving parents, a nice home, and plenty to eat—all wrapped up in a blanket of warmth and security. Her father had his own business and, as far as Doty knew, her family was considered well off.

Her mother had named her after a Chippewa princess named Mendota. The name meant "water" or "springs." Both mother and father had settled on calling her "Doty" instead of Mendota because Doty sounded more like a white woman's name. Since she had to live in a white man's world, the name Doty fit best.

Then Doty's whole world changed. When she was eight years old, her mother and father divorced. She never knew why her parents separated. Doty always wondered if the differences in her parent's races, her father being white and her mother being Chippewa, caused the separation.

Her mother had never seemed to fit in. She was looked down upon as less than a human. People were rude and disrespectful to her. Doty remembered people calling her mother names or refusing to speak to her at all. It was hard seeing her treated that way. Her mother had always been a kind and gracious woman and a loving mother. Doty loved her with her whole heart. She always thought that her dad had really loved her mother too.

Doty was devastated when her mother left. Confused and unsure, feelings of inadequacy that she must have been the reason for her mother leaving became her constant companion. She never saw or heard from her mother again. Doty often asked about her, but no one would say anything.

Her mother had simply disappeared from her life. Doty constantly wondered if this had been her fault. At eight years old, she felt her world of love and security had been replaced by abandonment and rejection. She felt all alone.

Life had also been hard for Doty because she was a half-breed, half Indian and half white. With her darker skin and black hair, it was easy to tell she carried Indian blood. As a child, other children had teased and made fun of her, especially in school. They even teased her about her name. They made up a chant to taunt her. "Dotty, Dotty, has to use the potty."

Day after day, the town's children taunted Doty. Whenever the teacher was not around or was busy with other children, they would call her names and say rude things. Finally, pushed to the point of anger, Doty turned on her classmates and yelled, "My name's not Dotty, its Doty with a long 'o'! Don't call me Dotty anymore! It's Doty!" She was the one that was punished.

The taunting continued. They didn't care that her dad had money. They didn't care that she dressed well and lived in a nice home. All that mattered was that she was different and being different was just not allowed. Doty never fit in anywhere; she was stuck in between the two worlds, Indian and white.

Between being a "half-breed" and being deserted by her mother, Doty struggled emotionally most of her young life. Her self-worth and confidence continued to erode. She withdrew deeper and deeper into herself not daring to run the risk making friends. To make friends she would have to trust someone, and she knew that trusting only led to rejection.

Soon after the divorce, Doty and her father moved to Emmett, Idaho to start a new life. Two years later, her father remarried. Doty figured her dad had done it right this time and married a white woman. Trudy, for all appearances, seemed to be a good wife for her father, but she had no love for Doty. She rather tolerated the child, enduring her presence in order to be with her father.

This cold indifference only grew worse once the baby came. While Doty never lacked for anything material, emotionally she was bereft. Her stepmother never accepted her, especially after her sister was born.

The one bright spot in Doty's life was Grandma Betsy. Her father's mother loved Doty and had stepped in to become the closest thing to a mother that Doty would ever have. Doty spent most of her childhood at her grandmother's home. The times spent there had become the only good times she could remember. Even though Doty felt love from her grandmother, it still had not erased the pain of the abandonment created by her mother's departure or the feeling of rejection from her father. She always wondered where her place was in this life.

Rosy began to rouse, and Doty's thoughts snapped back to the present. She looked intently at her daughter's face; her precious child's tiny mouth opened with a small yawn as her little arms and legs reached out and stretched. The image stirred Doty's emotions to the point of pain, her heart aching for all the things her daughter would never have. She wanted her children to have the best in life. She wanted them to be happy and safe and to have the security of a good home and a loving father. She wanted them to have everything they needed and to be surrounded with the warmth of a loving family. She sighed as she looked around the small shack; her reality was quite different.

Doty allowed her gaze to travel from her new daughter to the older girls still sleeping on the floor. She stared at her children as her thoughts drifted to the idea of God. God, an all-powerful, all loving Father. She shook her head against the thought. She had heard people talk about a loving God before, but if He really existed, why would He allow all this pain and suffering in her life?

She shook her head again and waved away a fly trying to alight on the baby's cheek. Then she chuckled softly. "If anyone could help us, God could." Still, questions about Him flittered through her mind.

Is there really a God? If I knew—if I could really believe, then I would ask Him to protect and provide for my family. But then again, if He was actually real, couldn't He see me? Couldn't He see all the things my babies need?

Swatting the fly out of the air, she put the thought of God out of her mind, telling herself that God, especially one like the townspeople talked about, could never really exist at all.

The baby started to fuss. Doty pulled the blanket back and raised the child to her breast to feed her. As the child suckled, Doty's mind wandered, and her thoughts turned again to her past…

1919

Doty was seventeen years old when she met Fred. When he looked at her it made her feel like she mattered. He was five years older and everything her father was not. At over six feet tall, Fred was broad shouldered and strong, a man who worked with his hands. She loved his dark brown hair and eyes, coupled with an outgoing personality that more than made up for her shyness. And the way he looked at her—he made her feel beautiful. His touch made her heartbeat quicken, her body tingle with anticipation. Fred was everything she wanted. Immediately, she fell in love, and it wasn't long before Doty knew she would spend the rest of her life with him.

Despite her family's misgivings, she loved Fred and felt he truly loved her. She knew that they were meant to be together. Their whirlwind courtship had led to an even hastier engagement.

Doty vividly remembered the evening she talked to her parents. Even now she could still sense the feeling of sweat down her back and sticky palms. She gathered with her father, stepmother, and half-sister in the lavish parlor of her father's home to discuss her engagement. She could still picture the fine velvet wallpaper and the ornate rugs that adorned the room as she anticipated telling them about her intentions to marry Fred.

"I said no!" Doty's father all but roared. Her stepmother sat by silently as she stared at Doty with that same cold expression.

Doty jumped up and snapped back, "No, all you ever say is no! You haven't even listened to me. Fred's a—"

Her father interrupted, "Too old for you and you're too young to get married. You're still under my roof and under my authority and until that changes, you'll do like you're told, young lady!"

Doty's anger flared. "I'm seventeen years old and old enough to know what I want!"

He paused and took a deep breath. "Look, Doty, you're still a child. I know things about the world…about men like Fred, he's just not good for you. There's something about him that I just don't like."

Trudy stood up. "Honey"—she turned to look first at her daughter, then over at Doty— "come, let's let daddy talk to Doty alone." With a cold indifference, Trudy glanced at Doty again, turned, and walked out of the room.

Disheartened, Doty spoke sharply to her stepmother as she walked away; "Go ahead and leave. I know you don't care about me, and this isn't your business anyway!"

Her father stood so fast that his chair flipped backwards, ripping a hole in the wallpaper. Jabbing his finger at Doty, he commanded, "That's enough, young lady! You will not speak to your mother like that! You will treat her with respect!"

"She's not my mother!" Doty stepped back, cowed by the fierce look on her father's face. In that moment, she believed that she would never have his heart, that she had truly been replaced by Trudy and an all-white sister. She looked from her father's reddened face to her stepmother's retreating back and made up her mind. She was surprised by the sudden feeling of resolve, of peace that overcame her. In that moment, she saw her father in a new—lesser—light.

I don't have to put up with this. "Yes, Father. If you'll excuse me, I'll just go to my room."

As she walked with measured steps from the dining room, her father called out from behind her. "If you marry

Fred…that wild, unrefined…he's a ruffian…!" He stammered and took a breath, calming himself. "If you marry that man, you'll never be welcome back into this house." The last impression she had of her father was of a man broken and confused, and perhaps something else…afraid.

Doty stormed off to her room and slammed the door behind her. Her resolve weakened. She grabbed a vase of roses that was sitting on the dresser and heaved it against the wall. The iron crystal shattered, leaving streaks of water, staining the wall as the varied hues of roses lay crushed and broken on the floor. Staring at the fragmented shards of crystal and crushed stems, she saw a reflection of herself, of her past life and wondered if it was a foretelling of her future.

She shivered.

With a sigh, she let a sarcastic smile creep across her face. "At least Mother had the kindness to actually leave." She looked toward the door. "But you, Father, you just pretend as if I don't even exist."

Father and his family…or Fred. She had made her choice. In reality, she had no choice to make; there was no future without Fred. It wouldn't be easy leaving her father, but she loved Fred and he was her future.

The next morning Doty woke early, rising while the rest of the house still slept. As the sun painted the eastern sky with shades of champagne and streaks of magenta, she made her way out of the house and loaded a few of her belongings into her Model T, a high school graduation present from her father. Gripping the steering wheel, she raised her face to catch the light of the rising sun, inhaled and released a breath. She smiled in greeting of the new day. She was surer of this than of anything else in her life. She stepped on the starter and opened the throttle. The back wheels spun and sent up a small cloud of dust as the Model T took off. Smiling, she drove to Fred's.

Hours later, sitting in the one-room that made up the small cabin, Fred reached his hand across the table and collected Doty's much smaller hand in his. She loved the contrast in their skin; his fair and her darker, richer tones. His, strong and rough from years of hard work taming a wild land, and hers, smooth and soft, reflecting the refined life of the more cultured class.

Fred cleared his throat and waited for her to look up at him. "Doty, ya know I love ya, but are ya sure ya want ta do this? Right now, you're angry because your pa won't let us get married. But runnin' away? I don't want ya ta feel bad about this later and think that ya got stuck with me or somethin'."

"Fred, I want to marry you." She squeezed his hand in both of hers. "Eloping…eloping is the only way we can get married."

Fred didn't argue. Grinning, he stood and opened the door for her and followed her to her car.

Fred drove her back to her father's house. Then turning to her, he reached out and gently touched her face. "Ya sure ya wa—"

"Quick," she said, cutting him off, "my father will be at work by now and Trudy will be back soon. I want to be out of here before she gets home."

Fred looked at Doty with a mischievous grin, eyes bright. "Okay, let's do it!" He ran to the rear of the Model T, released the straps holding the boot, a wooden trunk used for storage, and lifted it to the ground. Fred grabbed the trunk by its end straps and followed her into the house.

"Okay, fill it up." They quickly packed the rest of her personal items and were off.

Laughing, they drove directly to the justice of the peace. Smiling up at Fred, Doty had no second thoughts as she said, "Yes," promising herself to Fred forever.

Shortly after Doty and Fred were married, Doty's father and stepmother moved to Arkansas, back to where Trudy's family still lived. Doty never knew if they moved because of her or not, but either way, she never heard from them again.

She gave up everything for Fred: her home, her family, and the standard of life to which she was accustomed. She loved Fred more than life itself, and he was the one person, with the exception of her grandmother, who had seemed to accept her for herself.

Fred was kind and gentle to Doty before they were married. He was a good man—when he wasn't drinking.

It wasn't until months later, that she realized how right her father had been about him and how wrong she was. Fred was a mean drunk. The realization had hit hard. So had he. She had felt the back of his hand many times.

She touched the side of her face, remembering the last time she felt his hand. She closed her eyes as a solitary tear escaped, trickling down her cheek and falling from her chin. Doty leaned forward and kissed the forehead of her sleeping infant. Her two older daughters still lay sleeping on the dusty floor. She laid her head back on the pillow and allowed her thoughts to drift back again, trying to understand how she had arrived at this place in her life.

She remembered seeing the property for the first time with Fred as her husband. Doty had seen the land through new excited eyes. Although there was only a shanty on the plot, now it was hers—hers and Fred's.

The one-hundred sixty acre spread sat about six miles outside Emmett, Idaho, about fifteen miles from the Black Canyon Dam. Fred had worked on some of the improvements on the property, but there were many more things that needed to be done.

Doty brushed her hair back from her face as her thoughts returned to the present. Dust sifted in between the boards of the small forlorn-looking building, keeping the single room structure persistently dirty. The one cracked window did not allow much light in, creating a gloomy atmosphere. Hot, sultry air in the small shack made it difficult to breathe. In one corner of the room, she lay on a grimy double mattress on the floor, covered by a worn handmade quilt. Her eyes drifted around her home. Old wooden crates stacked in another corner created a makeshift table and chairs. An old cook stove stood in another corner, the wall behind it blackened from smoke and soot. A stack of firewood was piled on the floor beside the stove. In the remaining corner sat her wooden trunk, containing the few possessions she brought with her.

Doty wiped away the perspiration that trickled down her forehead. She closed her eyes as bleak images continued to flit through her tired mind. Her surroundings were a constant reminder of a life she had chosen.

She thought of the constant wind that sucked what little moisture there was from the land and of the dust that swirled around outside the shanty. The sky had been releasing less water than normal and the dry heat of the semi-arid desert was becoming even hotter and dryer. The only water available was from a hand pump that stood over a shallow well in the front yard; it had to be hauled by a bucket to the house.

The few remaining fences that existed on the farm gradually gave in to the incessant beating of the wind and fell to the ground, laying useless in the dirt. The door of the weathered outhouse swung back and forth as the wind blew through, carrying with it the stench of human waste.

This life did not match at all the dreams of an adolescent Doty. Before they were married, Fred had promised her a nicer, larger home with a barn and a garden. She had believed him and married him, trusting in his promises.

THREE

Doty loved her husband. However, times had been tough for him, and she believed that he had truly tried. The past few years of drought had been too many and the crops had been too few. The irrigation canals had not yet made it to their side of the valley, leaving them with only the water that rainfall and snow melt could supply. It had not been enough. She watched as each spring Fred worked the land and planted the seeds. She watched each spring as the sky, stingy with her gifts, released very little of the desperately needed moisture.

Over the last few summers most of the crops, battered by the heat and dust, had curled up and wasted away. Come fall, the harvest would be too small, and the money was never enough. Fred picked up every odd job he could, hoping it would somehow be enough to feed his family. But time and time again, he had been disappointed. Fred changed, as if something deep down inside him died. Mentally and emotionally, he seemed to wither away like the shriveled crops that dry up from lack of moisture.

Undernourished and weak, Doty had lost their first child, a little girl. The child had been stillborn and the pain of the child's death had left a deep scar in Fred's heart, adding to the wounds left over from his own youth.

The child in her arms stirred and Doty's thoughts suddenly jumped even further back to a few weeks after she and Fred were married. She recalled the only time Fred had ever talked about his own childhood and the atmosphere of abuse and neglect in which he had been raised.

She thought back to the evening that they had sat on their porch watching the sun's rays fade away. Fred rocked slowly in his worn rocker, deep in thought. Then without having been prompted, he had begun to talk. Doty, not wanting to interrupt, sat quietly beside him and listened.

"Ya know, Doty, my father wasn't a very nice guy. He beat me and was very abusive ta me in other ways. The memories of it make me feel all confused and twisted inside; it gives me feelings I don't even understand. I've tried to push the memories away, tried ta bury them deep down inside, ya know, to put them out a my mind and just forget. At first that seemed to help, seemed ta keep back the dark feelings." He sighed, but did not look at her, instead continued to stare out over the vast expanse of land. "But even now, the feelin's keep comin' back."

Fred stopped rocking, leaned forward with his elbows on his knees, and looked down at his feet. "There seems ta be a dark place in my soul where these shadows live. These feelin's…they're twisted and perverted." He ran his fingers through his hair and moaned softly as if in pain. "And they're always there. They're always there in my mind, even when I don't want 'em. They keep comin' back when I least expect it."

For a moment, Doty had been afraid for Fred. In her mind, she questioned the torment her husband was battling and wondered what it could mean for them. But, as she looked in Fred's face, she saw tears reflecting in his eyes. Her thoughts of fear disappeared, replaced with compassion for him.

"I don't wanna be like my father. I don't wanna do ta my kids what he did ta me. I just want the past behind me…out a mind, and forgotten! When the time comes, I wanna be a good papa ta my children."

When the second and third child were both taken through the ravishes of starvation, it had been the final straw. Something good and decent had been driven clean out of Fred. He blamed himself. Guilt, anger, and feelings of inadequacy overwhelmed him. He turned to the bottle for comfort.

What little money Fred did have was now mostly spent on whiskey. Since prohibition was in force, alcohol was illegal, and Doty was never sure where he came up with his bootlegged whiskey, but he always found a way to get his hands on it.

Doty looked down at Rosy asleep in her lap. She gazed at her newborn daughter, marveling at the sweetness of her innocent face. She gently touched Rosy's cheek with the back of her fingers while the child slept.

As she gazed at her baby girl, memories of the loss of her dear departed children slowly flooded her mind and brought tears to Doty's eyes. The pain inside her chest twisted and ripped her heart into pieces, again. Her arms would always ache to hold her little ones that had been taken away too soon.

At first, Fred had mourned the deaths of their children as well, but all too soon his pain had turned into anger. An anger spent mostly at Doty's expense. The more he drank, the more abusive he became at home with his constant barrage of insults, foul language, and beatings. Doty sank beneath waves of fear and control.

Remembering the last words her father spoke to her—
"If you marry that man, you'll never be welcome back into this

house,"—she knew she had nowhere to go and no one whom she could depend on. She was once again alone.

The one thing Doty was sure of was that her husband, the man she called Father, was a mentally and emotionally broken man, and she was under his absolute control.

FOUR

The morning after Rosy was born, Father woke up sprawled out on his worn rocker on the porch, one leg propped over an arm of the chair. On the other side, his arm dangled with his hand clutching an empty whiskey bottle. He opened his eyes, trying to get his bearings. His head ached and his mouth had that familiar quality of dryness that came after consuming great quantities of bad alcohol. The sunlight made his eyes ache, so he scrunched them closed, trying to keep out the offending brightness of the morning sun.

He dropped the whiskey bottle beside him and pressed his hands over his ears to silence the songs of the nearby birds. "Blasted critters…making enough noise to wake the dead." He groaned and winced. His eyes traveled to the empty bottle as he recalled the indulgence of the night before. "I know—more whiskey—that's what I need, some 'hair a the dog'!"

Picking up the whiskey bottle, Fred saw it was empty. With an angry curse, he threw it at the Tin Lizzie, the bottle shattering on the car's bumper.

As he stood, Fred grabbed the back of the chair to keep from falling, his momentum carrying him forward. He reached for the porch post and hauled himself up. Slowly, he staggered out to the hand pump in the middle of the yard and dropped to his knees. He put his head under the spout and pumped the water handle, letting the cold water run over his upper body and head, trying to wash away the night before. Fred shook his head, attempting to shake off his hangover and was rewarded with a throbbing pain for his trouble. He moaned and stood up, arching his back.

Dredging his memory, he suddenly swore, then cursed Doty. "Like I need another mouth to feed!"

A feeling of helplessness came over him. Mumbling, Fred asked himself, "What am I gonna do? I can't provide for the mouths I already got. Where's the money gonna come from?" Despair welled up inside him. "I need a drink." He wanted to yell and scream; he had to do something to release the anger and bitterness overwhelming him.

Inside the house, Doty shrank back into the shadows, hoping to stay out Father's line of sight.

"Besides," he said aloud, "this ain't my fault." He looked toward the house and cursed again. Speaking in a loud voice so that his wife and children could hear him, he began a string of epitaphs, each more degrading and brutal than the one before. He dropped to his knees and stuck his head back under the spout again as he pumped the handle, letting the water cool his head. "Blasted woman! I'm gonna have ta go look for another job...all these mouths ta feed." He swore again and stumbled toward the car. Fred stopped to look back, cursed and trumped back toward the house.

Doty peeked out the shanty door, waiting to see how he would react before offering him a hot cup of black coffee. In one hand she had the coffee and in the other she held Rosy, hoping Fred would at least ask about his new daughter.

Moments passed as she waited for some kind of reaction.

"What's its name?" Fred finally asked as he staggered over to the porch, took the coffee, and stared at his new child.

"The baby is a girl. Her name is Rose, but I'm calling her Rosy." She rocked her child protectively in her arms. "Do you want to hold her?"

Fred hesitated. "Not now. I need ta get ta town and start lookin' for work again." He guzzled his coffee, shoved the cup back into Doty's hand, and turned and shuffled carefully back to the Tin Lizzie. As he turned back to look at his new daughter again, Doty could see a look of helplessness in his eyes. She watched as he fumbled getting into the car and sighed with relief as he drove off towards town, knowing that while he was gone, she and the children would at least have a few hours of peace.

As he drove slowly through downtown, Fred noticed that it was strangely quiet. Only a few people rambled up and down the sidewalks; none of them seemed to be in a hurry. Glancing through the windows of the quaint storefronts as he drove by, he saw very few customers in the stores. *Hmm…not very busy in town today. Where is everyone?*

He drove on, finally coming to a stop at the local feed store. *Since there ain't no rain and no irrigation on my side the valley, I can't grow the crops, but maybe I can sell the feed at the feed store.*

Fred walked into the store and greeted the store owner as he shook his hand. "Hey, Joe, I'm lookin' for a little extra work. Do ya need any help around here? I'm a good worker."

"Hello, Fred," Joe greeted him. "I know you're a hard worker, but I'm sorry, I have more than enough help now. Crops have been bad and business has been awful slow."

Joe leaned against the counter and crossed his arms. "But I did hear last week that Hank, the foreman at the lumber mill, was hiring. Ya might check there."

"Thanks." Fred nodded his head. "I know Hank. I'll go talk to him." Fred got in his car and drove back across town to the lumber mill, stopping in the gravel parking lot in front of the mill's office. As he got out of the car and walked toward the mill, he could hear the buzz of the saws cutting wood. He glanced around at the large piles of recently cut logs sitting beside piles of neatly stacked lumber. The smell of newly cut wood lingered in the air and filled his nostrils. He took a deep breath, enjoying the fragrance of cut pine.

Fred entered the office and heartily greeted the foreman, "Hello, Hank." Fred reached out to shake his hand.

"Hi, Fred, how ya doing?" Hank smiled as he grabbed Fred's hand.

"I'm doin' okay. Say, I hear yer hirin', and I'm lookin' for work. Crops are bad, and I've a family to feed. I need work pretty bad. I'm a hard worker…"

Hank slowly scratched his chin and looked at Fred. "I just hired a couple a guys last week. I don't rightly need any more help. I'll keep you in mind in case something opens up, though."

Fred's shoulders sank and he exhaled dejectedly. Looking away from Hank, he wiped his face with a dirty hand and sighed. *Nothin's work'n…everything I touch goes bad.*

Fred turned back to look at Hank and held out his hand. "Thanks anyway," he said tight lipped.

As Fred turned quietly to leave, Hank called out to him, "Hey, wait a minute. I might need someone to deliver some lumber. Would ya be interested in that? It won't pay much, but it'll help keep a little food on the table for your family. Then if something else opens up, you'll be first on the list."

Fred stopped and spun. "You serious? Yes! I'll take it! When do ya want me ta start?"

"Tomorrow would be great. I've a delivery that needs to go out first thing in the morning."

Fred grinned, grabbed the foreman's hand with both of his and shook it hard. "I'll be here bright n' early! Thank ya! I really appreciate it!" Fred nodded once at Hank and turned and walked out, stepping with a little higher step and smiling from ear to ear. Tears of relief crested and ran down his weathered face.

Things are lookin' up. I have a job. At least now I'll have a little money for food so the kids can eat.

FIVE

"Shh…it's okay, Rosy…" Doty held the feverish little girl in her arms and touched her lips to the child's forehead to check her temperature. She gently laid a cool, damp cloth on the child's warm forehead to help bring down the fever.

Doty flinched when the front door slammed open. Kicking his way into the small shanty, Father staggered into the house, drunk again. "Where's dinner?" he demanded.

Doty looked up, fear darkening her eyes as concern for her children's well-being weighed heavy on her. Fred had worked hard over the past few months, eventually ending up with a full-time job at the mill. Things at home had gotten a little better. The family had regular meals, and Fred's anger had somewhat subsided, except for when he drank.

He had started acting a bit like his old self as he fulfilled his responsibilities of supporting his family. But from one day to another, Doty constantly lived in fear of his abuse and what might come next. She always wondered when he would again lose control of himself from drinking too much. It seemed that tonight was another one of those nights.

Annabel and Carolyn were sitting in the corner of the shack, playing marbles with pebbles. Doty was exhausted, frustrated, and short-tempered. She had not had a minute of rest all day. Sitting on the edge of the mattress, holding the sick child close as she rocked her, Doty barked back at Father, "I've been taking care of the baby; she's been sick all day. You'll just have to wait a while for dinner." As soon as the words were out of her mouth, Doty knew she had made a mistake.

Father slurred as he bellowed, "What kind a wife 'r ya? When a man comes home, he 'spects his dinner ta be on the table! Now git it ready!"

Doty retorted, "I'm sorry, but you'll just have to wait. The baby is really sick, and I need to take care of her!"

"You do what I tell ya!" Leaning over her, he angrily backhanded Doty across the face. The blow landed solidly on her cheek, causing her to lose her grip on the baby. Rosy slipped from her mother's arms and thudded to the floor. The child screamed.

Annabel and Carolyn stopped playing. They huddled together in the corner, trembling and watching in fear as Father's cruelty continued.

Doty scrambled to her knees and bent over the crying baby. "Stop! Stop, you've hurt Rosy!"

Horrified, Doty was in the act of picking up the crying child when Father grabbed her by her collar and snatched her to her feet.

"Leave the baby 'lone an' fix my dinner. When I git back in the house, my dinner better be ready. If it's not, you'll be sorry. Next it'll be the girls!" He threw Doty to the floor and stumbled out of the house.

Doty immediately crawled to baby Rose. "Shh…it's okay…shh…" she whispered. Adrenaline rushing through her veins, she gently picked up her daughter with trembling hands, holding tight so her grasp wouldn't give way. Sitting cross legged on the mattress, she cuddled the baby tight and patted her on the back trying to comfort her. "Shh…it's okay." Her entire body trembled as she rocked the crying baby.

The two older girls were sitting, horrified and wide-eyed at what they had just witnessed. They hurried to their mother's side for comfort. Doty tried to ease her children's fears, but she knew the only way to protect them would be to do what Father wanted.

Her hands still shaking, Doty wrapped the baby in a dingy blanket then handed the fussing child to her oldest daughter. "Annabel, take Rosy and rock her while I fix Father's dinner." The baby continued to whimper and cry as her big sister tried to calm her.

Doty's fear darkened, changing into something more menacing. She knew Father meant it when he threatened the girls. She slapped the bacon into the iron skillet. As the meat fried, the grease spattered, and the sound of sizzling began to fill her ears, Doty's breaths became shallow, speeding up. Her heartbeat seemed to race in unison with the crackling of the frying meat. Her mind churned as thoughts of leaving stormed through her head.

Doty knew women were subject to their husbands. Wives didn't leave their husbands, no matter what the circumstances…it just wasn't done. Abuse, physical or sexual, was never spoken of, whether the husband abused the wife, children, or both. Private matters were never made public.

I've had enough of his drinking and abuse! A plan started forming in her mind as she poured water into the coffee pot. *I'm tired of living in fear and worrying about the kids' safety. I'm taking them and leaving. Tonight!*

She sighed. The fact that there were very few jobs for women made it almost impossible for a woman to support a family. She also knew that Father would hunt them down, and she feared what he would do to her and the kids.

Doty cracked an egg on the edge of the frying pan, feeling the shell shatter in her grip. She shook the slimy substance from her fingers and picked out the larger portions of shell but stirred the smaller pieces into the mix, scrambling them in the sizzling grease.

In contrast to her mood, the delicious aroma of bacon, coffee, and eggs—the fragrances of love and of family—permeated the small room in mockery of the dread that filled her heart. Doty's stomach became queasy at the smell of the food. Eating was the last thing on her mind.

He's dangerous, and I've got to get us out of here!

That night while Father slept, passed out from too much whiskey, Doty silently got up in the early morning hours, packed the few possessions she and the girls had, and loaded their belongings into the car. She grabbed a gunny sack and filled it with all the food she had in the house. She then dug through Fred's wallet and found a dollar and some coins. *This isn't much money, but it will get me out of here. I don't know where I'm going, but wherever it is, it has to be better than here.*

The early morning rays of sun were just peeking over the distant hills as the coolness of the morning seemed to settle the rush of her adrenaline. Everything was packed and in the car. One by one, Doty carried the sleeping girls out to the Model T. Once she and the girls settled, she double checked to make sure she had everything she needed; she wouldn't be back.

"Okay," Doty whispered to herself as she grasped the steering wheel tightly and took some deep breaths. *It's time to get out of here before Fred wakes.* She stepped on the starter and cringed as the engine roared to life, hoping the noise wouldn't wake him up. She glanced quickly at the shanty door as uneasiness and fear racked her mind and body.

Slowly opening the throttle, she then drove away, not knowing where she was going or how she would even feed the girls, but at least they would be away from Father.

As the day dawned, hope of a new life, a possibility of a life without fear and abuse, began to take root.

The morning slipped away quickly as Doty drove across the Emmett valley at full throttle. Feeling like she couldn't get away fast enough, she was constantly glancing in the rearview mirror, watching for Fred.

After driving for a half hour or so, all three girls woke up. Doty pulled off the road at the bottom of Freeze Out Hill. Rosy seemed to feel better and more settled this morning than yesterday. The movement of the car had lulled her to sleep, but now she was wide awake and hungry. Doty sat in the vehicle and nursed the baby while the girls had some water and a piece of bread for an early breakfast.

After feeding the girls, she tucked Rosy back into the blankets on the seat beside her, started the car, and was soon back on the road. The new graveled state highway that went up Freeze Out Hill was faster than the back roads. So, she figured taking that highway to Boise would be the quickest way to put miles between her and Fred.

Doty didn't know where she was going; she just wanted to get away. But she did know that, sooner or later, Father would come looking for them, so she constantly watched for a good place to stop and hide if needed.

As she got closer to Boise, she began to feel a little better, her fear subsiding now that she had put some distance between herself and Fred.

Fred awoke late in the morning, his head throbbing, his mind spinning, and his memory hazy. He sat up slowly, knowing that he drank too much the night before. He knew he was paying the consequences, again. Unsteadily, he leaned against the wall and pulled himself up. He looked around for Doty. "Doty!" he called in a cracking voice. "Where's my coffee? I need ta get ta work!" He stumbled forward and looked around again. She was not in the house. "Blasted woman."

He scratched himself and mumbled as he continued shuffling forward. "Where's that woman? Where's the girls?"

He stumbled out the door onto the porch and surveyed the yard, looking for them. There was no sign of his family, and the Model T was gone. Wondering where they went, he staggered back into the house. Looking around the room, he noticed that all of Doty and the girls' clothes were gone. He glanced up at the shelves, there was not a speck of food in the house. Memories of the night before started flooding in.

Suddenly, he realized what had happened. *They're gone. They left me!* Anger filled every fiber of his body. "How dare she defy me! I'll teach 'er! They couldn't a left more than a few hours ago. I'll catch up with 'em and show her who's boss!"

Father quickly pulled on his boots, ran out the door, and raced across the field to the neighbor's house. "I'm gonna find her an' she'll be sorry," he mumbled under his breath.

Bill, his neighbor, was out in the field fixing a fence. "Hey, Bill," Fred yelled across the field, trying to catch his breath. "Can I borrow your car? My family didn't come home last night. I think they're stranded on the road somewhere," he lied.

"Sure, do you need help findin' them? I can go with you and help ya look," Bill offered.

"No thanks, I think I know where they are. I'd just like ta use your car." Fred ran over and jumped in the car, stepped on the starter, then took off as he yelled back, "Thanks, Bill! I'll get it back soon as I can!"

Father's eyes scoured the surrounding countryside as he sped down the rutted road with a dirt cloud racing after him. He watched for cars, people, tire tracks, anything that would give him a clue as to where Doty went. The farther he drove, the more his anger grew, the more his rage seethed.

Doty stopped at a gas station on the outskirts of Boise. Using some of what little money she had, she filled the gas tank and quickly continued on her way. She drove slowly through the small city, hoping not to get lost. She finally reached Highway 30 that headed southeast towards Glenn's Ferry. As she pulled out on the highway, all three girls curled up and were lulled back to sleep again from the gentle motion of the car.

Doty raced down the highway, anxious to put more miles behind her. She glanced in the rearview mirror often, checking to make sure Fred was nowhere around. After driving for a while, Doty's fear was subsiding, and she was beginning to feel more relaxed. *I'm almost to Glenn's Ferry. I've only got a little over ten miles to go.*

All of a sudden, there was a loud pop and the car lurched forward. The vehicle then started pulling hard to the right. Doty gripped the steering wheel tight, trying to keep the Model T on the road, but it began weaving back and forth. Her heartbeat sped up as she throttled back and slowed the vehicle down. "No! Not now! I can't afford to have anything go wrong!" Frustration and panic rose inside her.

She slowly guided the car off to the side of the road, got out, and examined the tires. "A flat tire! It'll take time to change it…time I don't have!" Exasperated, she took a deep breath that did nothing to calm her nerves. She searched the car for a car jack and tire pump but could find neither.

"A flat tire and I don't even have a jack or a pump!" In anger, she struck the fender with her fist and kicked the tire, twice. Dread filled her being. "Glenn's Ferry is still over ten miles away. I'm stranded…"

Doty heaved a sigh and helplessly leaned back against the car as she slowly slid down the door and sat on the ground. She pulled her knees up to her chest and put her arms around her legs, laying her forehead against her knees.

Her worries were playing out. Uneasiness filled her again. *I have a flat tire in the middle of nowhere with three kids. The road is deserted, and there's not a house in sight. Now what am I going to do?* Overwhelmed, she sat in despair for what seemed like hours, feeling sorry for herself.

Tears filled her eyes though she tried to blink back the liquid. She thought about Father and her bitterness towards him grew. *I'm not going to let him treat the girls and me the way he does anymore. I'm not!* Slowly, determination started rising inside her. Abruptly, she sat up straight, shoulders and head back. *No, I'm not doing this; I'm not giving up. I'll not let Fred find us. We need to get away!*

As the girls slept quietly in the car, Doty did the only thing that she could do. She stood up, brushed off her clothes, and held her head high. Trying to strengthen her determination, she spoke out loud to herself, "Hopefully the girls will sleep for a while. I'm going to see if we can catch a ride."

Doty leaned against the car door and waited. Eventually, a noisy old car came down the road. She stepped up to the roadside and waved her arms. The jalopy stopped. Doty walked over to the driver's side of the car. "Thank you for stopping. I have a flat tire and no way to fix it. I also have my three girls with me. Could you give us a lift to Glenn's Ferry?"

The couple in the car had four kids in the backseat. The driver looked at Doty with apologetic eyes. "I'm sorry, but we don't have room. However, the town is only about ten miles down the road; we'll send help back for you."

"Thanks, I would really appreciate that." Doty watched as the jalopy drove away, hoping they would send help soon. She leaned against the car door again and continued to wait.

Morning had already slipped away and the early afternoon was setting in, the breeze warming up. Leaning back against car, she watched the two older girls playing in the backseat as she rocked baby Rose in her arms. Annabel complained, "Mom, I'm hot and thirsty. Can I have a drink?" Doty gave each girl a drink, rationing the water.

The hot sun beat down on them, as the dry desert winds sapped the moisture from their bodies. Doty leaned against the car door, scanning the surrounding land and the deserted highway. A mirage gradually appeared in the distant landscape, its illusion shimmering in the afternoon sun. She heaved a deep sigh as she watched it. Her determination waned. With very few vehicles on the road, she figured it would be a while before help would arrive.

Eventually, Doty saw another car coming down the road. She laid the baby down on the front seat, stepped out to the side of the road, and waved her arms. Much to her relief, the vehicle stopped. "Thank you so much for stopping," she said excitedly as she rushed up to the car's window. "I have a flat..." She stopped.

The door flew open. Father stepped out of the vehicle.

His built-up rage burst into fury. He grabbed her by the front of her dress and slammed her against the car. Getting right up in her face, he swore and slapped her, knocking her to the ground. From inside the car, the girls screamed in fright.

He stepped away from her and clasped his hands on the top of his head, pacing in a circle, and then glared at her as she lay sniffling in the road. Placing one hand on his hip, he shook the other at her, pointing and yelling, "You're not gonna get away with treatin' me this way, ya blasted woman! And how dare ya leave me! I told ya that you better do what I say!"

He rushed over to the Model T and dragged the two older girls out. "I told ya that it'd be the girls next time!" he shouted.

"Daddy no! Please, Papa, don't!" the girls cried out, as Fred dragged them from the vehicle. He dropped the girls on the ground beside Doty. Alone now, the baby screamed.

"No!" yelled Doty. "Stop! Leave the girls alone! It's me you're mad at. I'm, I'm sorry..."

He turned toward Doty, walked over, and kicked her. She lay silent and still, scared he would kick her again. The girls curled up in little balls on the ground, afraid to move or even whimper. Overpowered, Doty lay in silence.

Without a backward glance, Father abruptly turned and headed back to the Model T to get the baby. Horrified, Doty cried out, "No! Not the baby! Please, leave the baby and the girls alone! I'll go back with you. I'll do whatever you say. Just please…don't hurt the children." Tears ran down her face as blood trickled from her split lip.

Father stopped, walked back, and grabbed Doty by the front of her dress. He snatched her up and slammed her against the car again. "Alright, ya better remember that if ya try this again, I'll hunt ya down and I'll kill ya. I'll kill ya'll! And if ya tell anyone about this, I'll do the same ta them too. Now git in the car!" His rage vented, he slowly started to settle down.

As she struggled to straighten up, Doty wiped the blood from her lip with the back of her sleeve. She stood slowly and helped the girls up from the ground. Fearful, the two girls climbed into the Model T, lay down in the backseat, and curled up in the fetal position, afraid to move. They knew not to make a sound.

Doty silently climbed into the front seat of her vehicle, sat down, and checked on Rosy. Thankfully, the baby had fallen asleep.

Father retrieved the tire jack and the air pump from Bill's car and repaired the flat tire.

In the silence of the wasteland, Doty sat in the driver's seat of the Model T and nervously waited. She listened to the clicking of the jack as Fred jacked up the vehicle, and to the air swishing from the hand pump into the tire. While Father patched the tire and put Bill's tools away, no one said a word.

When he finished fixing the tire, Father defiantly opened the passenger's side door of the Model T and picked up the baby. As he placed Rosy in the front seat of Bill's car, he hollered at the other girls and pitched his head. "Annabel, Carolyn, ya both get in the backseat of this car. You'll ride with me. That way your mother won't try anythin' foolish.

"Doty, you know this is all your fault! If ya hadn't run off, none of this would've happened!" Father released a string of swear words aimed directly at her. She closed her eyes and turned her face away from him. "Now, Doty, you drive the Model T back and I'll drive Bill's car!" he commanded. "I'll be following ya, so if you're thinkin' 'bout doin' anythin' foolish, remember, I've got the girls!"

Doty didn't reply.

Fred climbed into Bill's car and followed closely behind Doty. The whir of the engine and the crunch of the gravel on the road were the only sounds to be heard.

Doty felt helpless as she realized the violence that Father was capable of. She looked at the empty road ahead of her and she knew that she was alone, there was no one else to help.

By the time they arrived home, Fred had calmed down. His anger had mostly dissipated. After returning Bill's car, Fred walked home across his neighbor's freshly plowed fields, taking large strides, careful to avoid disturbing the fresh furrows. Picking his way through the fields, he had time to reflect on the events of the day. For a brief moment, his mind began to swirl with feelings of regret for his actions of cruelty. *How could I treat my family like that? They depend on me.* Fred, angry at himself, kicked a large dirt clod and watched as it exploded in the air. *I've got to pull myself together.*

But just as quickly as his regrets came, they disappeared and were replaced with resentment and blame. *Wait a minute, I ain't gonna accept the responsibility for all this. Doty's the one ta blame; she ran off with the girls. This is all her fault.*

SIX

1930s

Over the next few years, quiet whispers of guilt haunted Fred's thoughts and caused him to cut back a little on his drinking. He drank less, but he still waited anxiously all day, looking forward to the burn of that first swig of whiskey every evening. He waited for the soothing swallow that helped numb his mind, drown his emotions, and escape from the world he lived in.

Doty watched as Fred seemed to gain a little more control over his behavior. She could see that he was trying hard to be a better husband and father. During evenings and weekends when he wasn't working, he spent more time playing and working with the children. He would even drop the two older girls off at school every morning on his way to work and pick them up when he could. Fred also treated Doty with more respect and kindness.

The family continued to grow, and Fred and Doty now had six children. There was eight-year-old Annabel, seven-year-old Carolyn, six-year-old Rosy, five-year-old Willie, two-year-old George, and the baby, six-month-old Henry.

As their family grew, so did Father's responsibility. He managed to add two more rooms to the one-room shanty. There was now a bedroom for the boys and one for the girls; Fred and Doty still slept in the front room.

But even with Fred's temper under control, more than ever, he felt the burden of providing for his family. Over and over, he turned back to his only solace—liquor.

Doty continually lived in fear and uncertainty. Father's past actions were permanently imprinted in her memory.

———————≈———————

Fred came home one afternoon from work carrying a very large package under his arm. Wrapped in plain brown paper and tied with string, the package had lots of neatly printed letters on it. He set the parcel down on the makeshift table. "This package is from the post office. We'll open it after the chores are done." Fred grinned and headed out to do his chores. Doty watched Fred as he walked out, as the unexpected feelings of anticipation filled her body. Turning, she smiled and shared in the children's excitement.

Everyone crowded around the table and stared. No one dared to touch it, but each person examined it closely. Very seldom did anyone get mail, let alone a large package. It was the first time the children had ever seen a parcel come through the mail.

Rosy pushed her way through the small crowd to get to the table. At six years old, she had not learned to read yet. As she studied the letters on the box, her eyes widened with wonder. "Mommy, what's it say? What could be inside such a big box?"

"Prancing from one foot to the other, Rosy could hardly contain her excitement. Suddenly an idea popped into her mind. "I'm going to help Father with the chores so we can open the package sooner," she yelled as she ran out the door.

"Me too!" "Me too!" "Let's go!" the rest of the children chimed in as they all rushed out the door.

It was just a short while until they all came scurrying back, pulling Father by the hand, chores finished. The children crowded all around the table, excited to see what was inside the mysterious box.

"Are we ready to open the package?" Fred smiled as he watched ripples of excitement waft through the circle of children.

Voices of excitement echoed throughout the small room as the children pushed closer, crowding up against the table.

Doty chuckled; she was excited too. Picking up the box, she read aloud, "'From Grandma Betsy.' This is from my grandma, your great grandma. I've talked about her before. She raised me when my mother went away. I wrote her a letter a few months ago. I know you haven't met her yet, but I told her about all of you. Let's open the package and find out what's in it."

As Doty untied the string and removed the brown paper from the package, silence blanketed the room. The children were breathless. Even Doty couldn't begin to imagine what was in the box. When she opened it, she saw smaller boxes inside, each wrapped in colorful wrapping paper and ribbon. There was a letter lying on top of the gifts. Doty opened the letter and read it to the kids:

Dear Doty and Family,

Thank you for your letter. I am so excited to hear from you and to know that I have so many wonderful great-grandchildren. I would love to see and meet you all, but I am not able to travel, so I did the next best thing. I sent each of you something special.

There's a package with your name on it for each of
you. I hope you enjoy it.

Love,

Great Grandma Betsy

The second page of the letter was written to Doty. When Fred wasn't looking, she quickly folded it and slipped it in her apron pocket to read later.

One by one, Doty took the packages out of the box and set them on the table. Each package had a name on it. Never having seen parcels like this, the children were spellbound. No one said a word as they gazed at the beautifully wrapped gifts. The children glanced around at each other breathlessly, each waiting for their own present.

Doty picked up a package as she looked at her excited children and suggested, "Why don't we open each gift one at a time so everyone can see what's in it?"

"Annabel, here's your package." Doty handed it to her. Annabel carefully reached out and gently took the box. Slowly turning the gift over and over, she examined it then finally set it gently on the table. The other children watched in awe as she slowly untied the ribbon. Carefully, Annabel unfolded the wrapping paper from the box. The paper was a beautiful red color, and she wasn't going to tear it.

"Hurry up, Annabel, I want to see what it is," Carolyn whined impatiently. Annabel ignored her. She savored the moment as she lifted her gift from the flat box.

"Look, everyone, Grandma sent me journals and pencils! I've never had any of my own before!" The delight in her eyes was obvious. She hugged the precious items to her chest, laid them on the table, and picked up the wrapping paper. Folding the wrapping paper carefully, she neatly placed the journals and pencils on top of it and tied them all together with the ribbon as her eyes danced with excitement.

"Carolyn, here's your package." Doty handed it to her.

Carolyn grabbed her gift, as excited about the beautiful wrapping paper and ribbon as she was about the gift. After carefully opening it, she proudly displayed two books to a chorus of ooh's and aahs. The family took their time examining each one. Books were a luxury very few people owned.

"Willie, here's yours." Doty smiled and handed him his package. As Willie slowly unwrapped his gift, everyone was mesmerized. Being just as careful as his sisters, he untied it, unfolded the wrapping paper, and pulled out his gift. "A baseball! Grandma sent me a real baseball!" Everyone ooh'd and aah'd.

But Rosy couldn't focus. She didn't care what everyone else got. She wanted to see what Grandma Betsy had sent her. Finally, Doty called her name, "Rosy, here's your gift from Great Grandma." With trembling hands, the young girl took her package and sat down. She quickly but carefully took the ribbon and paper off. As she unfolded the paper, she gasped. Her mouth opened and closed, but no sounds came out. There, lying in the midst of the paper was the most beautiful doll she had ever seen. It was handmade and all fancied up in a blue bonnet, a blue and white ruffled dress, with lace shoes. She had never had a doll. After a few moments of silence, tears started running down her cheeks. Rosy hugged the doll. "I think I'll call her Betsy, after Great Grandma." The doll quickly found its home in Rosy's heart.

Doty unwrapped a handmade stuffed animal for each of the two younger boys.

That evening, after the children were in bed, Doty glanced out the open door of the shanty to make sure Fred was sitting in his rocker and engaged in his evening activity. She didn't want any interruptions. He was sitting on the porch, relaxing from a long, hard day, his hand clasp loosely around his bottle, his eyes gazing out into the darkening dusk. She took the second page of the letter out of her apron pocket and opened it up:

Dear Doty,

I was excited to hear from you. As I said, I am unable to travel due to my health. I am living at my sister's now. She has welcomed me into her home to take care of me. Because of this, I have to say no to you and the children. I would love to have you come live with me; however, it is not possible because I have no home of my own now.

I am sorry that you are in this abusive situation. I feel bad for you and the children, but there is nothing I can do to help you right now. Have you tried writing to your father? Maybe things have changed and he might be willing to help. I'll look around and see if there are other possibilities.

I Love You,

Grandma Betsy

Doty folded the letter in her lap and lowered her face. *Daddy will never let me come home.*

Quickly wadding up the letter, Doty tossed it in the stove to burn. She couldn't take the chance that Fred would see it.

Devastated, she sat down at the kitchen table. Hope of that possibility is gone. *Now what am I going to do? I've got to get these kids away from Father, but I don't have any other options.*

SEVEN

1933

The afternoon sun blazed through the windows of the general store as a cloud of dust worked its way through the opened door coating everything inside. Near the back of the store, crates of produce lay wilting in the heat as a swarm of flies hovered over the meat counter. The proprietor, Sam, a middle-aged man with a balding pate and a long, thin nose, looked as limp as his vegetables as he swept listlessly at the dust on the wooden plank floor with a straw broom.

Fred walked into the general store and saw his neighbor Bill with a group of townsmen all gathered closely around the radio, chatting. Dropping two pence on the counter, Fred grabbed a newspaper before pulling up an empty crate and joining the other men.

"Hi, Bill," Fred said as he sat down beside him.

Bill returned his greeting as they shook hands.

"I didn't expect to see you here. Figured you'd be out workin'," Fred commented as he saw a look of concern on his neighbor's face.

"Figured I'd come in so I could hear what the news had to say about everything that's going on in the country. I'm worried about my job and my land," Bill confessed.

"Me too." Fred nodded an acknowledgment to the other men.

Fred had made it a point to keep up on the country's economic issues. Over the last few years, he managed to remain current on the country's state of events as they unfolded by listening to the radio and reading the newspapers. Fred sat with the other men around the radio, chatting and wondering what the current events would mean for him, his job, and his family.

Sam swept his pile of dust and dirt out the door and then leaned his broom against the counter. "The news is coming on any minute," he announced. He turned the radio on, pulled up a crate and sat down with the men. A hush fell over the large room.

Turned to its highest volume, the thin voice still barely filled the room. The men all leaned closer to the small wooden box. As they listened to the broadcast, no one spoke; each wondered what his own future would hold.

Fred wiped the sweat from his brow with the back of his sleeve. With the newly purchased newspaper in hand, he leaned forward with his elbows on his knees and his head down as he listened to the radio announcer's brief summary of the past few years:

"Hello, fellow countrymen," the announcer began. "I'm glad you joined us for the latest on the state of our economy and our country. As you well know, The Great Depression, which began with the stock market crash in 1929, has deepened. Economists are predicting that the collapse has set in motion a chain of events that will keep the country and most of the world in chaos for the next few years. Unemployment is expected to exceed 13 million. Charitable services will increase as soup kitchens feed many of the destitute. Much of the population is now migrant in their own land as they search the country looking for work.

"Making the situation worse are the severe droughts and high winds that are creating massive dust storms which are caused by over plowed and overgrazed lands. These so called 'black blizzards' that are ravishing much of the country's farmland are continuing to increase."

The radio announcer paused, and the sound of rustling paper was heard in the background. He cleared his throat and continued, "The effects of what has become known as the Dust Bowl in the Midwest have changed the weather patterns all over the country. Ecologists are saying that this year, 1933, almost 75% of the country is experiencing bone-dry conditions. The Dust Bowl is worsening and the rainfall is decreasing even more. Many displaced farm families are being added to the chaos. The working class is broke. None have money to spare."

There was a short pause, then the announcer continued. "Please stay tuned for more news after this word from our sponsor."

A jingle for Pepsi Cola came on: "Pepsi Cola hits the spot! Twelve full ounces—that's a lot. Twice as much for a nickel, too; Pepsi Cola is the drink for you…"

While the commercial played in the background, Fred sat quietly thinking about the news he had just heard, then addressed the men that were sitting around the radio. "For the last three years, my farm has been hit by severe drought. The wind is strippin' the topsoil off the land. I'm goin' broke and I'm scared of losin' my crop again. And it's gettin' worse. No tellin' how long it will last."

"The rain certainly didn't follow the plow this time," Bill stated as he glanced around the circle of men. "The drought we can't control, but maybe we can change some of our farming methods."

Discussion continued as the men evaluated their own bleak futures. When the news was over, Fred stood and nodded goodbye to the men. He turned and walked out of the store, thinking hard about what he'd just heard.

Fred shoved his hands into his pockets. *This country's financial problems have been slow ta reach Idaho, but now it's hittin' us just as hard. Construction's all but stopped, so lumber ain't sellin', and the mill is cuttin' back. And with no rain, farmers can't produce crops. With no work, how am I gonna make a living?*

Hopeless, he bent over, picked up a rock, and heaved it as far as he could. He walked out to his Model T and opened the door. *Now what am I gonna do?*

Fred could feel his mind and emotions bowing beneath the weight of his responsibilities. *I'm tryin' my hardest, but it's a battle I'm losin'.* He agonized over the situation as he sat in his car. After of few moments, he grabbed his whiskey from underneath the car seat, pulled out the cork, and took a long draw on the bottle. After a few moments, he grabbed his whiskey from underneath the car seat, pulled out the cork, and took a long draw on the bottle. As Fred started the car, a dark feeling of foreboding settled over him.

Disheartened, he mumbled to himself, "At least I got somethin' at home to help me feel better. It's my right."

A week later, Fred came home from work at noon. He got out of the car, whiskey bottle in hand, and hesitantly walked up to the shanty. Stopping at the steps, he stood silently, took a deep breath, and slowly exhaled, then stepped up onto the splintered wood. Fred lowered himself into his rocker, leaned back, and began slowly rocking as he stared out over the dry acreage of wilted crops.

He ignored Rosy and Willie as they sorted their favorite rocks out on the ground by the porch step, and Doty, as she came out and sat in the old rickety chair beside him, holding baby Henry. Fred appeared to be in a trance as he watched the horizon, but his mind was working overtime as he tried to digest the information that he had received that morning.

He raised the whiskey bottle to his mouth and let the last few drops dribble onto his tongue. He swore and hurled the bottle across the yard as hard as he could, shattering it against the water pump.

The children flinched but dare not scream. Doty stood up, cradling the baby away from his father and made eye contact with the other children. Unspoken commands understood.

Fred stared at the glittering shards of glass as they lay scattered on the ground. As he glared at the broken pieces, all he could see was his fragmented life: a life of hardship, of abuse, and brokenness. *No matter how hard I try ta put my life back together, nothin' works.*

Fred blinked and glanced at Doty with a look of warning. *I'm not in the mood to put up with none of your belly aching.*

The excitement passed; the children returned to their play as Doty sat down quietly in the chair beside him again.

Fred continued to rock as he silently struggled about how to tell Doty. He finally stopped rocking and gazed out over his withering fields. "Doty." Fred sat silent for a long moment as he continued to stare out into the distance. After taking a few deep breaths, he reluctantly continued. "I-I lost my job at the mill today." He swallowed hard. "We were told a couple a months ago that the mill was cuttin' back production. Then they told us a few weeks ago that if business didn't pick up, they'd have ta look at closin' the mill." He rubbed the back of his neck with his hand as he lowered his head and stared blankly at the warped floorboards of the porch. "Today was the day. This afternoon they laid us all off and closed the mill."

Doty could see the desperation in Fred's face, and that scared her.

"I knew this was comin'." Fred slowly shook his head. "At least I got almost six good years a work at the mill. But there're no other jobs around here; I checked. I've been askin' around and gettin' information about possible work, and everyone I talked to said California's the place ta go."

He sat silent. His mind continued to mull over the situation and, at the same time, he tried to deal with his desperation. Fred stood, placed his hands on the back of his waist, and slowly stretched his tense, stiff back.

He stepped off the porch and squatted down, pulling up some dead grass to examine it, and then tossed it back down. "It's the end of July, and there's even less rain this year; and the crops are dyin' again. I have no job, and now we have six kids. How are we gonna survive? We need ta eat." Fred stood back up, then sat down on the edge of the porch in silence.

Doty said nothing, afraid she would say the wrong thing.

Fred reached into his pocket and pulled out a flyer. He unfolded it and handed it to Doty. "This here paper says that there's work in California. It says there's lots a work with good pay. Most of the jobs are pickin' fruit and tendin' orchards and farms. My foreman at the mill said he heard that the pay was really good there."

Doty quickly scanned the flyer then glanced back up at Fred. She could see a faint flicker of hope in his eyes.

He turned his head and looked directly at Doty. "Since I can't find work here, maybe I can git a job in California. I think we should go. What ya think?"

Doty sat in shock. Fred had never asked for her opinion before; she was not sure what to say. Yearning to get away from the desert and harsh life that she chose an eternity ago, hope began to rise inside her. She pondered her answer to the question before she spoke. *I need to get out of this place, away from being trapped on the homestead, from living in a shack, from being isolated and lonely.*

Fred looked at her, waiting expectantly.

Doty's thoughts tumbled with possibilities. *Maybe we could have a nice home and a normal life. And the kids...the kids have never been anywhere except this farm and the small town of Emmett. They need to see more of the world. This could be our chance.*

The desire for change grew quickly. Yes, she wanted to go—desperately! She hadn't even realized how badly she wanted to go until the chance presented itself. *I have to choose my words carefully. I have to say them in a way that Fred will feel he is still in charge and that it's his decision.*

Avoiding Fred's eyes, she looked down at her baby as he slept in her arms. "The kids have to eat," she said calmly, "and with no crops and no work, right now I don't see any other way to survive. I think you have a good idea. If we go, when would we leave?" She turned her questioning eyes back to Father.

"Soon."

Curious, Doty asked, "What would we do with the homestead? Sell it?"

He pondered for a bit. "No, we can't sell it." He shook his head slowly as he spoke. "We can't git a good price out a it right now with the economy down. Plus, if things don't work out in California, we got a place ta come back to.

Maybe there'll be more rain for the crops by then. That's what we need, more rain."

Deep down, Doty started to get excited. "How soon is soon?"

Fred thought out loud. "We'll take time to butcher a pig so that we'll have food ta eat on the way. Then I need time ta sell the other livestock so we'll have the money to git there." He again looked intently out over his parched acres and watched as the thin clouds drifted slowly overhead. "I'll need to check out the car to make sure it's in good 'nough condition to make it all the way ta California. We'll need to pack only the essentials 'cause we won't have much room in the car with the kids. We could probably leave in a week."

Doty's thoughts started racing. *A week! I'll be out of here in a week! There's so much to do. There's very little room in the car so I'll have to take only what we absolutely need. We'll need food, clothes...*Doty's thoughts started churning.

Getting up from his old rocker, Fred made his decision. "The matter's settled. We'll leave one week from today. I'll go butcher a pig right now so you can start packin' the meat in the mornin'." He went to the pig pen, chose the smaller of the pigs and butchered it.

Fred also butchered a couple of chickens for dinner. Very seldom did they have chicken to eat. The birds were mostly for laying eggs, but tonight was a special occasion. They would have a nice dinner this evening. Afterwards, he would break the news to the children. He would tell them that they were all going to California.

Doty took Henry back into the house and laid him down for his nap, then went out to the barn to retrieve items she needed to salt the pork. Talking out loud to herself, she contemplated, "Let's see, one five-gallon keg of pork will help feed the family for about a week. I'll fix two kegs, that should be enough to feed us until we get to California and Fred finds work." She put two empty kegs, a couple bags of salt, and all the other items she needed to salt the pork out on the work-table behind the shanty. She would be ready to pack the meat after Fred sliced it up. Meanwhile, it was time to fix dinner.

Fred brought in the two chickens. "Here, Doty, I butchered a couple a chickens for dinner. We might as well eat 'em. We can't take 'em with us."

Doty was delighted. "The kids will love the chicken." She eagerly accepted the hens. "This'll be a real treat for them." Immediately, she lit the fire in the cook stove, and set a larger blaze beneath the giant pot in the yard for scalding. When all was ready, she plucked and cleaned the chickens and put them in the oven to bake. Quickly mixing up the dough for her mouth-watering, homemade bread, she placed it in the oven to bake along with the chickens. She also opened one of the last jars of canned green beans and put a pot of potatoes on to boil.

As the chickens roasted and the bread baked, the aroma drifted out of the open window and wafted in the breeze outside. Soon the children, who were playing outside, smelled the delicious aroma. Play stopped, and they followed their noses into the small farmhouse. Rosy took a big whiff, then tentatively asked, "Mom, are we having chicken for dinner?"

"Yes, we are." Doty grinned. "Now go get washed up."

"Hey guys, did ya hear that! We get chicken for dinner!" Rosy announced eagerly. "Hurry, let's go wash our hands!" Smiles beamed on each of the children's faces as they scurried off to wash for dinner.

Soon, the children were crowded around the small kitchen table, sitting impatiently on the makeshift benches. Along with the bread, green beans, and potatoes, Doty set the chicken on the table.

"I get a leg!" Rosy yelled.

"I get one too!" hollered Willie, eagerly grabbing a drumstick from one of the chickens. Each of the other children started to reach for a piece

Doty slapped Willie's hand. "Not so fast, young man," she scolded. "All of you, wait until you're served proper. "

Willie pulled his hand back and sat impatiently. He drooled as he licked the juice off his fingers. The other kids, not wanting their mother's scolding, waited impatiently along with him.

When Father finally sat down at the head of the table, the children quieted down. After serving Father first, Doty then served each of the children a portion, making sure there was plenty for everyone.

The children pulled, picked, and gnawed every morsel of meat off the chicken bones. Then they licked and sucked on the bones until every bit of flavor was gone. "Mom, this is the best chicken I ever tasted! Can I have some more?" begged Rosy.

Doty got up and started to clear the dishes from the table. "I'm sorry, but it's gone; there's no more chicken."

Rosy sat quietly for a moment. Suddenly her face lit up and she jumped up and grabbed her mother's chicken bones. The other children dove into Father's with both hands, grabbing every bone they could get ahold of. Without saying a word, they started gnawing and sucking on those bones too.

"I guess it has been a long time since we had chicken." Doty looked at Fred and smiled. They both chuckled.

After the dishes were done, Fred called all the children to sit on the floor. They came quietly and sat cautiously, not knowing what to expect. "Kids," Father started, "the lumber mill closed today. I lost my job, an' I can't find work 'round here."

The older kids glanced at each other with worry and fear in their eyes, waiting to see if Father was going to take his anger out on them.

"I have ta make money so we can buy food. So, I decided that we should go ta California so I can look for work. We'll all be leavin' for California one week from today. I'll find a job and we'll settle there for a while." The children sat for a bit, letting the unexpected news sink in as they looked back and forth at each other, and then back at Father. Questions started forming in their heads.

"Are we moving to California?" asked Willie.

"Yes, we're movin'," Father confirmed.

"Is it near town?" questioned Rosy.

"No, silly," Carolyn said, laughing, "California's near the ocean. It's at the end of the country."

After a bevy of questions, there was finally a quiet pause.

Suddenly Annabel yelled, "We're going to California! Yay!"

Commotion followed. The children started jumping and hugging, screeching, and shouting. Then unexpectedly, their voices giggled and joined together, chanting, "We're going to Califor-nia! We're going to Califor-nia! We're going to Califor-nia…"

After a few minutes, when the children's excitement was spent, Rosy looked up into her father's face. "Father, how far away is it?" she asked.

Then even more questions followed. "Will it take very long to get there?" Annabel inquisitively looked at Father.

Wanting Father's undivided attention, Willie stood right in front of him and looked directly into his eyes. "I want to go! What can I take?"

Fred actually took the time to answer the children's questions. "It'll take quite a few days, but it'll be excitin'. You'll go places you never been before and see things ya never seen."

After an evening full of discussion and questions, Doty finally inserted herself into the commotion, "Alright, kids, its bedtime."

"Aw, do we have to go to bed?" Rosy asked.

"I'm not tired. I want to stay up and talk," Carolyn whined.

Father gave them his firm look that meant, "Do what you're told."

The children stopped immediately and went to bed, but sleep evaded them. Filled with excitement, their curious minds continued working as they lay in bed, trying to imagine their new life in California.

Rosy lay on her bed, wondering. *What will it be like? I've never been away from home before. Will we ever be able to come back again?* Pulling her blanket up to her chin, she finally drifted off to sleep with unanswered questions swirling around in her mind.

EIGHT

When Fred woke the next morning, the burden of the decision he made the night before had grown even heavier. As he lay in bed, jumbled thoughts cluttered his mind. The idea of uprooting his family and moving hundreds of miles away to a strange place frightened him, but he was somewhat excited for the change.

He sat up on the edge of his bed. Gazing at his wife, he watched her deep, regular breaths with envy. Thinking of all his responsibilities and everything he had to do, he felt like he could barely breathe. Running his hands over his face and through his hair, he tried to wipe the confusion from his mind, but the distressing thoughts stayed with him as he got up and dressed. He grabbed his knife and headed out behind the barn to finish the job he had started the evening before. *Maybe being busy will help me keep from dwelling on the situation. It sure couldn't hurt.*

He sliced the strips of meat from the drained carcass and placed them in a wooden box as he worked. When the box was full, he toted it to the house and gave the meat to Doty, who was now up and dressed. She went to work, smiling and humming as she rubbed salt into each strip of meat to preserve it and then placed it in the kegs. Fred gazed at her, irritated at her happiness. He shook his head and went back out to cut more meat.

After the kegs were packed full, Doty took the meat that was left and roasted it in the oven. *I'm not going to waste one precious bit of this meat. My family will enjoy roasted pork for the whole week. We will eat well for a change.*

Fred put the chickens in some crates and loaded them into the backseat of the car. After tying the farm animals to the back bumper in hopes to sell the livestock in town for a good price, he drove the Model T at a very slow pace so the animals could keep up. He left for town with the livestock following reluctantly behind, fighting the pull of the rope.

It took a while, but he finally found someone that would buy the animals, but not for even close to the price he was expecting. Infuriated, Fred headed back home. On the way, he stopped at the moonshiner's shack and used some of the money from the sale of the animals to buy a few bottles of whiskey for his trip.

Fred arrived home fuming as he barged into the house. Initially excited, the children quieted down as they took note of their father's mood. Fred slammed the door, let go of a string of swear words, and ranted to anyone who would listen. "Right now, there's not much demand for livestock. I was lucky to get 'bout a third of what those animals are actually worth!" He paced back and forth.

"Since the mill closed and most people lost their jobs, they've got no money neither. A lot of the people around here can't even feed the livestock they got and don't want any more ta take care of. An' others that are leavin' to find work elsewhere can't git rid of the animals they got." His pacing slowed as his anger turned to frustration. "Even if they could sell the critters, I hear the prices are down everywhere. Those of us that are takin' our families and leavin' to look for work are gonna need that money for gas and travel expenses." As he spoke, his anger gradually subsided. His pace slowed more, and he finally sat down on a crate, still irritated.

Doty signaled her children to go outside then turned to listen silently as Fred's words planted little seeds of worry in her mind. Stopping at the door, Rosy looked back at her mother. Doty smiled and waved the child on.

With the kids outside now, Doty focused again on Fred. She listened to him as he ranted; his words made her began to doubt that he had made the right choice. However, the decision was made. Doty knew that Father would not change his mind now.

But deep down, she continued to question his decision. *Will we have the money to get where we're going? Will Father be able to find a job once we get there? Where will we stay, and how will we eat?* Knowing that Father's decision was final, Doty tried to put the concerns out of her mind. Staying busy helped, so she pulled herself together and continued packing the items she knew they would need to survive.

The day before they left, Doty called the children together and instructed them, "Okay, kids, it's time for you to start your packing! Pack only your clothes."

"We only get to take our clothes?" whined Carolyn. "Can't I take my books?"

"And what about my journals and pencils?" Annabel joined in. "It'll be a good time to write." Not wanting to leave their treasures behind, the younger children echoed their siblings' wishes.

Looking at her children's downcast faces, Doty softened. "You can take one special thing. By the time we load what's needed, there'll be precious little room for anything else."

Rosy *knew* what she was going to take. She didn't have much, but what she had was precious to her. She was taking Betsy, the doll that Great Grandma had made for her. Her handmade doll was her prize possession. Betsy was the most beautiful doll Rosy had ever seen. It was the only doll she had ever owned, and she was definitely taking her. Hugging her doll tightly, Rosy was determined. "I'm taking Betsy! I won't leave her behind!"

"I'm taking my leather baseball." Willie tossed the ball into the air and caught it. "Then I'll have something to play with when we stop along the way."

The other children made their choices of things to take as well.

Only the essentials had been packed, things that would be needed as they traveled and when they reached their new home. Very little would be left behind, as they had little to start with. Doty packed the food, pots and pans, dishes, clothes, and bedding, and Fred packed his tools, a tent, and extra car parts they might need along the way. After making sure the car was in good running condition for the long drive, Fred pronounced everything ready.

Finally, the day came for them to leave. It took longer to get everything stuffed into the vehicle than Fred had planned. Doty had packed the car's wooden trunk as full as possible, and Fred strapped it to the back of the Model T. He loaded and reloaded everything at least three times, trying to get everything to fit just right in the car. Finally, he tied bundles on the top and back of the vehicle. By the time he was ready to go, the morning had slipped away.

Since it took until noon to get everything organized and loaded, they got a late start. The three older girls and Willie climbed into the backseat, holding tightly to their prize possessions. Fred, Doty, two-year-old George, and baby Henry were in the front. Finally, everything was loaded, the farmhouse was closed up, and everyone was in the vehicle.

Ready to leave, Fred sat silently for a few minutes staring at the homestead. He turned to his wife. "Doty, do ya' have everything packed and in the car?"

"We have everything we planned on taking. Some of our belongings are staying. I hope no one bothers our property while we are gone."

"Then let's go!" Fred's voice was full of anxiety. This was hard for him. The feeling of failure overcame him, again. He grabbed a bottle from under the seat, took a couple of big swigs of whiskey, corked it, and placed it back under the front seat with the rest of his stash. He did not want to leave his home and drag his family all over the country.

Doty could see in his eyes the anger and fear, even though he tried hard to hide it. She struggled too, not because of what she had to leave behind, but because of the uncertainty of the future. It was hard to risk her children's future and well-being on something she knew nothing about. It was hard for them both to leave their home, but they knew that they could no longer stay.

Taking a deep breath, Fred gripped the steering wheel and stepped down on the starter switch. The Tin-Lizzie sputtered to life. He pulled the throttle wide open, and the car coughed out a large cloud of smoke. The rear wheels spun; one of them found traction, lurching the vehicle forward. Fred turned from the farm driveway onto the main street, which was nothing more than a rutted road. A part of him could not get out of there fast enough, but another part loathed leaving.

Conflicting emotions continued to build up in his mind. He mulled over the feelings of leaving his home behind and entering the unknown. *What am I doing? I'm taking my family and leaving behind my home, my livelihood, and everything I own—*

and for what, a questionable future? He put his hand under his seat and touched the bottles to make sure they were still there, taking comfort in knowing his whiskey would drown out his feelings of desperation and fear.

"Goodbye, house," the children echoed each other in the backseat. "Goodbye, barn. Goodbye, dirt. Goodbye, home. Goodbye…"

Giggles filled the air.

Having left the homestead later than Fred had planned, it was already early afternoon by the time they reached Highway 30, heading west out of Idaho. As he drove down the gravel highway that led to Ontario, Oregon, his thoughts continued to be plagued by uncertainty over his decision to leave. He did his best to put the doubt out of his mind.

By mid-afternoon, the day was settling in to be a scorcher. Trying to put his troubles behind him, Fred forced himself to think of positive things. After reflecting for a while, he glanced at his wife then back at the road. "Doty, once we arrive in Ontario, we'll head towards Burns. Since that's where ya lived as a child and ya still got family there, I think it'd be good for you to see 'em again; ya haven't seen 'em for years." He looked at her and smiled. "Plus, your uncle owns a small hotel there. We should be able ta stay with them for a few nights."

Fred snickered under his breath as a smirk played around his mouth. *We won't have to worry about where ta stay or what ta eat, it'll be free room and board for a few nights.* He smiled again, cutting his eyes to the side, looking at Doty.

Talking as if this was all about doing something special for Doty, Fred continued, "That would give ya time to visit with your family and give the relatives time ta get acquainted with the kids. Why don't we stop at the general store in Ontario to call your aunt and uncle and let them know we're comin'? I bet we could stay as long as we want."

Surprised at the suggestion, Doty perked up, her lips curving into a small smile. Excited about seeing family, but scared that they might not accept her, she forced a larger smile for Fred's sake. "Really?" She adjusted two-year-old George in the seat. She looked at Fred questionably. "We can stop and see my family? I haven't seen them since I was a child. I don't even really know them anymore. Wonder what they'll think of us." All of a sudden, a yearning to see her family and reconnect with the past rose inside her. As she thought about it, anticipation slowly filled her body. She started to fidget and her legs grew restless. Needing to release the pent-up energy and excitement, she picked up baby Henry and rocked him heartily in her arms.

The four children in the backseat were still excited. They were chattering, watching the landscape, giggling, and enjoying the trip. Doty loved the sound of her happy children. She listened to the prattle as she watched the scenery slip by. Henry and George rode contentedly and seemed to enjoy the motion of the vehicle from the front seat. Henry cooed as Doty rocked him and George chattered. It was amazing what a change of scenery did for the family.

At around 25 miles an hour, Fred was planning on being in California in a little over a week and a half, depending on how long they stayed with Doty's relatives. The driving seemed to help him relax a bit as he mulled over his plans.

I'll start lookin' for a job in the lumber mills of northern California; havin' mill experience will help. If that doesn't pan out, I'll move on down state and look for a farmin' job or a job pickin' crops...anything to make money to feed my family. I'm sure I can find some kind of work.

As Fred contemplated, Rosy sat in the backseat singing. She loved music; she loved to make up her own songs. As she sang her own created tune, she danced her doll, Betsy, on her lap. "We're going to Califor-nia, to git a new house. Betsy will love it. I hope there's no mouse." The other children laughed at Rosy and her creation, but she didn't care; she loved singing. Ignoring her siblings, Rosy sang, and Betsy danced on her lap. The happiness was evident on Rosy's face and the music was inviting. Soon, all the kids joined her in singing her song.

Doty laid her head back, rested, and enjoyed the excitement that filled the car.

Fred craved his next drink.

The land was arid but beautiful. The deep blue sky adorned with slivers of pure white clouds gave contrast to the purple mountains in the far distance and the flat brown and tan scorched earth of the desert. Heat from the sun beat down on the parched terrain and was absorbed by the metal of their vehicle. As the wind wound its way through the car's open windows, it provided little relief from the high temperatures.

Eventually, the children's excitement settled down to a low chatter. They watched out the windows as the changing landscape passed them by, amazed at the new world they were seeing for the first time.

Because they started much later than they had planned, Fred didn't make it as far as he had hoped. It had been a long and emotionally tiring day. Now the sun was going down, so he had to find a place to camp for the night. The time and miles would have to be made up tomorrow. He slowed down and watched along the side of the highway, looking for an open field that would make a good place to camp. It would be a nice change, sleeping out under the stars.

Fred found a spot, pulled off the road into an open grassy area, and stopped. "I'll unpack and put up the tent while you make a campfire and cook dinner," Fred ordered Doty. "Annabel," Fred called out, "come give me a hand with the tent. "

"I'll help you, Fred," Doty offered.

"Did I ask for yer help? Do what I told ya."

Doty dropped her head, but quietly complied.

"Annabel," Fred called to his oldest daughter again. Annabel exchanged a look with Doty and Carolyn, but then hurried after her father.

Because of the eventful day, everyone was hungry and tired. As soon as they had eaten and the beds were made, the children and Doty crawled into the tent and under the covers. It wasn't long before they were sound asleep. As darkness surrounded them, Father sat quietly by the campfire and pulled out a bottle of whiskey.

The next day, Father was up early but struggled with a hangover. He was light-headed and dizzy. His head felt like it would explode, and the bright morning sun made his eyes ache. "I need a drink," he muttered to himself. Taking a few swigs of whiskey to doctor his hangover, he grimaced as the liquid burned its way down his throat, but then sighed as he felt the much-anticipated relief. "Ahh, the hair of the dog!" he uttered. Soon, he felt a little better.

The family ate breakfast, packed, and was soon back on the road. Cool morning air rushed through the open car windows, twisting and tangling the children's unkempt hair. This morning the kids were a little more settled. They sat quietly, gazing out at the beautiful, dry landscape, enjoying the cool morning breeze as it wafted across their faces.

For Doty, this was a nice relaxing time. She hadn't sat this still in years. The corners of her lips flattened out, and she let her mind unwind. She just reflected on life as she gazed at the passing countryside and hoped that this change would be good for her children.

The day was long, but it went by without a hitch. The children entertained each other as Rosy made up another of her little ditties and taught it to her siblings. The babies slept from the rocking motion of the car, and Doty, for the first time in a long time, felt hope.

NINE

That afternoon they arrived in Burns. Surrounded by farmland and ranches, the small picturesque town was a welcome sight. The hotel wasn't hard to find. There were only two in town, and Doty's uncle's hotel sat on the outskirts of the rural community. As they turned into the long, graveled driveway, all eyes cut immediately to the huge two-story hotel that resembled a large farmhouse. The large white building had a pitched roof and numerous windows with curtains neatly pulled back, dotting the front and sides of the hotel, upstairs and down. A big beautiful porch surrounded the building, its roof held up by pillars. Chairs and a porch swing were placed in the shade, creating a relaxing area for guests to sit and enjoy the day.

The children all pressed forward, leaning out the windows and chattering like excited birds. Doty smiled at her children. *This is a far cry from our three-room shanty.*

The family got out of the car slowly. Doty and Fred exchanged an apprehensive look, and with a breath stepped forward.

A middle-aged man and woman made their way out the main door of the hotel and Doty's eyes filled with tears. "Aunt Emmy? Uncle Ray?" She spoke hesitantly and took a tentative step toward them. Taking Doty into their arms, they squeezed her. After a moment, she slipped her arms around them and returned the hug. "It's been so long."

Standing behind them, Fred gathered the children near him and stood silently watching. Doty continued hugging her aunt and uncle as tears of joy and relief streamed down her face. "I've missed you all so much!"

Then she turned to her waiting family. "This is my husband, Fred. Fred, this is my Uncle Ray, my dad's brother, and his wife Aunt Emmy. And these are my kids…" Before Doty could say anything else, giggling, excited children began pouring out the front door of the hotel.

Aunt Emmy chuckled. "And these are some of your cousin's children. Come on in, and we'll introduce everyone. I'm glad you called ahead, that way we could all be here to greet you!"

As Doty walked into the house, there was an explosion of noise. Excited voices came at her from all directions. She was greeted by adults and children alike. Her cousins and their children were all present to see her. She had never expected a welcoming like this. There were hugs, introductions, and smiles—lots of smiles. She would have the next couple of days to get reacquainted, and there would be time for their families to get to know each other. Her lonesome heart seemed to burn a little brighter, and a beautiful glow escaped from her face. She couldn't remember the last time she felt so welcome. Fred stood near the door, taking in the scene. A shadow crawled over his features.

Doty was introduced to her cousins, Uncle Ray, and Aunt Emmy's children. She scarcely remembered them from when they all were young, but they were now adults like her. Not having seen them for so long, she didn't recognize any of them; everyone had changed so much, including herself. As her aunt and uncle introduced them one by one, each cousin greeted Doty and her family with a wide smile, a big "hello," and huge hugs. Their nieces and nephews also crowded around them, brimming with excitement. There were twenty-one in all.

What a wonderful family. Doty marveled.

The next two days were glorious. There were friends and relatives, food and laughter. The time slipped by quickly as they visited, reminisced, and enjoyed each other's company. The women enjoyed working together, baking bread and biscuits for Doty's family to take on their trip. The children played outside most of the time and got to know their cousins. The men sat around discussing the country's sad condition; the Depression, the drought and Dust Bowl, and the thousands of people forced to migrate to look for work.

But Fred made himself scarce. His current situation and past memories continued to haunt him. He stayed away from everyone and wandered around outside, fondling the whiskey bottle he carried in a pocket of his jeans.

"Where's Fred?" Uncle Ray walked over to Doty and sat down beside her on the porch swing. "I ain't seen much of that husband of yours at all. I'd like to get to know him a little before ya'll have to hit the road again."

"Uncle Ray…" Doty looked down at her feet as she spoke. "Fred isn't much of a social person. He's also fretting because he lost his job and is worried about finding work." She clasped her hands and placed them on her lap as she glanced back at her uncle. "Maybe it's better if we just let him be for now. When he wants to talk, he'll come in."

Ray studied Doty's face before answering, then dipped his chin, coming to resolution. "Alright," he said, reaching out a hand and gently covering Doty's. "I know it's been hard for you, and I do feel bad for Fred. I hope he can find some work soon."

A thought suddenly occurred to Doty. *I never even thought about asking Uncle Ray and Aunt Emmy if they could help us get away from Father and his abuse. I wonder if they'd be willing.* "Uncle Ray—"

"Mom! Uncle Ray!"

Hearing the panicked voice, Ray and Doty instantly looked up.

"Help! Somebody...help!" Rosy came running toward the house, screaming. "Something's wrong with Gabe! He's choking!"

Sitting on the porch just outside the screen door, Ray, Doty, and Emmy heard the scream and saw Rosy running towards them. They jumped up and ran to meet her; others followed. Doty's four-year-old cousin, Gabe, came staggering across the yard, gagging and clutching his throat. He collapsed to the ground, unconscious. Gabe's father came running over and scooped the child up, cradling him in his arms. The boy lay motionless and pale, his legs and arms hanging limp.

Hearing the screams, the child's mother ran from the hotel kitchen, her hands and arms coated with flour. Seeing that it was her son in trouble, she screamed, "Gabe!" and frantically raced over to his side. Her child was not breathing. As he lay in his father's arms, she started patting her son's face, attempting to get him to take a breath. "Breathe, Gabe, breathe!"

Gabe's father quickly laid him on the grass, and together, he and the boy's mother worked furiously to try and force air down their son's throat. His father reached into the child's mouth, hoping to locate what it was that obstructed the airway, but his fingers met resistance. The inside of his mouth was torn and bleeding; the throat was swollen shut.

Panicking, his father thumped him on the back; his mother tried to breathe into his mouth. Finally, he gasped and took in a breath. Gabe gagged as he continued to gasp and choke for air, but at least he was finally breathing.

Rosy stared intently as the adults continued to help the young boy. They worried over him, rubbing and patting his back, and watching the rise and fall of his chest as they cried tears of relief. She watched as Gabe struggled to breathe.

Fear filled her heart and her stomach soured. She knew what had happened. Rosy knew what Father had done: experience had taught her.

Gabe was only four, still a baby. He hadn't deserved this. She folded her arms tight across her chest and bit down on her lip as she fearfully looked around for the man who'd caused this pain. For a long time, she had fostered a hatred in her heart for the abuse that Father had already done to her—and to her family—now he hurt Gabe. And now he had also made sure that she and her family would not be able to stay with or see her cousins again.

Frightened and ashamed, she quietly retreated to the porch and folded herself into a ball, cowering in the corner where no one would notice her.

Coming from out of nowhere, Father staggered over to the boy and surveyed the chaos. "Poor lil' feller. Somethin's wrong with 'im," he slurred, smirked, and staggered off into the yard, chuckling.

Rosy glared at him as he turned and staggered away. She wondered, *Why-why did Father hurt Gabe?* She couldn't understand. In her mind, thoughts collided with each other, thoughts of confusion and panic.

Gabe's parents hurriedly loaded him into their car and drove to the small hospital on the other side of town as fast as they could.

As soon as Gabe and his parents were gone, Fred quickly approached Doty, grabbed her by the arm, and glared at her. Slurring, he hissed, "It's time to get goin'! Doty, start packin', we're leavin'…now!"

By the tone of his voice, Doty knew better than to argue with him. Memories of Father's threats, abuse, and other cruelties tumbled through her mind. Afraid not to do as Father insisted, Doty packed swiftly, loaded up her children, and said a hurried goodbye. Sad and ashamed, she did not want to leave, but she knew they couldn't stay.

Doty knew that when Gabe's parents got back, they would know what Father had done, and in their rage, they would look to punish him.

They will try to kill him…and they would put me and the kids out. Stuck in the middle of nowhere with nothing. Father is a mean, abusive drunk, and he just sexually abused a four-year-old boy, and now he has cut me off from the last of my family.

Just sitting beside Father in the car made Doty feel unclean, dirty, like she had been a part of his evil. Seeing the smirk on his face made her feel cold inside; he was depraved. Aversion and anger churned in Doty's mind, stirring her emotions.

Fred took a drink from his bottle and looked at Doty. "I guess you can't go back there again." He smirked again, took another drink, and turned his eyes back to the road.

As she sat in the front seat, she gripped the babies tightly, trying to keep them as far away from the beast as possible. In the rear seat the older children sat quietly. Doty tucked herself tightly against the passenger side door. *He's ruined Gabe's life; he's taken his childhood away the same way he's taken my children's childhoods away…*

Doty's hatred towards Father festered. Recollections of him molesting their own children roared through her thoughts as anger and bitterness filled her heart and mind. *But how can I stop him…?* Her whole body quivered with apprehension. *I want to confront him; I want to hurt him. I want him out of our lives.*

However, fear for her own children's safety restrained her. She knew if she said one word to him, it would open the door to release her anger, and she wouldn't be able to stop. And just one wrong word to Father would be all the reason he needed to take out his fury on her or the children. In that knowledge, she bit down on her thoughts and swallowed her words. She sat quietly, holding in her pent-up rage, hating herself because she knew that Father was comfortable knowing she would do nothing.

She felt tense, and her stomach constricted as she reflected on what Father had done to Gabe. She was heartsick, but Doty also knew that her family couldn't survive without Father.

As they drove out of Burns, Doty knew that she could never go back again.

Fred drove as fast as the Model T would go, watching in the rearview mirror for police cars. He knew they would be after him. He had to get across the California border— soon. Knowing it would take a couple of days to get there, Fred kept the throttle wide open. He needed to put as much distance between himself and the cops as possible. Recalling the details of the map, he would have to take U.S. Highway 97 to California, and then hit Highway 99 which would carry them down through California.

Why did I do something so stupid? Blasted Doty, I knew she was thinking about leaving me. Now I have to be on the lookout for the police too. He grabbed his bottle of whiskey from between his legs and after twisting out the cork with his teeth, guzzled it until the bottle was empty. He hurled the empty bottle out the window and watched as it shattered on the roadway.

Doty leaned tightly against the passenger side door, staring out the window. Though she had not spoken to him, Father could tell that she was churning on the inside. He waved a hand toward her as if cutting the air. *Let 'er seethe. She'll do what I tell 'er and keep er mouth shut or she'll answer to me.*

The vehicle was filled with silence and quiet desperation as no one, not even the children, made a sound or spoke a word.

TEN

Fred continuously glanced in the mirrors. His mind spun as he tried to assess the situation. *It'll take 'bout six hours to get from Burns ta Bend, then a little over six hours from there ta California. If all goes well, includin' all the stops we have ta make, it'll take a long day ta get to and 'cross the California-Oregon state line.* Father again glanced in the rearview mirror, then back at the road. *I think it's a better idea ta drive slow for two short days rather than hard and fast for one long one. I don't know what's happenin' in Burns, but if the police are after me, I don't want 'em ta find me.* He throttled the car back and slowed down. *I gotta keep a low profile, take it slow and easy, an' not draw attention ta myself in any way.*

Full of sadness for Gabe, Rosy stared out the window as she rode quietly in the backseat of the car with the other children. Her compassion for her cousin was strong. Unsettled and confused, her insides churned as her heart ached for him. She cut her eyes to the back of Father's head, and anger swelled again at what he had done. Powerless, she swallowed her thoughts and turned again to look outside at the passing landscape.

They had been driving for about three hours when Rosy noticed that the scenery was gradually shifting. Slowly, pine and juniper trees came into view. As she watched, the arid desert gradually transformed into forested mountains with tall trees, green grasses, and beautiful flowers.

But now Rosy was emotionally and physically exhausted from the trauma and the hours of riding. Sitting in the backseat, she pulled her legs up to her chest, wrapped her arms around them, and curled up facing the door. As she stared out the window, her feelings slowly changed along with the scenery of the countryside. Her inner turmoil gradually dissipated, leaving her empty, numb of all feeling. Her thoughts swirled with excuses trying to explain away her father's actions; *Maybe it wasn't as bad as it seemed. Maybe Gabe did something to deserve it. Maybe Father was just drunk. Maybe…maybe…maybe…* No matter what she came up with, nothing would explain away what Father had done. But she was tired now—tired of thinking, tired of riding, tired of hating, tired of being scared, tired of worrying, tired of being tired. She gradually closed her eyes and slowly drifted off to sleep.

That night, just outside of Bend, they made camp along the highway. Pulling into the campground, Father was still followed by fear as he muttered under his breath, "I'll park the car back behind the tent where the police can't see it if they come by." He pulled the car as far back into the campground as possible.

"Doty, I'll set up the tent while ya fix dinner. It's been a long day, so let's eat and get ta bed so we can get an early start in the mornin'!"

Without uttering a word, Doty begrudgingly obeyed. As soon as dinner was over, everyone went to bed except for Father.

He didn't sleep much that night. Father dozed off and on as he sat in the vehicle, watching for the police, hoping they weren't hunting for him. The next morning, he woke the family up early, quickly packed, and was back on the road.

Everyone was quiet again that morning. They could read Father's mood and knew he would still not tolerate anything—no talking, no fighting, and no bickering.

As he drove, Fred started relaxing some. A few swigs of whiskey and fresh morning air helped to clear his head. After driving for an hour or so, he finally spoke, "This mornin' there seems to be a lot of traffic. I bet it's mostly migrants headin' ta California ta look for work."

Doty didn't respond. Fred looked at her, hesitated, and glanced up, checking the rearview mirror again. He then sat silently as he drove, attempting no more conversation.

Seeing that there were no cops, he felt a little safer this morning as he blended in with the heavy traffic. However, as he drove, he still kept a close eye on the rearview mirror.

Suddenly, in the distance, Fred heard a faint siren. As the siren grew gradually louder, the hair on the back of his neck stood up; fear engulfed him. Looking in the rearview mirror, he saw a Model A police car with lights flashing, pulling up quickly behind his car. His heart skipped a few beats and then started pounding as his chest tightened. He couldn't say a word.

The police car continued to follow close behind; the cops had found him. Filled with dread, his heart beat rapidly as panicked thoughts raced through his mind. *What should I do? Should I stop? Should I try ta outrun the cops?* His muddled mind swirled as he continued to stare into the rearview mirror. Then he reasoned, *If I don't stop, they'll chase me down anyhow. Besides, I can't outrun the police with a car full a kids.*

Nervously, Fred decided to take the chance and pull over. His knuckles were white as he gripped the steering wheel. Cutting his eyes quickly to the side, he glanced at

Doty; he saw both fear and relief in her eyes. Just as quickly, his eyes returned to the rearview mirror.

Doty sat silently in fear, grasping her baby with one arm, gripping the door handle with the other hand, and clenching her jaws. As her heartbeat sped up, dread of how Father would react filled her gut, but at the same time, she felt relieved, hoping this might all be over soon.

Unwillingly, Father pulled the Model T over to the side of the road, stopped, and sat anxiously waiting for his arrest, his eyes darting around looking for a possible quick escape. Then unexpectedly, the police car rapidly pulled out around Father's car, raced past him, and continued on its emergency call.

Fred gasped, then exhaled with a sigh of relief as his trembling hands gradually released the tightness of his grip on the steering wheel. Sitting silently, he closed his eyes, rested his forehead on the wheel, and tried to gather his wits. For a long moment, Fred dared not even to move. *Breathe, just breathe.* His heart slowed as his breaths deepened and his body began to relax from the perceived close call. Raising his head, he inhaled, smiled, and without so much as a spoken word, he turned the wheel to the left, and pulled back out onto the road. No one uttered a word.

With his mind on high alert, Fred continued to watch for the cops. His eyes were constantly bouncing back and forth between the sideview and the rearview mirrors as he drove, and he stopped only when absolutely necessary. That night, they camped about fifty miles from the state line. It had been a nerve-racking day and a half, but they were almost to California.

The next morning, Father turned on to Highway 99. He smirked, knowing he was safer, having crossed the state line. He hadn't seen any more police; chances of the cops coming after him now were very slim. He grinned to himself and sped up.

───────≈───────

After finally arriving in California, Fred turned his attention towards finding a job. Watching the landscape as he drove, he pointed toward the green forest covering the mountainsides. "Look at that, Doty—trees everywhere. There's money to be had here fer a fellow who's not afraid ta work."

When she didn't answer, he turned his attention back to the road. Smiling and humming to himself, he tried to organize his thoughts. *In northern California, there's lots of loggin' in the forests. I'll drive us south a ways, down Highway 99…*

After his plan had come together in his mind, he looked at his wife, who still hadn't looked in his direction. He shook his head. "Tsk, tsk, tsk."

Eventually, Doty grudgingly asked, "Now what? Now that we're in California, what're we going to do?"

Fred glanced at her then looked back at the road. "I'm gonna find a job. I'll find us a little mountain town and check at the lumbermill. There's gotta be work in the mills."

Fred nodded to himself. "Yep, that's what I'm gonna do. Every town we go through that's got a mill, I'll stop and see if they're hirin'. I can work on the green chain or cut trees or anythin' else they need me to do. I just want a job."

Doty could see the hope start to grow in Fred's eyes.

Traffic streamed up and down the major highway as Fred fell in line with the other vehicles. "Look at all the traffic," he exclaimed, overwhelmed by the busyness of the thoroughfare. "Ain't never seen these many vehicles on a highway." Having never driven in heavy traffic before, he drove cautiously as he watched for 'Hiring' signs and for cops.

As the family continued on their way, Doty studied the migrants on the road. Most vehicles on the highway were heavily packed with household goods. A few were parked or broken down along the sides of the roadway. Some people had pitched tents while others hitched rides to get somewhere. Realizing that she and her family fit right in with the caravan, her stomach churned. *I guess this is my way of life now, whether I like it or not.*

The first town they came to was Yreka. Fred drove slowly all around the small town, looking for the lumber mill. He spied a middle-aged white man walking down the side of the street. The man was unshaven, wearing dirty pants, and a soiled shirt, but he strode with purposed steps. Pulling over and flagging down the local, Fred smiled his friendliest. "Hello, mister! Could you tell me if there's a lumber mill 'round here? I'm lookin' for a job."

The man stopped and smirked. "You and hundreds of others," he replied, rubbing his chin. "Everyone's lookin' for work. And yeah, there's a mill, but they ain't hirin'."

"Where's it at? I need ta check anyway. I need a job really bad," Fred answered as he gestured at the kids in the backseat.

"It ain't gonna do ya any good, but do what ya have to. Turn left on the next road and go a mile or so. You'll come right to it. I wish ya luck!" The man nodded at him, spitting a stream of yellowed tobacco juice between his teeth, he turned away and continued his trek.

Fred thanked the man and headed directly to the mill. Pulling into the parking lot, he parked beside the building. The place looked deserted. He got out of his vehicle and quickly looked the wooden structure over. It was dilapidated and in need of serious repair; the windows were broken, the paint peeling, and the roof needed patched. The mill's office door, warped from the heat, hung crooked on its hinges. It stood part way open, revealing nothing but the shadows inside. Fred walked to the entrance and peaked in, knocked, and hollered, "Anyone here?" There was no answer.

Pushing on the door, it swung open slowly, groaning on rusted hinges. Fred walked in and was assaulted by a hot, dry stink. An older man with gray hair that hung limp across his forehead, sat hunched behind a rundown desk. The man's hands rested limply on the bulge of his paunch. He sat, unseeing, staring through the cracked pane of a window that was covered in layers of dirt and grime.

The office was in disarray; files and empty supply crates were stacked in several different clusters around the small space. A stack of disheveled papers lay scattered across the desktop. The man didn't respond to Fred.

"Hello, sir? I'm Fred."

There was no answer.

"I've come lookin' for a job and was hopin' that you were hirin'," Fred spoke respectfully. "I've worked at a mill before, and I know what I'm doin'. I could sure use a job."

The older man slowly turned his head toward Fred and looked at him with surprise. Batting his eyes and swallowing before answering, he let his eyes travel the length of Fred before coming to rest back on his face.

"I'm sorry, we're not hiring. In fact, I had to close the mill and lay off fifteen men a few weeks ago." He started to shuffle the papers on his desk and then gave up. Looking towards Fred again, he shook his head. "Construction is down and lumber's not selling. No one's buying or building because they've no money. There're no jobs here, and I'm afraid you'll not find work of any kind anywhere around here." He turned his head back toward the window and silently continued his forlorn gaze through the dirty pane.

"Thank ya kindly," Fred replied with disappointment in his voice. Dejected, he turned and walked out the door. He returned to his car, slipped into the driver's seat, and continued down the road without saying a word.

After a few more miles, they came to another rural community. Fred drove through the small lumber town, and his hopes rose again. "Look, there's a sign that says, 'Hiring'." As he drove up and stopped beside the mill building, he could tell that it was deserted too. The door was hanging on one hinge, windows were broken out, and through the glassless window frames, he could see birds nesting in the rafters. Fred did not bother to get out. He started the car and continued on his way as the children slept in the backseat.

"We've been driving for hours." Doty sighed. "When the kids wake up, they'll be hungry. We should find a place to stop and eat lunch."

Begrudgingly, Fred agreed. "I guess it'd be nice to get out and stretch a bit. I'm gettin' kind a hungry too." He slowed down, looking for a place to pull off the road. It wasn't too long before he saw a nice shady spot under a grove of trees. He pulled over and parked.

When the lulling motion of the vehicle ceased, the children began to rouse. Seeing that they had stopped, they bounced back to life. The youngsters piled out of the car with renewed energy, running, giggling and, playing while

Doty fixed lunch. Soon, a meager meal of biscuits, pork, and water was ready for them. The family sat in the shade under a tree and enjoyed what little food they had by eating it slowly, savoring every bite, and making it last as long as they could.

Willie finished his lunch first. Licking his fingers, he yelled, "Hey! Let's play catch. I'll go get my baseball out of the car." Full of energy, he jumped up and ran to the vehicle. Racing back with the ball, he started tossing it to the other children. Fred and Doty joined them, and the entire family was soon enjoying a game of catch.

"Father! Here, catch!" Willie threw the ball to Fred and Fred threw it to Doty. She jumped and missed it, the ball landed in a nearby stream and started to float away. As Doty ran to grab the ball, she slipped and fell in the water. Sitting in the icy creek, she started giggling as Willie ran to get the baseball. Fred chased it down the opposite side of the stream.

Before long, they were all laughing, all playing in the stream, soaking wet.

These times of reprieve, of laughter and family fun, gave Doty a glimpse of what normal life could be like—a life she longed for.

After playing a while, they loaded back up and headed out on the road again.

The continual search for work wore on Fred's nerves. All he wanted to do was drink, but knew he couldn't until the end of the day. He didn't want any potential boss smelling whiskey on his breath.

Three small towns later, he still had not found work. Fred released a string of swear words then looked over at Doty. "In every town there's countless people lookin' for work. Stores, restaurants, and most other businesses are already closed or are closin'." He shook his head. "Everyone I talked to had the same story. There ain't many jobs, and the jobs that do exist are already filled and don't pay much."

Doty didn't bother answering; she simply looked away.

It had been a long, hard day of driving. The family was exhausted and everyone was ready to make camp early in the evening. As Fred drove slowly down the busy highway, searching for a place to camp, he found that most campsites were already taken. The few empty places that were along the forested highway were somewhat hidden and hard to see. Finally, Doty spied a larger campsite that had only one small tent on it. "Maybe we can camp by those people." She pointed at the space.

Fred pulled off the highway, into the campsite, and stopped. "Hello!" he called out.

A young man, clean and tidy, stepped out of the tent. "Hello to you," he called back. "Can I help you with something?" A young woman followed him out and stood beside him, smiling.

"Yeah, is anyone else campin' in this space? If not, do ya care if we camp out here for the night?"

"You're welcome to stay," replied the young man. "We'd enjoy the company."

"That's mighty kind of ya. Thanks!"

Fred parked the car and helped Doty and the kids out. Turning to the young couple, Fred extended a hand. "Hello, my name's Fred, and this is my wife, Doty. These are our two youngest kids." Fred nodded towards the younger boys. "This is Henry and George." Doty carried baby Henry on her hip as he stretched and yawned. George fussed and struggled to get away as Fred held his hand tight.

Nodding towards the other four children running around, Fred gave a small smile. "Our other four are out exploring."

"My name is Stewart, and this is my wife, Amelia." The young man stepped forward and shook Fred's hand, "We're glad to meet you."

Amelia smiled as she watched the children run around in the campground. "That's quite a family. We don't have any kids yet," she commented. We just got married three months ago." She turned to Doty and Fred. "Right now, Stewart and I are looking for work."

"Have you had any luck?" asked Doty. "Fred is looking, too, but there doesn't seem to be any jobs around." She glanced at Fred as she shook her head. "We came through northern California so he could find a job in a lumber mill, but the mills and most businesses are closed down."

Reaching into his pocket, Fred pulled out the worn flyer and handed it to them. "We've seen these fliers that say there's work pickin' fruit in central and southern California. So, if I can't find work in the mills, we'll head down there ta look for work in the orchards and farms." The young couple looked at the flyer, then at each other.

"Well," said Stewart as he handed the flyer back to Fred, "there's jobs, but there's also hundreds of people looking for work."

"The jobs only last a few weeks," Amelia added. "If you get a job picking fruit in an orchard, it's not long before all the fruit is picked. The more people picking, the shorter the job. Once the fruit is picked, you have to move on to find another job."

As Fred listened, he looked discouragingly at Doty.

"Even though the wages are low," continued Stewart, "the employers know that they can find someone to do the work. And if one person isn't willing to work for that amount, there are many others that are because they need food for their families. They'll work for whatever they can get. A little money is better than no money. And the struggling families move wherever they can find jobs."

Fred sighed, looking defeated as he watched all the vehicles speeding down the highway. "There's an awful lot a people on the road, an' seems they're all lookin' for work. I guess I'll just keep tryin'. Findin' a job's gonna be harder than I thought. We better get back to camp. We'll need to be up early so we can get on the road. Thanks for the information; I appreciate it. It's been nice talkin' with ya."

"See you in the morning." The young couple smiled and waved as Fred and Doty left.

Wishing the couple goodnight, Doty took George and Henry back to camp to put them down for the night, and Fred went off to find the other children. He found them collecting leaves in the meadow by their camp. Coming from an arid area with hardly any trees, leaves were captivating to the children. They were fascinated with the different shapes and colors.

"Father, look!" exclaimed Rosy. "Look at all of these different leaves." She held up a number of them. "Here's a green leaf, a yellow one, and a red and green leaf…" Chattering, the four children continued to collect leaves as they explored on the way back to their tent. Showing their leaves to Father, each child shared their newly discovered treasures. He listened to the chatter all the way back to camp.

When they arrived at the tent, Fred found an empty crate. "Let's put the leaves in this box," he suggested. "Maybe ya'll have time ta find some other leaves when we stop tomorrow. Ya could make a leaf collection and dry 'em. I'll show ya how." The children excitedly discussed the idea as they headed to the tent and got ready for bed. Fred placed the treasure box of leaves safely in the Model T. After the children were tucked into bed and sound asleep, Doty joined them.

Disheartened, Fred struggled with the idea that finding a job was going to be harder than the job itself. He sat in the front seat of the car and pulled out his bottle of whiskey, mumbling to himself, "I'll have ta look 'round ta find another distillery. This is my last bottle, and I have ta make it last. If I don't find work, I ain't gonna have any whiskey an' my family won't have food."

He took one long, slow swig, swished it around in his mouth, and slowly swallowed it. He could feel the burn of the alcohol as it slid smoothly down his throat. "Ahh," was all he said as he corked the bottle and slid it back under the front seat.

Fred sat in the vehicle for a while, contemplating how he could find a job. In the quiet of the night he lost focus and dozed off, then woke with a start as a passing car backfired. After a moment, he got his bearings. Realizing he had to get some sleep, he quietly joined his family in the tent and fell into a restless slumber.

ELEVEN

They were packed up and back on the road as quickly as possible the next morning. The sky was clear, the air fresh, and the morning cool and beautiful. Fred inhaled a whiff of fresh air as it wafted in through the car's window. With the start of the new day, he looked forward to the possibilities of what the day might bring.

As they traveled down the scenic highway, the evergreen trees started to thin out, and large green fields appeared. Fred gazed at the countryside, amazed at the acres and acres of cultivated land. "Doty, look at the farms and orchards." Fred pointed at the acres of fruit trees. "This area would be a great place ta work."

In the distance, he saw a sign. His heart started beating a little faster. "Maybe they're hirin'," Fred muttered to himself. He slowed down as he approached the sign. "Look, Doty!" he exclaimed. "The sign says 'Hiring'."

Continuing to drive slowly, he gazed out over a large, beautiful, apple orchard with trees full of shiny ripe apples that were ready to be picked. In front of the orchard there were numerous cars parked in a large dirt parking lot with a long line of men who were waiting to be hired. "I'm gonna stop here. Maybe I can get some work." Fred pulled in by the other cars and parked. "You wait here. I'll be back in a while." He jumped out of the car and rushed over and stood in line with the other men. Doty and the kids waited impatiently in the Ford.

A table had been set up outside the orchard perimeter and was manned by shift bosses. The line of migrants waiting for jobs moved quickly. Fred slicked his hair back with his hand, tucked his shirt in, and waited. He watched as each man in front of him stepped up to the table and was told that the orchard owner paid ten cents a bushel, take it or leave it. Few turned him down. It was a low wage and it was not fair, but it was their only option. Their families had to eat.

Fred stepped up to the table when it was his turn. He was told, "We pay ten cents a bushel for picking apples, take it or leave it."

"I'll take it," said Fred.

More instructions came. "Don't bruise the apples. If they're bruised, they're no good to us, and you won't get paid for them. Handle the apples carefully."

"Is there some place 'round here for my family ta stay while I work?" Fred inquired.

"There's a Hooverville about two miles down the road. You can set up your tent and stay as long as you work or need a place to stay. Next!" the orchard boss yelled.

Confused, Fred asked, "Wait a minute. What's a Hooverville?"

"It's a campground where migrants can stay. It's a shanty town. Next!" the man yelled again.

Fred turned, rushed back to the car, and jumped in. "They hired me! Can you believe it? I actually got the job!" Fred vigorously slapped the steering wheel with both hands, yelling, "Yes!" He tried to be serious and not grin, but elation radiated from his face. "And there's even a campground a couple a miles down the road. It's called a Hooverville. It's where workers and their families can stay. Ya can stay there with the kids while I work." He grinned as he started the vehicle.

Doty was excited but she was relieved too. *A place to stay and money for food; right now, what more can I ask for?* She let out a sigh of relief and smiled a small, crooked smile.

As Fred headed down the highway, a giddiness rose up inside him; he couldn't quit smiling as he watched for the Hooverville. Ahead in the distance, he could see the campground. The highway curved and led right by it. He slowed down and turned at the turnoff, then stopped to survey the rundown, shabby encampment.

The Hooverville itself was large but seemed dirty and trashy. He studied the dwellings; there looked to be around a hundred camping sites of one kind or another. There were a number of tents mixed in with other dwellings made of cardboard, tarps, boards, blankets, and anything else the migrants could find to create temporary homes that would protect them from the sun, wind, and rain. A creek ran through the middle of the large camp where the people could fetch their water. The migrants themselves, hanging around the dwellings, were mostly gaunt and dirty.

Fred shook his head and sighed. "Well, it's not exactly the kind of place I had in mind, but it'll have to do for now." He looked apologetically at Doty. "I guess it's at least a place to stay."

"I'm just excited to have a place to unpack and camp for a while." Doty gazed out over the village and examined her new neighborhood. The children sat on their knees in the backseat, looking out the car windows, just waiting for their chance to jump out and run as soon as the car stopped.

Following the road, Fred wound slowly around the encampment, looking for an empty campsite; he soon found one. The site was large enough to hold a tent, vehicle, and had a large campfire area. As he pulled in to park; suddenly, a large grubby man with a scrubby beard rushed out into the middle of the campsite. Putting his fists on his hips, he stood, glaring at Fred. "Hey!" shouted the man. "You can't have this space! It's taken! It's mine!" He looked angry and ready for a fight.

Furious, Fred grabbed the handle of the driver side door and shoved it open. As Fred stepped out to confront the man, Doty quickly grabbed his arm. "Father, look! There's another camp spot over there. It's twice as large and a lot nicer. Let's grab it before anyone else does."

Fred turned and looked at the other site, then hesitantly got back in the car. Giving the large man an irate glare, Fred angrily backed out of the first space and pulled into the larger one. As soon as he stopped, the children piled out of the vehicle and ran around, exploring the campsite.

After unloading the car as quickly as he could, Fred jumped in and started the vehicle. Looking back at Doty, he called, "I'm not sure how long I'll be able to work today, but I'll be back this evenin' sometime." He took off, heading back to the orchard. As he passed by the man still standing in the first campsite, Fred glared at him.

Doty set up camp and watched the two younger boys while the older children took off exploring. The children wandered around Hooverville, examining every kind of temporary housing they came across. It didn't take them long to explore the camp and get acquainted with the other children that stayed there.

When Fred arrived back at the orchard, he parked, and surveyed the area again. There were acres and acres of apple trees, hundreds, maybe thousands of trees, loaded with ripe apples. The branches on the trees drooped from the weight, some brushing the orchard grasses and some touching the ground. *This job should last a while, that is if they don't hire a bunch more people. I hope it'll last a long time, longer than two or three weeks like everyone says.*

Fred walked back to the table where he was hired. The foreman gave him more instructions. "Here's a bucket to put the apples in. When you pick the apples, place them— do not drop them—place them into the bucket. And do not dump the bucket of apples into the bushel basket. PLACE the apples carefully in the basket or you'll bruise them. We will not pay for bruised apples."

With bucket in hand, Fred followed his boss into the orchard. "Start picking here at this tree," the boss instructed. "Then continue down this row." He turned and left.

"Hmm…", Fred smirked as he mumbled under his breath, "I know how ta pick apples. It's simple and something that anyone can do." Hungry, he grabbed an apple and bit into it. As the sweet flavor of the fruit filled his mouth, the juice dribbled down his chin. It had been months since he had eaten fruit. He savored every bite. Having had very little breakfast, he filled up on apples as he worked. They would have to hold him over until dinner.

Fred worked quickly, ignoring the instructions. He wanted to make as much money as possible so he picked the apples and dropped them into the bucket as fast as he could. When it was full, he hurriedly dumped the apples into the basket, and filled another bucket, and another.

After a short time, the bushel basket was full. He carried it over to the barn to check it in. "A dime a basket," he commented to himself. "A few more a these, I'll be able ta get a bottle a whiskey."

When Fred set the basket down on the table, the foreman picked up a couple of apples and inspected them. "Look at the apples! You dumped them!" the foreman cried. "You bruised the apples. You need to place them gently in the bucket and the basket. We can't use those apples now. You'll not get paid for 'em!"

Angrily, Fred grabbed the basket of fruit, took it back to the orchard, and dumped all of the bruised apples onto the ground. "There goes a whole dime an' my whiskey," he mumbled irritably under his breath.

But then an idea popped into his mind. *Hmmm,* he thought, *instead of throwin' these away, I could take 'em back ta the kids. They need fresh fruit and they'd love it. The kids would have somethin' healthy to eat, and I could use all the money I earn ta buy my whiskey.* He grabbed a bruised apple to eat on the way back through the orchard.

By late in the afternoon, Fred began to realize that eating too many apples was becoming a problem. He abruptly dropped his bucket and ran to the outhouse, just barely making it in time. *Now I've gone an' done it; too many apples gave me the trots. I'm not gonna get many more bushels picked today.* He ran back and forth to the outhouse the rest of the afternoon. *I'll have to remember.* He chuckled to himself. *Tomorrow…don't eat so many apples.*

When Fred left the orchard that evening, he stopped and loaded some of the discarded fruit in his bucket to take back to his family. He said nothing to the boss about taking the apples, suspecting the boss would want him to pay for them.

He returned to his campsite with the fruit. He carried the bucket and walked up to Doty first, handing her an apple. Her mouth dropped open in surprise. A large grin spread across Doty's face as she accepted the fruit, elated.

"Apples! You brought apples! Thank you!" After rolling it around in her hands to look at it, she polished the bright red fruit on her skirt before she took a bite.

As she bit into the apple, Doty closed her eyes and let the sweet juices flood her mouth and saturate her taste buds. The liquid ran down her throat as she swallowed. She smiled with satisfaction. *I can't remember the last time an apple tasted so good.*

Rosy, seeing the fruit, eagerly ran up and stood by her father. He handed her an apple. "Wow! Thanks, Father!" she cried out. "Look guys! Look at the apples Father brought us!"

Immediately, he was surrounded by his children, each crowding and pushing to get an apple. One by one, Fred handed out the bruised fruit, making sure each child received one.

Fred smiled as he watched his children gobble the fruit down and slurp up every drop of the sweet juice they could. Feeling good that he could provide some nutritious food for his children and his wife, he took another apple from his bucket and polished it on his shirt.

A movement caught the corner of his eye and he glanced up to see children from the surrounding dwellings gradually wandering over and standing quietly in the shadows. Their sad, vacant eyes mirrored their empty stomachs. As they watched, Fred knew each silently hoped to receive an apple too.

Fred's heart went out to them. He knew the feeling of an empty stomach, of hunger and starvation, of having your body crave food. He looked at the apples that were left and then around at the hungry children who were gazing at the damaged fruit.

He couldn't help himself. Fred handed his apple to the closest child, a young, scrawny, unkempt boy. The child's eyes grew huge as he reached out with his grimy hands and gratefully accepted the apple. Smiling from ear to ear, the boy took a big bite. As Fred watched the child practically inhale the fruit, he knew what he had to do.

He passed out the rest of the apples to as many children as he could. He would get more apples from the orchard tomorrow. That way, the ruined fruit would not go to waste, and the children would have something to eat.

"Father, I'm still hungry," whimpered Rosy. "Can I have another apple?"

"I'm still hungry too. We haven't eaten since breakfast," repeated Willie. The rest of the siblings chimed in, all wanting more food.

"Sorry," said Fred sadly, realizing an apple was not much food and that his own children were still hungry too. "The apples are all gone. I just gave 'em all away."

From a distance, the grubby man watched as Fred passed out the apples; his anger was now gone. A six-year-old girl that must have been the man's daughter took a huge bite out of the apple she had received. Gratitude filled her father's face.

Doty began to fret as Fred gave the last of the apples away. Their food was almost gone. When she had packed the food, she had only room enough for a couple of weeks. It had taken Fred longer to find a job than they expected. What were the children going to eat? There was one biscuit and a small piece of salt pork for each person for dinner. After that there was enough for one more scant meal the next day. Then the food would be gone.

Father would have to get paid soon, or Doty would have nothing to feed her family. She thought about the haunting shadows of hunger in the eyes of the other children in camp. *I don't want my children or the other kids to starve.* A sense of powerlessness filled her. *There's nothing I can do to feed them.*

Thoughts of her own children that had died from hunger years before flooded her mind. Waves of anguish crushed her soul all over again. *I thought I put the past behind me.* She tried to push the emotions away.

But now, her current children were facing the same hardship; hunger and possible starvation. Clouds of despair hovered over her.

Later that evening, after the family had eaten and gone to bed, Fred pulled out his bottle of whiskey from under the front seat. *It's almost gone.* Sitting down in the car, he stroked the bottle, knowing he had to drink it sparingly. He took one, long, slow, swig, letting the whiskey linger in his mouth and wash over his tongue. Savoring the taste, he closed his eyes and swallowed, feeling that familiar burn as the liquid ran slowly down his throat. He laid back and relaxed as the warm feeling filled his body.

"Excuse me," came a man's voice.

Fred jumped.

"I need to apologize about this afternoon," the man said as he stopped just outside the driver's side window.

Fred recognized him as the man that challenged him for the campsite earlier.

The man looked down and then back at Fred. "I was angry, and I took it out on you. I'm really sorry for how I acted."

"Yeah," Fred said and met the man's gaze. "I did nothin' to you."

"I know, there's no excuse for my rudeness. But I just got here when you did, and we needed the place to stay." He put his hands in his pockets, then looked down at the ground as he kicked the dirt. "I'm sorry." There was a long pause. "These last few weeks have been real hard for me. I've been lookin' for work for weeks now. We've come up through southern California, and all I can find are small jobs that pay just enough to buy the gas to go look for the next job. We've been out of food for the last couple a days, and it's really tough to watch my family go hungry. Tomorrow, I'm headin' out to look for work again."

As Fred listened, he felt bad for the man. He could see the desperation in his eyes. He also knew the feeling of responsibility that came when your child was starving and there was nothing you could do about it. Fred had to speak up. "I got a job pickin' apples a ways down the road. There's lots of apples, and I think they're still hirin'. Ya can go to work with me tomorrow and try for a job if ya want."

Fred knew he shouldn't have said anything. He knew the more men that were hired, the sooner the apples were picked, and the shorter his job would be. But he also knew what it was like to have hungry children.

Tears crested on the big man's eyelids and flowed from the corners of his eyes. "You would do that for me after the way I treated ya?" He reached out his hand and took Fred's. "Thank you, sir. Thank you." He shook Fred's hand so hard it hurt. "Oh, my name's Ben."

"I'm Fred. You can ride with me. I'll see you bright an' early in the mornin'."

Ben nodded and turned to walk away. He stopped and turned back to Fred. "By the way, thank you for feedin' my daughter the apple this evenin'. It's the only thing she's had to eat in two days."

Fred paused, lifted his almost empty bottle of whiskey and handed it to Ben. "Here, have a swig. I think you could use one."

Ben accepted the bottle gratefully and took a long, slow drink. "Thanks. I needed that more than ya know." He tipped his head toward Fred, handed the bottle back, and turned and left.

Fred corked the bottle and slipped it under the car seat again. Sitting in the driver's seat, he leaned back and rested his head. As he closed his eyes, sleep quickly over-took him.

The next morning, Ben was standing by the Model T when the sun came up. He was obviously anxious to get started. Grabbing a couple of pieces of what little salted pork was left, Fred handed one to Ben. "Here, you need some breakfast so you'll have energy ta work." Ben accepted the food gratefully and thanked him. They hopped into the car and drove to the orchard.

Fred watched as Ben made his way to the foreman's table. Not long afterwards, Ben walked energetically into the orchard with a bucket of his own. As he placed apples into his basket, he smiled over at Fred. "Thanks again for this. All I can think of is that my kids will be able to eat tonight."

Fred stared back at Ben. *And I can get me a bottle of whiskey.* But out loud he said, "No problem, we gotta take care each other."

At the end of the day, Fred and Ben walked around the orchard and picked up the bruised and damaged apples off the ground to take back to the camp for their families. They each filled a basket.

"Where do you think you're goin' with those apples?" yelled one of the orchard bosses as Ben and Fred walked out of the orchard toward the car. "You stealin' our apples?" Furious, fists clenched, the boss stood in front of Ben and Fred, blocking the way.

Ben nervously explained, "We just picked up the apples that are bruised and damaged. They'll just rot on the ground, and our families are hungry. We were takin' them back to our place so they can eat."

The boss walked up to the baskets and picked through the apples, checking to see if Ben was telling the truth. Then he mellowed a bit. "The apples are ours! You can't take them. If we let you take them, everyone else will be taking apples too. Then they'll even start taking the good apples from the trees."

The two men just stood in place silently with looks of desperation in their faces. They didn't say a word.

Hesitating, the boss seemed to realize how badly they needed the food. He could read it in their eyes. Knowing the apples would just lie on the ground and rot, he glanced around making sure no one was watching, and then he spoke quietly to Ben and Fred, "You can take them this time, but if you try it again, I'll have you arrested for stealing." He turned and walked off. The two men quickly took their baskets of apples to the vehicle, hoping to avoid any more confrontations.

After placing the baskets in the car, they walked over to the table and collected their pay for the day. Fred had enough to buy a bottle of whiskey. Ben wanted food for his family.

"Hey, let's go ta town," Fred suggested to Ben. "It's just a few miles away. Maybe the store's still open, and I'll find out where I can get some moonshine. I'll stop ta pick it up on the way back."

"Sounds great! Let's go!" Ben smiled. The two men jumped into the Model T and eagerly headed to town.

Their first stop in town was the general store. It was late, and the store was just closing; they barely got there in time. Ben jumped out of the car and ran into the small store. While he shopped for food, Fred sat impatiently in his car. In a few minutes Ben was back with groceries.

"I had enough money to buy some eggs and flour," Ben said, excited that he could feed his family. He carefully set the food on the floor of the backseat. "Eggs are good protein and cheaper than meat, and with the flour and eggs together, we can make bread or pancakes; and we'll have apples to go with it. We'll have a good meal tonight." His face beamed with eagerness. "Let's get outta here so I can go feed my family!"

As soon as Ben climbed back into the car, Fred throttled up and took off.

Ben settled himself in the front seat. "Hey man, you gonna grab some food stuffs for your family?"

Fred didn't answer at first, instead starting down the roadway. "Naww, we're good for now." After speeding through the small town, he turned down a deserted road, leaving a small dust cloud behind.

"Where're we goin'?" enquired Ben.

"I've done some askin' around town an' I found out where the still's located. Since prohibition is bein' enforced, it's hidden back in the hills."

Following the rough dirt road for a couple of miles, Fred pulled up to an old rickety shack hidden in the trees. He jumped out of his car and ran into the building. With a bottle in hand and a smile on his face, he hurried back to the vehicle.

That evening, as Doty fixed dinner, she stretched the remaining food as far as she could. Using the last of the salted pork and the few remaining biscuits, she served her children the only meal they had eaten all day. Now the food was gone.

When Fred came home late that evening, he proudly walked up to Doty and set his basket of bruised and partly rotten apples on the make-shift table of apple crates. "Look what I brought home again. I picked 'em up off of the ground. They're a little bruised but mostly good," he said smugly.

"Apples!" she cried, grateful to have more. "We need the food; I just set the last of our food on the table. We have nothing left."

Picking through the apples carefully, she found a nice one, washed it, and ate it. The apple was the only thing she had eaten all day. "I'll make applesauce out of the rest of them. That'll help them last longer."

She nibbled on a piece of peel as she sorted through the apples. *Father should be getting paid soon and we'll be able to buy more food. Hopefully, this should last until then.*

After the children were in bed that evening, Fred sat down and relaxed by the fire. He pulled out his almost empty bottle of whiskey and took a long drink. Ahh…" He tossed the empty bottle into the fire, watching it disintegrate into fragments.

He got up, sauntered over to the Model T, and pulled out the new bottle from under the front seat. When Doty saw him with it, she stood in disbelief. *How can he buy whiskey when we have no food, when the children are hungry?*

She became furious. Flashes of the distant past, of her babies starving to death, roared through her mind. She glared at him and watched as he uncorked the bottle and took a swig. The immediate recollection of the constant look of hunger in her children's eyes sparked rage inside her. Fury swelled within her chest. Her lips tightened; her jaws clinched. Suddenly, she could stand it no longer.

She stalked over to Father and grabbed the bottle out of his hands. Enraged, she yelled, "Father! Our kids are going hungry! The food's gone, and we won't eat tomorrow, except for rotten apples…and you're spending money on booze!" As she yelled at him, she knew it was a mistake, but she couldn't help it.

Father's face reddened. His eyes grew wide. He snarled, snatched the bottle back, and backhanded Doty across the face. She crumpled to the ground.

"Don't you dare tell me what to do, woman!" he bellowed. He glared at Doty as she lay in the dirt, and then turned and stumbled off, fondling his bottle. "How dare she yell at me and grab my whiskey," Father mumbled.

The yelling and fighting had caught the attention of the folks in the surrounding camp area. They watched in shock as the angry couple yelled at each other and they saw Fred hit Doty. When Fred stumbled off, a few of the closer neighbor ladies rushed over to help Doty.

Ben and his wife watched the scene from their own tent across the road. They understood how Fred and Doty both felt. But Ben couldn't understand how Fred could treat his wife that way. As Ben and his wife looked at each other, they shook their heads sadly, and turned and walked away knowing there was nothing they could do.

———————≈———————

Doty stayed in the tent, fuming, until Father left for work the next morning. She refused to even speak to him. After he left, she spent her morning at the campsite, watching the children play in the distant stream. They were kicking and splashing in the cool water. *At least the kids have some applesauce to eat and fresh water to drink. But that's not enough.* She applied a cool wet towel to her bruised cheek.

That morning Fred and Ben drove to work separately.

After Fred sobered up, he felt guilty about what he had done the night before. Doty's eye had turned black during the night, and her face was swollen and bruised. The children were hungry and begging for something to eat.

Racked with guilt, Fred looked at Doty. "When I get paid today, I'm gonna go ta the store an' buy some food for the family. In fact, every day after work when I get paid, I'm gonna buy more food ta make sure they have something ta eat."

Doty didn't respond.

Fred harrumphed and kicked at the dust. "Woman, this job is just about over, and we'll have to move on soon."

When Doty still didn't respond, he turned and walked away. *I'll show her. I'll get her some darn food.*

He was determined to do better than he had.

TWELVE

A few days later, the family found themselves on the road again. Driving down the highway, Fred and his family passed farmlands and orchards as they watched for 'hiring' signs. They gazed out the windows at the passing landscape. With the green fields, clear blue sky, and temperatures in the 70's, it was another beautiful day. The fresh air wafted through the open windows, and a peace settled in the car, a peace that seemed to promise another new beginning. Even Fred relaxed and was, again, looking forward to his next job—whatever that might be.

After riding for about two hours, Doty spotted a sign nailed to a post. "Look, Fred, there's a sign up ahead. It's newly painted and says, "HIRING". And there's an arrow pointing to that dirt road."

Fred pulled off the highway, onto the road, and into a driveway that led to a large parking lot where he parked the car. He got out and surveyed the surrounding fields. There were hundreds of acres of all kinds of vegetables that looked ready to be picked.

He turned to Doty as she sat in the car. "Look at all the crops ready for harvestin'. Maybe I can get a job here. If I can, the job should last quite a while. Wait here with the kids while I go check." Just like before, Fred joined the men waiting in line, hoping to find work. As more vehicles continued to arrive, men swarmed out of their cars and raced over to get in line. Fred had gotten there just in time, right before a rush of jobless men.

While standing in line, Fred fidgeted. *I need work real bad.* He slipped his hands in his pants' pockets to keep them still. *My family's future depends on it.*

He shifted his weight from foot to foot, waiting nervously as the line in front of him grew shorter. When he finally reached the table where the field bosses sat, a little hope rose up inside him; he knew they were just starting to hire. He addressed one of the bosses, "Hope you're still hirin'. I'm lookin' for work. I got a wife and six kids and they need ta eat." Fred held his breath.

The field boss announced heartily, "You're hired. We can use all the workers we can get. The crops are ready and need to be picked quickly."

The tension Fred felt gradually drained from his body as he exhaled slowly. Relief came over him, knowing he had proved Doty wrong again. He would feed his kids and get another bottle as well.

Back up the highway, Fred had passed another Hooverville. He hurried to the car and drove his family back to the encampment. After finding a campsite, he dropped them off, unloaded the car, and returned to the fields immediately to start work.

As Doty stood in their new campsite, she looked around the Hooverville. She sighed and mumbled, "This place is dirtier and trashier than the last place we stayed in. But it'll be our home for a while, and I guess we'll have to make the best of it."

Standing beside her mother and hearing her comment, Rosy glanced around the dilapidated encampment and then up at Doty, concern on her young face. Not receiving any further comment from her mother, Rosy eagerly ran off with the other children to explore their new home.

By now, Doty was an expert at setting up camp. The tent was up and the camp was organized in about an hour. Since it was late morning and her job was done, she took the two youngest children and did a little exploring herself. While she was walking around the campground, she became more grateful for her tent home as she examined the numerous homes made of cardboard, blankets, pieces of wood, and anything else that the people could find to construct a shelter. A sudden gust of wind blew through the camp, tearing a few chunks of cardboard from a dwelling and carrying them throughout the campground.

Doty walked around, anxious to meet a few friends. Seeing a woman fixing a meal over a campfire, Doty walked up behind her. "Hello?"

Surprised, the woman turned with a start, then smiled. "Oh, hello. Is there something I can do for you?"

"Hi, my name's Doty. We just got here today, and I wanted to meet some other folks." She let go of George and reached out to shake the woman's hand.

The woman wiped her hands on a dirty towel and then shook Doty's. "I'm Velma. Go ahead and have a seat." She pointed to a nearby rock. Doty sat down.

Velma, dressed in an old, dirty calico dress with her greasy hair pulled back in a bun, seemed very shy but friendly. She said timidly, "I'm glad to meet you. We've only been here for three days. My husband has just started working at the farm down the road."

"That's where my husband's working too." Doty raised baby Henry to her shoulder and patted him on the back. "I hope this job lasts for a while. We've only been in California a short time. This is Fred's second job here. His first one we had just gotten settled in before we had to move again because the apples were all picked." Henry giggled as Doty kissed him on the cheek.

Velma handed Doty a cup of coffee then sat down on an apple crate across from her. "Yeah," Velma agreed. "This job'll probably last about three weeks. It depends on how many men they hire. There looks to be a lot of them. As you probably know, the more men, the shorter the job. We've been doing this for five months now and have moved every two to three weeks."

Doty shivered at the familiar words. This was not the life she had expected when she left the homestead. She had envisioned a better life: a small house, a place for the children to play, and a steady job for Father. Instead, she got a transient lifestyle, a hard existence, and was uncertain from where the next meal would come.

George sat down in the dirt and started to play. Henry laid his head quietly on Doty's shoulder as she rocked him. Holding Henry with one arm, Doty sat the coffee down and slicked her hair back, then reached down and brushed dust off her dress. "Is there any water around here? I need some drinking water and some water to wash up."

"There's a fairly large creek on the far side of the camp. The water's good for drinking if you get it above the camp. Otherwise, everyone's bathing or washing clothes in it." Velma self-consciously looked at her own grimy dress, then brushed back her stringy hair with her hand.

George poked at his baby brother. Henry started to cry. Doty gave George a stick and directed him to draw pictures in the dirt. Trying to comfort her fussing son, Doty asked, "Velma, do you mind if I nurse Henry? He's hungry; it's time for him to eat."

"No, I don't mind, not at all. Go ahead and feed him. I can tell he's hungry."

Doty unbuttoned the front of her dress and began nursing him as the women continued chatting. They talked easily about everything from children to their husbands' work.

Doty really liked this woman. Velma seemed to have it all together. She had been a migrant a lot longer than Doty and knew how to make do. Doty wondered to herself about the future: what would it look like, and what jobs might be available? "Velma…maybe you can answer a question for me." Doty paused, half afraid to ask. "My family's' been here in California for just a few weeks now. In a few months, the farming season will be over and the jobs will be getting fewer. What will you—we—do when the crops are harvested and winter comes? Will there be any jobs then? How will we survive the winter?"

Velma just looked at Doty, shrugged her shoulders, and took a sip of coffee. She shook her head slowly and didn't say a word. She had no answer either.

The women sat in silence.

Finally, Velma replied, "I guess we'll have to deal with the problem when we get there. We'll find some way to survive." She again grew quiet.

Feeling the conversation was over for now, Doty stood and handed the empty coffee cup back to Velma. "Thank you for the pleasant morning. It's been nice to have another woman to talk to. I need to get back to camp and make lunch for the kids. Hopefully I'll see you later." Doty gave her a smile, took George's hand, and headed back to her camp with the two boys.

Velma took the coffee cup. "I've enjoyed the morning. Hope we can talk again."

Rosy and Willie came running into camp about the time their mother arrived back at the campsite; each of them was carrying a huge fish. "Hey, Mom! Look what Willie caught!" Eyes sparkling, the two children squirmed and danced as they held up their prize to show their mother.

"Look at our big fish!" boasted Willie.

Amazed, Doty gazed wide-eyed at the two fish, and her mouth fell open.

"We wove limbs together and made stick nets out of them," Willie explained. "Then we put the nets across the creek. The fish got caught between the sticks and couldn't get away!"

"Willie dragged them out," Rosy bragged, proud of her younger brother. "We're starved. Can we have them for lunch?"

"Wow, I didn't know you kids were fishermen." Doty quickly laid Henry down in the tent on a blanket so she didn't wake him and gave George his stuffed bear to play with. Turning back to Willie and Rosy, she gave them her undivided attention. "I'll tell you what. I'll fry them for lunch if you go see if you can catch some more for dinner."

"Okay!" the two children shouted gleefully. They handed Doty the fish and ran off to catch more.

"It's been a long time since we had fish. I hope the kids can catch more," Doty said to George as he clung to her leg with one arm and cuddled his stuffed bear with the other.

Annabel and Carolyn wandered into camp and walked up to Doty while she was cleaning the fish. Surprised to see the fresh catch, Annabel asked, "Mom, where did the fish come from?"

Carolyn gazed at them. "Boy, those are huge. Do we get to eat them for lunch?"

"Willie and Rosy caught them and yes, I'm fixing them for lunch. Why don't you girls stoke up the fire for me?"

It wasn't long before the fire was blazing and the fish were on to fry. As Doty watched the fish cook, she was filled with joy and thankfulness. *Real food…the kids and I will have a decent meal today. There's plenty here to feed us, and with a piece of bread each, it should be more than enough.*

Within the hour, all of the children were back in camp and ready to eat. "We didn't have any luck in catching more fish because now everyone else in camp is down at the creek trying to catch their own fish in our fishing hole," Willie explained with disappointment.

"That's okay, Willie. You can try again later at a different place. Right now, let's eat the fish that you did catch. It looks and smells delicious." Doty's mouth watered as she dished out a serving of fish and a piece of bread to each child.

"Hey, guys, let's eat!" announced Willie as he grinned and eagerly took the first mouthful. Each person savored every bite of the fish. The pan-fried bread added just the perfect touch. For the first time in weeks, the children's bellies were full and satisfied.

"Hey, Willie, that was delicious. Let's go further upstream to see if we can catch some more fish for dinner," Rosy suggested.

"I want to go too," Carolyn chimed in.

"Me too. I want to catch some fish," Annabel added.

"Let's all go." Willie grinned.

All four older kids jumped up and took off toward the creek. As they ran out of camp, their excited voices bounced off each other:

"Show me how to catch the fish," Carolyn said.

"I know where to catch a whole bunch for dinner," Willie boasted.

"Where did you catch these?" Annabel asked.

Their voices faded off.

Fred came home late that evening. He was tired, hungry, and grouchy from a long day's work. "What's that smell?" he asked irritably. "Something sure smells good. The neighbors must be cooking fish."

Doty and the children just smiled at each other.

"We waited to eat dinner with you." Willie beamed. "Come see what we caught today!" The kids started giggling as they grabbed his hand and dragged him over to the campfire, excited to show Father their catch of the day.

Upon reaching the campfire, Fred handed Doty a few blemished tomatoes that he had picked up off the ground. Then glancing at the campfire, he saw it; a large pan full of fried fish. His eyes brightened, and a smile grew on his face. He hadn't had fish for so long that he had almost forgotten what it tasted like. "Where did ya get the fish?"

"We went fishing in the creek today. Look at all the fish we caught!" Willie smiled from ear to ear. "Look how many!"

The other children continued to giggle, happy to show off their catch.

Fred smiled. "'Tween you kids catchin' the fish and your mom cookin' them, this looks to be a great dinner," Father complimented, his mood changing. The family sat down together to eat.

The children sat around the apple-crate table and smiled as they waited for Father to take his first bite. Fred put a small chunk of fish in his mouth and chewed slowly, then he sucked the juice out of it. He let the flavor linger in his mouth. Munching, he mumbled quietly to the kids, "I don't remember the last time I ate fresh fish." As he swallowed the bite, he could feel it slide all the way down to his empty stomach. One bite after another, he enjoyed every bit of it. Doty and the children also ate slowly, trying to put off the moment when the simple feast would be over.

After dinner, Fred suggested to the children, "If you kids catch more fish, I'll teach ya how to smoke and dry 'em. We could have fish to eat for quite a while."

Doty sat, listening to the discussion. The prospect of more fish sounded wonderful to her, but she wondered how long before the stream was fished out. If Father's plan worked, the family could have more to eat beside biscuits and spoiled fruits and vegetables.

After the children went to bed that evening, Father was in the best mood Doty had seen him in for a long time. However, the question she had asked Velma that day still troubled her. She wanted an answer; she needed to know what to plan on. After mulling it over, she decided to ask, knowing there would be no better time than the present.

Fred relaxed as he sat down by the fire and took a swig of his whiskey. She sat down beside him. Doty had to consider how to ask the question; she knew that she needed to ask in just the right way or Father might take it wrong. He might think that she doubted whether he could take care of them; and if she asked in the wrong way, it could bring on his anger.

She chose her words carefully. "Fred, how was work today?"

He frowned. "It was back-breakin'. I bent over all day long pickin', and my back aches."

She hesitated. "How long do you think this job will last?"

Uncertain, he thought for a minute. "Two more weeks, maybe a little longer. As usual, it depends on how many more men they hire."

Now seemed like the right time to ask the question that haunted her. She took a deep breath and released it slowly. "Father, what will happen when all the crops are harvested, when winter comes? What then? Will there be any work?"

A look of hopeless desperation appeared in his eyes. She had seen that look many times before. It made her wish she hadn't asked, but she waited for an answer.

"I don't know…" He looked straight in her face. "I'm just trying to get through this day by day. I'm doing the best I can…" Then suddenly the anger and rage flared. "Now don't ask me again!" he bellowed, "and leave me alone!"

Doty stood up and quietly walked over to the tent. She stopped, turned, and looked back at Father. She could see in his eyes the unanswered question haunting him. He had no answer either. As she went to bed, she knew she shouldn't have asked Father; he had enough to worry about.

Anxious about the future, she tossed and turned all night.

THIRTEEN

Two weeks later, Fred's job ended. He and Doty packed up the family and headed out to find another one. After that job was over, Fred found another…and another…

"Ya know, Doty, it's been a long season. We left home the end of July. It's been over four months now." Fred hefted the trunk onto the back of the Model T and strapped it down. "I've lost count of how many jobs I've worked over the past few months. Now we're off to find another. I'm exhausted."

Doty finished packing the last crate. "And I'm tired of moving so often." A sigh of weariness escaped her mouth. "It's been a long, tiresome season." Her eyes were tired, and her body was fatigued. Fred loaded the last of their belongings into the car.

After checking to make sure everything was packed and everyone was in, Fred sat down in the driver's seat and closed the car door. "Fall is almost over, and it's still the same old story. We have to move on again." He gave a quiet, discouraged sigh, stepped on the starter, and pulled out onto the road.

Doty studied the look on her husband's face as he drove down the highway. It was easy to see the tiredness in his gaunt, tanned face and his droopy, bloodshot eyes. She also noticed that his hair was mussed, his clothes were dirty, and his broad, muscular shoulders sagged. His hands struggled to grip the steering wheel. Fred was completely exhausted.

Doty could see that the last few months had taken its toll on him.

Glancing at Doty, Fred continued to speak his thoughts. "If I'm lucky, I might be able ta find one more job 'fore the season ends. But since it's the end of the fall harvest season an' there're fewer fields of crops ta harvest, that means there's fewer jobs and more men that want the work."

Fred stopped at every field and orchard that looked like they might be hiring. But no jobs were to be found. He became discouraged.

After job hunting all day, Fred pulled into a nearby Hooverville and found a campsite. Sitting by the campfire that evening after his family was in bed asleep, he was troubled and stressed, unable to unwind. *I need another job soon,* he fretted.

As he stared into the campfire, thoughts of the past months started to flash continually across his mind; he couldn't shake them. It was like a nightmare that never ended. He picked up a rock and fiddled with it, and then threw it as hard as he could out into the darkness.

He took a swig to help his mind slow down, but the alcohol seemed to let the thoughts flow freer. *We've been in California for almost five months, an' now it's the end a fall.* Fred picked up a stick and stirred the fire. *It's a transient way of life that I can't get used to.* He watched the bright embers float up into the inky darkness of the night. *And now fall and the harvest season are comin' to an end…an' my job's over. The future seems ta hold nothing but hunger for me an' my family.*

Doty lay wide awake in the tent on her blanket, her body weary, but her mind wouldn't stop. *What will we do if Father can't find any more work? The kids need food.* The possibilities of the future scared her. *I'm so tired of all this. I just want to go home.* Tears started to trickle from the corners of her eyes.

After a few more days of looking for a job, Fred was distraught. He finally gave up. The family was asleep for the night, and he sat in the Model T in the dark, watching the heavy rain pour down around him. He raised the bottle to his lips, took a large gulp of whiskey, and winced as he listened to the rain pound on the car. *The rainy season is here an almost every day brings rain; we're always chilled to the bone.*

Shivering, he pulled his blanket tighter around himself. *If we had a dry place ta stay, the wet weather would be a nice relief from the summer heat. But in the tent, we're always wet and chilled. We're miserable.*

Fred sat in a daze, staring out the windshield of the car.

The next day, rain continued to pour down all morning but it stopped in late afternoon. The evening was cool, and the sun was low in the sky. But Fred didn't notice as he walked out of the Hooverville and down a worn path to the stream. Fred slapped at a bug as it landed on his arm. He needed to figure out what he should do next.

As he wandered down the path thinking and trying to come up with possibilities, he paid no attention to where he was going. Suddenly his feet were wet. Looking down he saw he was standing in the edge of the stream with water up over his ankles. He smirked. *I guess I better watch where I'm goin'.* He gazed at the water as the current rippled and gurgled around his feet. *The stream is wider and deeper than it was this mornin'…it's risin' quickly! The fall rains are here; that means winter'll be here soon.* He felt panic as the realization hit him again. *Time's short. I gotta figure how to take care of my family durin' the winter.*

Hustling back to the camp, Fred yelled, "Hey! Kids! Come here!" He motioned for the children to hurry. "The stream is full of trout right now, and they're hungry. We're going fishin'!"

He quickly made some poles from willow branches and string, and Willie made another trap. Fred led the children back to the stream. Every time someone threw a hook into the water, a fish grabbed it. The children jabbered excitedly.

"Hey, kids, shh. Stop your chatterin', "Fred mumbled under his breath. "You'll scare the fish away." The children lowered their voices, but continued whispering.

"This is the best fishin' I've ever seen!" Fred declared quietly as they caught one fish right after another. "They'll feed us for a while." As the sun slipped behind the mountains, the small group of fishermen finally gathered up their booty and marched back to camp. Fred's fears seemed to settle some; at least they'd eat for a few more meals.

"Hey, Doty," bragged Fred, as they marched into camp, "look at all the fish we caught. We've got 'nough fish for dinner and some extra for smokin'. Fred stoked up a fire and sat chatting and joking with Doty and the kids that evening as the fish smoked.

After dinner was over and the children were all asleep, Doty, exhausted from a hard day, stood and headed for the tent. She stopped, turned to her husband, and watched him for a moment as he sat quietly tending the fire. "Goodnight, Fred," she said quietly and smiled a small smile.

This had been a wonderful evening; she yearned for more of them.

FOURTEEN

The next morning, Fred sauntered over and sat on a rock beside Doty as she continued to smoke the fish. Without saying a word, he reached out and took a piece of the already-smoked fish off a plate, picked off a chunk, and placed it in his mouth. The salty, smoked fish flavor made his mouth water. Fred stood up and wandered back and forth in the camp site as he munched and pondered. *I managed ta save a few dollars for gas, whiskey, and a little food, but I don't have near 'nough to get us through the winter. I've thought about this for weeks. I have ta make a decision soon, but I can only see one option.*

Fred took another bite. "Doty, this fish is real good. Best smoked fish I ever tasted."

She smiled at him while placing a chunk of the fish in her own mouth. "You helped too."

He nodded his head at her and continued his pacing.

Doty sliced bread for breakfast and set it out with some of the fish. It was time for the children to get up. The family would have a special treat this morning.

Fred walked over and looked longingly at the delicious breakfast. He picked up a slice of bread and another chunk of fish, rolled it up together, and took a bite. He complemented Doty again as he chewed slowly, enjoying every mouthful. "Mm…Hey, Doty, this really is tasty. We did good!"

"Yes, we did. It's delicious," Doty answered as she chewed another mouthful of fish.

Munching on his fish sandwich, Fred strode out of the campground, down the road, and back to camp again, feeling like he'd failed. "He knew he had to tell Doty they were going home.

He finally pulled her to the side and spoke to her quietly, his eyes directed toward the ground. "Doty, I have no more work." His tone was flat and resigned. "Since there's no more jobs, I've made a decision."

Doty's heart skipped a beat. She looked at him questioningly.

Fred paused, then determinedly took a deep breath, raised his head, and looked straight into her eyes. "Doty, tomorrow morning, we'll eat breakfast and head back home."

Doty was speechless. A wave of relief swept over her as a seed of hope started to grow. There was not much at the homestead, but at least she would have a house, a place to call home. She never thought that she would be so excited to be heading back to the arid, desolate acreage and the small shanty. A smile crept over her face. "I'll be packed and ready to go as soon as possible."

Suddenly, there was an outburst of young voices. "We're going home? We're leaving tomorrow?" The children had been listening from the tent. They came running out and started dancing and jumping around, chanting, "Home, we're going home, we get to go home…we're going home…" The childish excitement was contagious; even Doty joined in as she grabbed hands and sang and danced with the children.

Fred stood back, watching the merriment, as a familiar darkness pulled at the edges of his mind. He smiled at his children, but the light never reached his eyes.

Eventually, the children settled down, but they continued jabbering about what they would do when they got home. Everyone was ready for a "normal life" and excited to leave this one behind. Everyone, that was, except Fred.

Fred knew what was waiting for them—nothing…nothing except hunger and possible starvation. The thought terrified him.

It was another hard decision that weighed heavily on him. There was no work or food back home either. The more he thought about it, the more his uneasiness and doubt grew as he watched his family celebrate. The more they celebrated, the more he questioned his decision, and the angrier he got knowing that he really had no decision to make. There was no work or money to feed his family, no matter where they went.

Look at 'em dancing around like ever'thing's just fine. But it's me that's gotta make it work. I'm the one that gets blamed if it don't work out. Me. It's always me. He slapped his hand on his thigh.

Fred dropped down on a nearby rock, placing his elbows on his knees. He planted his face in his hands. As his back muscles tensed and his jaws tightened, he inhaled a few deep breaths, trying to calm his fear and uncertainty. His head started to ache as the shadows in the back of his mind began to take shape, again.

A knot formed in the pit of his stomach. "You kids knock it off!" he yelled. "Settle down and be quiet!" His body began to tremble. He couldn't contain his demons any longer.

Glaring at Doty, he suddenly released his stress as he lashed out at her. "Ya know, Doty, this is your fault! If it wasn't for you, I wouldn't be in this situation! I wouldn't have all these kids and all this responsibility!"

Everyone froze, the joy forgotten. Doty shushed the children and began moving them away from Father.

In a rage, Fred sprang up from the rock, grabbed Doty by the arm, and backhanded her. The blow landed solidly against her cheek.

Doty reeled with the blow; pain shot through her head and neck. Blood streamed from a cut in her lip as he shook her. The blood trailed down her neck and absorbed into the collar of her dress.

Blind with rage, Fred cursed and swore at Doty, his words intended to cut a slice from her heart.

Not knowing what she had done to trigger him, she cowered, waiting for the next blow.

As Father raised his hand to hit her again, a small voice rang out, "Stop! Father! Please don't hit Mommy! Please don't hurt her!"

Father looked toward the voice. Rosy stood by the campfire. She had tears in her eyes. The other kids were standing in fear behind her. The horror in their eyes brought Father back to his senses.

What...what am I doing? He looked again from Doty to his children. Turning away from them, he gripped his head between his hands and stalked back and forth before the fire, growling as he paced. *What am I doing? This isn't all her fault!*

Fred pulled at his hair; his eyes wild. He squeezed his eyes shut, fighting for control. He screamed at no one in particular, "How long will this last?"

When he finally came to himself, he noticed the neighbors in the nearby campgrounds staring at him. He grabbed his bottle, turned around, and walked out of the campground into the darkness of the nearby orchards.

When Doty woke up the next morning, Father was still gone. She left the tent quietly, careful not to wake the children. Sitting on the large rock by the tent, she basked in the morning sunlight. Her jaw and face ached. She touched her cheek and cringed from the pain. The swelling and tenderness told her that her face was bruised and that she had a black eye, but she couldn't think about that right now. Her children needed breakfast. Taking care of her bruises would have to wait until later. The children's voices could be heard coming from the tent. She needed to feed them quickly and then start packing. She knew when Father came back, she had better be packed and ready to go.

She cut the only loaf of bread she had into thin slices and served it to her children along with the smoked fish. After eating, Doty and the children started packing their belongings. Soon, everything was packed and ready to be loaded in the car. Doty impatiently sat and watched as the children anxiously raced around the camp area, releasing their pent-up energy before they had to sit in the car all afternoon.

In the late morning, Father finally wandered back into camp. The tension from the day before was strong between him and Doty. Without speaking, they quickly loaded the vehicle, and before long the family was on their way.

Fred wouldn't chance going home the same way they came a few months before. He could not go back through Burns. He couldn't take the chance of running into the police or Doty's family; they may still be watching for him. He would travel north to Sacramento and catch Highway 40 over the Sierra Nevada Mountains. It was longer than the way they came, but he didn't feel he had a choice.

"Mom, I'm hungry. We haven't had lunch yet," Rosy whined.

"Me too. I'm hungry too," Willie mimicked Rosy.

Doty glanced quickly at Father but never said a word. Neither acknowledged the children's comments. After driving for a while, Fred came to a small grocery store and stopped for gas and food. While he filled the car with gas and went into the store, his family got out of the car to stretch their legs.

Father plopped bread and apples on the counter and pulled out his wallet. "I need ta pay for this food and the gas. Also, I was wonderin' where I could buy some whiskey."

The clerk paused for a moment, weighing Fred's words. Looking out the window and seeing his family by the car and the money in his hand, the clerk decided that Father was an acceptable risk. He knew whiskey was illegal, but the clerk reached under the counter, grabbed a bottle of moonshine, and set in on the counter anyway. After paying for his items, Fred turned to leave.

"Hey, hey, look at that." The clerk had a leering grin on his face and his attention was fixed out the main window. "A man would sell his right arm for a few minutes with that young beauty—" The man quieted when he turned and saw the look on Fred's face.

"That's my daughter." Fred grabbed the clerk by his collar and pulled him against the counter. "I ought to wring your neck, you lit—"

"Wait—wait, I'm sorry! I didn't know she was your daughter. Look, I meant no offense. Here, take your money back, and let's just forget I said anything."

Fred released the man and pushed him back against the wall. The clerk eyed him and nodded again at Fred's money still on the countertop.

Fred grabbed the money and pocketed the bottle of whiskey. Without saying another word, he turned and left the store.

"Here, I got lunch for us." He handed Doty the bag of groceries. "Let's go." As Doty went through the bag, Fred's thoughts returned to the exchange that had happened in the store. He looked at his daughters and felt the money in his pocket.

Doty grew angry at Father, again. There were only apples and bread in the bag. Her eyes fell on the bottle he held under his arm. She shook her head in disgust. In her heart, the root of bitterness grew. *At least he bought us something to eat. We'd have enough money and more to buy what we need for the trip home if he'd quit buying liquor.* She wanted to say it out loud but didn't dare. She gingerly ran her fingers across her face, which was still bruised and swollen from the day before.

"Thank you," she replied, trying not to irritate him. Doty looked at her hungry children's hollow eyes as they quietly begged for food. She rationed what little food they had, saving the smoked fish for dinner. Her heart ached for her hungry children as she tore the bread into small pieces and handed each child a piece, along with an apple and a drink of water.

Fred casually took his wallet out and counted his money. "I don't have much money saved up. There's enough for gas ta get us home but not 'nough to feed us more than a day or so. We'll have ta stop along the way to fish, hunt, or come up with food some other way." He put his wallet back in his pocket, started the car, took a swig from his bottle, and headed down the road again.

Taking note of the extra money still in Father's wallet, Doty wondered where it had come from. As she rode in the front seat, her thoughts of spending even more time in the close quarters with Father reinforced her anxiety. She scooted over and leaned against the car door, glaring out the window. *The trip will take longer now; we'll need to hunt and forage along the way.*

FIFTEEN

It was a beautiful fall evening as they drove down the highway through the mountainous landscape, but no one paid much notice except Doty. Leaves shivered as a light breeze wafted its way through the branches. The wind tickled the golden grass as it danced across the surface of the meadows in the fading sunlight. Streams of clear water tumbled and darted over the rocks, then meandered quietly through the fields of grass.

Relaxing as the scenery passed by, Doty's thoughts turned towards home. *I'll miss the mountains and meadows. It'll be hard going back to an arid desert with hardly any water, but we're going home.* Her thoughts comforted her as silence engulfed the car.

That evening, driving through the countryside, Fred and his family came upon some poverty-stricken migrants. These casualties of the Depression were camped in a small tent village. This was another Hooverville, and like so many others, it provided temporary shelter as people moved from town to town looking for work. The names may have been different, but the faces reflected the same strains of worry and hardship.

Yet, this camp was different. It was not dirty or trashy like the ones in which the family had stayed in recently. "I've heard about these camps." Fred slowed down and surveyed the campgrounds as he drove by. "This is a government Hooverville. Look over there." He pointed at the encampment. "See the well-maintained roads an' the clean and neat look a the place? These camps are subsidized by the government and provide runnin' water and toilets for the residents. But the charge and care a' the place are left to the migrants 'emselves."

"And look at the gorgeous countryside." Doty gazed in awe at the tent village. "It's a beautiful area with the meadows, forest, and creek. And look at all the tents scattered throughout the meadow. There looks to be around a hundred or so." She observed children running and playing while the women cooked dinner. The men sat in small groups and discussed issues.

"It sure is a pleasant place to stay for these people," she added, "especially during these hard times." Doty's heart yearned for a peaceful place to relax and forget about her worries.

Fred drove slowly by, surveying the area as the children gawked out the windows from the backseat, watching the other children play. Doty loved the camp's relaxed feeling. "I really like this place; it's nice and peaceful. Why don't we stay here for a while?"

Fred pulled over to the side of the road and stopped. He looked around the campgrounds as the occupants of the camp stopped what they were doing and curiously watched the newcomers.

"Good idea," Fred agreed. "In fact, there's a place over there that we can camp in tonight," he said to Doty, pointing to an unoccupied campsite at the edge of the meadow close to the road. "That empty area right there would be a good place to put up the tent." He backed the car up, turned slowly into the spot, and parked. The car doors immediately flew open, and the children piled out. The children were ready to burst from all the pent-up energy and emotional trauma from the past days.

"Hey, let's go play with the other kids!" Rosy yelled. Rosy, her brother, and her sisters ran off and disappeared among the small crowd of eager youngsters that were watching and waiting for these new playmates to join them.

The village people didn't have much, but they were rich in compassion and friendship. Doty's family was welcomed with open arms and greeted with kindness. Doty felt their affection. *What a wonderful change; my family is receiving the warmth and love of others.*

She left the two youngest to sleep in the front seat while she helped Fred put up the tent. After their camp was set up, Fred wandered off through the campground, exploring.

It only took a short time for her youngsters to get acquainted with the other children in the camp. That evening, her children ran and played for hours with their new-found friends. The chattering and giggling were a welcome respite that brought joy and pleasure to Doty's heart.

After a while, Doty unpacked the smoked fish and bread and called her children to come eat. It was another meager supper of fish, bread, and water, but at least now the children had a little food in their stomachs.

But Doty worried. *In another few meals the fish will be gone; then what will we eat?*

In the thickening dusk, Doty pulled her hair over her black eye hoping no one would notice in the dark. She picked up the baby, took George's hand, and walked over to meet a couple that was camped next to them.

"Hi, I'm Doty," she greeted her neighbors. Letting go of George's hand, she reached out to shake hands. "My family and I just made camp a little while ago."

"Hello, I'm Liza, and this is my husband, Jack. We're glad to meet you." Liza, a middle-aged woman with dark hair, wiped her hands on her apron then grasped Doty's hand and shook it, trying to ignore the bruise on Doty's face.

"Have you been here long?" Doty asked as she cuddled baby Henry. George clung to her skirt.

Liza's husband, Jack, smiled as he stepped forward with one hand on his hip and reached out with the other and shook Doty's. "Yes, we've been here for about a month. Didn't I see your husband 'round here? We'd like to meet him too."

"He's here somewhere. I'm not sure where he went. He's probably chatting with someone." Doty contemplated as she spoke. "I'm sure he's asking about work."

"There's not much work around here, but the hunting and fishing are good. That's why we're camped here. It will make a good place to winter," Liza informed Doty.

Doty was glad to hear that. *If we can't make it home, this would be a good place to stay.* She immediately pushed the thought aside. *No, I'm going home…*

The time flew by quickly as Doty and the neighbors continued chatting. She really appreciated having someone to talk to and enjoyed the evening, but underneath her joy lay a lingering concern; *Where's Father?*

It was growing darker. As Doty watched her children, she could see that they were tiring from play. She smiled. *They'll sleep well tonight.* Finally rounding up her brood, she sent them to the tent to get some sleep. Reluctantly, they went to bed, but exhaustion quickly won out. Almost as soon as their heads hit the blanket, they were sound asleep.

Doty sat on the ground quietly outside the tent, listening to the children's peaceful breathing as she waited for Father. The sun set behind the wooded mountains; darkness had slowly crept in and given way to the bright stars overhead. She leaned against a tree near the tent and gazed up at the twinkling stars and the full moon. Her body relaxed as she closed her eyes. *What a peaceful evening.*

The camp was quiet except for the crickets chirping and coyotes howling in the distance. For the first time in many weeks, she could feel herself start to relax and let go of her worries and concerns.

But her pleasant time of relaxation didn't last for long. Eventually Father showed up, sat silently down beside her, and didn't say a word. The anxiety she felt when he was around returned.

Suddenly, a woman's piercing scream cut through the still night air. Fear immediately pulsed through Doty's veins. *What's Father done now?*

The woman screamed again, "Help! S-Someone help! My daughter's been raped! P-Please, she's been beaten and is b-bleeding! Someone, help us!"

People started running everywhere, some to help the girl, some to check on and protect their own families, and others to hunt for the culprit. Horror and confusion spread quickly throughout the camp.

"Time to go," Father said quietly to Doty. "Start packin'." Then he yelled loud enough for everyone to hear, "No one's gonna rape my kids, we're leavin'!" He turned his head and snickered.

Afraid to ask questions or say anything, Doty quickly packed up their belongings, woke the kids, and loaded them into the car as fast as she could. She noticed a number of unfamiliar boxes stacked on the floor of the backseat and tied to the wooden trunk on the back of the Model T. *Where did those boxes come from?*

Father jumped into the vehicle, started it, and sped off, leaving a cloud of dust and the tent village behind in complete chaos.

Fred opened the car's throttle all the way, racing as fast as he could go. Afraid of being followed, he had to put as much distance as possible between him and the tent village before the people realized that he was the one that raped the girl and took their food. One thought rumbled through his mind; *At least now I have enough food to last for a while.*

He drove all through that night while the children slept, and Doty withdrew into herself.

As Father raced away, thoughts of his actions raced with him and started to catch up. Memories of the past started to haunt him as they stormed through his mind. Scene after despicable scene ran over and over through his head like a garish nightmare he could not escape. The face of the young girl he'd just raped made its way to the front of his crowded mind. Her screams that he muffled, the look of fear, combined with the smell of her blood assaulted him. Then, the memory of Gabe…of what he'd done to that little boy and the damage it had caused Gabe and his family…Doty's family. Finally, the faces of his own family, of Doty, of Rosy and the rest of his kids, how he mistreated and abused them, of the suffering they experienced because of him.

He slapped the steering wheel and ran a soiled hand roughly across his face as guilt plagued him. *Why did I do that? Why do I act like that? It's the whiskey, I know it is!* He swallowed, forcing his feelings of guilt down.

However, strangely, in a way, Father was pleased with himself. Because of his actions, he now had enough food to feed his family for a while; he even had money to spend on gas and whiskey. In the place of guilt and recrimination, feelings of smugness and pride began to take root and grow.

But soon the conflict returned. *I actually stole food from good people and left them to go hungry.*

He grimaced, trying to justify his actions. *But now my family will eat.*

As the guilt rose inside him, he again quickly pushed the feeling down. He shook his head hard, fighting to stave off the reality of his actions.

The conflict between right and wrong, survival and death, repeated itself in his thoughts over and over, causing his mind to spin. *What am I doing?*

Unable to deal with the conflict and guilt, tremors began deep down inside his body and slowly migrated outwards to his hands; soon his whole body was trembling. Fred swerved over to the side of the road, slammed on the brakes and skidded to a stop.

Doty and the children gasped as loose articles careened forward, crashing into them.

Closing his eyes, Fred squeezed them tight. Grasping his head with both hands, he held it tightly and shook it back and forth. *My head aches, I feel like I'm losin' it! I'm goin' crazy!* He knew the only thing that would stop him from completely losing his mind was his whiskey. He fumbled underneath the seat, retrieved his bottle, and inhaled large swigs.

Doty stared at Father. *What is wrong with him? He's acting even stranger than usual.* She felt a sense of foreboding grow inside her.

Father then stuffed his bottle back under the seat, grasped the steering wheel, and rested his forehead against it. He sat motionless, giving the whiskey time to pulse through his body and relax his tremors. Finally lifting his head, he reached for the Model T's throttle, opened it up, and sped off.

SIXTEEN

After the morning rain, the forested mountains smelled of fresh pine. The evergreen trees glistened as sunlight reflected from the dew on the dark green needles. It was only mid-morning, even though the sun was already high. The day was cool and heavy with moisture in the air.

Fred continued down Highway 40, which would take them through the Sierra Nevada Mountains and into the Nevada Desert. After driving and drinking all night, he was exhausted and intoxicated. Between the alcohol and the marathon drive, Fred felt sticky and irritable.

Doty sat in the front passenger seat, caring for the two youngest boys. In the backseat, the four older children started bickering amongst themselves.

"You kids, knock it off!" Fred snarled. "Be quiet! I'm tired a your fightin'!" There was immediate silence.

The long hours of driving gave Fred too much time to think. *I took my family ta California hopin' for a better life, but we got nothin' to show for it! If anythin', we're even worse off than before. How'll we survive?*

Doty noticed Father's knuckles turning white as he gripped the steering wheel. His body twitched, and his expression grew darker. Seeing his irritability grow, fear of his cruelty caused Doty to draw as far from him as she could. She grasped Henry tight and pulled George close to her, pressing herself against the passenger door. She had no desire to provoke him in any way. As they traveled for miles through the mountainous landscape on the crooked dirt road, the family's silence was as piercing as a knife.

Then, up ahead, Father spotted a slender young woman with a small boy who looked to be about four years old. They were walking down the dirt roadway hand in hand. Father pulled the Ford up behind them and stopped. "It musta been their car we saw alongside the road a couple miles back. Ya'll wait here!" he demanded. He quickly got out of the car, walked up to the woman, and started talking as his family sat in the car and waited.

Doty watched as the interaction between Father and the woman became intense. *What is he saying to her? What is going on?* She could tell that the young woman wanted no part of whatever Father was saying.

The woman, holding her son close to her, shook her head no. Father then suddenly grabbed her arm. She yanked her arm free and slapped him. He raised his hand and backhanded her across the face, knocking her and the boy to the ground. As she held on to her son and fought back, struggling to get away, Father ripped the young boy from her grip and threw him to the ground. He dragged her, as she kicked and screamed, toward a large rock at the side of the road, and they disappeared behind it. After a few minutes, there was an ear-piercing scream that echoed through the forest, followed by a long and deafening silence.

Doty didn't know what to do. Father's threats of the past echoed in her mind. In the mood he was in, she never doubted that he would follow through with his threats to harm her children or anyone else that angered him. So, she sat in fear and waited, daring not do anything.

The woman's young son sat in the dirt road and sobbed uncontrollably.

Willie suddenly flung the car door open and jumped out. "Father! Father, where are you?" he yelled.

In sudden panic, Doty screamed as quietly as she could, "Willie! Willie, get back here! You'll get in trouble with Father! Willie!"

Ignoring his mother, Willie took off running, calling again, "Father, where are you?"

Then Fred could be heard yelling angrily from behind the rock. "Get back in the car!" But Willie continued, running behind the rock to find his dad.

"Willie!" Doty screamed. "No! Come back!"

"I told ya to get back in the car!" Father yelled.

There was a child's scream. And then stillness.

Doty sat in the car, expecting a whimpering Willie to come running back. *He must have really made Father upset. You'd think he would learn to do what Father says.*

"Willie? Willie!" Annabel called out the car window. "Where are you?"

There was no answer.

Finally, Father came from behind the rock. He walked over and picked up the sobbing boy who was still sitting on the road. He carried the boy over to the car, opened the back door, and threw him into the backseat. "That's Willie from now on!" Father bellowed.

Rosy shouted at Father, "That's not Willie! Where's Willie? Where did he go?"

Father grabbed Rosy out of the seat by the front of her blouse, rage in his eyes. He slapped her across the face. "Listen to me! That's Willie now!"

Frightened and hurt, Rosy started to weep. "W-where's Willie?

"That's Willie! From now on, that's Willie!" Father repeated, pointing to the boy.

As Rosy cried, Doty looked at Father, astonished. "Father! What did you do? Where is he? What's happened to Willie?" Doty's heartbeat started to race.

The expression on Father's face showed it all.

Suddenly, Doty realized she would never see her son again. "NO! NOT WILLIE, WHERE'S MY SON?" she screamed at Father. "WHAT DID YOU DO?" She jumped out of the car and ran toward the rock to find her son.

Father tossed Rosy back into the seat and slammed the door. He raced after Doty. Catching up to her quickly, he grabbed her tightly around the waist. She flailed and clawed at his arms with her fingernails as he carried her back towards the car. "LET ME GO! I'VE GOT TO GO FIND WILLIE! PUT ME DOWN! LEAVE ME ALONE!" Doty screamed. "I'VE GOT TO GET WILLIE! I'VE GOT TO FIND MY SON!"

He shoved her back into the front seat and slammed the door. Glaring threateningly at her, he yelled, "Don't get out of this car unless you want the same thing to happen to them!" He pointed at the children who sat cowering in the rear seat.

"What do you mean? WHAT DID YOU DO TO WILLIE?"

Doty's whole body trembled. Her hand quivered and was barely able to grab the door handle as she tried to open the car door. *I have to get out! I have to find my son!*

Father raced around to the driver's side of the car. He jerked the door open and jumped in, stepped on the starter, and opened the throttle. "We're gettin' out a here!" he bellowed. He gripped the steering wheel as the tires spun, spitting out a large cloud of dirt and gravel.

Deep down, Doty's primal maternal instinct rose up inside her; survival of her children was her top priority. "NO! I HAVE TO GET WILLIE!" Doty screamed as the car gained speed. After quickly turning and handing the baby to Annabel in the backseat, Doty pushed George behind his brother, and grabbing the door handle, pushed the door open, and leaped out. Father slammed on the brakes as Doty tumbled out of the car. As she hit the ground, gravel bit into the palms of her hands and her knees. The impact of landing on her hands shot pain through her wrists and up her arms. Blood spurted from her gashed palms and skinned legs. Ignoring the pain, she quickly jumped up and sprinted back to look for her son.

Father jumped out of the Model T and chased after Doty. Her toe caught. She stumbled and fell, landing hard. When Father caught up with her, he grabbed her by the arms, shaking her, and then slapped her across the face, dragging her back to the car. "Don't ya dare run from me!" He threw her into the front seat and slammed the door shut. "Ya'll stay in the car if ya know what's good for ya! Don't try that again!" He jumped back into the Ford and sped off.

"NO! NOT MY WILLIE! WILLIE…" she cried out in horror. "WE CAN'T LEAVE HIM BEHIND! WILLIE!" she screamed louder, pounding her fists on the car window. As her reflection stared back at her, she pressed her face and hands against the glass, her ragged breath fogging the window, the palms of her hands leaving smears of blood. "No, not my Willie…not Willie." Her body shook with sobs.

It was then that something snapped inside her. Doty's emotions froze. Her mind, no longer able to cope with what was happening, went blank. Needing to escape reality, she withdrew into herself as the shock set in. A growing numbness blunted her emotions.

Not understanding what was going on, the children sat in confusion and fear in the backseat.

SEVENTEEN

It was early afternoon when they left the forested Sierra Nevada Mountains behind. Fred sped through the scorched Nevada desert, glancing in his rearview mirror often to make sure no one was following him. His stomach knotted, and his bowels cramped. Every muscle was rigid with tension; his heartbeat was pounding hard in his ears. Now filled with horror, he could not comprehend what he had just done or what had driven him to those actions. Looking behind him, he focused on the boiling cloud of dust he left behind, its swirling mass reflecting his inner turmoil.

As the Model T trudged up and down the desolate hills, reruns of the horrifying morning played over and over in Doty's mind. She sat in shock, and the children slept restlessly in the backseat.

Rosy sobbed in her sleep, grasping her doll, Betsy, tightly in her arms. "Willie? Willie! Where are you?" she whimpered over and over.

As Father listened to her whimpering, emotions of guilt and anger stormed through his mind. He ran his fingers through his hair, trying to rid himself of a throbbing headache. Finally, Father slammed on the brakes; the car skidded to a stop in the middle of the road. He leaped out of the vehicle, jerked the back door open, and grabbed Rosy, pulling her out of the car by the arm. He marched her up the side of a hill and sat her down on a large lava rock that overlooked the desert.

Only half awake, Rosy sleepily looked around. Confused, she asked Father, "What's going on?"

He demanded, "You stay here on this rock! You're goin' to sit here until you quit cryin' for Willie! We're leavin', and I'll be back when you accept that there boy as Willie!" He marched back down the hill to the automobile, grabbed Rosy's doll from the backseat, and threw it at her as she sat on the rock.

Back in the car, the "new" Willie sat terrified. Cowering on the backseat, his large eyes searched the strange faces around him and darted constantly to the window. Tears streaked his dirty face as he continued to cry.

Father looked at the boy through the side window and sneered. "You're mine now," he tormented. "You gotta do whatever I say!" Father sneered again, jumped in the car and sped away down the road.

"Wait!" cried Doty. "What are you doing? We can't leave Rosy here by herself in the desert!" As soon as the words were out of her mouth, she knew Rosy would be the next target of his anger.

"It's either leave her here, or I'll do to her what I did ta Willie. You choose! I'll not put up with her snivelin' behavior!" Father growled. "When I think she's learnt her lesson, we'll go back an' get her."

So, Doty remained silent. Her emotions numb, she would do whatever it took to save Rosy. Thinking of what Father *would* do to Rosy made it easier to accept the fact that he was leaving her behind. Doty knew that Rosy had a better chance of surviving in the desert than at the hands of Father right now.

Concerned for her remaining children, Doty sunk into silence. Their survival was top priority.

The desert breeze tousled Rosy's hair while she sat on the rock and looked from the steep hillside out over the parched land. She whimpered as she watched the dust cloud from the Model T float slowly down the dirt road and disappear. Soon, all was quiet; her family had left.

What did I do? Why are they leaving me? Confusion and fear filled her heart.

Her horror quickly changed from fear of Father to fear of being alone. Overwhelmed, her tears continued to stream down her face. "Where am I?"

The stillness of the desert was overcome by the soft sound of a slow, steady breeze as it leisurely wafted around Rosy, whispering against her ears. She listened and waited as she gazed out over the open valley and the distant hills, watching for that dust cloud to return. *I'll do what Father says and not get off this rock; then he'll come back for me.*

Eventually, the quiet beauty of the desert seemed to settle her soul. Her sobbing gradually subsided. She could breathe again. She sat…and sat, waiting for Father to return. "I won't cry when Father comes back, and I'll call the boy in the car Willie, even though I know it's not him." Determined, Rosy took a deep breath and released it.

Rosy spotted her doll, Betsy, laying in the dry grass and dirt. The doll was covered in dust and lay facing her, waiting to be rescued. "Betsy, if I get down from the rock and get you, Father won't come and get me," Rosy quietly told the doll. "You'll just have to wait for Father too."

Restlessness began to overcome her. Rosy could feel the heat penetrating her body as it radiated from the dark stone. Finding it uncomfortable to sit on the large boulder, she wiggled and squirmed, then crossed and uncrossed her legs numerous times, trying to alleviate the heat on her legs and bottom. Her face, burning and flushed from the scorching sun, was also becoming chapped by the dry desert breeze.

Doubts and uncertainties fluttered through the young girl's mind as she sat for what seemed like hours. *Has Father forgotten me? I'm sure Mom would remind him that I'm waiting.*

She closed her eyes, hoping to hold in the tears which were perched on her bottom lids again. *I've been waiting forever.* A deepening fear started to fill her heart, a fear that she would never see her mother and siblings again. Rosy sat silently on the rock as these thoughts and feelings played over and over; she was unable to shake them.

Then gradually, an unexpected feeling came over her. She felt a peaceful presence surround her. This presence seemed to tenderly and lovingly envelop her little by little. At the same time, it quieted her soul. A feeling of security began to fill her being and take her fear away.

She did not understand. Sensing there was someone with her, Rosy looked around. It felt as though someone had their arms around her, making her feel safe. Despite seeing no one, her fears gradually subsided.

A peace engulfed her and settled in her little girl's heart. "Hello? Anybody there?" she called. Seeing no one, she wondered, *Could this be God?* She looked up into the sky and searched the heavens. Whispering aloud, she spoke to a God she didn't know. "God, is that You? Do You really exist?"

Silence enveloped the countryside.

"I heard 'bout You before…heard others talk about You. But I don't know anything 'cept that You're supposed to love people." Rosy looked around again. "I've never felt

You with me before. But I think this must be You. Are You protecting and taking care of me?"

Rosy sat for a long moment, listening with her soul. Gradually, a large cloud drifted through the sky and came to a stop right above her in front of the sun. The cloud's cool shadow hovered over her and didn't move, protecting her from the sun's blistering rays. Relaxing, she laid down on the rock, curled up, and closed her eyes.

When Rosy awoke, it was early evening, and the sun was lower in the western sky. She was hot, her throat was parched, and she desperately needed a drink of water.

However, nothing had changed.

The sense of peace remained with her. She still sat on the rock, the sun still shown, the cloud still hovered, and the breeze still blew. In the vast emptiness of the desert, she was still alone—and still she felt the peace and security in her heart that she decided must be God.

Rosy gazed over the land and thought of her family again. Bursting out in tears, she cried out, "God, I want my mom…" As tears escaped from her eyes, she wiped them away with the back of her hands, still feeling those protective arms wrapped softly and gently around her.

Relaxing in the security of that presence, her thoughts slipped back to her current situation. *I dare not get off this rock. If Father comes and I'm not where he told me to be, he'll drive away, and I'll never get to go home again.*

So, she sat all alone, still feeling safe and protected.

Then, thinking back on what little she knew about God, Rosy began to make up songs about Him to entertain herself. She didn't know much about Him, but she knew what she wanted Him to be and to do. She wanted Him to continue to be with her. She wanted Him to protect her, to give her water, and to bring her a ride home. And most of all, she wanted to feel her mother's arms around her again.

Taking a breath, she started singing her own made up songs of her wants and needs to God. At first, her songs were quiet, almost a whisper, but as she sang and the feeling of God's presence became more real, she began to sing louder and stronger. Looking up to heaven as she sang, she knew God was there.

If I sing loud enough, God will hear me. She sang her heart out, asking Him for her needs and for His protection, and most of all, to be with her mother again. But eventually her voice grew hoarse, she became tired, and silence muffled her songs. Resigned, she continued to sit and stare out over the dry empty land.

Then something caught her eye. Rosy noticed a movement in the distance. It was a cloud of dust coming from the direction that Father had driven. She giggled giddily. "God heard me! Father's coming back!"

The dust cloud came closer and closer. *I don't dare get down from the rock. Father will drive right by if I do.* She waited quietly as the car came into view. *Wait, no…that's not our car, it's a different car!*

Soon the vehicle was right below her. *It's driving right by! They didn't see me! I have to stop them!* "STOP!" she screamed as loud as she could. "WAIT, I'M HERE! HELP ME! STOP!"

The car came to a sudden stop, backed up, and parked right below the rock. There was a middle-aged, well-dressed couple in the car. The man sat in the driver's seat while the woman got out and quickly walked up the hill towards Rosy. "Young lady, what in the world are you doing out here in the middle of the desert by yourself?" she asked, amazed.

"Father forgot me." Rosy broke out into tears. "He left me here and forgot me."

"Which way did your father go?" the woman asked.

Rosy pointed east.

The woman took Rosy's hand. "Come with me, we'll find your father. There's a town quite a few miles back. We'll look for him there. What's your name?"

Quietly she replied, "Rose," then stronger, "Rosy!"

"Hi, Rosy, my name's Lila Roberts and my husband's name's Charles. Let's go find your family." Her rescuer gently took her hand and helped her off the rock.

Rosy knew in her heart that God had brought these people to save her. She climbed down from the rock, grabbed her doll, and followed the woman down the hill and into the vehicle. The kind woman gave her a cold drink of water and talked to her tenderly.

Sitting quietly in the backseat of the car, Rosy hugged her doll. The man turned the car around and headed back in the direction that Father had gone, trailing his own dust cloud.

Lila turned to talk to Rosy, but Rosy didn't feel like talking. "Sweetie, what are your father and mother's names?"

"Mommy and Father."

Lila tried again, "What kind of a car do they drive?"

Rosy thought before she answered. "It's black and has a wooden trunk tied on the back of it." She hugged Betsy and then sat silent and still.

After a few minutes of driving, Charles asked, "Do you know where they're going?"

"They're going home without me. Father forgot me." Rosy started to cry, answering the question only because she had to. All she wanted right now was her mother's arms around her.

Lila reached to the backseat and took Rosy's hand. "It's okay, sweetie. I'm sure we'll find them." Charles raced as fast as he could back down the road for an hour and a half before they reached the next town. To Rosy, it seemed like eternity as she sat in silence, staring out the window.

Finally arriving in the town, they drove slowly around the streets, looking for Rosy's father's car. After about fifteen minutes of surveying the local parking lots and watching traffic, Rosy pointed and yelled, "There it is! There's my car at that store, and there's my family!"

Father was just going into the grocery store. Doty and the kids had gotten out of the car to stretch. Trying to comfort the new 'Willie', Doty stood with her arms around his shoulders as the other children stood quietly in front of the store.

The Roberts's pulled into the store parking lot and stopped. Rosy didn't wait for them to turn off the engine. Grabbing the handle, she slammed the door open and quickly jumped from the car. "Mommy! Mommy, she yelled, "I found you! Mommy!" Rosy raced toward her mother. Lila and Charles followed quickly behind her.

Doty looked up when she heard the familiar voice yelling "mommy" and saw a small figure leaping from a car and running toward her. "Rosy?" Recognizing the small figure as her daughter, Doty erupted into tears and collapsed to her knees. "Rosy!" With trembling hands, she brushed away tears and hugged herself before stretching out to grasp ahold of the figure that was fast approaching her.

"Mommy! Mommy!" Rosy raced across the parking lot towards the outstretched arms of her mother. She threw herself at her mom, latching her arms around her mother's neck and burying her face against her breast. She held on, intending never to let her go.

Doty grasped Rosy tightly, hugging her with shaking arms. A look of joy and relief crossed Doty's face as she closed her eyes tight and clutched her daughter. She whispered, "Rosy, you found us. I was afraid that I'd never see you again!" Both mother and daughter wept with tears of joy.

Doty was grateful to have this precious moment with Rosy while Father was in the store. Relieved and knowing her daughter was safe, a wave of gratitude passed through Doty's being, followed by a surge of fear for the young girl's life.

The other children eagerly surrounded Rosy and grasped her and hugged her, thrilled to see their sister again—all the other children, that is, except the new Willie. He stood by the car and solemnly watched the family reunion. "Where's my mommy?" his lips whispered silently.

Rosy was the first to notice Father walk out of the store carrying a bag of groceries. He was surprised and shocked to see her, and he seemed unsure of what to say.

Seeing her father, Rosy suddenly cried out, "Father, you forgot me! I stayed on the rock, but you forgot me. These people found me and helped me find you!"

There was fear In Doty's eyes when she heard the innocent accusation.

Father furiously turned his head to the side and quietly released a string of curses. Handing Doty the food, he then forced a smile, walked over to the couple, and extended his hand. "Hello, I'm Fred."

"I'm Charles Roberts." He extended his hand and shook Fred's.

"Thanks for bringin' Rosy back to us." Father tried to grin. "There's so many kids in that vehicle that I guess I didn't even realize she was gone. It's a good thing we had a flat tire. I stopped ta fix the flat and we decided ta get out an' stretch for a while. Otherwise, ya probably would've never caught up with us."

Mr. Roberts gave Fred a skeptical look. "That and the fact that I drove as fast as I could to try and catch up with you." Charles put his hand on Lila's shoulder. "This is my wife, Lila." Father tipped his head in acknowledgement.

"I'm glad we found her." Lila looked suspiciously at Fred. "She was pretty scared, sitting out in the desert by herself."

The couple looked at each other questioningly, then back at Fred, but said nothing more. Mr. Roberts tipped his hat to Doty, and the couple left. Doty looked up as the couple passed her. Charles leaned close to his wife and whispered, "I hope we did the right thing."

Doty looked at Father and saw anger in his eyes. Neither said a word. They all got into the car, gave each of the kids a chunk of bread, an apple, and some water, then drove out of town.

Rosy sat silently, thinking of the rock in the desert, of God, and of the loss of Willie. The boy they now called Willie sat quietly beside her with yearning in his eyes. Rosy took the boy's hand and looked at him with understanding. When their eyes met, he leaned toward her, and the two cried quietly together. Beside them, Annabel and Carolyn stared out the window, not saying a word, while the two youngest slept restlessly in the front seat between Father and Doty.

Doty was so overjoyed at having her Rosy back that she swallowed hard, pushing down the anger and pain from before.

However, the fear remained.

———————≈———————

The next week of travel passed slowly. Each person yearned in their own way to be home. Those few days and nights were the hardest for the family yet. Even when they camped, their dreams echoed the horror of the last few months, and the new Willie just cried. Each distanced themselves from what had happened, turning their thoughts toward a better future. But the past was not easily forgotten.

The numbness had worn off and the grief and regret in Doty's heart at the loss of Willie would not be ignored or silenced. The shards of her broken heart could not be put back together again. *Every time I think of you, Willie, it hurts worse, and the broken slivers cut deeper into my heart. I want to be home, out of this car, away from everything and everyone. I want to be by myself so I can cry and mourn for you…*

I'm so sorry, my love.

Rosy rode silently in the backseat of the car, yearning for her brother. Her heart broke for him. *I miss you so much, Willie. Please come back. I don't know what to be without you.* Rosy didn't cry; she had no more tears to shed. Her whole body ached with grief, but it seemed numb to life. She decided to accept the 'new' Willie and try to help him instead.

The boy was confused. He didn't understand. He wanted to know who these people were, where they were taking him, and where his mommy was. His eyes glimmered with unshed tears. Overwhelmed and afraid, he had no choice but to do as he was told. He sat silently between the girls and wondered what would happen next.

Fred couldn't get home fast enough. As he followed the road, his eyes surveyed the familiar landscape. *A few more miles an' we'll be there.* He opened the throttle as wide as possible. *I'm puttin' the past behind me. I'm gonna make us a new beginning.*

EIGHTEEN

When the homestead came into view, the children erupted with excitement. Everyone except Willie.

"Mom! We're home!" yelled Rosy. "Look, Willie," she continued to yell, forgetting which Willie she was talking to, "we're home!"

"Where's my mommy?" Willie looked with big eyes as the acreage and shanty came into view. Confused, he looked at Rosy. "This ain't my house."

"It's where we live," Annabel smiled as she put her arm around Willie. "It's your home now, too."

Falling into silence, Willie stared out at the parched acres and clear blue sky. Anxious to get out of the car, but still afraid, he pressed back against the seat.

Carolyn pressed her face and hands against the window, grinning from ear to ear as she watched her home grow closer and closer.

Doty gazed at the homestead, her heart beating a little faster as a new hope for a normal life and a stable home sprang up inside her. She turned and looked in the backseat, watching the children's reactions. Her heart broke for Willie as she saw a look of despair on the young boy's face.

Doty sighed. *I never thought I would be so glad to see this place.* Holding the baby in one hand, she placed the other hand on the door handle, ready to open the door as soon as the vehicle stopped. She needed space.

Fred brought the car to a stop in the dirt driveway, breathing a sigh of relief. As soon as the vehicle stopped, doors flung open and the family rushed from the car. Fred turned to look at the boy who hadn't moved. "Look here, kid. This is yer home now and that there is your momma. From now on your name is Willie, ya hear me? If'n you don't do like I tell ya, I'll beat the skin off ya. You hear me?"

The boy stared up at Fred, but still didn't move.

Fred got out and snatched open the rear door. "Get out. And stop yer moping around."

Welcoming the wide-open acres of their own space, the children screamed, hollered, and giggled as they chased each other around the yard. It was a time for celebration; they were home at last. Doty joined them as she swung baby Henry in circles, both of them laughing and giggling. Fred watched as Doty and the children happily reclaimed their home.

Fred turned silently to gaze out over the barren farmland. The desert breezes whistled through the dried fields, raising small puffs of dust. He could see that nothing had changed. *The fields are still parched and desolate; there's still no water and still no way to make a living.* Fred slapped his thigh and closed his eyes in despair.

They think the nightmare is over. They don't understand nothin'…

Fred helped Doty unload the car. Doty toted the household items into the house and started to clean and organize her home. Fred unpacked his belongings and then meandered out to the barn and fields to check things out. All the children had run off to explore their old familiar places—all the children, except Willie.

Still standing where Fred had left him, Willie stood and stared at the homestead. He wandered toward the front porch and sat beside the wooden step. Everything scared him. "I want my Mommy," he whimpered.

After a moment, he made his way into the shanty and shuffled up to Doty. He stopped in front of her and stood with his hands in his pockets. Looking up at her with sad eyes, he demanded in his little boy's voice, "Where am I, and where's my mommy?"

Doty's heart broke for the boy. "Oh sweetheart…" She knelt down in front of him and gently took his hands. She looked at him with tearful eyes and said sadly, "I get to be your mommy now, and we're your new family, and this…this is your new home."

His eyes filled with tears. "But I want my mommy…" he whispered. He hung his head and wept, his body jerking with each sob. He collapsed against Doty. "I want my mommy…"

Exhausted, he cried himself to sleep.

Doty collected the boy in her arms and rocked him. "You'll be okay. We all will. We'll take care of each other." *He'll accept his new life. He has no choice.*

Coming in, Rosy saw her mother with the child. Remembering how she'd felt alone on the rock, she sat down on the floor beside the young boy and took his hand into hers. She sat silently and pressed her face against his cheek.

After a while, she took his hand and placed in it the shiniest rock from her and Willie's collection. The boy's eyes opened, and Rosy smiled down at him. "Willie, you get to be my new brother."

The boy frowned. "My name's Johnny, not Willie."

Rosy put her hand over his mouth and looked to see if Father had heard. She shushed him and said, "No, Father said your name is Willie now. We don't want him to hurt you, so just be Willie, okay?" When the boy didn't answer, she continued, "Let's you and me go collect some new rocks. We can start a new collection."

Willie nodded his head, so taking him by the hand, Rosy led him out the door. "I'll teach you everything I know. We'll be best friends."

Doty watched the children from the porch. With tears in her eyes, her heart ached for her Willie and for this little boy.

From the shadow in the barn's door, Fred seethed as he watched Rosy lead the boy from the house, thinking what she would tell the child. In contrast to what he thought, seeing the boy didn't help him forget what he'd done to his son, but only reminded him of the level of cruelty he was capable of.

It's that boy's fault. I'll teach him.

Fred meandered around the homestead, examining it. The 160 acres and its ramshackle house of weathered, warped boards still stood nestled in the large valley, surrounded by distant foothills. Dust from constant winds still sifted through the cracks between the sun-bleached boards and the broken window of the shanty.

What few livestock that had once offered a measure of support were now gone. Not even a meager crop was available for food or sale, and no kitchen garden had been tended. The house and outbuildings needed repaired. The desert land with its wind, dust, and lack of rain continued to make it impossible to produce a living from the earth. The children still wore their tattered hand-me-down clothes and ran around with dirty, callused feet because shoes were still a luxury they could not afford. Nothing had changed.

As Fred wandered around the acreage, he suddenly noticed the dried tops of a few root plants from last summer's garden. He knelt down, dug the soil from around the dried onion tops, and tugged on them. The onions came up. They had survived the summer. He then started digging up potatoes and carrots. "Yes!" Fred spun around, dirt flying and hollered, "Hey, Doty—quick—come see what I found. Bring a shovel. I found food!"

Doty hustled to the barn, grabbed two shovels, and ran over to Fred. "Here's a shovel, I brought one for me too. I'll help." She handed one to her husband and eagerly began to dig along beside him.

As they dug, they managed to fill up a few crates with potatoes, carrots and onions. The more food they dug, the faster Fred's heartbeat. *More food for my family; things are lookin' up a little. There's enough root crops here, along with the food I stole, ta feed the family for weeks. But I still need a job. I'll start checkin' around.*

The next day, Fred headed to town, hoping he could find work. Stopping at Bill's house on the way, Fred noticed a few gaunt farm animals wandering around in the fields. He knocked on the door of the shack and waited for an answer. "Anyone home?" he yelled as he slowly pushed the door open; no answer. He tried again, "Hello?" Stepping into the small cabin, he left footprints on the floor in the dust with every step he took. The house's creaking floor and the bare, dust-covered shelves gave it a feeling of abandonment. The family had packed up and moved on.

Fred walked out and stood on the doorstep. Occasional gusts of wind whipped around him and the deserted shack as he watched a cow, pig, and some chickens roam around in the fields looking for plants, bugs, anything that would suffice for nutrition. *Can I really be that lucky?* His heart skipped a beat.

Fred also noticed that Bill's truck was parked in the barn. *Hmm, I wonder why Bill left his truck?* He inspected the vehicle. *This is a good truck. I wonder if Bill's coming back?*

Fred continued on his way into town. Even knowing that most of the stores had closed some time ago, he still had to check for job possibilities. The general store and feed store were the only ones open. Fred walked into the general store. "Hello, Sam. Where's everyone?"

Startled, Sam quickly turned to him. "Well, hello, Fred. When did you get back?"

"Got back yesterday." Fred reached out and shook Sam's hand. "No luck in California. Had ta come home. There any work 'round here?"

Sam shook his head no. "Sorry. Most everyone's moved on to find work. They couldn't make a livin' here. Since there's no jobs here, there's no money." Sam leaned back against the counter and crossed his arms. "There hasn't been much rain either, so most of the crops have died. Only those folks livin' way out by the reservoir that get irrigation water are still around, but they won't be for long; there's not much water left even there."

Fred mulled over the information for a minute before he continued, "Sam, my old neighbors, Bill and his family, are gone, moved out, an' have turned out their livestock. Will they be back?"

"Don't 'spect so. I heard they went up north to live with family and are stayin' up there. They headed out last summer right after you and your family left, butchering only what meat they could take with them. Since most everyone's moved on, there's no one else to keep the animals, so the animals were left to fend for themselves."

Fred grinned to himself. *Food! I've found a way to feed my family for a little while longer.*

"If no one wants 'em, I can sure use them. I think I'll round 'em up, and take 'em home. If nothin' else, I can butcher them for the meat." Fred smiled and turned to leave. "And by the way," he turned back towards Sam. "Bill left his truck, too. If he's not comin' back, I could sure use that too. It's a Ford Model AA farm truck and in a lot better condition than mine."

Sam walked Fred out the door to the street. "Bill used to be well off when he moved here a few years ago, but like the rest of the country, things went downhill for him." Sam's shoulders lifted with a shrug. "Bill took his other car—he needed it to take his family—and packed his belongings in it too. He tried to sell the truck, but no one could afford to buy it, so he left it here. I don't know what to tell you about that. You be the judge. I don't think he's coming back, but I don't know for sure."

"Thanks, Sam. I think I'll pick up the truck. If Bill comes back, I'll give it back to him. Let me know if ya hear of any job openin's." Fred added, "And if anyone asks, I'm takin' the abandoned livestock."

On the way home, Fred stopped, and rounded up the animals. He put the chickens in an old crate and put them in the backseat of the Model T, tied the cow and pig to his bumper, and very slowly led them back to the homestead.

As he drove the animals home, Fred began to consider other possibilities. *Other families may have left food too. I think I'll scavenge the other abandoned farms for food and other things.*

After he arrived home with the animals, Fred walked over to Bill's house. He climbed into the truck and drove it around to other deserted homes in the area, looking for anything that would be helpful. He found a few more animals, more root crops, and even a few canned goods.

Fred also stopped at the school. It had been closed for quite a while by this time. While he was rummaging through the building, he had an idea. *I'll take the schoolbooks an' other materials home an' give them ta Doty. She graduated. She should be a good teacher. Maybe she could continue the children's schoolin'*

When Doty saw the books, she accepted them thoughtfully and began flipping through the pages of a teacher's manuals. Then she examined all the other materials. Over the next couple weeks, while Fred continued to scavenge the neighborhood, Doty poured over the books day and night. Seeing education as the best way for her children to escape Father, Doty was determined that they would get the best education possible.

After two weeks, she was ready to begin. "Okay kids, school starts today. Come on over and sit down."

All of the children crowded around the table; the four oldest slid into the makeshift chairs while the younger children ran around chasing each other. Doty gave each child at the table a small chalk board and a stick of chalk.

Each day, she was ready with a new lesson. She was determined they would be more than ready when school reopened. Doty finally felt that she was doing something positive for her children.

NINETEEN

1934

Over the next couple of years, Doty rationed what little food Fred brought home, making it last as long as possible. Now the meat was gone except for one old sow. Father couldn't fish, the streams were dry, and any wild animals that should have been around had left the area long ago.

Sometimes, if he was lucky, Father might catch a rabbit or kill a rattlesnake to bring home. Every now and then, he would make the fifteen-mile hike out to the Black Canyon Reservoir to hunt. Occasionally, he might bag a deer that had come out of the hills for a drink of water, or maybe he would shoot a quail or two. But since there was very little water left in the reservoir, his chances of bringing home food were always slim at best.

Fred opened the barn door and shuffled inside. On the left side of the door were two stalls; one was empty and the other contained a small pile of hay. Inhaling deeply, the scents of the hay and manure flooded his sinuses, bringing back flashes of memories of open fields and better times. He exhaled as he lumbered to the other side of the barn, lifting a coiled rope hanging from a large nail on the wall. *No matter what I do, it's never enough for 'em. Always lookin' at me…accusing me. Like I ain't doing all I can.*

He clutched his head in his hands, squinting his eyes against the pain of memories and phantoms of his past actions. He cursed. *Three children already dead…and Willie.*

Willie…the name rang in his mind like a klaxon, shrill and uncomfortable. He shook his head again, trying to rid himself of the pain. *They got ta leave me alone.*

Still holding his head, Fred sunk to the dirt. As he sat in agony, suddenly the words of the store clerk, that he bought whiskey from on the way home from California, started echoing in his mind, *"Hey, hey, look at that. A man would sell his right arm for a few minutes with that young beauty…"*

Father shook his head and tried to push the concept away. He walked out of the barn to the pig pen, opened the gate, and put the rope around the sow's neck. This was the last meat they had.

The children's chores were finished, and they were outside enjoying the morning as they ran around, chattering and playing in the yard. As Fred began to lead the pig out of its pen and towards the large cottonwood tree behind the barn, he stopped. He stood silently contemplating and wrestling with his tormented thoughts as he watched the children play "Follow the Leader" around the yard. The store clerk's comment kept resurfacing, the very idea that he had been trying to forget.

Is this my last resort, the only other way I can feed my family? As he watched the children run around, Father finally weighed the idea. *I guess it won't be anythin' new to the kids. They're already used ta what I do to 'em. It'll just be someone different.*

Fred settled on what he had to do; it was this or let his family starve.

"Hey! You kids, git over here!" he shouted to the children. *I have ta make sure they do what I say.* "Get over here an' sit down on the ground!" He pointed to a spot nearby. "Now."

The children called Fred Father, but it was not a name of love or respect. To the family, it was a neutral name to negate any and all warmth toward him. They held a strong fear of him in their hearts and minds. The children avoided him as much as they could, but there were times when they dare not, and this was one of them. When Father spoke, they obeyed.

The children immediately stopped their play and walked slowly toward him, not knowing what to expect and afraid to find out. "Coming, Father," Annabel quietly replied. Carolyn, Rosy, and Willie followed her reluctantly with their eyes turned to the ground. Their tattered clothing hung loose on their undernourished bodies as they shuffled through the dust toward Father.

"You kids get over here and sit down!" Father impatiently shouted again. "Hurry up!"

They glanced at each other with fearful eyes. Moving a little faster, the children gathered beneath the tree and sat down. They huddled together, taking each other's hands for reassurance and security.

As soon as they were sitting on the ground, Father bound the struggling pig's hind legs together with the rope. He threw the loose end of the rope over a tree limb and pulled the pig up, hanging it upside down. The old sow squealed and squirmed, struggling to get free, but she was held tightly by the sturdy rope and tight knot.

"You kids watch this!" Father demanded as he grabbed the pig, wrapped his arm around her head and held her tightly. Lifting his long sharp knife, he slashed the animal's throat, then let go. The pig's body thrashed and jerked. As the crimson blood gushed from its body, so did its life. The warm, metallic smell of the draining blood slowly rose and hovered over the children and the surrounding area. Soon, the sow quit squirming and hung motionless. Using his knife again, Father slit open the sow's belly. The blood continued to stream from the lifeless body onto the parched earth, splashing onto Father's pants and in the faces of the silent children. As the kids watched the blood ooze from the pig, the color slowly drained from their faces.

Then turning to the children, Father avowed emphatically, "From now on, ya do what I say, or this'll happen to you! Ya hear me? Answer me!" His threat filled each child with fear. They had all seen Father slaughter animals, but now his words and behavior were different. As they looked at Father with horror in their eyes, they slowly nodded their heads.

Rosy looked into her father's face. *Was this what he did to Willie?*

Father dragged an old washtub from behind the barn, cut the dead animal down from the tree, and dropped it into the tub. The children stared as Father slowly skinned and butchered the pig.

Rosy closed her eyes and turned her head, unable to watch.

Spattered with the pig's blood, the children sat motionless. Horrified at what they had just seen and heard; silent tears rolled down their cheeks, leaving streaks on their dirty faces. The graphic scene and piercing words had penetrated into their very being and would stay with each of them for the rest of their lives.

Watching and listening from a distance, Doty stood outside the shanty door. Shivering in horror and fear, she had no doubt that Father meant exactly what he said. As Henry and George sat in the house on the floor playing, tears ran down Doty's cheeks. *I know our survival depends on Father…he's provided even the little bit of food that we do have. But how can I continue to let him hurt my children? How can we live like this?*

From across the yard, Father met her gaze.
He smiled.

TWENTY

1937

It was a typical summer day on the homestead. The heat from the morning sun stirred the air, causing a wind to blow through the valley, quickly drying the morning dew and depleting what little moisture was left in the young corn plants. This spring, rain came a little more often now, but it was never enough. The vegetation was gradually turning from the beautiful, small, green corn shoots to brittle, scorched yellow foliage. Even the grass on the valley floor hunkered down to avoid the sun and moisture-stealing air.

Rosy, who was now ten years old, had the tasks of feeding and watering the animals and milking the cow. Sauntering out of the house, she headed out into the early morning heat. The wind tousled her hair as the dust and hot air dried her eyes, making them burn. Squinting to avoid the drying wind and the already-blinding sun, she scampered to the barn to get the milk bucket. The rickety old barn door was so huge it took all her weight to drag it open just a foot or two.

She squeezed through the small opening and grabbed the wooden bucket from one of the stalls. Then taking the bucket to the old iron hand pump in the front yard, she poured the water, which had been intentionally left in the bottom of the bucket, into the pump to prime it. After hanging the bucket's handle over the pump's spout, Rosy pumped the iron handle up and down. Water was sucked up out of the shallow well, gushed out of the spout, and tumbled into the wooden pail.

She toted buckets of water back and forth, again and again, to each of the livestock, pouring it into their troughs, being very careful not to spill it. Water was precious; she dared not waste a drop.

After pumping a little more water into the bucket, she squeezed back through the barn door and set the bucket back in the stall. Rosy's eyes shone with delight as she shuffled to the back of the barn. The top part of the Dutch door that led to the corral, was already open. She unlatched the lower part of the door and swung it open too.

"Now, my favorite chore…" Rosy stepped into the corral. She took hold of the cow's halter and gently coaxed the animal into the barn. "Come on, Star, it's time for milking." She patted the black star-shaped spot on the animal's forehead and led her to the milking stall. A small portion of grain was poured into a bucket for Star to munch on during milking.

Rosy loved the familiar smells of the barn, and she relaxed, resting her head against the cow's warm, soft flank while she busied herself milking. The wind made a hollow sound as it whistled through the cracks in the barn walls, and it reminded Rosy of a sad song.

She had thought often about her time on the rock and had made up songs to God just to show her gratefulness. She still knew very little about God, but the memory warmed her, so she sang songs just for Him to hear.

As she milked, the rhythm of her hands became rhythm for her song. The wind whistled and hummed the background music. Quietly she sang, "Oh God are You up there…can You hear me…do You care? I know You're somewhere…I know You love me…I know You're there."

The milking and the singing continued as she relaxed and enjoyed her time with a God she didn't know.

Milking finished, Rosy released the cow from the enclosure into the fields. Star was free to wander and graze on whatever else she could find to eat.

Rosy returned for the milk. As she took the precious liquid into the house and gave it to her mother, something occurred to her. *Maybe this is a way that God is taking care of my family and me, by providing milk through Star.*

With chores finished, Rosy and her siblings rushed outside to play tag. Doty didn't worry about them playing outside; it gave her some peace and quiet for herself.

"Rosy, you're it!" her siblings yelled.

Rosy didn't hesitate. "Then you better run!" She giggled and took off after them, chasing the other kids all around the yard. They ran and laughed as their feet kicked up the fine dust.

"You're it!" Rosy called, as she tagged Carolyn.

Rosy turned and ran away as Carolyn chased her and yelled, "I'll get you back!"

The chase was on as the children ran around the old farmhouse bantering back and forth.

Then, in the distance, the children heard a vehicle approaching. They stopped their game and listened, watching the road. Shortly, they saw Father's car speeding down the driveway toward home, followed by a large cloud of dust. Fear filled their eyes. Instantly, Rosy panicked. *When Father drives that fast, it means something bad—usually that he's drunk.* "Run!" yelled Rosy. "Run!" The children took off in all directions, unsure of what was coming next.

It was too late. The vehicle raced into the dirt driveway and slid to a stop. Father jumped out of his car and yelled, "Rosy! Get over here, now!" Rosy stopped and watched as the other children kept running, disappearing into a cloud of dust and leaving her behind.

She slowly turned around and hesitantly walked toward her father. She knew what was about to happen; the past had taught her.

I want to keep running too. Rosy held her head up and threw her shoulders back, determined not to cry. *I want to run so far away that Father can never catch me, and I can find a hiding place where he can never find me.* But she knew the consequences were too great. *I guess it's my turn. I'm 'it' again. I hate you, Father, for making me do this.* She shivered as bitterness and anger filled her whole being.

Another man stepped out of the passenger's side of the car. He grinned when he saw the young girl. He studied Rosy from head to toe. "She'll do," he said.

Rosy loathed Father for what he made her do. She hated the men touching her and the abuse they inflicted on her. She despised her father, but she feared him even more.

Father slurred as he demanded, "Rosy, go with 'im to the outhouse. You'll do whatever he says…anythin' he wants—ya do! Do ya understand?"

Rosy hung her head but didn't answer. Memories of Father's abuse to her, of other men's cruelty, and of Father's demands when he butchered the pig, raced through her mind. She knew she didn't have a choice.

"Answer me!" he commanded.

Her voice trembling, she answered, "Yes, I understand…"

She slowly turned and unwillingly followed the stranger.

Sometime later, the man returned from the outhouse, Rosy shuffling slowly behind him, tears streaming down her cheeks.

Her abuser walked up to Father and flipped him a large coin. "She did great!" He smiled, then walked away, heading back toward town.

Tears continued to flood down Rosy's cheeks. Her body hurt and ached. She felt dirty, but not from the dust and grime. With her head down, the young girl turned and walked away. She walked unhurriedly out into the open fields, then lifted her head high, pulled her shoulders back, and started to run. She ran and ran until she couldn't run anymore. Falling to the ground, she lay in the dust and the dry dead grass. Sobs from somewhere deep down inside her gut rose and caused her torso to convulse with each sob.

The dry grass stabbed her skin, but she did not feel it. The scorching sun beat down on her; she did not notice it. The dirt and dust covered her body; she didn't care. Rosy lay on the ground and cried and cried until she could cry no more.

"God, where are You? I need You…" she cried out as she lay in the field, unable to understand.

Father walked into the house and plopped the large coin down on the kitchen table. "Here's some money for food," he said smugly.

He turned and walked out.

Doty stood silently looking at the coin, then glanced up at Father's back as he walked out the door. She knew where the coin had come from. She hated him for what he made her girls do. She hated him for making her use the coins. She wanted him dead. She wanted him out of their lives. She wanted to scream and yell at him. *No…you can't do this to the girls! Leave them alone! I hate you! Get out of our lives.* But the words would not come. They stuck in her mouth like cotton. She stood still, voiceless, unable to speak, overcome by fear of retribution.

Instead, she silently watched him walk out the door. *But we need him.* Anger and pain welled up in her eyes and ran down her face.

At least we have food; the kids will eat...

———————————

Money and food were still very scarce. Fred worked the fields, trying to grow his crops and he also worked odd jobs when he could find them. Over the next few years, every now and then, Fred would bring a man home, or a man would knock on the door, asking for Fred. Fred would then send one of the girls to the outhouse with him. The girls did what they were told, afraid of the consequences if they didn't. Any money earned went to pay for food and Fred's whiskey.

TWENTY-ONE

The year was 1941, eight years since Fred and Doty's family returned from California. The Depression was over, and the country was starting to rebuild itself. The rains were back, and farming was a viable occupation again.

Working in the field in the early morning, Fred steadied the plow behind the family's mule as it worked through the hard-packed soil, readying the land for planting. As the sun rose, its golden rays slowly spread up and out, chasing the morning shadows away. On the opposite side of the large field, Rosy and Willie used their spades to break up the dirt clods.

Rosy had found a spot a few feet away from Willie and chopped the hard chunks of soil as she worked along beside him. She smiled, relieved that she didn't have to work beside Father. "The ground is holding more moisture this year," Rosy acknowledged. "I wonder if we'll get a good crop this summer." She chopped another clod, then picked up a few rocks and tossed them in a pile beside her.

Willie stopped and leaned on his spade, inspecting the damp soil. "I heard the drought was over. Last year, we had more water than the year before. Hopefully, we'll even receive more water this year." Willie plunged the spade harder into the soil.

As Rosy worked, she glanced over at Willie. She could see that her younger brother was already growing into a good-looking young man. He was dark haired, slender, and at a mature 13 years old, he was already 5'8" tall. His muscular arms and broad shoulders gave witness to the fact that he was a hard worker.

While Willie worked, he glanced across the field at Father. The distant panorama view of Father plowing suddenly brought back to him a glimpse of his young childhood. "Rosy, I just had a flashback of another man. I don't know—" he rubbed a hand across his face, "—but it feels like he was my real father. It doesn't make sense. I guess I'm just trying hard to put the pieces of my past together." He stared at her with a mixture of longing and fear.

As the two worked together side-by-side, Willie picked up more rocks and tossed them into the pile. He stopped to rest and turned to Rosy. "Do you remember anything about my young childhood, about when I first came here? I don't remember much at all, just flashes. It seems like I just showed up here, but nothing before that. I know that my mother died, but no one ever said how she died. I remember Father picking me up along the side of the road and putting me in the car. That's how I came to live with you."

Rosy wasn't sure what to say, so she didn't say anything. She didn't dare speak what she did remember in fear of Father's retribution.

Receiving no response, Willie continued, "I don't remember my mother's face. Rosy, who am I? What about my real father? No one ever says anything about him." He looked toward the field, and a frown darkened his face. "The only father I remember is Fred."

"Willie, at that time I was a young child too. I'm only a year and a half older than you, and I don't remember much more than you do. All I knew was that your first name was

Johnny. I never knew your last name, and no one knows anything about your real father."

Willie thought out loud, "Why doesn't Fred like me? He's mean to me, and I don't know why. I wish I knew what to do."

Rosy could tell that deep down inside, Willie really wanted to be accepted, that he wanted Father's approval and would do anything he could to get it.

Fred watched the two chatting as they worked across the field. He did not like what he saw and spat into the dirt. "I'll put a stop ta that. They won't be gangin' up on me."

Guilt and anger warred inside him, and Fred knew only one way to beat back the ghost of conscience that haunted him. "Brother and sister, huh? I got somethin' for that." He began to laugh.

One afternoon, while studying in her bedroom, Rosy heard Father's footsteps shuffle up to her door and stop. She could tell he was drunk as he mumbled under his breath. Experience had taught her how to survive. She moved quickly into a corner to hide and huddled silently, hoping he wouldn't see her. It didn't work.

Father walked into her bedroom, staggered over, and stood in front of Rosy, staring directly down at her. He had half a bottle of whiskey in his hand. At fourteen years old, Rosy was wise beyond her years. She sat quietly, knowing that something bad was coming.

"Willie, get 'n here, now!" Father demanded at the top of his voice.

After a moment, Willie hesitantly entered the girls' bedroom and shut the door.

"Ya' sit down an' lis'n ta me," Father slurred, barely able to form the words.

Willie looked first at Rosy, then sat down on the worn mattress, not making a sound.

Father began his spiel. "Boy, you're old e'nuff that ya need ta know how ta satisfy ya' self with a female. Rosy's gonna teach ya how." Father grabbed Rosy and pulled her up out of the corner.

"No! Leave me alone! Get your hands off me!" she screamed. Fighting as hard as she could, Rosy kicked and scratched, struggling to get away.

"Ya do what I say!" Father yelled. He grabbed her dress and ripped it off her shoulders. She continued to scream as she slugged Father in the face. He threw her onto the mattress and held her down. "Willie, get over here!" His grip tightened.

"No!" she shrieked as the struggle to get away continued. "No...Stop...Leave me alone...!"

Doty heard the noise and knew what was happening. She ran to the closed door and stood outside of it, pressing her forehead against the worn wood. Hearing the voices, she shivered as her blood ran cold through her veins. *Father wouldn't do this...he wouldn't...*

Doty grabbed the doorknob but didn't turn it. She wanted to make Father and Willie stop. She looked instead at her stomach and the unborn child she now carried. With her hand covering her stomach and her forehead still against the door, Doty stood and cried silent tears. She finally turned and walked away.

"Mom! Help! Help me!" Rosy screamed. Her mind raced. "Mom! I need help!" *Where is Mom? Why doesn't she come?* After a long struggle, Rosy finally realized it was useless to fight. Having no choice, she lay exhausted and defeated on the mattress, resigning herself to what was going to happen. Rosy glared at Father; she loathed him. Hatred oozed out of every pore in her body. She wished he was dead!

Father stood over her, daring her not to move. She closed her eyes and turned her head away…

Getting off of her, Father smirked. "Okay, Willie, get over here. It's time for ya' to learn." Father slurred, "Rosy, show Willie how ta treat a girl!"

"No! Not Willie!" Rosy cried out. "He's my best friend and my brother!" She jumped up and ran towards the door, but Father was ready. He grabbed her and threw her back down on the mattress.

"Willie get over here," Father yelled as he stood over her.

Afraid of Father, Willie reluctantly did what he was told. Standing over Rosy, he stared at her for some time, neither one of them speaking or moving. He knew what Father wanted him to do. "But, Father…" He looked at Rosy and back at Father, questions and fear visible in his blue eyes.

Rosy looked at Willie and remembered the look on Father's face as he watched them work together in the field, and she knew why Father had done this.

As she lay silently on the mattress, staring fearfully into Willie's eyes, Rosy saw a gradual change come over him. His eyes slowly filled with darkness as a slow, leering grin came across his face. He caved…slowly, finally giving into Father's will.

"NOOO…" she screamed. "No! Not you, Willie!"

That day, Rosy lost her brother and best friend for the second time and gained another abuser.

Fred was satisfied. *Now things will be like they ought ta be. No more of this best friend stuff. The boy can never turn against me now.*

Fred nodded at Willie and clapped a hand of approval on his shoulder.

Doty stood silently as Father and Willie left the bedroom. Neither man paid her any attention, instead walking past her as if she didn't really matter. From inside the room, quiet crying reached Doty's ears, and she walked in carrying warm water and blankets, closing the door behind her.

TWENTY-TWO

1943

Over the next few years, rains came more often, and as the time passed, the weather returned to normal. Fred stood on the porch with his hands on his hips as he gazed out over the fields of wheat and barley. Doty walked out of the house and stood beside him.

"Look at that, Doty." Fred gestured with his hand at the expanse of his fields. "The fields are green and producin' more crops than we could even dream of. We'll have a good harvest this year. Maybe we can make some money." He smirked. "And I can make all the whiskey I want."

Doty frowned at the remark and tried to ignore it.

"The creeks are full, and we have plenty of water." She looked out over her vegetable garden. "So now my garden should produce lots of vegetables too, and I can do a lot of canning." Doty put her hand on her bulging stomach, grabbed an arm of her rickety old chair, and sat down carefully. "And…we can take all the showers we want. All we have to do is stand in the rain." She chuckled.

Fred grinned, then became more serious. "I think I'm gonna start raisin' more livestock. That would bring in more profit." One side of Fred's lips curved up slightly, forming a small, crooked smile. *My hard work is finally startin' ta pay off. Maybe my life will become a little easier.*

He crossed his arms. "I heard on the radio this morning that with the rains back and with the domestic programs from President Roosevelt's New Deal, jobs are openin' up.

The economy's recoverin', and life's gonna get back to normal." Fred looked at Doty's large vegetable garden and studied it. "An' like you said, even your vegetable garden's flourishin'."

He proudly gazed out over his acreage again and rubbed the back of his neck as he looked over at his wife's belly. The expression on his face changed from pride to concern. *But with another baby coming, we'll need money more than ever.*

Doty didn't get into town by herself very often, but when she did, she loved the freedom of being away from Father and the children. She loved shopping, looking around in the stores, and chatting with the townsfolk. She felt free to be herself, but these times were very few. Despite her fears of what people might say about her daughters and Father, she was determined to have a good time.

During one of these rare moments of freedom, Doty strolled down the sidewalk, window shopping. A woman stopped, placing a hand on Doty's forearm. Doty looked up in surprise and fear.

"Doty, is that you?"

After a moment, Doty recognized the woman. She was astonished to see her old schoolmate. "Trudy? I haven't seen you in years!" She smiled, hesitantly.

Trudy reached out and pulled Doty into a big hug.

Stepping back from the embrace, Doty asked, "Are you living in Emmett again? I thought you moved away for good."

Trudy smiled brightly. "We moved back. My husband couldn't find work anywhere else. Besides, we have a farm here, so at least we have a house to live in."

Doty didn't want Trudy to suspect that anything was wrong at home, so she smiled a big smile and was careful of what she said. "Trudy, that sounds like what happened to us. We moved back from California because Fred couldn't find work either. And now, even though the rain is back and the crops are growing, money is still short, so we're looking for jobs for our girls."

Doty rested her hands on her protruding stomach. "This is my tenth child and we need all the money we can get. My girls, Rosy, Annabel and Carolyn, are in high school. They're old enough to help out, but there just doesn't seem to be any work around."

Trudy put her finger to her lips as she stopped to think. "Doty, it seems I heard that there are jobs open at the Mary Secor Hospital." Looking up, Trudy frowned in concentration. "Yes. They're looking for girls to help with the laundry. The hospital doesn't pay much, but I think they provide room and board. The girls could work there and still finish high school."

Doty's ears perked up. She couldn't believe what she had just heard. Doty's thoughts started racing. *I really need to get the older girls out of the house. They could move out and have a place to stay, work, and finish school. Maybe this could be the way they can get away from Father. This could be the answer I've been looking for.*

"Thanks for the information, Trudy! I'm going to go check on it right now! I'll talk to you soon." Doty practically ran to the car, jumped in, and raced to the hospital. She was breathless when she dashed in the front doors of the building.

As Doty burst through the doors, the charge nurse who had been seated behind the large curved desk, jumped to her feet, seeing the obviously pregnant woman panting and cradling her distended stomach. "Oh dear," she exclaimed, thinking that Doty was in labor. "I've got you, honey." She grabbed a wheelchair and rushed over to where Doty had finally come to a stop, heaving for breath and looking wild. She stopped beside Doty and moved to help her into the wheelchair. "Hello, I'm Nurse Bella. Here, let's get you sitting down, and I'll wheel you into delivery!"

"Oh no," Doty chuckled around breaths. "I'm not here to have my baby…not yet. I'm not in labor. My name is Doty Pearse. I'm here to ask about a job."

The nurse's eyes traveled over Doty again, surprise coloring her face.

"Oh, the job's not for me." Doty chuckled again. "I'm looking for jobs for my three daughters. I hear that you are looking for girls to work in the laundry."

"Yes, we are." Nurse Bella began to smile as understanding dawned. "Are your girls still in school?"

"Yes, they're all in high school, but I heard that the job came with room and board…and I hoped they could work while they finish school." Doty looked imploringly at the woman.

"That's true, but it's not just a job. It's nurse's training. They go to school and finish high school, but they also take nursing classes and train to be practical nurses."

Suddenly, Doty could see freedom for her girls. But just as quickly, her excitement dimmed as another thought came to mind, and she spoke it out loud, "How much does all this cost? How much money do we have to come up with?"

Nurse Bella smiled. "It doesn't cost anything. The girls work here at the hospital and earn their own way through school, and they receive a small income to help support themselves. They'll receive a check every Friday. But they have to go through a government training program to do this. Nurses are badly needed in this country right now with the war and all, and this is a way for us to get trained help and for the girls to earn a nursing degree and have a good career."

Doty could not believe her ears. This is more than she had imagined possible. The girls would be safe and cared for while getting a high school and college education. "I have three girls that would love to do this. When could they start?" Doty's excitement bubbled over, and she could hardly contain herself.

"Well, we need help at the hospital now. Can you bring them into the hospital for interviews in the morning?"

"I'll have them here tomorrow morning, bright and early." Doty shivered with delight.

Bella chuckled, "Not too early! Say, nine o'clock?"

"Yes, yes! Nine would be good!" Doty eagerly grasped the nurse's hands and gripped them hard. "Thank you! Thank you so much."

Nurse Bella walked over to the front desk, picked up some papers, and handed them to Doty. "Fill these in and bring them back with you. If everything works out, maybe we can even get the girls started tomorrow. We're that desperate. We're in need of help as soon as possible."

As Doty walked out the front door of the hospital, tears of joy spilled down her cheeks. *I can't believe this; these are perfect jobs for my girls.*

Her thoughts raced as she drove home. *How am I going to tell Father? I'm sure he'll be angry.* Her body shivered with a mixture of relief and fear as reality set in. *Yes, he'll be mad, but I'm going to get the girls out of there no matter what Father does. It's about time I stood up to him. If not for myself, then for my girls.*

That afternoon while Father and the boys were out working in the fields, Doty called Rosy, Annabel, and Carolyn into their room. She closed the door to make sure no one else could hear. "Please, sit down." All three girls looked questioningly at each other and then at their mother as they sat down on the mattress.

"Girls," Doty spoke very quietly, "you've never deserved this kind of life. I'm sorry I haven't done my job and protected you, but I couldn't. We had to survive. And now…the way things are going, I'm afraid that you'll end up pregnant by Father or someone else." Doty paced back and forth.

The girls looked from one to another but said nothing. They grasped ahold of each other's hands and sat quietly.

"I need to get you out of this house, and I think I've found a way." Doty sat down on the mattress by her daughters. "I've been looking for quite a while, and this morning while I was in town, I found possible jobs for all three of you at the hospital. It's a new government training program to train nurses.

The three of you can live there and work to earn your keep while you finish high school. You will also be training for a career in practical nursing. If the interviews go well, you could start tomorrow. You'll stay at the hospital and work while you finish high school and take nursing classes. The education is free! The hospital will even pay you for working.

The girls just looked at each other for a few moments. Then, smiles slowly spread across their faces.

Rosy spoke up, thinking maybe she misunderstood. "You mean that the three of us would move out of this house? We'd be living and working at the hospital while we finish high school and take classes to learn to be practical nurses? School's free and they would pay us to work—and they want us to start when?"

Doty nodded. "Yes, yes, Rosy, and yes. And if you get the job, you can start tomorrow." Her excitement grew along with her daughters. "Pack tonight and tomorrow I'll take you over there for an interview in the morning."

Out of habit, Doty looked around the room, then lowered her voice. "And please don't say anything to Father. I haven't told him yet."

When Doty left the room, the three girls immediately jumped up and started packing. It didn't take long; they didn't have much to pack. As the realization started setting in, they grasped the fact that this was the last night they would spend in Father's house. Tomorrow they would be on their own, away from Father, and they would have the freedom to build a life of their own.

"We'll be out of here tomorrow," whispered Rosy, "but what about Mom and the other kids? They still have to live with Father's abuse."

The girls looked questioningly at each other; no one answered.

That night, the three girls quietly discussed the move and the job with each other in their room behind the closed door.

In a loud whisper, Carolyn said, "I can't believe that we are getting out of here."

"We won't have to worry about Father anymore." Annabel smiled.

Rosy released a slow, deep sigh. "We can finally get a good night's sleep." She grabbed her doll, Betsy, and hugged her. Her heart felt light, and relief flooded her soul. *Our lives are about to change for the better. I'm getting out of this place, and I won't have to worry about Father anymore. I'm going to be free!*

Rosy's thoughts raced as she closed her eyes in anticipation, trying to imagine her new life. The conversation between the girls went on for a while until they finally fell asleep, already dressed and ready to leave in the morning.

Rosy slept holding Betsy.

Early the next morning, while Father was sleeping off his drink from the night before, Doty quickly loaded the younger children into the car and dropped them off at the neighbors' house to spend the day. She needed to make sure they would be safe. The boys were already in the fields getting a leg up on the chores.

When the girls walked out of their room, Doty was arguing with Father. "They're moving out?" he yelled. "You're taking the girls without my permission?" Father's face was flushed, and his eyes flashed with anger. Still hungover, he steadied himself on the back of a chair.

Doty grew furious. "I've stood by too long and watched as you abused your own daughters and taught your boys to do the same! No more, Fred Pearse! No more! Now, I'm taking my daughters out of this house, and I'm getting them into that school."

Father raised his hand as if he would hit her. This time, Doty didn't back down. "Go ahead. Hit me again; it's what you're good at. Either way, me and the girls are leaving. My black eye will be one more thing I have to explain to the sheriff when I explain to him what you've been doing to your girls."

Father stepped back and lowered his hand.

Showing no fear, Doty stood directly in front of Fred, face to face. "Besides, getting the girls out of here, you'll have fewer mouths to feed. They'll be taking care of themselves."

Father looked at Doty, then at the girls who were standing back, holding their bags. The all too familiar rage began to crawl across his face, and he shook with anger. Doty had never stood up to him before. She had been afraid of him their whole married life, but not this time.

Studying his face, Doty was somewhat surprised that Father appeared to take a measure of pleasure in seeing her confront him when she knew what could happen. She waited for the backhand that would knock her to the floor. But she stood her ground and did not cower. Her eyes locked into his, daring him to hit her.

The girls watched in horror as Father glared at their mother. There was a long pause. Then, surprisingly, Father's attitude changed. His anger dissipated. The expression on his face slowly changed as a new twinkle in his eye replaced the angry expression. "Ya know what?" he realized out loud, "You're right. I won't have ta worry about supportin' them anymore. They'll have their own jobs."

He turned and smirked at the girls as a determined glare of authority flooded his face. "And…" he pointed to himself as he spoke gruffly, "any extra money you girls earn will be comin' back ta me. Ya hear me?" They didn't answer.

As the girls stood outside their room, the fear for their mother subsided. Father grinned at them. "I hope you girls like your new jobs. Take yer bags and go! Goodbye. Three kids gone—that means much less responsibility. I think I'll go celebrate!"

When he turned to walk out the door, a painful look came over his face. He stopped and rubbed his temples, shook his head, and ambled out the door.

"Quick," whispered Doty. "Let's get out of here before he changes his mind. Hurry!" The girls quickly grabbed their bags and headed to the car. They stopped midstride when they saw Father standing by the driver's side with the door open. Grinning a crooked grin, he retrieved his bottle from underneath the seat, turned around, and walked off.

Uncertainty and apprehension filled Doty and the girls as they quickly climbed into the vehicle and sped off, each glancing back to see if Father really meant what he said. He held up his whiskey bottle to them as they drove off, saluted them with it, and took a large swig.

Doty pulled out of the rutted driveway, onto the country road, and headed towards town. Together, the girls quietly watched Father and the shanty shrink in view and fade into the past. When they disappeared, the girls grinned at each other and suddenly started shouting together, "We're free, we're free!" Full of exhilaration, the girls threw their hands in the air and cheered. Tears of joy ran down their cheeks as their bodies quivered with excitement.

Rosy gazed up at the sky. *We're free from Father! Maybe there is a God!*

Driving towards town on the country road, Doty trembled. Her fear was subsiding, but her hands still shook as she tried to steer. The confrontation with Fred was over and she had stood her ground, but it had taken an emotional toll on her.

Doty pulled over to the side of the road and stopped. She sat, trying to regain her self-control. *I can't believe I did it. I stood up to Father and I'm still alive.*

The baby jumped in her womb and started kicking. She laid her hand on her stomach. "Oh, little one, everything is okay. We both just need to settle down." She stilled herself, taking deep breaths. She could feel her heartbeat start to slow.

The girls continued to chatter happily about their new life's possibilities. They didn't even notice the car had stopped. While Doty sat and listened to them, she could hear and feel their excitement. A bit of pride rose inside her. *I did it. I finally did it. I got the girls out of there. Now they'll be safe and cared for if—no—when they get the jobs.*

But Doty struggled. Her emotions still ran wild. Now she was losing her girls. *My heart can't let go. I'll miss them so much. But I don't have a choice.* Refusing to cry, she started the vehicle and continued on her way to the hospital, knowing that this was the best thing for her girls.

It was a new chapter in their lives…and hers.

TWENTY-THREE

The girls slowly got out of the car and fixed their eyes on the huge structure.

Rosy gazed at the large brick, two-story building in awe. "I've been by the hospital before, but I've never been inside."

"Just imagine, this might be our new home." Annabel looked over at her mother. "It's unbelievable!"

Curious, Carolyn wandered down the sidewalk, exploring the landscape around the side of the building. "Hey guys, come look at the courtyard." She yelled. "It's an enormous rose garden." The girls followed Carolyn around the side of the building.

"Wow! Look at all the rose bushes," Rosy exclaimed. "There's all different kinds and colors…and all the shade trees! I've never seen a garden this beautiful!"

The girls gazed at the stunning landscape. Annabel clasped her hands in front of her. "I hope we're allowed to spend time here." She turned and looked at her mother gratefully. "Mom, thank you! Thank you for all of this!"

"Let's don't get ahead of ourselves, girls." Doty stepped out. "We need to interview first. Let's go! They're waiting for us." She couldn't help but smile as she led the small parade down the sidewalk toward the entrance.

The group of women entered the front doors. There to greet them was the head nurse. "Hello, ladies! I'm Nurse Bella. I'm so glad to meet you." She extended her hand to shake hands with her new acquaintances. "Your mother has told me a little bit about you. I'm anxious to learn more."

The girls smiled. Politely, they shook hands with her as they introduced themselves.

"Hi, I'm Annabel."

"And I'm Carolyn"

"And I'm Rosy."

Grinning from ear-to-ear, all of their faces glowed.

"Welcome to Mary Secor Hospital," Nurse Bella addressed all three. "I understand you're all interested in nursing careers."

The girls chimed in with hearty agreements. After chatting for a bit, Nurse Bella announced, "I'd like to talk to each of you individually, to interview you and find out if this is a good fit for you." Nurse Bella called each of them, one by one, into her office.

After the interviews, she stepped out of her office and announced, "Well, girls, welcome to Mary Secor Hospital. I think each of you will be a great addition to our staff and make a great nursing student. You each have the job!"

A smile immediately spread across Doty's face from ear to ear and relief flooded her being. But at the same time, her eyes simmered with unshed tears as excitement, doubts, and uncertainties all fluttered through her mind. *I have to let them go for their own good. Hopefully, with a promising future ahead of them, they can put the past behind and move on with the assurance of a good life.*

The girls, trying to contain themselves, grinned huge grins and hugged each other and their mother as they shuddered with excitement. Rosy quivered as the new opportunity overcame her. "Thank you, Nurse Bella! Thank you for giving us this chance." She stepped up to

Bella and gave her a huge hug, a hug so tight she tipped Bella's nursing cap off to the side of her head.

Nurse Bella grabbed her cap, cleared her throat, and smiled warily. "You're welcome." She looked long into Rosy's face, and she could see her tenderness and compassion. "Rosy...I think you'll make a wonderful nurse."

Choked up, Bella cleared her throat again. "I have everything ready for you girls." She removed a bobby pin from her hair, adjusted her cap, and pinned it back into place. "Your classes and training will start tomorrow. I'll fill you in on the details as time goes on. Right now, you just need to settle in and get acquainted with your new home."

The girls exchanged glances with each other and their mother. With a subdued squeal, Rosy grasped Annabel's hand and squeezed it.

"Follow me. I'll show you your rooms." The five women headed down the hall. "We have only two rooms at present, so two of you will have to share a room," she explained as she led them through the hospital.

Carolyn grabbed Annabel's arm. "Annabel and I will share a room. We're best friends."

"Carolyn!" Doty glanced at her younger daughter.

"Mom, that's okay," Rosy stated. "In fact, it's great. I would love to have my own room and be by myself. I think I would really like that."

Nurse Bella cleared her throat. "Well, don't get too excited. We have two beds in each room, so we have room for one more girl. In fact, you might wind up sharing it with my daughter. She's applying to the program as well."

Rosy dipped her chin and cut her eyes at the head nurse. "Sorry Ma'am."

Nurse Bella looked kindly at the girls. "This way. Let me show you around the hospital on the way to your rooms." While walking down the hallway, a familiar aroma flooded the women's senses.

Carolyn took a big whiff. "Do you smell that? It smells like Mom's baked chicken!"

"The cafeteria is just down the hall." Nurse Bella pointed as she spoke. "We have the best cooks around, and that's where your meals are provided." She took a deep breath through her nose, smelling the aroma of the morning's breakfast as she glanced over at the young women and smiled. "Working here, you'll get three meals a day."

"My mouth is already watering." Annabel licked her lips. "That's where I'm heading as soon as I get unpacked; I haven't eaten yet today." Rosy and Carolyn smiled in agreement.

Doty peeked into the cafeteria as they walked by. Servers stood behind counters, dishing out large servings of food. The knowledge that her girls would be well fed helped settle some of Doty's concerns.

Continuing the walk, a strong and unfamiliar smell filled the air. "What is that strange smell?" asked Rosy.

"The hospital always smells that way," Bella replied. "That is the smell of rubbing alcohol, antiseptics, and cleaners." Bella gave the girls their first lesson as she explained the reasons for such cleanliness. Their new boss continued the tour through the building, showing them every department and ending the tour at their rooms.

While the girls settled themselves, Nurse Bella announced, "I'll give you today to get unpacked and familiar with the hospital. Just walk and look around, ask the nurses questions, and make yourselves at home. Tomorrow, we'll start your training bright and early at seven o'clock. Meet me in the laundry room." Bella said her goodbyes and left the girls to get situated.

Carolyn and Annabel entered their room, and Rosy and Doty stepped into Rosy's. As they each looked around, they all found that both rooms were luxurious and beautiful compared to their own home. Each room had two beds, two dressers, a closet, a bathroom, and a table with two chairs.

Rosy studied her new room in amazement, then ran her hands across the smooth walls. "Mom, look. There are no cracks or slivers!" She inspected the closet and flushed the toilet while Doty followed, examining her daughter's new home herself. As Rosy sat down on the bed, she found it was clean and comfortable. "Wow! This is the nicest place that I have ever stayed in…and it's more than I ever dreamed possible," Rosy whispered under her breath.

Doty gazed around the room, and a calmness settled inside her as she left to go see Annabel and Carolyn's room.

Rosy finished unpacking her things then sat on her bed, looking around again. She picked up Betsy and hugged her. *This is hard to believe; it's all happening so fast and seems too good to be true.* "Just imagine," she whispered to herself. "I'll be in school fulltime, be learning a good career, and starting a new life. I even have a room of my own for a while, until I get a roommate."

She reached out and gently ran her hand over the soft blanket on her bed. *And I don't have to worry about Father anymore.*

As she laid back and relaxed on her bed, her mind wouldn't stop. She reveled in her thoughts. *I've never even considered the possibilities of being a nurse, but now it seems to be my future, my wonderful future. I love taking care of others; this will be the perfect job for me.*

Gazing out the basement window and looking up to the sky, Rosy wondered, *Maybe God has heard my prayers.* "Thank you," she whispered again to a God she didn't know.

Elated, the girls came running out of their bedrooms chattering, about the accommodations, cafeteria, and their new life. Doty held back her tears as she watched each girl revel in excitement. She needed to tell them goodbye, but she didn't want to leave. She had to get out of there before she changed her mind. She finally spoke up. "Girls, I loved seeing your rooms and am excited for you about your new jobs. But I need to go now. I'm sure Father's patience is running thin and I need to check on your brothers and sisters."

The girls rushed forward and trapped their mother in a group hug, holding it extra-long. "Mom…" Rosy could hardly speak. "We're going to miss you so much."

Annabel's body jerked with a sob as she kept her arms around her mother's shoulders. "Thank you, Mom, for getting us this job and helping us move out and away from home. I'm sorry you have to go back; I know it's hard for you and the other kids."

Carolyn couldn't speak. She couldn't voice the words to tell her mother how much she loved her and would miss her. She stood quietly as her heart broke.

Tears started streaming down everyone's faces.

"Don't worry girls; you'll see me quite often." Doty tried to smile as she sniffled. "Every time I come to town; I'll stop by to see you." One-by-one, she gave each of her daughters a hug. Clearing her throat, Doty declared, "Girls, I know it's hard to leave the old life behind, but this is a new beginning for all of you. Just remember that you have each other to lean on, and I love you."

Doty gave them all one more hug and then with her head up and shoulders back, she turned and headed down the hallway, around the corner, and back to her old life. She couldn't let herself look back.

Doty's heart ached as she left her girls behind. Satisfied that they were safe and taken care of, her thoughts turned to home. She knew she had to go back; back to Father and the abuse, back to the knowledge that her younger children were still not safe, and back to wondering what the future would hold. She looked down at her belly, and her stomach churned.

That night, Rosy couldn't sleep. She lay awake, anticipating her new life and expecting to meet her new roommate. *My life is really changing. It was just yesterday I was worried about Father.*

Rosy was up early and out exploring the hospital while waiting for work to begin. She was startled when someone called her name. At the far end of the hall stood Nurse Bella with a younger woman.

Nurse Bella and the woman strode toward Rosy with quick, purposed steps. "Oh, Rosy, I have someone I would like you to meet," Bella called.

Rosy straightened her blouse as she waited for the Head Nurse to reach her.

Bella came to a stop and inclined her chin toward her companion. "This is my daughter, Martha. She is going to be your new roommate. You'll also be going to school together, working together, and taking nursing classes together. I'm sure you'll get to be good friends."

Rosy and Martha looked at each other and smiled. "I'm glad to meet you," the girls said in unison. The three women chuckled.

Bella stepped away from the girls. "Rosy, why don't you show Martha to your room. I need to get back to work."

"I'd love to." Rosy pitched her head and grinned. "Come on. Follow me. It's down in the basement." Rosy and Martha headed down the hallway, chatting.

It didn't take long for the girls to get acquainted. They talked about their lives and family, though Rosy remained silent about the darker side of hers.

As Martha unpacked, the girls chatted. "It'll be great sharing a room with just you, Martha," said Rosy. "All my life I've had to share with my brothers and sisters. I have four sisters, four brothers, and my mom is going to have another baby. There will be ten of us kids."

Martha looked surprised. "Ten!"

"What about you?" Rosy looked at Martha as they put their clothes away. "Do you have many siblings?"

"Yes, but I feel more like an only child. I have three brothers and one sister. Two of my brothers are in the Navy and one's in the Army. My sister is married and already has a child."

Martha changed the subject. "Where were you born?" She didn't give Rosy a chance to answer; she answered her own question. "I was born in Kansas and moved to Colorado. Because of the drought and dust storms in Kansas and in Colorado, we moved here to Idaho, but that was before the drought reached here. With no rain, my dad had to get a second job and work his fields. But now, since the rain is back, things are looking up. His crops are doing well, but he still works both jobs. He farms and works in the feed mill. What does your dad do for a living?"

Rosy took a breath for her new friend. She wasn't sure what to say. "Well…we have a homestead outside of town. Father farmed and worked at the lumbermill until it closed—"

Martha interrupted. "I wonder if my dad knows your dad. I'll have to ask him."

Rosy's heart skipped a couple of beats. Oh, please, don't be one of the men Father brought to the house. *If he's one of the men Father brought home, what will that mean for me and my job?*

"I don't think they know each other," Rosy replied quickly, hoping to discourage Martha from asking. "Don't worry about asking him."

Quickly changing the subject, Rosy returned to their previous conversation. "When Father lost his job at the lumbermill, we went to California…"

The girls continued their chatting, the question of their fathers meeting forgotten.

Seven o'clock the next morning, Bella addressed the girls, "Good morning, ladies, and thanks for being on time. This morning, you will start your on-the-job-training. For the rest of the summer until school starts, the days will consist of learning the different skills you'll need to know to help take care of the patients. Today, I will give you your first lesson. It's about how to do the hospital laundry. Over the summer, you will not only learn how to do the laundry: you will learn how to clean the rooms, feed patients, and other skills that are necessary to work in the hospital. First, we start with the laundry…"

As Rosy watched and listened, she thought of her mother at home, who toted water and scrubbed the clothes. *At least we have running water here at the hospital.*

In the following days, the girls listened to instruction and worked long hard hours, learning and practicing the basics of patient care.

At the end of the first week, Nurse Bella handed out the girls' first paychecks, which they eagerly received. Bella explained, "I know it may seem small, but your room and board comes out of your paycheck every week."

The girls exchanged excited looks as Rosy mouthed to her sisters, "We get all this?" They quickly slipped the checks into their pockets.

When Nurse Bella left, Annabel whispered to her sisters, "I'm hiding my money. Father's not getting any of it. He'd just spend it on whiskey."

"He's not getting any of mine either," Carolyn agreed.

As Rosy listened to her sisters, her heart went out to her mother. *I think I'll give Mom some of mine. She needs things that she has never been able to buy, but Father won't get any of my money either.*

TWENTY-FOUR

Several weeks later, Rosy sat visiting with her mother at the family's home. The hot summer breeze floated through the open window, leaving behind its stifling heat. Rosy sat across the table from her mother as her younger siblings played outside. As she spoke, she pulled a handkerchief from her pocket and wiped the sweat from her forehead. "Mom, I can't believe that summer's almost over and our high school and nursing classes are starting next week. It's been a busy summer of training and working at the hospital, but once classes start, it'll even get worse."

Doty smiled, glad to have the company and even happier to see her daughter.

Rosy glanced around the shanty, wondering where Father was. "During the school year, we'll have classes all day and work at the hospital during the evenings and weekends. I won't be able to see you as much, so that's why I came over today." After chatting for a while with her mother, Rosy glanced around the shanty again. "Where's Father?"

"He's out working in the fields with the boys." Doty motioned towards the open door. "The boys are getting old enough that they can do a man's work now. The extra hands really help."

Rosy stood and walked over to the window. She could see Father and the boys working in the fields. Relieved, she took a deep breath, turned, and headed back to the table and sat down with Doty again. Then quickly glancing out the door to make sure Father wasn't heading toward the house, Rosy reached into her pocket and pulled out three one-dollar bills. "Mom, I want you to have this. I know that you need a lot of things you can't afford." She folded the money into Doty's hand. "This is for you and the kids…not Father! He'd just spend it on whiskey. I'll try to get you a few dollars every month."

Doty was at a loss for words. Overwhelmed by the unexpected gift, she shook her head no. Putting her hand to her mouth, she choked back a grateful sob. "N-no, that's your money, you earned it." She cleared her throat. "Rosy, thank you. But I can't take your money; you need it." Doty tried to hand the money back to Rosy.

"Mom, this is for you." Rosy curled her mother's fingers tightly around the dollar bills and pressed her mother's hands into her lap, "I've saved it for you, and I want you to have it." She gave her mother a hug. "I love you, Mom."

As Rosy glanced out to check on Father, again, Martha drove into the driveway. "My ride's here, Mom. I have to go, but I'll see you soon." As she drove away, she waved to her mother, and threw her a kiss.

Doty sat stunned, staring at the folded dollar bills in her hand. She peeked out the door, looking to where Father worked in the distance, then at his whiskey bottle sitting on the table.

Nodding her head, she cautiously slipped the money into her apron pocket.

Rosy thrived; she had never been happier. She had a best friend, a safe place, a good job, free schooling, and a little money to help her mother. But she thought often of her mother and she knew what her family was going through with Father. Though happy with her new situation, Rosy still felt guilty that she wasn't there for her younger sisters.

But every time she thought about Father, the hatred and bitterness towards him returned. She couldn't put it out of her mind, and she wasn't sure she even wanted to. She would never let anyone use her again. Ever.

It was Sunday morning again, and again Nurse Bella had come by to pick up Martha. Martha would arrive back at the hospital in the evening. Curious, Rosy asked, "Martha, what do you do all day on the Sundays that you don't work?"

Martha smiled. "My mom and dad pick me up on their way to church, and after the service I go back to the house for Sunday dinner."

"Church, huh?" Rosy looked a little confused. "You know, I've never been to church. What's it like?"

Surprised, Martha repeated, "You've never been to church? I thought everyone had been to church. Well, church is where we go to worship God. We sing praises, but mainly we learn about God. Our pastor teaches us what the Bible says."

Rosy had a questioning look in her eyes. "The Bible's a book, right?"

Martha's mouth fell open. "A book? Yes…but it's more than that. The Bible is God's word that He gave us so we could learn about Him. It's about Jesus…You do know who Jesus is, don't you? Well, it's about Jesus and about the Holy Ghost."

Rosy began shaking her head. "Martha, I'm not sure there even is a God. I've really not heard much about Him at all."

Martha leaned forward and grasped Rosy's hands. "Have you at least heard about Jesus, God's Son?"

"No, not really. I've mainly heard the names Jesus and God used as swear words." Rosy hesitated and lowered her face. "Martha, would you be willing to tell me about this Jesus?" As Rosy waited for an answer, her thoughts momentarily slipped back to the presence she had felt when she sat on the rock in the desert.

Martha smiled. "The Bible teaches us many things about God." She picked up a small leather-bound book and handed it to Rosy. "This is my Bible. You can read it if you want."

Rosy held the book in trembling hands. *Could this book be about the same presence I felt on the rock?*

"And if you would like to go to church with me and hear what God has to say through the preacher, you're more than welcome." Martha waited patiently for an answer.

Rosy pondered for a bit, then responded, "I've always wondered if there really was a God, I've heard very little about Him and would like to know more."

"Well, why don't you come to church with me, and you can learn about Him and make up your own mind," Martha replied softly. "God speaks to each of us in His own way. You can make your own decision about Him."

Rosy looked at Martha, hesitated, and with a determined look on her face, announced, "I'd love to go. Maybe I can get some answers to my questions. If there really is a God, I want to know about Him."

Sunday came. Rosy asked nervously, "Martha, what should I wear to church? I don't have any nice clothes."

"Whatever you have will be fine. But if you want, you can wear one of my dresses." Martha walked to the closet and took out two dresses. "You can choose. I'm sure they'll fit you."

"Thank you, Martha. Mine are so old and worn. I'd feel so much better wearing something nice. Can I borrow the yellow one? Yellow is my favorite color."

"Sure." Martha smiled and handed it to Rosy. "Yellow looks great on you."

Rosy slowly ran her hand over the soft cotton fabric and traced the delicately stitched white lace with her finger. *Someday, I'll have a dress like this—a new one with lots of lace.*

Waiting for Martha's parents to pick them up, Rosy paced back and forth. "Rosy, relax. It's gonna be fine. You'll have fun," Martha said calmly, trying to help relieve her friend's nervousness. "Everyone's so nice, and you'll learn new songs, meet lots of nice people, and maybe get some of your questions answered." Martha waited, but Rosy didn't offer anything as to what those questions might be.

Rosy was skeptical at first, but she thought about it as she paced. *Well, I love to sing and would like to learn some new songs. I like people and want to know more about God. Maybe I'll enjoy it.* The more she thought about going, the more convinced she was that she should go.

Rosy walked into the church with Martha and her parents. It was a small church with about 35 to 40 people in attendance. The people were wandering around, chatting with each other. When they noticed Rosy, many of them came up to her and introduced themselves. She immediately felt welcome.

The pianist started playing, which signaled the start of the service. The congregation quickly took their seats in the pews. Rosy had never seen a pew before. After examining the new seat, she sat down on it and wiggled, making herself comfortable as she sat next to Martha and her parents. She anxiously glanced around at the sanctuary and watched the people in the congregation. *This isn't so scary; everybody is so friendly. I can do this.*

The music continued for a few more minutes and then stopped. A hush fell over the congregation as the song leader stood up in front and announced, "Please turn to page 168 in the hymnal."

Martha picked up a song book, opened to the page, and shared the book with Rosy. The music started again, and the leader led the singing; everyone joined in. Rosy sang along the best she could, not knowing the songs. The songs spoke of love and forgiveness. They were about the God she didn't know.

After the singing was over, the congregation sat down as the preacher came to the podium. "Good morning, and welcome to God's house. I'm Pastor John. We're all glad to see a few new faces here today. "

Rosy's face flushed with embarrassment, even though the pastor wasn't looking at her. She didn't want any attention drawn to herself, so she lowered her head.

Pastor John opened his Bible and laid it down on the podium. "Today we'll be talking about God's creation and how we fit into His plans."

This was the part Rosy had been waiting for. She listened intently as he began.

The pastor grinned. "But first I'd like to announce that my family and I have a new addition." The congregation went silent. Pastor chuckled. "Yesterday afternoon, my cow, Gertrude, gave birth to a beautiful little heifer."

"Congratulations!" yelled one of the parishioners. A few people chuckled.

"Thank you," came his reply. "My six-year-old son and I helped with the birthing process. As the calf was born, my son became very curious. He asked me, 'Dad, what's that rope for?' I explained, 'That's not a rope, it's the umbilical cord. That's how the baby calf was fed while she was inside her mother's tummy. It's attached at the calf's bellybutton and food goes through it from the mother to the calf.' I could see in my son's eyes that he was processing all of this.

"At dinner last night, my son sat quietly contemplating while he ate. After a while, he looked questioningly at his mother and asked, 'Mom, when I was in your belly, did my bellybutton have taste buds?'"

The congregation laughed as the pastor's son hid his face against his mother. Even Rosy chuckled at the boy's question.

After the congregation settled down, the pastor continued. "I lay in bed last night thinking about that new life, how that calf was one of God's creations. God is the only one that can create life. We can nurture it, alter it, even end it, but only God can create it. Today, we're going to talk about God and His timeless plan for us, His creation.

"Our God is the one and only sovereign God. He is all-knowing, all-powerful, eternal, and absolutely free—free to do whatever He wills to do, anywhere, at any time, to carry out His eternal purpose...and WE are His timeless plan of creation.

"Before time existed, before creation, God was there. He created us out of His vast store of love and designed us to have relationships with Him. He wanted us to experience His love and, in return, to love and follow Him willingly. He wanted a relationship with those who would be willing to walk with Him, to fellowship with Him.

"But before He created us, God had a plan in place. He knew we would need a home, so He planned and created the heavens and the earth. Since God is all-knowing, He also knew we would sin, so He planned a way of salvation through his Son, Jesus." Here, the preacher paused. "Our God, the God of the universe, our creator, designed our existence. Everyone, please turn with me in your Bibles to the scripture for today, Genesis 1:1."

Martha opened her Bible and shared with Rosy.

Pastor John read the first verse, "'*In the beginning, God created the heavens and the earth.*'

"As we read on in Genesis, the Bible tells of creation, of how God created the earth and life on it."

After reading and discussing the next few verses, Pastor John came to the part of the creation of man.

"Then God created man. Genesis 1:26 says, '*And God said, 'Let us make man in Our image, after Our likeness...*' and verse 27 states, '*So God created man in His own image, in the image of God created He him; male and female created He them.*'

"God created man and woman in his own image; we are a likeness of God, made to resemble Him! We are different from among all of God's other creatures because we have a body, soul, and spirit. Your body is the material part of you. Your soul is your mind, will, and emotions. And your spirit is the true essence of who you are, the part that longs for a connection with God. You can reason, you can make choices, and you are created for His fellowship."

Rosy was amazed. *God created me in His image…What exactly does that mean?*

These were new thoughts to Rosy. It made her feel good to know that God created her. *He created me; plus, He wants to be my friend.* She shifted in her seat uncomfortably trying to figure out what to do with this unexpected information. *Then why did He let Father hurt us so?*

The pastor continued, "God created us according to His own plan. Although through sin we have ruined our perfect relationship with Him, God still loves us and wants us as His very own. In Psalms 139:13-16, Scripture tells of our creation." He read it very slowly so the congregation could digest it. "Verse 13 says, *'For Thou hast possessed my reins: Thou hast covered me in my mother's womb. 14. I will praise Thee; for I am fearfully and wonderfully made: marvelous are thy works; and that my soul knoweth right well. 15. My substance was not hid from Thee, when I was made in secret…'* "

The pastor paused to let the words echo in the people's minds. Turning the page, he continued with verse 16. "*'Thine eyes did see my substance, yet being unperfect; and in Thy book all my members were written, which in continuance were fashioned, when as yet there was none of them.'* The second part of this verse may be hard to understand, but it is saying that my days that God designed for me were written in His book before any of them came to be.

"In essence, these verses are saying that God chose to create you. He knew you before you were ever created. He planned you and oversaw your creation. In fact, every single atom was created by Him as He carefully knitted them together to make your body and its parts just the way He wanted them. He watched as you grew in your mother's womb. You are no mistake; you are here because God created you and placed you here, on this earth, in this place, at this time.

"Psalms explains that before you were ever created, while you were forming in your mother's womb, God had your days written down. He knows how many days He gave each of us on earth. He has designed them...and He has given us a choice on how to live them."

The pastor stepped out in front of the podium with his Bible in hand. He cleared his throat and continued, "And even today, He oversees our lives. He walks with us each day as we go through this life. His Spirit is constantly with us, teaching and guiding us...if we choose to listen.

"He could have created us to obey His every command, but God wanted us to choose to follow Him, so He gave each of us free will. We are free to make our own choices. He wanted us to love Him and fellowship with Him willingly. We now have that choice.

"But God knew the future. Yes, He knew we would make poor choices, that we would sin. When we do things that we know are wrong, things against His will, it makes God sad. It separates us from Him. God cannot look upon sin, and it severs the relationship between Him and man. But God loved us so much that He planned and made a way of salvation through Jesus Christ."

Pastor John flipped through the pages in the Bible to his next Scripture. "Romans 6:23 states, '*For the wages of sin is death; but the gift of God is eternal life through Christ Jesus our Lord.*' Since the wages of sin is death, as sinners we deserve to die. But God loved us so much that He sent His only Son, Jesus Christ, to die in our place for our sins.

"In John 3:16, Jesus says, *'For God so loved the world that He gave His only begotten Son, that whosoever believeth in Him should not parish, but have everlasting life.'* Christ's death covers our sins and unites us with God. Now, instead of receiving death for our sins, God has given us life through Jesus Christ—eternal life—beginning the moment we believe in and accept Him. Pastor John quietly and slowly stepped behind the podium and laid his Bible on it, giving the congregation time to process what he had just told them. He flipped through the pages to chapter 14 in John.

"And…on top of everything else, He is now preparing a place for us, and some day He plans to come and take us to live with Him. John 14:2-3 says, *'In my Father's house are many mansions: if it were not so, I would have told you. I go to prepare a place for you. And if I go and prepare a place for you, I will come again, and receive you unto myself; that where I am, there ye may be also.'*

"But remember, God has also given us that freedom to choose, and we need to make a choice. We can choose to accept God and His gift of eternal life with victory over sin and death, or we can choose to reject Him. If we don't accept Him, we reject Him."

Closing her eyes, Rosy concentrated and listened closely, wanting to remember everything she heard.

The pastor continued, "God is a God of love. He loves us and wants to be in our lives. If you want Christ in your life, peace in your heart, and joy beyond your comprehension, accept His gift of love. All you have to do is admit you have sinned and ask forgiveness, believe in your heart that Jesus died for your sins and rose again, and confess with your mouth Jesus as Lord of your life. He is a gentleman and waits patiently for His invitation. His fellowship and gift of eternal life awaits your decision."

The pastor quietly closed his Bible, walked to his chair, and sat down, giving the congregation time to internalize God's Word.

Rosy wasn't sure what to think. *According to what the pastor said, God planned for me. He planned a home for me, designed me, and loves me. Rosy ran over the points of the sermon in her mind. Wow, this is overwhelming.*

She folded her hands in her lap. *And if I accept Him as truth, He gives me the gift of eternal life with Him, prepares a room for me, and plans on coming back to get me.* She scooted back in her seat and glanced around at the congregation as she contemplated what she had heard.

I have never heard of such things: sin, forgiveness, eternal life, choice. Is this really true, or are these people just plain crazy? Rosy sat in silence, reflecting.

Somewhere, deep down inside, Rosy hoped it was true. She wondered again if God had been with her when she had been left by Father, maybe that unknown presence on the rock really had been God.

Even though this seemed to make a sort of sense, it was still too much for Rosy to process all at once. *I need more time—time to think about what all this means. I need to learn more.*

After church was over, the girls decided to walk the short distance to Martha's family's house for Sunday dinner. Martha lifted her face to the warmth of the sun. "Well, Rosy, what did you think? Did that answer your questions?"

Rosy just shook her head. "It answered some questions but it also created lots more. I need to learn more about God to understand. Maybe I'll keep coming to church with you, if you don't mind. I want to learn more about this God of love."

Martha was thrilled. "That would be wonderful!"

As the months passed, Rosy continued to attend church. She listened to how she was God's creation, and how much God loved her. She listened intently to the sermons and began taking notes. During the week, she looked up the scriptures in Martha's bible, and pondered what it all meant. Deep in her heart, she was beginning to believe that it must be true, that there really was a God, that Jesus died for her and her sins. She wanted to believe. But the more she thought about it, the more confused she became.

But if this is all true, where was God when I needed Him?

This was the one thing that really bothered her, the one thing she couldn't shake as she looked back over her life. *If God is supposed to be such a great, loving, and powerful God, why did He allow Father to do the things he did? Why did He allow Father to rape me? Why did He let Father kill Willie? Why did He let all those men use me and my sisters...?*

The questions came to her almost as fast as she could think. Overwhelmed by anger and a deep sadness, Rosy closed the Bible and collapsed on her bed, dissolving into tears.

God, where were You?

Entangled by bitterness and hatred, unforgiveness reared its head. Rosy couldn't forgive her father—or God. Doubts drove its roots deeper, crushing at her soul.

God, You could have stopped it all if You wanted to. You could have given me a good father. How could You love me and still allow all this to happen?

As Rosy continued to attend church with Martha, she couldn't shake her doubts, but she kept searching for answers.

TWENTY-FIVE

Rosy discovered that she loved spending time with her mother as long as Father was not included. Now that she and her sisters lived in town, their mother made an effort to see them as often as possible. Over the months, Rosy, along with her sisters, spent many precious hours together with their mother. This togetherness gave them a chance to develop the mother-daughter relationship they never had.

One day, when Doty left the hospital after visiting the girls, Rosy pulled her sisters aside. "Did you see how fragile Mother has become?"

Her sisters looked at her with blank expressions. "That woman that raised us," Rosy continued, "used to look so strong…putting up with Father's abuse, taking care of all us kids virtually by herself, and now she looks almost broken. I never really thought about what everything was doing to Mother."

Rosy contemplated their new situation and how much their mother had done for them. Looking at things from her new perspective, Rosy came to understand that not only had her mother struggled physically and mentally, she struggled emotionally most of all. Rosy was also coming to understand that she would need to forgive her mother as well.

As Rosy looked at her sisters, she squeezed their hands. "I know mom did her best, but I still have feelings of anger because she never stopped Father from abusing us."

Annabel tried to pull away, but Rosy redoubled her grip. "Please don't shut me out. Just listen to me," Rosy pled with her sisters.

Carolyn added, "But you just said mother was so weak, and—"

"I know, I know," Rosy said, cutting her off, "I'm just saying I have those feelings. Sometimes I feel such hatred and bitterness towards Father, and I get mad at mother for not stepping in and protecting us. She's our mother; it was what she was supposed to do."

When her sisters did not respond, Rosy thought again about her mother's brokenness. "Maybe Mom did all she could. Maybe she was as much of a victim of Father as we were."

Annabel and Carolyn still said nothing, but simply looked at their younger sister. In that moment, Rosy knew that if anything was going to change, it would have to begin with her.

———————— ≈ ————————

On an evening in mid-October, as Rosy sat studying in her room at the hospital, there was a quiet knock on her door. Careful to mark her page, Rosy put her books away as she nibbled on the end of her pencil, a bad habit she'd picked up while being schooled at home by her mother. Repeating equations to herself, she made her way to the door and opened it.

Surprised to find her mother standing silently in the hall, Rosy smiled. "Mom! This is a surprise. Come on in. I was just studying." Rosy held the door open for her mother as Doty took leaden steps making her way across the threshold. Rosy reached out and greeted her with a big hug, but she stiffened when the hug wasn't returned.

Doty was trembling.

"What's wrong, Mom?" Rosy asked in alarm, closing the door.

Her mother, pale and solemn, braced herself on the back of a chair for balance, and with slow deliberate steps, made her way over to the bed. She more fell than sat down as a gust of breath escaped her pursed lips. She could hardly speak. "Y your father is in the hospital…He was j-just admitted into Emergency here."

Rosy knelt in front of her mother and grasped her trembling hands. "Mom, what happened?"

It was hard for Doty to speak. "Father…F-Father was complaining of a bad headache all morning. She paused and swallowed hard. This evening as h-he was heading to the barn to do the chores, he fell on the ground and h-had a seizure. Then he went unconscious. I t-tried to wake him up, but he wouldn't wake up; he didn't even move."

Doty paused to pull her chaotic thoughts together. "There was no smell of alcohol on his breath, so I knew he hadn't been drinking. I told the doctor he had been complaining about bad headaches lately." Her jumbled thoughts spilled slowly from her lips. "The kids helped me get him into the car to bring him here. He's still unconscious."

Anxious, Doty could feel her heart pounding wildly in her chest, and she could hear the blood coursing through her ears. "The doctors don't know what's wrong. They've taken some tests but have to wait for the results, and right now they're taking more. He's still unconscious in emergency." She fidgeted with a button on the front of her dress as her eyes focused on the floor. "One doctor told me that it doesn't look good."

Rosy sat down on the bed beside her mother and wrapped an arm around her, pulling her close.

Doty sat in shock, staring into emptiness. After a long pause, she whispered quietly, "In his condition, they're not sure how long he'll survive."

Silence blanketed the room. The two women sat quietly, trying to digest the news.

"Rosy…" Doty asked after a moment, "would you go get Annabel and Carolyn? I need to let them know what's happening, and I'll let the other kids know as soon as I get home."

Rosy walked quickly down the hall to her sisters' room and knocked on the door. Jumbled thoughts competed in her mind as she tried to reconcile how she would tell them. In the end, she decided to let her mother do the telling. She led Annabel and Carolyn back to her room.

Rosy stopped at the door, leaned against the door jamb, and let her sisters go in first. As the two girls sat near their mother, Doty was finding it hard to speak. With vacant eyes, she gazed down at her own clasped hands as they laid in her lap. She continued to stumble over her words, trying to explain to Annabel and Carolyn about their father.

Rosy closed her eyes and listened while her mom told her sisters about Father. She finally stepped into the room, closed the door behind her, and quietly sat down. Her sisters sat stone-faced and stared at their mother. From her position, Rosy tried to wrap her mind around how she felt. She looked at her sisters, whose faces matched her own, and finally back at her mother.

Silence encompassed the room.

Suddenly, Doty blurted out, "I don't know whether to be relieved or scared if Father dies. He won't be here to hurt us anymore, but he won't be here to support and feed us either. I'm afraid…what am I going to do?" Tears rolled down Doty's face. Rosy wrapped her arms around her mother. The four women sat in silence, none of them sure about how they felt.

After the initial shock wore off, the women were emotionally confused and exhausted. It was late and the girls could see that their mother was worn out.

"Mom, you need some rest," Carolyn said compassionately. "Why don't you go home and get a good night sleep…if you can."

Annabel gently took Doty's hands. "I agree, Mom. Besides, you still need to tell the kids about Father, and they'll need you at home."

Rosy gave her mother a tender smile. "We'll keep in contact with the doctors and nurses. If there's any change, we'll let you know."

Doty blinked vacant eyes and then focused on Rosy's face. "Yes, you girls are probably right. I suppose that's best."

The three girls walked their mother out to the car. Doty sat down in the driver's seat. "I don't feel like I should leave, but you're right. I need to be with the children right now to help them through this."

Rosy and her sisters hugged their mother good-bye and watched as she drove off. Rosy couldn't help but wonder what this would mean for their future.

As the girls headed down the stairs to their rooms for the night, Rosy stopped and looked back toward the nurse's station. "Hey, you guys go ahead. I'm going to go check on Father first."

Both Carolyn and Annabel stopped to look at her but said nothing. Instead they continued silently down the stairs. When they were gone Rosy headed to the front desk, hoping that Nurse Bella would still be there.

As Rosy approached the desk, she was relieved to see her boss sitting behind the counter, flipping through patient charts. Rosy leaned against the counter and waited for Bella to look up.

Nurse Bella glanced up, and, seeing Rosy, she quickly laid down the files. "Oh, Rosy...I heard about your father, I'm so sorry. There's not a lot I can tell you right now. The doctors are still working with him."

Rosy realized she was crying, and wiped her own tears away with her hand.

Nurse Bella rose quickly and, coming around the desk, gathered the young lady in her arms. Relenting, Rosy rested her head on Bella's shoulder and cried.

Slowly raising her head, Rosy wiped her tears again with the back of her hand and stepped back, looking questioningly into her boss's eyes. "Nurse Bella, what can you tell me about Father? I need to know."

"Come with me to my office, Rosy, and we'll talk."

Rosy followed the nurse down the hallway. She needed a better understanding of Father's condition to help her deal with her own conflicting emotions.

The office door clicked as it closed behind them. Bella sat down behind her desk in her small and sparsely furnished office as she motioned to Rosy. "Please, have a seat."

Rosy sat down in the chair across the desk from Bella, waiting apprehensively to hear the details of her father's condition.

Bella sat quietly for a few seconds, looked at Rosy, and took a deep breath. "Rosy, the doctor has already talked to your mother, but you need to know also. We don't know the cause of your father's condition. It could be caused by a number of things. It could be caused by his drinking, or a stroke, or something else. We just don't know. So far, all the tests the doctors have run have come back negative. The doctor said he did regain consciousness for a little bit. He opened his eyes and blinked a number of times. The doctor did some quick tests, but your father closed his eyes and became unresponsive again." Bella paused. "His prognosis is not good. We don't know how much time he has left."

For a moment, Rosy sat, silently processing the information. "Thank you, Nurse Bella. I appreciate your time." Rosy stood and walked out of the office, still troubled about her father's illness.

———

Doty sat at Fred's bedside while he slept. She had been there for hours, trying to grasp the meaning of everything that was happening.

Fred is dying.

Doty leaned forward, put her elbows on her knees, and rested her forehead in her hands. She sat motionless with her eyes closed, her confused thoughts going wild. *What am I going to do without him? How can I feed the children?*

Anger swelled in her chest as she looked at her sleeping husband; anger and fear for him leaving her in this situation. She hated him.

The sound of someone clearing their throat made her look up. Rosy stepped around the curtain. "Mom?" she said in a quiet voice.

Jolted from her thoughts but relieved, Doty stood up and opened her arms for Rosy. At that moment, they both needed someone to lean on.

Rosy gently pulled back from the embrace and studied her mother's face. Seeing the desperation in her mother's eyes, she wondered if it was mirrored in her own face. "Mom, can we talk? I just came back from talking to Nurse Bella."

Doty nodded wordlessly.

The two women walked to the cafeteria for a cup of coffee. They sat at a table in a corner away from everyone else. Rosy took her mother's hand in hers and looked into her eyes. "Mom, I love you, and I'm here for you, whenever you need me."

"Thank you, Rosy." Doty looked at her daughter and gave her a small, crooked smile.

"I spoke with Nurse Bella last night and again this morning," Rosy reported to her mother. "They still don't have any answers." The two women sat quietly for a long moment. "Mom, now—now—we need to help each other get through this. The doctors say Father doesn't have long. If you want, I'll stay here with you." As the words came from Rosy's mouth, she shuddered. The last place she wanted to be was at Father's side, but she couldn't tell her mother that.

After a few more minutes of discussion, they sat in silence, sipping their coffee. Once they had both finished their drinks, Rosy walked Doty back to Father's room and gave her mother a hug before she left. "I need to get to work, Mom, but I'll be around the hospital if you need me. Just let the person at the desk know if you need anything or want to get ahold of me."

"Thanks, Rosy." Doty walked over and sat down by Fred, and sat silently watching him.

As Rosy walked out, the floor nurse walked into the room to check on Fred. Standing just outside the doorway, Rosy turned and glared at her father as he lay motionless in bed. She wrestled with her feelings. As a patient, her father needed the necessary care. The task had fallen to her. But she was not sure she could give it to him. She felt no pity for the man. She knew she would have to bury her anger and resentment and do whatever needed to be done. But she wouldn't like it.

Memories swirled in her mind—memories of his drunken stupors, his night wanderings, the abuse he inflicted on her and her family. Father's actions were burned into her heart and mind. *Why should I take care of him? He used us and let strangers use us for money. He killed my brother and taught the new Willie to use me too. Just the thought of him makes me feel dirty. I feel sick looking at him.* The muscles in her jaw tightened as she continued to glare at him through the room's open door.

Remembering she had a job to do, Rosy took a deep breath, released it, and turned to walk away.

As Nurse Bella was walking down the hall, she stopped when she saw Rosy standing outside her father's room. She watched as Rosy glared through the door at her father. It was Rosy's job to attend him, but Bella could see the play of emotions war on Rosy's face. Bella walked over to where the young woman stood, causing her to jump with a start. "Rosy, I'm going to have Martha take over the care of your father. That way, it'll be easier for you and your family."

Her lips taught, Rosy looked at Bella gratefully. "Thanks, I appreciate that. It's really hard for me to be around him right now." She turned her back to her father's room and rushed down the hallway as quickly as she could, unable to deal with her emotions as she grappled with her own demons.

Two weeks after Fred was admitted to the hospital, Doty was called to his bedside. She sat by his bed, staring at his emotionless face as Nurse Bella monitored his vitals. They watched as his breathing gradually slowed and became shallow. The two women kept Fred company and talked quietly to him as he lay unconscious.

Doty became antsy and stood, pacing back and forth at the bedside. She watched as Fred lay motionless. He looked as if he was merely sleeping. Anger rose inside of her. All her married life, this man had used and abused her and her children and now he was leaving her with nothing. Lying in his bed, Fred looked small and helpless; all his threats and bluster were gone. There was nothing left of the man she'd feared. She hated him. She wanted him dead.

One by one, the three girls joined their mother and stood quietly at their father's bedside. As each girl stared at Fred, Doty could see a reflection of her own emotions in their faces.

Carolyn glared at Fred, anger and hatred visible in her eyes. She sat with her arms crossed and her chin up.

Now that she saw him like this, Annabel looked at her father with a mixture of anger and apathy.

Rosy sat by her mother trying to comfort her. She didn't even want to look at her father. She put her arm around her mother's shoulders and held her tight. The man they'd called Father had never truly been a father to them. In all three girls, fear of what would happen next played on their emotions.

After a while, Fred's breathing became even slower and shallower. "His time is getting close," Nurse Bella said in a thin voice.

Confusion, anticipation, hatred, fear, anger, unforgiveness, and many other emotions filled the silence of the room.

Finally, Fred's chest rose as he took a large gasp of air, then released it. Doty forgot to breathe as she squeezed Rosy's hand tightly. She watched Fred's chest rise and fall with his last breath. Clinging to Rosy's hand, Doty whispered, "Don't let go."

Together the ladies watched as Fred breathed his last. As he laid there, the only regret Doty felt was that she never took the chance to tell Fred how she truly felt. Watching Nurse Bella pull the sheet up and cover Fred's face, Doty released a deep sigh of relief. *He's gone…*

I'm glad he's dead. We'll be better off without him. Suddenly, Doty was filled with guilt. She let go of Rosy's hand and covered her face with both of her own. *He's my husband and I shouldn't be thinking like this, but I can't help it. At least the kids and I are safe now.*

The hatred and bitterness she felt was real. She couldn't and wouldn't cry for him.

Doty and her girls stared at the sheeted body lying on the hospital bed and the realization slowly set in that Fred—Father—was actually gone.

Doty shuddered. "Now I'm alone."

She ran her hands up and down her upper arms as she struggled with unanswerable questions. *I've never had a job; I've always depended on Fred. Now I'm responsible for the family. How will I even feed my kids?*

A few days later, the doctor called Doty into his office with a report of the cause of death. After hearing the report, Doty asked Rosy, Annabel, and Carolyn to meet her in the hospital cafeteria to talk about the results. Since Nurse Bella read the report too, Doty asked her to come so she could answer any questions they might have.

After they were all seated at an isolated table in a corner of the large room, Nurse Bella ordered coffee for all of them. Bella and the girls sipped their coffee as they waited silently for Doty to begin.

Doty contemplated, trying to find the words she needed to say. "Girls…" she paused. "The doctor received your father's autopsy report today. I met with him and he gave me the results of their findings." Doty sat still for a moment, finding it hard to speak. Finally, she pulled the report from the envelope and placed it on the table. "The doctor told me that Fred died from a large brain tumor."

After a moment of silence, Rosy looked at her mother. "Mom…did the doctor know how long he'd had it?"

Doty shook her head. "He didn't know, but he thought it might have been developing for many years."

Rosy grasped her coffee cup with both hands, absorbing its warmth. She took a breath and turned to Bella. "Nurse Bella, could the tumor have made him abusive and mean?" Rosy swallowed and lowered her eyes.

"We don't know for sure"—Nurse Bella scooted her chair up closer to the table—"but it's possible." She leaned forward, placed her elbows on the table and grasped Rosy's hands gently, careful not to spill the coffee. "Rosy…your mother told the doctor and me about Fred's abusive behavior. The tumor very well may have caused those actions, but there could have been many other reasons that made him act the way he did. The doctors don't know."

Nurse Bella released Rosy's hands and rested her own hands on the cafeteria table as she interlaced her fingers. She studied the girls' forlorn expressions. "We know so little about tumors. Research is just beginning, and it will take years of study before we can even begin to know the effect that things like cancer and tumors have on the brain. Depending on the kind and size of the tumor and where it's located, it could affect how the body functions or how the brain works."

Seeing the uncertainty in Doty and her daughters' faces, she tried to answer their unasked questions. "Fred's tumor was large and there was nothing we could do to help him, except keep him comfortable. I'm so sorry." Bella reached over and gently squeezed Doty's hand, then sat silently, giving everyone time to absorb the information.

Even knowing that the tumor may have been the cause of Fred's cruelty, Rosy could not bring herself to accept his behavior or forgive him for the things he had done. Those memories fueled her hatred for him. She despised him for abusing her, her family, and so many others.

I'm glad he's dead.

On a small shelf of land on the side of the grassy hill, an old picket fence surrounded the quiet resting place of souls that had gone before. Rows of stoical tombstones stood tall in the old country graveyard overlooking the valley. As the towering stones gazed out over the freshly plowed fields of the valley floor, they stood guarding their trust, the graves given them to protect. In the distance, clouds seemed to hover over the foothills, watching and waiting.

It was midmorning on a late October day. The cool autumn breeze helped buffer the warm sunshine. The fragrance of sweet grass and dogwood trees from the surrounding hillsides flooded the small graveyard.

Doty, Rosy and her siblings sat in the country cemetery, chairs in a row, facing the wooden casket that sat beside the open grave. A few neighbors stood behind the family, their presence showing sympathy to Doty's family for their loss. The parson stood by the grave, ready to begin the service.

Doty sat silently at the end of the row. Her face was expressionless, her emotions numb. She stared at a cluster of three hand-carved gravestones that marked the resting places on the ground next to Fred's open grave. She looked longingly at the names of her long-lost children on the three grave markers, and her arms ached to hold them close to her breast again. It didn't seem fair that Fred was the one that got to rest beside them in his grave.

The hatred and bitterness in Rosy fought with the loss of what should have been a father figure. Trembling, she pulled a handkerchief from inside her dress sleeve and wiped the beads of sweat from her forehead and neck.

She sat and stared at Fred's motionless body as it lay in the open casket by the waiting grave. She had made herself come to the funeral, but only to make sure he was dead. In a corner of her mind, he was still a threat. *I have to have closure. I saw him die with my own eyes, but now I need to see him in the casket...dead and buried. I need to know for sure that he is really out of my life.*

Turning her eyes away from the sight of her father's body, Rosy looked out over the fertile valley. *It's such a beautiful morning...the cool wind, beautiful sky, and gorgeous view. I guess that makes today a perfect day to bury him. Too bad he can't enjoy it, 'cause where he's at it'll be sizzling hot and miserable.*

She smirked. *Hmm...where did that come from?*

The eulogy was short. A few words of sympathy from the neighbors were given, and the service was over.

At the end of the ceremony, the mourners lined up and walked slowly by the open casket, saying good-bye to the deceased. Rosy waited to be last. After everyone said their good-byes, she reluctantly walked over to the coffer. While standing over his body, she watched to make sure he was not moving. Fred lay rigidly in the wooden box; his eyes were closed, and his hands lay neatly across his heart. Rosy glared at him as he lay motionless. All doubt was erased from her mind.

He's dead...

As she stood over him, sarcastic thoughts tumbled over in her mind. *How ironic...he's a perfect picture of gentleness and peace now. At least I don't have to worry about him anymore. He's out of my life for good.*

Or is he?

As she continued to stare at him, she felt the bitterness and hatred towards him burn deep in her mind, heart, and soul.

After everyone but the family had left, the gravediggers sealed the wooden casket and placed it in the grave. Doty stood, and without looking back, turned, and walked away.

Rosy waited until everyone was gone. Picking up a handful of dirt, she tossed it in the grave, hesitated, then picked up another handful and threw it at the casket. "I'm glad you're gone. You represent a part of my life I hate. Just go away and leave me alone." She paused, composed herself, then turned and followed after her mother.

TWENTY-SIX

1944

Over the next few weeks, Rosy spent as much time as possible at home with her mother. The boys were in their teens and old enough to work the fields while the older girls helped take care of the house and the little ones. In the spirit of the times, a neighbor lady offered to babysit the little ones when the girls were in school. Everyone gradually learned their new rolls and life fell into the rut of the new norm.

Rosy worried about her mother and decided to bring up the issues with her. "Mom, what are your plans going forward? You're gonna need more than the farm can produce to take care of yourself and the kids."

Doty looked up but didn't answer. The familiar faraway look was clearly visible in her eyes. She began to shake her head.

Rosy took her mother's hand. "Mom, you can do this. I can help you. I know you've never worked outside the home, but you're a capable woman." Rosy smiled brightly. "Just like how you found a job for us at the hospital, I'm going to help you. I know a lot of people in town, and I will find someone who will hire you and help teach you. Just like you found for us."

Doty fixed Rosy with her gaze. "I don't know, Rosy. I don't think I could work as a nurse like you girls. I'm too old for that."

Encouraged, Rosy sat forward. "Oh no, nothing like that, but it'll be someone who will be patient and help you as you get past all that's happened."

Rosy put the word out to her friends and co-workers. Within a week, Rosy got a visit from one of the doctors on staff. She had worked with him for the last two years and really liked him. He was a good and kind man. "Rosy, I won't be on staff here at the hospital anymore. I'm going to open my own private office. I'll need a receptionist and I hear your mother is looking for a job. Is she still available?"

"Yes, she is. I know you've heard about my father's passing, and life has been hard on her since then. If you don't mind doing a little training, she would be fantastic. She's a very hard worker, and she taught most of us kids by herself even while helping our father run the homestead. If you're willing to be a little patient with her, I can promise you, you won't regret it."

The doctor smiled. "I would love to give this a try."

"Doctor Brown, that would be wonderful!" Rosy ran up and hugged him, then thought better of it. "I'm sorry, I shouldn't have done that." She blushed.

He smiled. "Can you bring her in tomorrow so I can meet her? I think I can help her, and she can help me."

Rosy breathed a sigh of relief. "I'll bring her into the office bright and early tomorrow. Thank you so much, Doctor Brown."

The next morning, Rosy brought her mother into the medical building. They stopped at the door of the doctor's new office. Doty took a deep breath and read the name printed on the window, "Dr. Charles L. Brown." Her emotions spiraled, and she looked over at Rosy. "I have no idea what I'm doing here." Her stomach knotted as her hands trembled. "What if he's like your father?"

"Mom, he's nothing like Father. You're ready for this?"

Looking at Rosy, Doty put her hand on the doorknob and released a breath. "I guess I'm as ready as I'll ever be." She took another deep breath, stood up straight, and opened the office door.

Dr. Brown welcomed Doty warmly. His kindness and compassion eased her nervousness. After a short interview, she was hired, and her training began that day.

He was very patient with her as he began teaching her the basic receptionist skills. By the end of the day, she began to relax and feel a little more comfortable in his presence. The first few days were difficult for Doty as she struggled to learn the new skills. She was also nervous dealing with people—especially men.

Dr. Brown watched and evaluated her work constantly. One day, as Doty sat at her desk, he stood beside her to assess her work. He leaned over and placed one hand on the desk and one hand on the back of her chair. His fingers accidently brushed her shoulder. She stiffened. Not sure what was going on, she sat rigidly, waiting to see. Seeing her tense up, the doctor removed his hand from the chair and stood back, not wanting to make her feel uncomfortable. It took a while, but she gradually relaxed again.

As her nervous tension slowly dissipated, Dr. Brown began to wonder what the struggles of Doty's past life had been. He could see in her a fear and lack of trust. After a few weeks like this, Dr. Brown decided to try and help her along.

Coming out into the receptionist area, he slid a chair over and sat across from her. Startled, Doty recoiled in her chair. "Dr. Brown?"

Raising his hands, Dr. Brown leaned forward and put his elbows on his knees, then clasped his hands together. He took a breath and looked into her face, feeling great sorrow for the fear he saw there. "Doty, you've worked with me for a few weeks now"

"Oh, Dr. Brown, I really need this job. Whatever it is, I'll try harder."

He laughed softly. "No, no, it's nothing like that. You're doing fine. I love your work. It's just that I can't help but see that at times you're very uncomfortable in my presence."

Doty dropped her gaze but did not respond.

"I've been a doctor for a long time, and as a doctor you hear a lot of stuff."

Doty's head snapped up, and her eyes darted around the room. She looked like a trapped animal.

Dr. Brown pushed back and held up his hands again. "Doty, I haven't heard anything in particular about you, but I can tell something's happened to you…and to your girls. He gave her a gentle smile. "I need you to know that I care about you and I would never hurt you."

Doty sat quietly and watched as Dr. Brown stood up and pushed his chair back, tipped his head at her in respect, and walked across the hall to his office.

When he was out of hearing range, she quietly replied in a strangled voice, "Thank you."

Within the first few weeks, Doty mastered the needed skills and was proficient at her new job. Dr. Brown was pleased with her work. One day, all smiles, he complimented her, "Doty, you're the best receptionist I've ever had."

The words made her body tingle. *That's the first complement I've had in years.* She felt giddy inside. *But I'm also the only receptionist he's ever had.* She smiled to herself.

Doty grew to love her job through the months. She really liked working with Dr. Brown and the patients. In fact, her fear of Dr. Brown started to diminish as she worked with him every day and got to know him better. She came to care about him as a friend and a boss.

1945

The end of February came. What little snow there had been had melted. The weather had warmed some, but the clear skies and chilly temperatures gave proof that winter was not over yet.

After work one evening, Doty had some errands to run. By the time she arrived home, it was dusk and past dinnertime. The children had lit the wood stove to warm up the shanty when they had gotten home from school. Now the house was warm, but the stove was out. The lanterns were lit as the children sat at the table finishing their homework.

Doty opened the iron plate on the stovetop and shoved a few chunks of wood into the fire box and stoked up the fire again. As the flames grew, sparks and embers escaped the stove. Rising on the warm air, a few embers rose up to the ceiling and nestled into the crevices of the dried wood. No one noticed.

Doty put the metal plate back on the stovetop and started to cook dinner. It had been a busy day, and she knew the children were exhausted. She let out a huge sigh. "Has everyone finished their chores?" She flipped the pancakes in the pan.

There was a weary chorus of "Yes" from the children. By the time Doty set dinner out on the table and the children had eaten, it was dark outside and time to go to bed. Each child drifted off to their room and was soon sound asleep. Doty joined them and curled up under her covers. She quickly dozed off and fell into a deep slumber.

The embers silently smoldered in the crevices of the ceiling boards for a while, and then, without warning, they burst into flames. Within just a few minutes, the fire had crawled across the wooden ceiling and ignited the tar paper roof.

Smoke quickly filled the structure, waking up Abigail first. Coughing and gasping, but still half asleep, she tried to figure out what was going on. She quickly realized there was too much smoke to be the stove. Terrified, she screamed, "MOM! MOM! FIRE! THE HOUSE IS ON FIRE!" Gasping for air, she crawled out of bed. Coughing and gagging, Abigail screamed as loud as she could, trying to wake everyone up, "FIRE! FIRE! WAKE UP! WAKE UP! GET OUT OF THE HOUSE!" Her sisters jumped up in confusion. Blinded by the smoke, they groped their way to the door and ran outside.

Abigail ran to the other rooms, screaming louder to wake her brothers and mother. "FIRE! GET OUT OF THE HOUSE!"

Doty woke up quickly to Abigail's screams. Her first thought was the children. In a flurry of confusion, coughing, and gagging, with her baby cuddled against her, Doty hustled the boys and Abigail outside.

The children rushed from the burning building, escaping into the night. Doty rushed behind them and stopped at the doorway. Squinting through the smoke, she looked out into the yard and did a quick head count; the children were all out of the building and safe.

As Doty ran from the flaming building, she collapsed. The baby fell to the ground and sat crying beside her. Her children dashed over and dragged her and the baby away from the burning house. As Doty lay motionless on the ground, the wind and fresh air gradually filled her lungs, and slowly she regained consciousness.

Doty sat up. "My baby! Where's my baby?" She was gasping for fresh air. Willie handed his mother the young child. Seeing her baby safe, she settled down some. The children gathered together around their mother, making sure she was okay. As they clustered together to keep warm, they silently watched their home go up in flames.

The splintering dry wood burned hot and quick. The whole house was soon engulfed in flames. Suddenly, it collapsed. The walls gave way and the roof fell in, sending a plume of ashes, embers, and smoke high into the air. The home disintegrated into a pile of cinders and ashes.

Hopeless, Doty and the children sat staring into the flames. They were devastated as they watched their home turn into smoke and ash. The loss echoed through Doty's being. *Everything is destroyed. Now what will we do?* She turned to check that nothing else was on fire. *At least we still have the vehicles and barn.*

Eventually, the fire died down and the smoke dissipated, leaving embers glowing in the night. The night chill deepened, and silence surrounded the dark, shadowy landscape.

Finally, Doty spoke, "We still have the barn, so at least we can take shelter there and get out of the cold breeze. We can sleep there for the rest of the night. Tomorrow, we'll figure out what to do."

Trying to keep warm, the family huddled together on a pile of hay in the barn. The night was long. No one slept. Eventually, dawn appeared, and the sun's rays gradually peeked between the cracks in the wall boards and through the barn door.

Doty got up quietly, put the baby on her hip, and slowly crept out of the barn to examine the devastation. The first thing she saw was the black soot-covered woodstove, the only thing standing in the midst of the charred remains. On the ground lay singed mattress springs, broken dishes, and mounds of burnt cinders.

As each person got the nerve, they slowly stood up and crept out into the new day. Each walked over and kicked around in the cinders, examining the charred remains. They looked for anything that represented their past life.

All was lost.

Doty turned and faced her children. "Willie and George, you stay and keep an eye on the place and take care of the animals. The rest of you get in the car. We're going to town," she ordered. "Maybe we can find some help there." The younger children silently climbed into the car. Leaving Fred's truck for George and Willie, Doty started the Model T and took off down the rutted road. The drive to town seemed longer than usual, the road bumpier, and the mood more depressing.

She pulled up in front of the police station. The small group piled out. They were a motley-looking group with their soot-covered night clothes and straw speckled hair. "Stay out here," Doty instructed. "I'm going in to talk to the police. Maybe they can help us and tell me what I need to do." She brushed off her nightgown, lifted her head high, and entered the station.

The children stood by the car. Passersby stared at the grubby-looking gang. Many people stopped to talk to find out what happened. Before long, they were surrounded by sympathizers who wanted to help.

Soon, Doty walked out of the office with a police officer. "Doty, I'm sorry that this happened. We'll check out your farm and get back to you." He handed her a note. "In the meantime, here's the name and address of the woman that is in charge of the used clothing store in our community. She will set you up with clothes and baths for your family. The hotel will give you free room and board until we figure out what to do. I'll go ahead and contact the rest of your family and let them know that everyone is okay."

"Thank you very much, officer." Doty looked at the note as she turned to the children. "Kids, let's get back in the car. I need to contact some people."

A group of sympathetic town's-people stood around talking as they drove off, discussing a way to help the poverty-stricken family.

Later that morning while the family was eating breakfast at the hotel, the police officer walked up to the table, removed his hat, and sat down with them. He looked around the table at the children and then at Doty. He took a deep breath and gradually released it.

"Doty, I sent men out to check your place. You're right. It was completely destroyed. I know you can't afford to build again, and there's no way you can sell the land right now with the economy the way it is. Your two boys said they would make themselves a place in the barn's loft to stay and take care of the farm. As they bring in money from the crops, they're planning on building another house, but it'll take a long while to raise all the money—"

Everyone looked up at a sudden commotion at the door. "Mom," Rose cried as she rushed into the room. "Are you okay? Are any of the kids hurt? Mom, what happened?" Rose's voice broke with emotion.

Doty opened her arms to her daughter. "Settle down, Rosy. We're all fine," she said in a comforting tone. Rosy looked around the table at her siblings for reassurance, then back to her mother.

"Tell me what happened!"

Doty told her about the fire and getting settled in the hotel. Rose hugged her mother and wouldn't let go for a long time. "Mom, I'm so glad you're all okay." Rose grasped her mother's hand with both of hers. "Please let me know what we can do to help."

Doty was tired and looked it; Rosy could see that her mother was exhausted. She touched her mother's face. "Get some rest. I should get back to work so I'll talk to you later. I'm so thankful that everyone's okay." She kissed her mother's forehead, hugged each of the kids, and turned and left.

After a few days had passed, Doty was visited by the same officer she had met the morning of the fire. "I've talked to one of the churches here in town," he began slowly. "They love to help people in situations like yours." He smiled as he fidgeted with his hat, thinking about how he would tell her the good news. "Umm…There is an abandoned house outside town. The owner said we could have it if we would move it. The church's congregation, along with other people in town, have offered to move it and set it up for you and your family. The trouble is that your homestead is over eight miles away and they can't move the house that far. So, one of the members has donated a small plot of land here in town if you don't mind living in town instead of on your acreage."

Doty was dumbfounded. "I don't…I don't believe this." She could hardly speak. "Why is everyone being so kind? They don't even really know me."

The officer smiled. "The townspeople know that you and your family have been through a rough spot. They want to help you as much as they can." Doty's eyes filled with tears. The officer continued, "The people said they can start today if you decide to do this. You can stay here until the house is ready." He put his hat back on. "Do you want to go see the lot for the house? That way, you can decide if you would like to live in town." Doty swallowed hard as she nodded her head.

The officer drove Doty over to the small section of land. It was about a mile away from where she worked and just two blocks away from the kids' school. "Officer, it's perfect." She cried when she saw it. "How much will all this cost me?" she inquired, knowing this was too good to be true.

"I told you, Doty; it won't cost you a thing."

Doty felt faint. For a few minutes, her voice would not come. The officer could see she was feeling overwhelmed by all that had occurred. He stood silently fiddling with his police hat. Finally, Doty said softly, "This will be a wonderful place to live. Yes, we'll take it."

Rosy met her back at the hotel, and Doty filled her in on everything that had just happened. She told her about the new clothes, the house, and everything the people at the church had promised to do. "People are being so generous to us. I don't know how we would make it without them."

Rosy took her mother's hands, and together they cried with both joy and relief.

Shortly after Rosy had left, Doty and the children laid down for an early afternoon nap. It had been an emotionally exhausting day. Doty laid in bed, restless, having a difficult time believing what had just happened. Her thoughts slipped back to the hard times on the homestead: the old, dirty shanty, the hard work on the farm, the hunger and poverty, and the abuse—Fred's abuse—that she and the children survived. *Now the fire…It all seems like I've been living a nightmare.*

Doty continued to rest. Numerous times, she rewound the past few hours over in her head; she eventually made a decision. *With Fred gone, my own job, a new house, fewer kids, this is a good time to start over, to start a new life. That's what I'm going to do. I'm leaving the nightmares behind me and looking forward to the future.* She finally relaxed and closed her eyes; her mind envisioning what life could be as her thoughts trailed off.

Doty and the younger children stayed at the hotel for the next month. Willie and George quickly made their home in the barn's loft and stayed to do the needed work on the homestead. The two boys visited the family in town often.

Over the next few weeks, the congregation worked hard to get the new house moved and the remodel finished.

One afternoon, the kind police officer that had been helping Doty out, walked into Dr. Brown's office. "Doty, your house is finished. I've come to take you over to see it."

Surprised, her eyes grew large and her mouth dropped open. She glanced questioningly at Dr. Brown. He smiled and nodded his head, giving her permission. Immediately, she grabbed her purse, raced across the waiting room, and followed the officer out the door.

Doty walked into her new house alone, everyone giving her a moment to take in the enormity of the blessing. She stopped just inside the doorway and looked around; the house had been furnished. With careful steps, she made her way into the kitchen and turned on the tap. "Oh my, hot water. No more boiling water over a fire." Tears streamed, unnoticed, down her cheeks. Making her way through each of the rooms, she flicked on the lights and sucked in her breath as the glow of electric lights flooded each area. She pressed her back to the wall and stood that way for a long moment in silence. "Electricity, hot and cold water, an indoor bathroom…they even left clothes for the kids and me." Doty shook her head in unbelief.

Doty could find no words to express her thankfulness. As she marveled at all that was done for her and her family, overwhelming thoughts of gratitude swirled through her mind.

These people are so kind and generous. Most of them don't even know me or my kids, and look what they did for us. Some even invited us to church. I don't know what they believe…as a matter of fact, I'm not even sure what I believe either. All I know is they helped me and my kids when we really needed it.

Standing outside the house with the townsfolk, Rosy stood by her mother and looked around at these strange, yet wonderful people. "Mom, I've never known people to love like this. They just reached out and accepted us; it's like they love you no matter who you are or what you've done."

She pondered these thoughts even as the memory of the presence at the rock returned to her mind. *Is this what God's love is really like? Maybe I should give God and His love a chance.*

———————— ≈ ————————

At the end of March, the cold winter weather gave way to the warm sun, the cool breeze, and the scent of the spring grasslands. The fresh air and beautiful morning all added to Rosy's excitement.

On one of these beautiful March days, Rosy went to see her mother. She stepped out of the car and turned to Martha. She was almost giddy. "Thank you so much for the ride to my mom's. When will you be back?"

"I'll be back in an hour or so. I'm swinging by my folk's place for a little bit. Enjoy your visit." Rosy closed the car door and waved as her friend drove off.

Rosy burst into the door of Doty's new house. "Hi, Mom!" she announced smiling as she gave her mother a huge hug.

Doty's eyes brightened. "Rosy, it's good to see you. It's been a long time."

"I'm sorry it's been so long, Mom. I've been really busy with school and work." Straightening, Rosy's eyes darted around the somewhat familiar surroundings. "I have the morning off, so I thought we could visit, just catch up on things." She looked around again, unwittingly expecting to feel Father's presence even though she knew he was gone. "Where is everyone?"

Doty watched as her daughter's eyes traveled around the room. "It's Saturday so the boys are out at the homestead building a fence, and the younger kids are outside playing." She laid a hand on Rosy's forearm. "This is such a nice morning, much too nice to be cooped up in the house. Why don't we go sit on the front porch and chat?"

Doty filled two glasses with cold water from the faucet and led Rosy to the porch. She handed a glass to Rosy and sat down in a chair as she motioned for her daughter to sit in the rocker.

Above them, the sky was a brilliant blue with thin wisps of clouds trailing one another through the azure atmosphere. One of the rare cool breezes wafted across the porch, bringing with it the fragrant scents of early spring. Sitting back in her chair, Doty waited for Rosy to speak.

Rosy glanced out into the street. "Ya know, Mom. It's sure different living in town, in a neighborhood with other houses." She stood up and stepped to the edge of the porch as she scoured the area. She examined the closeness of the neighbors' houses. "The neighborhood feels so safe and comfortable. And look, you can even see both downtown a couple of blocks in front of you and the farm fields behind you."

"It's a change—a good change." Doty gazed happily around the neighborhood. Rosy could tell that her mother had settled comfortably into her new home and surroundings.

Rosy turned, walked over, and sat down by her mother. Suddenly, recalling the reason she came over, Rosy's eyes lit up and a smile quickly spread across her face. "I came to tell you something." She started to giggle with excitement. "You know I've been going to high school, nursing school, and nurse's training for almost two years now. Last week, I was talking to one of my instructors. And…guess what?" Rosy beamed; she was so thrilled she couldn't contain herself. Twisting and squirming in her chair, she grasped the edge of the wooden chair's arms.

"Mom," she grinned, her voice quivering with excitement, "I'll graduate this spring with high honors from high school as long as I keep my grades up for the rest of the semester." She clenched her hands and shuddered with excitement. Her grin spread across her face from ear-to-ear. "And I'm on course to graduate in the summer with high honors in nurses training too." Unable to sit any longer, Rosy shot up from her chair and threw her hands out to her sides. "I never thought I could ever do anything like this."

Overwhelmed, Doty leaped to her feet and hugged her daughter. "Oh Rosy, I'm so proud of you!" Embracing, the two women shared a single look of radiance, brought on by the joy of Rosy's success.

"And guess what else," Rosy continued. "Since I'll be turning eighteen soon, when I graduate from nursing school in August, I'm guaranteed a job. And I hear nurses are in great demand." Grinning, Rosy flipped her hair back.

Doty gazed at Rosy and saw the eagerness and passion in her daughter's face. "I knew you could do this. You'll be a fantastic nurse. I'm so proud of you." Doty hugged her daughter again tightly.

TWENTY-SEVEN

Since the townspeople had invited her, Doty decided to go to church. That Sunday, she found herself and her younger children standing outside the small-town church wearing their nicest new-used clothes. As they started walking up the steps, Abigail pointed "Wow, look at the cross at the very top!" The small group stopped as all eyes turned and gazed up at the tall steeple and white cross. Impatiently, Doty rushed up the steps. "We need to hustle, kids," she said while shooing them inside. "We're already late." Deep down, Doty was glad she was late. That way she wouldn't have to speak to anyone.

The pianist had already started playing, signaling the beginning of the church service. Doty led the children to the rear of the sanctuary where the small group sat shyly in the back pew. This was all new to them. Doty and the children slowly surveyed the congregation, taking in everything.

Doty's gaze stopped suddenly. Seated only a few rows ahead of them were Rosy and her friend Martha. Catching her mother's eye, Rosy waved, her face bright with pleasure. Doty smiled weakly and returned the wave.

When the pianist finished, a hush fell over the congregation as the song director stood up in front and announced to the worshippers, "Please stand and turn to page 177 in the hymnal." Doty looked around and noticed the other people pick up a small book from the slot of the pew in front of them. Looking down, she saw a copy of the same book in front of her. She took one and handed it to the children to share, then opened another one for herself. The music started again, and the leader began singing; everyone joined in as the children flipped through the pages of the hymnal.

Recalling the song from her childhood, Doty sang the hymn with the worshipers. Thoughts of the love that these people had poured out on her and her family spun through her mind. A warmth grew in her heart, filling her with gratefulness. She wondered why these people would be so generous to a perfect stranger.

As Doty watched the song leader and tried to sing along, a movement in the corner of her eye caught her attention. She turned toward the motion. Taken by surprise, Doty gave a small gasp. *Oh...I didn't know that Dr. Brown went to church.* She released a quiet sigh. She watched him walk to a pew a few rows in front of her and join in the singing. She couldn't help but notice that his six-foot, slender build looked very handsome in his dark gray suit.

During the service Doty had a hard time focusing. She looked around, seeing many of the people that had shown her and her family such love and generosity. Many of them had given not from their abundance but despite their own need. These thoughts kept swirling through her mind and no matter how hard Doty tried to focus on the sermon, she had difficulty paying attention. The fact that her eyes kept drifting toward the doctor made it even harder.

After the service was over, Rosy rushed up and gave her mother a hug. "Mom, I'm excited to see you here." They chatted for a bit while Rosy stood and watched happily as, one-by-one, the people of the congregation came up and welcomed her mother and the kids. Seeing that her family was in good hands, Rosy waved a good-bye and left with Martha. "I'll talk to you soon, Mom."

After most of the people had left, Dr. Brown came up to Doty. She gave him a shy smile. She felt her cheeks turn pink.

"Hello, Doty. I'm glad to see you here." He reached out to take her hand. She reached out and shook his, but he didn't let go.

"Thank you. I was invited by Mr. and Mrs. Campbell, and many others who helped out with our house." She glanced down at his hand and then back at him. "Doctor, I didn't know you attended church here."

Doty shooed her children from underfoot. "You kids go play." It wasn't long before they had found playmates of their own and had wandered off outside.

Giving her a gentle smile, he squeezed her hand. "You need to call me Doctor in the office, but when we're not in the office, please call me Charles or Charley. My good friends usually call me Charley."

Doty blushed and gave him her shy smile again. He let go of her hand. Surprised, she found herself wishing he were still holding it.

"I'm curious, Doty. Since this is your first time here, what did you think of the service?" The doctor waited patiently for an answer.

Doty reflected for a few seconds before replying. "You know, the people here gave from their hearts to build a house for me. They gave their time, money, and many other things. From what I heard today in the sermon, that's a good example of God's love. These people gave me the best gift they could."

As the worshippers gradually left the building, Doty and Dr. Brown continued chatting as they followed, walking slowly.

Doty continued, "That kind of love goes along with today's sermon. The pastor talked of how God loved me so much that He gave me the best gift of all; He gave His own Son to die for me and my sins. I'm not sure what to think about all that…not yet at least. Of course, I've heard all this years ago as a child, but today…well, it sounded different."

As she thought about it, the idea of Jesus loving her so much that He had died for her was a strange notion; one that warred against her personal experience. *I've been denied love my whole life…my mother abandoned me, my father chose his new wife over me, and then…then Fred.* She closed her eyes against the pain. *Am I really worth loving?* She shook her head.

She looked up to see Charles smiling at her. He reached out and took her hand. "Then I can look forward to seeing you next week?"

Doty smiled. "Yes, I'll be back next Sunday."

"Great! I'll see you at work in the morning." He released her hand as he winked at her, said good-bye, and walked over to his car.

With her eyes riveted on him as he walked off, her heart started rushing. Realizing what she was doing, she turned with a jerk and checked to see if anyone had been watching her. Then just as sudden, a sullenness settled over her. *I can't—I refuse to get involved with another man. For the first time, I'm in control of my own life and it's going to stay that way.*

"Hey, kids, come get in the car. It's time to go."

That Monday, Dr. Brown sat at the desk in his office that was nestled in the back corner of the medical building. One wall of his office was covered with bookshelves full of medical journals and other leather-bound digests. Opposite of that was a large window framed by dark tan drapes. The walls, a light tan, held wood framed medical certificates and a copy of his medical diploma. The room was just large enough for his desk, chair, and two other chairs for his patients. On top of a filing cabinet in front of the window sat a potted ivy with long tendrils of leaves that reached down towards the floor. The lush plant helped give the office a calm, welcoming atmosphere as the sun rays brightened the room. His office door opened into the hallway that led into the receptionist area and waiting room.

The morning patients had come and gone. Dr. Brown was working at his desk, transcribing his medical notes from the morning. As he glanced up and out his office door, he saw Doty across the hall sitting at her desk, head down, busily working. Laying his pencil down on his notebook, he leaned back in his chair and studied her. His eyes rested on her, taking note of her beauty. He saw a quiet, gentle, broken woman that was trying hard to make a good life for herself and her family.

His heart filled with compassion and perhaps something more. She had only worked for him for a few months, but as he gradually got to know her, he began to realize what a tender, loving woman she really was. From the rumors around the hospital and the hints he observed in her, he knew she had been through a lot; but exactly how much or how bad, he didn't know yet. *How can I help her get over the losses…how can I get to know her better?*

Dr. Brown watched as Doty, with her brow furrowed and lips pursed, brushed back a strand of hair that had fallen across her face. When she smiled with the completion of the task, he felt his heart skip and he knew he was in trouble. *The first time I met her, I realized that there was something special about this woman.* That familiar feeling was stirring inside him.

Doty glanced up when a patient walked up to the counter. With effort, Dr. Brown took his eyes off Doty, picked up his pencil, and returned to his work.

At noon, Dr. Brown walked through the empty waiting room to the front door of the office. As he opened it to leave, he turned to Doty. "I'm heading to lunch; would you like me to bring anything back for you?"

"No thanks, I brought my own lunch." *He's so kind and thoughtful.* Doty smiled as a familiar feeling of affection stirred inside. She fought hard against the emotion but was losing the battle. The doctor tipped his head politely and left.

The office was closed during the noon hour, but Doty usually stayed and ate her lunch at her desk. Staying during lunch time gave her time to get caught up on paperwork. After she ate, she pulled out patient files and began to work on them. Once finished, she took them into Dr. Brown's office to be filed.

As she entered the office, she stopped, catching a slight hint of the doctor's cologne, a light woodsy odor. Doty inhaled slowly, enjoying the fragrant scent. After her filing was finished, she turned to leave, but as she did, she saw an opened book lying on the doctor's desk; the book looked familiar. She walked over and picked it up, careful not to lose his place.

Hmm…it's a Bible. She had never read one before and had never thought much about it really. Marking the page with her finger, she thumbed through the pages and stopped and read a verse or two. She ran her fingers across the onion-skin paper and her thoughts traveled back to the sermon from the day before. *Maybe I should get a Bible of my own. I'd like to know more about God.* She laid the book back on the desk.

As she lay it down, Doty carefully opened it back to the page where the doctor had left it. As she started to walk away, she glanced down at the book, this time noticing that a verse on the page was underlined. Curious, she picked it up again and read the verse out loud to herself, " *'These things I have spoken unto you, that in Me ye might have peace. In the world ye shall have tribulation: but be of good cheer; I have overcome the world.'* "

Not exactly sure what it meant, Doty reread the verse over and over, trying to understand. *Is this God speaking, saying that He'll give me peace? That would be wonderful. Peace in my life is what I need more than anything else right now.* Wondering, she put the book down still muttering to herself, "I'll have to ask Dr. Brown exactly what this means."

"Ask me what?" the doctor ask as he walked into his office.

Startled, she jumped.

"I'm sorry, Doty. I didn't mean to scare you." He chuckled. "But what did you want to ask me?"

She could feel her face flush, feeling like she had been caught snooping. She gazed down at his desk to avoid looking him in the eye. "Oh, nothing…I need to get back to work."

As she started to walk past him, Dr. Brown asked kindly again, "Doty, no…really, what is it? What's your question?"

"Um…" she wavered, knowing he wouldn't let her off the hook. She turned to face him, blushing. "I-I was filing some patient folders and saw your Bible on your desk. I read the part you had underlined and was just wondering what it meant." Clasping her hands behind her, she stared at the floor, embarrassed. She waited for his response.

Dr. Brown sat on the edge of the desk, picked up the Bible, and silently read the verse to himself. "Have a seat, Doty. I'll try to explain it to you." She perched herself on the edge of a chair in front of his desk. He sat down in the chair beside her.

Not wanting to make her uncomfortable, he handed her the book and scooted back a little. She relaxed but was somewhat confused. Was she nervous being around him because she was fearful of men or because he was Charles and stirred a peculiar feeling inside her?

"Doty, the first thing you need to know about this verse is that the red letters mean that these are words that Jesus actually spoke. All the words in the Bible that are in red letters are Jesus' words.

"I'll explain the verse one section at a time." Dr. Brown read the first part out loud. "*These things I have spoken unto you...*' This section tells us that it is Jesus speaking to us. '*...that in me ye might have peace.*' He is telling us that if we look to Him, He will give us peace."

Doty wanted to make sure she understood. She repeated, "So, Jesus is telling us that He will give us peace...in our hearts?"

The doctor smiled and nodded as he read on, " '*...In the world ye shall have tribulation.*' The word tribulation means trouble. This phrase means that as long as we're on the earth, we'll have troubles."

Flashes of Doty's hard life flitted through her mind.

"This last part is the best." He smiled as he read the last section, " '*...but be of good cheer; I have overcome the world.*' This part means be joyful, happy, because Jesus overcame the world." The doctor paused to think, then continued,

"When Jesus was crucified on the cross and rose from the dead, He conquered sin and death. He is in control of everything in this world—"

"Doctor," she interrupted, "so you're sayin—the Bible's saying—that if we trust Jesus, in spite of all our troubles, He will give us His peace? That we should be happy because He has defeated all the bad things in this world and is in control of everything?"

"Yes, Doty. That's what I'm saying. That's what Jesus is saying. No matter what you have been through, if you turn it over to Jesus and trust Him with it, He will give you a peace in your heart that only He can give. He has overcome all the evil in this world. And Doty, when you trust Him, He will walk with you and heal your mind and your heart. He will help you learn from your past and teach you to trust Him more."

She straightened, this time more from a feeling of excitement than of fear. To Doty it seemed so simple but also a bit complicated. *Perhaps,* she thought, *if I understood what Charles was thinking when he underlined the verse.* "Dr. Brown, why did you underline that verse?"

He closed his eyes and paused, then spoke softly, "A number of years ago, my wife died from heart problems. It was a hard time for me. Finally, after many months of pain and heartache, I turned to God and gave Him my life, my heart, everything I had. I received a peace and joy in my heart I never thought possible."

Doty was warmed by the look of peace Charles had on his face as he spoke of coming to know the Lord. But she had been caught off guard when he'd mentioned having been married. Was it wrong for her to be glad that he was single now?

Doty envied him. She could see the peace he had in his eyes. Just then, memories and confused emotions flickered within her, bringing with them the hurts and sense of failures she felt as a mother and wife. *I wish I could find a peace like that.*

She stood. "Thank you, Doctor, this gives me a lot to think about. But I should get back to work now." Turning, she quickly walked back to her desk.

Dr. Brown watched her walk away as he prayerfully reran their conversation over in his head, wondering what he said had that might have upset her.

The next morning when Doty came to work, she found a Bible laying on her desk with a note signed from Charles. Pausing, she smiled and looked around before picking it up. Holding the book to her breast, she lifted the note and read the brief message.

Doty, I enjoyed reading with you yesterday and thought you might enjoy having a Bible of your own. Of course, I am available to help you if there is anything you don't understand.

Charles

TWENTY-EIGHT

When Doty arrived home that evening, she placed the Bible on her coffee table, sat on the couch, and leaned back to rest as she closed her eyes. She could hear the children chattering happily in their rooms. After a few moments, she slowly opened her eyes and looked around her house, still having a hard time believing that this was all hers.

This house is as nice as the one I lived in as a child, just not as fancy. For a few minutes, she blocked everything else from her mind as she stood up and meandered through the house, taking it all in again.

After checking on the children, she returned to the sofa and sat down. Doty picked up her Bible and started flipping through it. She glanced at the names of the books and checked out the concordance. *There's so much to read.* Overwhelmed, she closed the book and put it back down on the table. She stared at it for a minute, then reached out and flipped it open again. Leaving it on the page where it opened, she picked it up and started reading.

She looked at the chapter name and number. "Hmm, Luke 12." As Doty started reading aloud, verse 24 jumped out at her. " *'Consider the ravens: for they neither sow nor reap; which neither have storehouse nor barn; and God feedeth them: how much more are ye better than the fowls?'* "

She smiled. *God does feed the birds and gives them places to stay…and now He has given me a place to stay and a job so I can feed my family.*

"God," she whispered into the silence, "was that really You?"

She continued reading aloud as another verse, 27, spoke to her. "*'Consider the lilies how they grow: they toil not, they spin not; and yet I say unto you that Solomon in all his glory was not arrayed like one of these.'*

"I'm not sure who Solomon was, but if he was arrayed in glory, he must have been dressed really well." She chuckled and quietly whispered to herself, "And I think the only thing more beautiful than lilies are roses. I wonder, was it actually God that provided my family and me with more clothes than we need?"

Suddenly, Doty realized God was providing for her and her children. She thought about all that she now had: the house, her job, food, clothes. "God," she whispered, "it's You! You've been providing for us. You've given us everything we need."

She read on to verse 29. God spoke to her through verses again. "*'And seek not ye what ye shall eat, or what ye shall drink neither be ye of doubtful mind. 30, For all these things do the nations of the world seek after: and your Heavenly Father knoweth that ye have need of these things. 31, But rather seek ye the kingdom of God; and all these things shall be added unto you.'*

"These verses tell me that God knows what I need, and not to be doubtful." Something started stirring in Doty's heart. It was a feeling that all this might be true…but doubt lingered near.

Doty hesitated and then looked up toward heaven. "Jesus, if this is You providing for us, thank You. Thank You for taking care of my family." Hoping and praying that it was God providing, tears trickled down her face as her fear of the future started to fade away.

The next Sunday, Doty and her family were in church again. When Dr. Brown walked in, he stopped and glanced around at the congregation. She took a shallow gasp and held her breath. *There's Charles.* She felt a gentle stir of warmth in her heart. *I hope he sits with us.*

As soon as he saw her and the children sitting in the back pew, he walked over to them and gave a polite nod. "Good morning, Doty, kids. Do you mind if I sit with you this morning?"

The children giggled and scooted down to make room for him to sit by their mother. As he sat down beside her, his leg brushed against hers. Her body stiffened. Suddenly, she felt her blood rush through her veins, creating goosebumps all over her body. Looking kindly at her, Charles whispered, "Good morning, Doty."

"Good morning, Charles."

Every Sunday from then on, Doty and the children saved a seat for him.

She began to realize that Charles was nothing like her father or Fred. Charles was a good God-fearing man. He was kind, patient, and accepting of everyone he met. He treated people with respect and gentleness, especially her and her children. The more she got to know him, the more her trust in him grew. In fact, her feelings of trust and affection for Charles were growing no matter how much she tried to deny or ignore them. She wasn't sure what to do with these emotions.

Doty had questions when she studied her Bible. The only person she knew that could answer them was Dr.

Brown. Trusting his gentle, understanding nature and his knowledge of the Bible, she often stayed after work and asked him about the things she didn't understand.

One Friday afternoon after the office had closed for the day, Doty timidly walked into the doctor's office. She sat down across the desk from Charles with her Bible in hand. Seeing the Bible, he slipped some papers in a file and quickly placed it in his desk drawer, then sat waiting. "I see you have some more questions for me." He grinned. "I hope I can answer them."

She sat quietly for a moment before she spoke. "Charles, thank you for spending this extra time with me and teaching me about God. You've helped me see how He has walked with me through my life, my hardships, and how He provides for me." Gazing down at the Bible, she shyly thumbed through the pages. "Charles, I'm tired of trying to deal with my horrid past and my confusing emotions. I want peace in my life." Tears that perched in the corners of her eyes along with the sad, pale look on her face told it all. "I'm so tired. Fred was a horrid man. He was abusive to me and to the children, and I-I never stopped him. I-I failed my children. I feel like I can't get away from my past. Sometimes, I feel almost numb inside? Other times, I get so angry that I feel like spewing at everyone, including God. But God is the one bright light in my life right now."

Charles stood and came around his desk, sitting beside her and taking her hand in his. He looked straight in her eyes. "Doty, nothing that you did or didn't do changes how God feels about you. He loves you."

She paused, trying to find the right words. *And what about you, Charles? Will you think any differently about me?*

She released his hands and picked up the Bible as she focused her thoughts. "Charles, I-I've decided…I've decided that I want to ask Jesus into my life. I want to be forgiven, and I need to forgive Fred. I want to be free from my past, and I want that peace and joy in my life. I believe that Jesus is the only one that can give me that." She cleared her throat. "Ch-Charles, how do I ask Him to be my Savior?" She glanced up into his eyes.

He smiled. "Doty, it's simple. Just tell Jesus your heart. Ask Him to forgive you and to be part of your life."

"W-will you pray with m-me?"

"Of course, I will. I'd love to."

Doty placed the Bible in her lap as Charles reached over and took both of her hands in his. Together they bowed their heads. A peace surrounded them as the tears, colored by the past, poured from her eyes. "Dear J-Jesus, I need You. Please come into my life. I need Your strength, Your love, Your forgiveness." As the tears streamed down her face, God's peace began to fill her heart. "I believe that You died for me and that Your blood will cleanse me; please forgive me for all the wrong that I've done…and help me to forgive others that have hurt me, especially Fred… Amen."

The two sat quietly for a moment, enjoying what had to be the presence of God. Then Charles whispered, "Amen."

The doctor gave her a reassuring smile and slowly let go of her hands. "Doty, you've told me of your feelings of anger and bitterness from the past, and I'm so sorry this happened. But there's one thing you need to know: those feelings can hold you captive for a short time or a lifetime if you let them. Ask God to help you deal with those emotions. You can allow the people who have hurt and abused you to control your life, or you can change your life for the better."

"How can I do that?"

"You have to forgive them, even Fred. Pray and give these memories and emotions over to God every time you have them."

"I'll try. I really want the peace Jesus promises. But what if the problem is me? What if I can't forgive myself?" She lowered her face as new tears ran freely.

Charles took her hand again. "Doty, nothing has changed. God already knows everything you did or didn't do."

She lifted her tear-wetted face and looked into his eyes. He smiled. "And it won't change how I feel about you either." Fearing he said too much, Charles looked away and a silence grew between them.

Doty dried her face. *Could it be?* "Thank you, Charles." She rose to leave. "Thank you for everything. I'll see you at church on Sunday."

Doty went into the office a little early one morning to pull the files of the patients for that day. She knew this was going to be a busy one; Dr. Brown had back-to-back patients. But there was one patient file she couldn't find. She had looked everywhere.

Maybe Charles put the file in his desk. That's the only place left to look. She stepped into his office, opened the drawers, and pulled out some file folders. As she was looking through them, in the bottom of one drawer she saw a file with her name on it. *Hmm…Why would he have a file on me?*

She pulled the file out of the drawer to look at it and glanced out the office door to make sure no one was around. Doty flipped the file open and slowly looked at the forms. *Here's my job application, notes of my interview, and my education history.* "What's this?" Pulling a paper out, she glanced over it. She gasped. *This is a transfer of papers of ownership from Charles to the town council for my property. But I have a deed and transfer of the land from the town to me. What's going on here?*

Then it dawned on her. *Charles had owned the land and donated it to the town council so they could donate it to me.* "He donated the land for my place."

Suddenly, she heard the front door to the office open. *I can't let him know that I know.* She quickly slid the papers back into the file, slipped it back into the bottom of the drawer, and closed it just in time. Acting like she was going through the patient filing cabinet when the doctor walked into his office, she said, "Good morning, Doctor. Do you know where the file is for Dan Stone? He's coming in today, and I can't find his paper work."

"Morning, Doty." He pulled the file from under his arm. "I took it home to study it last night." He handed it to her.

"Thank you." She turned and rushed from the room.

All day long, Doty thought about the deed and wrestled with her feelings. She wondered why he gave her the land. *Is Dr. Brown trying to help me?* Another idea popped into her mind. *Or maybe he's trying to control my life like Fred did. Dr. Brown did give me a job and has authority over me in my job and income. And maybe now he's trying to control where and how I live.*

Anger and rebellion surfaced. *I'll never allow another man to control my life ever again. How dare he try to manipulate and control me.* Betrayal and fury spun through her mind.

That evening, after she got away from the office, her emotions eventually settled down. While fixing dinner, a notion flitted through her mind:

Pray about it.

She pushed it aside. Quickly, uneasiness settled in and wouldn't go away. Not knowing what else to do, she finally prayed a simple prayer, *God, let me know what is going on. Is Charles trying to control me...or help me?*

Thoughts concerning Charles ran through her mind. He had been nothing but kind and considerate to her. For the first time since looking at the file, she began to feel that perhaps she had overreacted. Eventually, her fear and anger gradually dispersed. She was left with a feeling of affection and gratitude for Charles. She suddenly realized that he was doing everything he could to help her. *Is this his way of caring for me?*

Doty looked up questioningly toward heaven with a dawning hope in her heart.

The next day after work, Charles and Doty chatted as he walked her from the office out to her car. When they reached the car, he opened the door for her. "Good-bye, Doty. Have a great evening." When she turned to him to say good-bye, her eyes rested on his gentle, compassionate face.

Emotions filled her chest. *I don't understand, no matter how much I try to ignore my feelings, they keep coming back. Is this love? Am I in love with Charles?*

Fear from memories of the past made her body shudder. She cried out to God in her heart and was rewarded by a sense of peace as a thought passed through her mind; *Maybe I should give this a chance.*

Looking up into his eyes, she knew she needed to take it slow in getting to learn how she really felt about this man. "Good-bye, Charles. I'll see you in the morning."

She glanced at the rearview mirror, noticing him watching her as she drove off.

Charles smiled as he watched her leave. Sitting in his car, he began speaking his thoughts aloud, "I've fallen for that woman." His heart skipped a couple of beats as he heard his own words. "Yes, I have. I'm in love with her." He nodded to himself in agreement. "And I have been for a while. But I can't tell her. I'm afraid I'll scare her off. She tenses every time I even get near her or touch her."

He looked up and prayed, "Lord, I've trusted You with my life for years now. And I continue to trust You. I want Your will in my life. Please walk with Doty and me and show us both Your will for each of our futures."

Charles started his car and headed for home.

Doty sat on her porch with Rosy one Saturday morning, chatting. "Rosy, it's early April, but it's been a beautiful and extra warm spring, so the church has decided to have a potluck at the Emmett park this afternoon." She brushed a fly from her arm. "The kids and I are going. Why don't you come with us? You can hang out with your friends if you don't feel like sitting with your mother."

At first, Rosy didn't think she could go; she had studying to do. But the more she thought about it, the more fun it sounded. "Mom, I'll make time to go. It would be fun to relax a bit. I'll go ahead and catch a ride with Martha if she's going."

By noon, the sun was high, bringing with it the warmth of a calm spring day. Most of the park and the picnic tables rested in the cool shade of tall maple trees. From the distance, the rushing of the river that bordered the park, could be heard.

Almost the whole church showed up for the potluck. The mouthwatering aromas of the homemade food floated throughout the picnic area. It was a perfect day for the picnic-get-together.

Charles sat at a table, eating his lunch with Rosy, Martha, and a few others as he watched Doty scampering around and chatting with friends. In fact, she hadn't stopped chatting long enough to eat her lunch. Her plate sat piled high with food, untouched, on the picnic table beside him.

As Rosy took a bite of potato salad, she observed her mother laughing and talking with others. Amazed, she spoke to Martha and Charles as she chewed, "Look at her. I can't believe Mom." Rosy licked her lips and swallowed her bite of salad. "It's incredible. She's a completely different woman. Did her accepting Jesus do that to her?"

Both Martha and Charles smiled and nodded.

Charles gazed fixedly at Doty and muttered to himself, "Her whole demeanor has changed. She is no longer the shy, nervous woman I hired a few months ago." He crossed his arms and smiled a small crooked smile. *It's amazing what God's Spirit can do. God is healing her.*

Even seeing her from a distance, he could feel the warmth in his chest grow. He wanted so much to put his arms around her and hold her. Though he felt that she cared for him, too, he had kept his distance all these months and held his peace, giving her time to deal with her past and accept her new life.

Now as he watched, he sensed it was time to let her know how he felt. After saying a silent prayer, he gathered his courage, stood up and walked over to where Doty was chatting with a friend.

Rosy arched a brow at Martha, and both women smiled. "Here he goes." chuckled Martha.

Rosy acknowledge, grinning, "It's about time."

Charles crossed the distance with a few confident strides. "Excuse me. Doty, may I speak to you for a moment?" His words sent her gaze quickly to his face; she looked at him curiously.

"Sure." She nodded her head once, then turned to her friend. "It's been nice talking to you. I'll see you later." She stepped over to Charles. "So, what's on your mind?"

"You mind going for a stroll?" His gaze tangled with hers.

Sunlines crinkled in the corners of her dark brown eyes. She smiled. "I'd love to." As they strolled through the park, Charles fought to keep his heartbeat steady. He felt a trail of perspiration trickle down the back of his neck that had nothing to do with the warm spring day. He pulled a handkerchief from his pocket, wiped the back of his neck, and stuffed the handkerchief back in his pocket.

As they walked, Charles hesitantly reached down and gently took her hand, waiting for her reaction. He felt a slight quiver.

He stopped in the shade of a large maple tree and turned toward Doty. Taking both of her hands with his, his eyes were riveted with hers. He managed a shallow breath. "Doty." His heartbeat quickened as he fought to get his feelings out. "I knew you were a special woman the day I met you. Over these last few months, I've grown to care for you—a lot. I can't hold my silence any longer." He took a deep even breath to calm his nerves. "And I care for you more now than ever." There was a pause. Charles cleared his throat and swallowed. "D-Doty, w-would you be my girl?"

Doty's mouth dropped open. As she met Charles' gaze, tears of joy filled the corners of her eyes and tumbled down her cheeks; she finally admitted it to herself. *I really do care for—maybe even love—Charles, and he cares for me.*

Suddenly, anxiety filled her body as her past life with Fred flashed through her mind, a life of abuse and control. She couldn't breathe. Wrestling with her memories and feelings, immediately she sent the anxious thoughts up to God. *Lord, months ago I told You that I'm starting a new life…and I'll not let Fred or my past ruin it. Maybe this is my second chance at love and life.*

She inhaled a determined breath and gathered her courage. Speaking softly, she looked straight into Charles' eyes, "I-I really care for you too." She gave him one of her shy smiles and paused. Her face began to glow as a beautiful smile appeared.

"Charles, I would love to be your girl. But please promise me that you'll be patient with me. I'm still learning how to live a normal life, and I'm still learning to live for God."

As love and compassion shined through Charles' eyes, he tenderly wrapped his arms around her and gave her a gentle hug. She stiffened, closed her eyes, and relaxed, laying her head against his chest. He held her tenderly as the world withdrew from around them and the noises receded. Their hearts entwined; all they could see was each other.

After holding her for a long while, Charles let go and looked around nervously, suddenly aware that they were still in the park. Stepping back, he took Doty's hand. Feeling the warmth of her smaller, gentler hand grasp the palm of his larger stronger hand, he smiled, knowing she was going to be okay. Doty nestled her hand in his gentle grasp as they strolled off through the park hand-in-hand, a sweet silence surrounding them.

Rosy sat at the picnic table, watching as Charles and her mother strolled across the park toward the river. Folding her arms, Rosy relaxed them on the top of the table and took a deep, gentle breath as relief, joy, and happiness for her mother rose inside her.

Mom's going to be all right…but what about me? Is Jesus really the answer?

Part 2

And we know that all things work together for good to them that love God, to them who are the called according to his purpose.
Romans 8:28

TWENTY-NINE

Spring 1945

Rosy was folding sheets in the laundry room when Martha burst through the door. Startled, Rosy dropped the linen and pressed her hand to her heart. "Martha—you scared me…what…it's not your shift. I'm working this morning."

"I know, I know." Martha grinned widely. "I came to see if you can come over for dinner tonight?" Her whole body shivered with excitement. "My brother, Coop, is coming home from the Army tonight, and I want you to meet him. Mom is having a welcome home party and dinner and is inviting the whole family over. I'm hoping you can come too."

Rosy hesitated before she spoke, not sure if she should go. "Martha, I would love to go, but this is a family gathering, and I'm not family."

"Rosy, please come. You're my best friend, and I want you to meet my brother."

The anticipation in Martha's eyes that begged her to come made up Rosy's mind. "Well, okay, if you really want me to. What time?"

"How about you ride home with me tonight after work? I'll bring you back after dinner. It shouldn't be too late. You'll love Cooper. He's five years older than me and gorgeous," said Martha.

"Okay, I'll be ready." Smiling at Martha, Rosy picked up the clean laundry, put it away, and left to continue her rounds. "See you later."

Rosy, standing off to one side, watched as the whole house seemed to buzz with excitement. Bella and her husband, Don, were especially excited to have their son home. "Your mom looks like a bee scurrying back and forth around here."

Martha laughed and placed a hand on her friend's arm. "She's been busy all day, cooking Coop's favorites." Don brought in extra chairs and set up the dining room. All around Rosy and Martha was controlled madness.

The aroma of the roast, fresh baked bread, and huckleberry pies flooded the house, stirring everyone's taste buds. Homemade applesauce and a bevy of desserts lined the counters of the kitchen.

"Martha, Rosy," Bella called out from the kitchen. "Come in here and help me with the finishing touches for Cooper's meal."

Rosy inhaled a deep breath, drawing in the aromas. "Boy, everything smells delicious and looks fantastic." The girls made their way over to the table. "What do you need us to do?" Rosy asked.

"One of you can crank the handle on the ice cream maker…" Bella looked at Rosy and pointed to the ice cream maker in a wooden bucket sitting on the floor by the kitchen counter. And Martha, you can make some gravy."

Rosy sat down by the ice cream bucket and started churning the ice cream. Martha opened the kitchen cupboards, pulled out ingredients, and started making the gravy.

"Where is Cooper? He's late." Martha said, frustrated.

"It's too bad your other brothers aren't home from the Navy yet. When will they be home?" Rosy asked Martha.

"I don't know. They joined the Navy a year before Coop was drafted, but they're in for 3 years, and Coop was in for two. We haven't heard from them lately, but I think they should be home soon. Hopefully, the war will end; then we can celebrate again with more huckleberry pies." Martha grinned and licked her lips.

<hr />

They all sat down at the dinner table, waiting for the arrival of their guest of honor. Impatiently, Martha fretted. "I wonder where Coop is. He should have been here an hour ago."

But the joy and excitement never dimmed as Rosy and her friends continued chatting, joking, and laughing. Feeling right at home, Rosy gazed around the table. These are kind, gentle people. *There's a beautiful spirit in this family. It's so different than mine.*

The girls were entertaining everyone by telling funny stories of school and work when suddenly the door burst open. A man in an Army uniform with a duffle bag over his shoulder stepped through the door and into the room. Dropping his bag on the floor, he threw his arms into the air, and yelled loudly, "I'm home!"

Martha jumped up and raced over to hug her big brother, but her mother was faster, her father right behind. Bella and Don grabbed their son and hugged him tightly.

Martha came from behind and hugged all three. Tears of joy were streaming down everyone's faces.

Everyone, except Rosy, quickly rushed over and clustered around Coop to welcome him. There were hugs and kisses, tears and laughter. "I can't believe I'm home," Coop murmured softly. "I wasn't sure if I would ever see you guys again." As his family surrounded him, hugging on him, crying tears of joy, he closed his eyes, took a deep breath, and inhaled their affection. "It's so good to be home."

Enjoying the celebration, Rosy sat quietly at the table, watching. She gazed at Cooper. He was the most handsome man she had ever seen: tall and muscular, wavy brown hair, and stunning blue-green eyes. The combination of man and uniform took her breath away. She couldn't take her eyes off of him.

Coop was glad to be home; he had been waiting for this moment for two long years. As he glanced at the kitchen counter that was full of his mother's cooking, his stomach growled, hungry for a good homecooked meal. He took a deep breath, taking in the familiar aroma of his mother's cooking. "Hey, Mom, everything looks great, and I'm starved. Boy, I'm ready for some of your delicious homemade food. Let's eat."

"Coop's right!" Martha shouted. "It's dinner time, and I'm hungry too."

Rosy smiled, and from across the room, Coop saw her for the first time. Rosy dropped her eyes, looking away.

She's the most beautiful woman I've ever seen. He stared at her dark hair as it curled around her face like a frame. He noticed her rich brown eyes and began to stutter. "Ah...um...yeah." As he stepped tentatively in her direction. She quite literally, took his breath away. *Who is she?*

Martha grabbed her brother's hand and dragged him over to meet Rosy. "Rosy, this is my brother, Coop. Coop, this is Rosy, my best friend."

He smiled at her and reached out to shake her hand. "Hello, Rosy." He locked eyes with her. "Martha, she's as beautiful as you." His voice was warm and salacious.

Rosy could think of nothing to say, so she just reached out and shook his hand. Finally, the words came, "Hi, Cooper. I-I'm happy to meet you. So, you're back from Europe."

Continuing to hold Rosy's hand, Cooper stood gazing at her; he didn't let go.

"Uh…yes, I am. I just came in this afternoon on the train from back east. It was a long trip," he paused and grinned. "Sure am glad to be home." Suddenly, he realized that he was staring. Embarrassed, he let go of her hand.

Rosy blushed.

"If you two are done introducing yourselves, the rest of us would like to eat," Bella said teasingly. She took her son by the arm and directed him toward the table. When everyone was seated, somehow Coop found that he was sitting next to Rosy. Martha smiled at her brother.

Don stood. "Let's give thanks." Everyone quieted down, took hands, and bowed their heads. "Thank You, Lord, for bringing Coop home safely to us. I pray You'll be with our other sons, Dan and Larry, and protect them. Please bless this time of celebration, and bless this food to the use of our bodies. Amen. Now let's eat!"

Martha and Bella headed into the kitchen. A moment later, the table was covered with roast and potatoes, along with all the side dishes.

Coop licked his lips. "I haven't eaten like this since before I left for the Army. Mom, this looks great."

It was a wonderful evening. Rosy felt welcome and special. She got to know Coop a little as his family sat around the table, listening to his stories of the war.

Rosy decided to join in. "Cooper? Martha and I were chatting, and she told me that while you were in Germany, you blew up a bank?" Rosy giggled. "Is that true?"

"Oh, yeah." Coop chuckled. "That was interesting. Since I was in the military police, my job was mainly law enforcement and security. That included maintaining order in the German towns where the fighting had been. One time, my unit was policing a small town where the fighting was over, and the German infantry had just pulled out."

Coop cleared his throat and continued. "There was almost nothing left of this town. It had been bombed, and most of the buildings were blown to pieces. The only things left were piles of rubble and a small number of partially standing buildings. The town was completely demolished and mostly deserted."

Coop's eyes glazed over, past the family, and into nothingness, as his thoughts slipped back to the past. "As our unit infiltrated the town to check it out, my buddy and I noticed that the town bank was completely destroyed; it was nothing but a pile of rubble. But in the middle of all this rubble, a large safe stood by itself, untouched by the bombing.

"After surveying the area, making sure there was no one else around, my partner whispered, 'Hey, Coop, let's blow up the safe and see if there's any money in it.' He had this mischievous grin. It sounded like a great idea to me, so we stuck some dynamite behind the handle of the safe, lit it, and ran and hid behind a pile of rubble for cover." The side of Coop's mouth pulled up and formed a crooked smile.

"When it exploded, most of the safe was blown into fragments. Shocked, we watched as shrapnel, coins, and paper money was propelled out in all directions. Then slowly, a cloud of bills came floating down from the sky. Money was everywhere. We looked at each other in disbelief and at the same time said, 'Too much dynamite!' "

Coop chuckled again. "But that was just the beginning. This is the best part. Suddenly the German people appeared from everywhere. They came out from behind piles of rubble, out of bombed-out buildings, and from anywhere a person could hide. We didn't even know they were there. As they ran from their shelters, they started yelling, giggling, and laughing, grabbing at bills that were floating from the sky and picking up scattered coins from the ground. It was quite a scene. My buddy and I laughed hard, watching the fun and excitement in the people's faces as they raced around, grabbing all the money they could get their hands on. Even the children stuffed their pockets full." Coop smiled at the memory.

"After the money was all snatched up, the German people came up, shook our hands, and patted my partner and me on the back, thanking us.

"I really felt bad for them because their homes were destroyed, and I hoped the money would help them survive until they could rebuild." Coop smiled a gentle smile. "I think my partner and I made a few friends in Germany that day."

"Then you admit it, you robbed a bank!" Martha laughed. "And now I have a bank robber for a brother! Boy, I'm never going to let you live that down!"

The rest of the group snickered as they gave Coop a hard time about dynamiting the safe.

The celebration and fun continued late into the evening.

The party was over too soon for Rosy. "Martha, I don't want to, but I need to get home. I have a lot of homework to do for school tomorrow. Would you mind taking me?"

"Okay, let me get my purse and keys." Martha headed for the door.

Coop stood and took Rosy's hand. "It sure was nice meeting you. Hopefully I'll see you again." He walked her unhurriedly toward the door.

"Maybe, you never know. It was nice meeting you too." She smiled shyly at him.

"Are you coming, Rosy?" Martha asked, digging in her purse for her keys as she stood in the doorway. Coop tipped his head and winked at Rosy.

"Yes, I'm coming." Rosy slowly removed her hand from Cooper's. He watched as she turned and walked out the door.

Once the girls were outside, Martha grabbed Rosy's hands. "What do you think, Rosy?" she asked as she squirmed excitedly. "Isn't he gorgeous? He's a great brother. You two would make a wonderful couple."

Walking arm in arm, Rosy leaned toward her friend. "I have to admit, your brother's best-looking guy I've ever met." She sighed. "But I don't have time for guys right now. I just want to get through school and become a nurse."

"I knew it!" Martha beamed as she released Rosy's arm and hurried to the driver's side of the car. "I knew you two would hit it off."

As Martha continued talking, Rosy's thoughts trailed to her past. Recollections of her father, her brothers and other men molesting her started tumbling through her mind. She felt the familiar darkness gradually begin to rise and hover over her. She shook herself and raised a hand to Martha. "Martha. Wait a minute. I'm not looking for a boyfriend. Yes, Cooper seems nice, but right now, I don't have time for a man." She hesitated, not wanting to hurt her friend. "Thank you for introducing us, but please just leave it at that."

Rosy withdrew into herself and became quiet.

THIRTY

Two days later, Martha and Rosy took their lunch hour at work together. As the girls ate in the hospital cafeteria, they chatted about Wednesday evening. "Rosy, everyone enjoyed having you over for dinner." Martha slurped a spoonful of her soup. "Especially Coop."

Rosy eyed her friend over her sandwich. "Thank you," Rosy said graciously and took a bite of her sandwich. "But I told you I wasn't ready for anything like that." Out of the corner of her eye, she saw a movement; someone was walking toward their table. She glanced to the side, and her stomach flip-flopped. Cooper. She gasped. Choking on the bite of sandwich, she started coughing. As she reached for her glass of water to wash the food down, she tipped the glass over.

Coop quickly set a small box down on the table, came up behind Rosy, and started patting her on the back to stop her from choking. Laughing, Martha hastily sopped up the water on the table with napkins.

After Rosy finally swallowed the bite, she settled down. Embarrassed, her flushed cheeks glowed red. *How could I do something so stupid like that in front of Coop?*

"I didn't mean to sneak up on you." Coop chuckled as he sat down with them at the table. "I just wanted to surprise you two girls with dessert for lunch."

"You certainly did surprise us." Martha grinned. "What's in the box?"

"Mom sent it." Coop opened the container. "Three pieces of huckleberry pie. It's left over from Wednesday night."

"Oh wow, thanks, Coop," Martha reached out with her finger, wiped some huckleberry juice off of the box, and licked her finger. "Mm...my favorite pie." Each of them served themselves.

Not wanting to choke again, Rosy took tiny bites, keeping her head down and her eyes on her pie, while the other two chatted.

Coop struggled with trying not to stare at Rosy and at the same time trying to make conversation. He was unsuccessful at both.

Coop looked over at Rosy. *She's even more beautiful with those rosy red cheeks.*

Finished with her pie, Martha put her fork down. "It's time for us to get back to work. We're a couple of minutes late now, so we better get going."

"Yeah, I need to go too. Dad's probably waiting on me to help fix fences." Coop stood and pushed his chair in. "I hope we get to do this again." He smiled, tipped his head at Martha, and winked at Rosy, making her blush again.

Knowing the girls were watching, he turned to leave, and walked off in his soldier stride with his shoulders back and chin up. Unexpectedly, he stepped on his boot lace, tripped, and stumbled, doing an awkward dance with feet and arms flailing. He grabbed a chair to stop himself from falling. The girls covered their mouths with their hands and giggled.

He knelt on one knee and tied his boot lace. As he stood up, he nodded to the girls again and walked away, embarrassed. *Now I know how Rosy felt.*

Martha smiled inside after watching Coop and Rosy during lunch. *Yup, they're crazy about each other.*

The next morning when Rosy was working in the laundry room, Martha sauntered in. "Hey, Rosy, I have an idea. It's senior prom in a couple of weeks. Why don't you invite Coop? I think he'd love to go with you."

Unsure if she was ready for anything on that level, Rosy was uneasy. Tendrils of her past threatened to pull her down again. She quickly pushed them away. "I've only met him the two times…I'm not sure."

"Come on, what do you have to lose?"

Rosy sighed. "I don't know. I don't really know him very well…Maybe he's not even interested. And besides, isn't the guy supposed to ask the girl?" She finished folding a sheet and placed it on the shelf with the others. "Anyway, I don't have a dress to wear."

Martha waved her off, leaned against a dryer, and crossed her arms. "Rosy, he's crazy about you. He said you were beautiful, remember? And I have a dress you could borrow, and what better way to get to know each other. It would be a wonderful first date." Martha grinned impishly.

Rosy pulled another sheet out of the dryer and started folding it. "I wouldn't feel right asking him. It's just not proper for girls to ask guys out. And he's five years older than me." Rosy continued to make excuses, but deep down inside, she was beginning to like the idea, and she really liked Cooper.

Martha rolled her eyes. "What if I suggest it to him? I can tell him you would like to go, and if he asks you, you'll go with him."

Rosy's heart jumped. She really did want to go with Cooper. "You'd do that for me?" The more she considered it, the more she liked the suggestion. But deep down inside, she was scared; whispers of the past gradually grew louder. Trying to silence the haunting voices, her resolve set in. *Father's already ruined my past life! I'm not letting him ruin the future too. If Mom can put the past behind her, so can I! I'm going to do it. If Coop will take me, I'll go.*

Determined, Rosy pulled her shoulders back and stood up straight. "Martha, I think I would like that." Her decision was made. "Would you ask him if he'd be interested in taking me?" With her mind made up, Rosy could feel excitement seep into her nervousness.

Martha grinned. "You bet. I'll tell him tonight when I see him at dinner at my parents' house. I'll let you know what he says."

Excited and nervous at the same time, Rosy worried as she pondered the idea. *He barely knows me. Why would he even want to ask me out?*

Having fallen asleep before Martha returned home that night, Rosy awoke early the next morning. All night, she'd dreamt of her and Coop out for an evening together. Barely able to keep her eyes open, she dragged herself into the shower. Groggily she mumbled, "Hopefully, a shower will wake me up."

After showering, Rosy put on her bathrobe and felt a little better. While standing in front of the mirror, combing her wet hair, thoughts of Cooper crept into her mind. She could think of nothing else. *I wonder what he told Martha.*

What if he comes by after work this evening? She continued combing her hair, trying hard to put him out of her mind.

Shaking her head, she puffed out a breath of air. *I have to get ready for work.* When she came out of the bathroom, she quickly laid out her nicest dress on the bed so she could be ready in case Cooper decided to come by that evening.

Martha was up and getting ready for school and work, too. Rosy tried to be patient and give her time to get dressed, but finally, she couldn't stand it any longer. As Martha slipped on her work shoes and pinned on her uniform cap, Rosy blurted out, "Martha, did you ask Cooper about the prom? You came home late last night, so I didn't have a chance to talk to you."

Before Martha could answer, there was a knock at the door. "Who in the world would come over this early in the morning?" Rosy hustled over to answer the door. Unexpectedly, she found herself standing face-to-face with Cooper. She couldn't believe her eyes.

Flabbergasted, her mouth dropped open. "Cooper…" Her heart skipped a couple of beats and then sped up.

Standing in the doorway, he grinned at her. "Good morning, ladies." Behind Rosy, Martha stood giggling.

Rosy bit her lip. *He looks just as good in overalls as he does his uniform.*

Coop stood with his hands on his hips. "I apologize for coming over so early, but I wanted to catch you before you took off for the day."

Nurse Bella, his mother, had escorted him to the girls' room and now stood behind him, arms crossed, a stern look on her face. He turned and glanced back cautiously at her and then turned back to Rosy. After taking a shaky breath, he cleared his throat and looked nervously into Rosy's eyes. "Rosy, I…uh…know that we don't really know each other very well yet, but I hear that your senior prom is coming up…and I would very much like to take you. Would you go with me to your prom?"

Rosy stood speechless. This man did something to her. For a moment, she stood stunned, then stuttered, "I-I would like to go with you." Then, pausing, she took a deep and determined breath, looked directly into his eyes, and confidently repeated, "Yes, I would love to go with you."

"Then it's a date." Cooper's face lit up. "I'll pick you up next week on Friday at seven o'clock." He looked over his shoulder at his mother standing behind him, then looked back at Rosy. "I guess I should let you girls get ready for work. I'll see you later." He winked at Rosy and then looked at Martha. "Thanks, sis. I owe ya one." He tipped his head, smiled, and left.

Nurse Bella watched him leave, then turned to Rosy. Stern look gone, she gave Rosy a smile and walked away.

Rosy fell back onto her bed and just lay there. *I can't believe what just happened. Cooper made a special point to come all the way over here at 6:00 in the morning just to ask me to the prom. He actually wants to go with me.*

Suddenly Rosy realized, "Oh no! Look at me!" Embarrassed, she jumped up off the bed and looked in the mirror. "Coop just saw me with my hair wet and stringy, and I'm still in my bathrobe!"

Martha beamed. She sat down on the edge of her bed. "Wow, Rosy, he must really like you if he still asked you out while you were looking like that." She giggled.

Rosy's cheeks flushed a bright pink.

Smiling, Martha continued, "I'll bring that dress from home for you. You can try it on tonight, but I'm sure it'll fit you. It's a beautiful dress, and you'll look gorgeous in it." Martha raced out the door, heading to work. "See ya later!"

Rosy sat on her bed, still in shock, having a hard time believing what just happened. *Wow! Maybe he does like me.*

"Rosy? Rosy...Rosy!" Nurse Bella stood at the open door and put her head in. "You are coming to work today, right? Let's get a move on!"

Rosy snapped back to reality.

She jumped up, dressed quickly, and rushed out.

The next week was hectic for Rosy. Between work, school, and homework, she was so busy that she didn't stop. But in everything she did, she was distracted. All she could think of was Cooper.

While Rosy went on with her busy life, she fought off unwanted thoughts that constantly pushed in around her, making her heart beat faster. She felt sick to her stomach. *What is Coop going to expect from me? Will he be like Father and the men he brought home?* She tried to push those thoughts away but was unsuccessful. The unwanted thoughts and old feelings hung around and found a dark spot in the back of her mind, hovering and waiting.

On the day before the dance, Martha practiced fixing Rosy's hair in a number of different ways. "How did your sisters fix their hair when they went to their prom?"

Rosy shrugged. "They both wore their hair down."

Martha squinted into the mirror. "Well, I like it this way best, curled and piled on top of your head with curls down in the back. It makes you look older," she said, standing back to admire her work.

Rosy looked at her hairdo in the mirror, turning her head from one side to the other. "I think I like it best this way too. Will you fix my hair like this for the prom?"

"Sure, I will. We'll make you gorgeous!" Martha grinned. "That way Coop won't be able to take his eyes off of you all evening."

"Who are you going with?"

Martha laughed. "James asked me. I think he might be the one." Both girls giggled and clasped hands.

"Martha, I've got another problem." She looked in the mirror at Martha's reflection as she spoke to her. "I've never danced before. I don't know how. What will Cooper think of me if I can't dance with him?"

"You can't dance?" Martha looked a little surprised. "Well, why don't I teach you right now? Let's turn on the radio."

For the rest of the evening, Martha taught Rosy the jitterbug, waltz, and the swing dance. They practiced each dance over and over. Rosy learned quickly and easily. "I sure hope I can remember these dances tomorrow at the prom."

"You're already better than Coop," Martha chimed in as the music played and she twirled Rosy around as they did the jitterbug. "You may have to teach him to dance again. It's been a few years since he has had a chance, and I'm sure he's out of practice."

Friday evening came at last. It was almost seven o' clock, and Rosy was ready. Her borrowed gown had a tight-fitting, black bodice with off-the-shoulder short sleeves and a long, full, black skirt with white polka dots. She wore new black heels that accented the black in the dress. Her dark brown hair was curled and piled on top of her head with small ringlets down the back of her neck and curls on the sides by her cheeks. Eyeliner and lipstick were the touches that brought everything together to bring out the elegance in her.

Martha stood back, dressed in a pink and silver strapless combo of her own, and applauded Rosy, clapping her hands cheerfully. "Perfect!" she exclaimed. "You look stunning. Now all you need is this—the final touch." Martha pulled a necklace from her pocket and held it up. "This is my mother's. She said you could wear it."

The fine silver chain held three diamonds, a large diamond in the middle and a smaller one on each side. Rosy's eyes sparkled. "Oh, Martha, it's beautiful!"

"They're not real diamonds, but they sure look like it." Martha placed the necklace around Rosy's neck and hooked it. As the diamonds in the necklace lay against the black background of her gown, they glistened. "Oh, Rosy, that's the perfect touch. You're so beautiful," she whispered. "Every guy there will want to dance with you. Every man, that is, but Jimmy." The girls giggled.

Martha reached out and brushed an errant curl of Rosy's hair back behind her ear. "Rosy, Coop's a lucky man!"

About that time, there was a knock at the door. Rosy panicked. "It's Cooper! Martha, I'm so nervous. I've never been on a date before. What do I do?" Rosy wrung her hands as she bit her bottom lip.

"Shh…calm down, Rosy. It's gonna be okay." Martha smiled at her friend. "First you open the door and let him in. He'll take over from there."

Rosy stood nervously and stared at the door. There was another knock. She walked apprehensively to the door and opened it. Cooper was standing in the doorway. "H-Hi Cooper." Rosy melted as she saw him standing there, looking very nice in his black suit and tie.

When Coop saw her, his eyes grew big. "Wow, you're even prettier than you were the first time I saw you, if that's possible." He smiled broadly and stepped into the room.

"Here, I brought this for you." He set a little gold box on the table and opened it. After taking out a corsage of small yellow roses, he carefully pinned the spray of small flowers on her dress. The yellow flowers, accented with soft white baby's breath, were the perfect complement to her gown.

"Thank you, Coop. Yellow roses are my favorite."

"You're welcome." Cooper offered her his arm. "Shall we go? We don't want to be late. I want to dance every dance with you."

Rosy turned to Martha. "Thanks for all the help, Martha. I'll see you at the dance." As she took Coop's arm, she smiled shyly at him. Her heart jumped when he placed his hand over hers. His touch sent a tingle through her body. She wasn't ready for the surge of emotion she felt. As she walked out the door arm-in-arm with Coop on their first date, a thought came to her. *Cooper may be the man of my dreams.* She put the thought out of her mind immediately.

As they walked out the door, she asked, "Cooper, how did you know that I like yellow roses?"

"I have my ways." He glanced quickly back at Martha and smiled as he opened the passenger's side car door for Rosy.

While he walked around to the driver's side, Rosy's thoughts wouldn't stop spinning: *I'm on my first date with Cooper, wearing my first formal gown, and going to my first dance.* She marveled at this new life she was living.

After a short drive, they arrived at the high school. As Coop offered Rosy his arm again, she beamed. She felt beautiful walking beside him, like she was floating on a cloud in her own little dream world. But when they arrived at the gym door, her bliss disappeared; anxiety set in. Her heart started beating faster and uneasiness filled her body. This was all so new to her.

Standing with Rose in the doorway of the gym, Coop could tell she was nervous by the way she clamped her hand tightly around his arm. He gently tightened his hand on hers for reassurance. As she looked nervously into his eyes, he grinned at her and nodded his head. "Let's go," he whispered.

Cooper proudly led her through the doorway and into the building. Immediately they had the attention of most of the people there. The guys stopped and stared at Rosy as she breathlessly glided into the ballroom, holding onto Cooper's arm. The girls gazed as Cooper, an older, handsome, man with the muscular physique and the manner of a soldier, escorted the beautiful young woman.

Cooper led Rosy over to the refreshment table and filled two cups with punch. Music filled the room while they stood, sipping their drinks and watching couples dance. Coop turned to speak to her. But when their eyes met, everything in the room gradually faded into the background; all he could see was Rosy. He closed his eyes and took a deep breath. When he opened them, the sights and sounds of the room flooded back to his senses. His heart began to beat quicker as he gazed into her eyes.

When the song stopped and another began, Cooper politely took Rosy's cup and placed it on the table beside his. Taking her hand, he playfully bowed as he asked, "May I have this dance?"

Her skin tingled, sending shivers up her arms. She smiled and nodded her head yes. He clasped her hand tighter and led her onto the dance floor. When he put his arm around her waist, her mind went blank. All her newly learned dance steps disappeared. All she wanted to do was melt into his arms.

As they stepped out on the dance floor and he put his arms around her waist, he ached to pull her close and hold her tight. Their eyes met again; their gaze tangled. Her gentle touch caused every nerve in his body to quiver. Cooper swirled her around to the music, then pulled her close. He never took his eyes off of Rosy the whole dance; he couldn't. He stayed by her side all evening and danced every dance with her.

Rosy felt she was living her dream. *I never want this evening to end.*

The time flew by; the prom ended before they knew it. Disappointed that the dance was over, Cooper tenderly took Rosy's hand and escorted her out to the car. "Rosy, it's been a wonderful night. I've had the honor of escorting the most beautiful and kindest woman I've ever known."

Rosy blushed and looked into his eyes. "Thank you for bringing me, Cooper. I've had a wonderful time too."

He held her hand as he slightly bowed and opened the car door for her. "Your ride awaits, Miss." He chuckled.

"Why thank you, sir." She playfully tilted her chin up and put on airs, pretending to be a woman of high society. Then she giggled.

Cooper drove Rosy back to the hospital. After he got out of the car and opened the door for her, they stood on the sidewalk in awkward silence, staring at each other. Finally breaking the stillness, Cooper asked, "Rosy, would you like to go for a walk in the rose garden? It's a beautiful evening."

The stars twinkled through the dappled darkness and light posts lined the sidewalks, lighting the way through the garden. The night was calm and warm.

"Cooper, I'd love to." He reached out and offered his hand to her. She welcomed it with tenderness as she gently placed her small, soft hand, into his large callused hand.

As the two strolled in the night air, they chatted about the evening and just enjoyed being with each other. After a short while, Cooper stopped, took both of her hands, and looked softly into her eyes. "I had a wonderful evening tonight. Thank you for going with me. And I was wondering…would you like to go out to dinner next Friday?"

Rosy felt like she was still floating on a cloud, this just topped off the night. She didn't hesitate. "Yes, I'd love to go out with you, Cooper."

"It's a date then. I'll see you Friday, and by the way, you can call me Coop if you want; most everyone else does."

"Okay." Her eyes glistened teasingly as she smiled. "I just might do that."

He continued to hold her hand as he walked her to the front entrance of the hospital. When he started to leave, he turned to her, smiled, and winked.

She watched him walk back down the sidewalk into the darkness. Then she slowly closed the door. Rosy's thoughts drifted back over the evening as she floated down the hallway to her room. She fell back on her bed and lay staring at the ceiling. For the first time, she didn't think about her past; she began to imagine what her future might be.

***

Coop and Rosy went out to dinner the next week—and the next week, and the next. They started dating regularly. Rosy loved being with him. He made her feel so special, so beautiful, so safe. He was good to her; she never felt threatened by or fearful of Coop. In fact, she felt the opposite of how she had felt around Father, fearful, nervous, and full of hatred.

Rosy worked and studied hard, and Coop admired her for that. He loved her determination to succeed. In fact, he loved everything about her. Not only was she beautiful, she had a gentleness about her. He admired her compassion for others and marveled at her amazing spirit.

But there was another side of Rosy that kept nagging at Coop in the back of his mind. He noticed at times she would withdraw and become quiet and reserved. He also noticed that she didn't talk much about herself or about her family. The only person she spoke about was her mother, but there was rarely a mention of her father. He reasoned that maybe she didn't talk about her dad because he had died so young. Coop decided not to press the issue. At times, he could see a sadness in her eyes and wanted to comfort her, but he didn't know how.

Oh Rosy...how I wish I could fix what's hurting you so...

THIRTY-ONE

Coop came running down the hospital hallway, yelling, "Hey, Martha! Rosy! Did you hear?" He grabbed Martha and swung her around in a circle, then excitedly hugged Rosy. "The war in Europe is over! It's over!" The three cheered, yelled, and hugged, as they joyfully celebrated along with the other people in the hospital hallway.

Martha clasped her hands and squealed, "That means our brothers might be coming home soon!"

Rosy lay in bed, exhausted. It had been a trying day. Sleep eluded her, again. She was so tired she couldn't sleep. Her mind never seemed to stop. *My time is taken up with work, classes, homework, and church. She tossed and turned in bed. I have so much I need to do and not enough time to do it. And somehow, I need to make more time for Coop. I only see him on Saturdays. Something has to change.*

Systematically, she ran her schedule through her mind over and over again. *I can't give up my work and classes, and I won't give up seeing Coop. I can come up with only one option. I guess church and God lose out.* Feeling that this may not be a good choice, she felt a slight check in her spirit but pushed it down, justifying her decision. Her relationship with Coop needed to be a top priority.

She quit attending church and started spending more time with Coop. Every other Sunday, she worked at the hospital, and the other she spent with him.

Martha became concerned. One morning before work, she sat on her bed, leaning back against the headboard. She glanced at the Bible laying on the dresser and then at Rosy. Martha knew she should talk to Rosy about church but sat quietly, fidgeting with her hair as she contemplated what she should say.

Rosy sat at the small table, studying. Martha finally stood and walked over, pulled out a chair, and sat beside her. "Rosy, why don't you come to church with me anymore? We all miss you. I've had many people ask me why you weren't there, and I didn't know what to tell them."

Rosy flipped through the pages of her science book and then closed it. "Martha, I do miss going to church. I learn so much when I go. However, I need to spend more time with Coop, and he's not interested in going. I asked him if he'd like to go with me, but he refused. He said something about not wanting to go to church to worship a God that lets millions of people die in the war. He questioned why a good God would allow it. I wonder that too. I'd love to come, Martha, but honestly, I'd rather spend the time with Coop."

Martha rested a hand on Rosy's arm. Tears fell on her hand when she looked up. "I know the war changed Coop. He used to love going to church, but Rosy, he needs God and so do you."

A sadness for Rosy started growing in Martha's heart. She knew God had to be Rosy's own choice. Martha stood and pushed the chair in. She smiled a sad smile. "Thank you for being honest with me, Rosy. I'm sorry you're not coming anymore. If you change your mind, let me know. I want you to remember, I'm praying for you both."

Martha left for work; her heart heavy. *Did I do the right thing introducing them? Coop is a good man, but both him and Rosy need God.* "Lord Jesus, please touch their hearts and help them to see that You love them and they both need You. I pray for their salvation."

Bombs fell in a constant rain of dark destruction. In the near distance, shelling, artillery fire, and the rapid tat-a-tat of rifle disrupted the night. Private First-Class Cooper Grear stood knee deep in dead bodies and mangled leftovers of both ally and enemy remains. A thick, frozen mist slowly settled in around him and over the dead soldiers that lay on the scarlet snow-covered battlefield. Private Grear ran across the snow-packed fields from body to body, looking for wounded men he could carry back to safety. As he looked down, he noticed his own combat boots had holes cut in them and that his toes were sticking out, black and frozen.

"Private Grear," shouted the sergeant, "load up those bodies onto the flatbed truck and get them outta here!"

A small truck sat idling just a few feet away, steam rising from its engine in the cold air. Grear began dragging the dead and mangled bodies to the truck one by one and struggled as he piled them, like cordwood on the flatbed.

As Grear tended his gruesome duties, blood flowed from the lifeless bodies, dripped down his arms and chest, and flowed down the sides of the truck. While wiping the darkening blood from his face with his hands, which were themselves covered in blood, something strange and out of place caught his eye. Small and clean, ivory in color, it contrasted with the blackness of the congealing blood. From a distance, the object seemed to glisten. Letting go of the body he was loading, Grear rushed over to see what it was that had captured his attention. Forgotten, the body fell unceremoniously from the flatbed, arms flailing, and struck with a dull thud on the frozen ground.

As Grear slowly walked closer examining the object, he could see it was a woman's ring on an ivory-colored hand. Startled, he rushed to get closer. He stooped over as he inspected the hand; it had been blown off at the wrist and was still oozing blood. Staring at the hand, deep down inside, Grear could feel the interwoven relationship of the promise of life and the finality of death. Rocking back on his haunches, he rubbed his hand across his face; his breaths were suddenly shallow and rapid. And in spite of the cold, a hot sweat broke out across his forehead. The sight of the severed hand shook him to his core. Using all the self-control he had, he bent over, and with a tenderness that betrayed his position, he picked it up. The fingernails were clean and well-manicured, and the simple ring adorned the ring finger of the hand. Compassion for the unknown woman filled Grear. "What do I do with this?" he whispered under his breath.

Through the frosty mist, he saw a faint outline of a bombed-out church in the distance. Grear rose to his feet and headed toward the church. *Maybe there's a priest or someone there. They'll know what to do.*

Resting the woman's hand across both of his, he stumbled through the field of the mangled bodies. With great caution, he picked his way through the dead bodies as he rushed over to where the church stood like an island of peace in the middle of chaos. The mist closed in around him as he entered the broken-down building. Near the transept stood a priest, his cassock clean and pressed. Grear couldn't say a word as he gently handed the severed hand to the holy man. The priest accepted the hand graciously, nodded to Grear, and disappeared into the mist.

As Grear turned to leave, a beautiful woman slowly materialized in front of him in the thick fog. She silently reached out to him. He could see that her left hand was missing, blood oozed from her wrist. Horror rose inside him.

"Go! Go back!" he yelled. "It's not safe here! I'm sorry. I'll get your hand back! I'll…" He turned and ran back towards the church, slipping into the thickening mist while looking for the priest.

Half-awake and full of fear, Coop cried out, "Hey, Holy Man…"

Startled by his own voice, he woke up trembling. Once awake, he realized the nightmare had returned, again. He swung his legs off the side of the bed, sat up, and hid his face in his hands. "No, not again." *Why do these dreams continue to haunt me? How many times do I have to relive the pain of the war?*

He slumped back onto the bed, lying awake until he quit trembling. Forcing the grim images back below the surface of his conscience, he knew that as bad as the dream had been, it paled in comparison to what he had actually experienced. His adrenaline finally dissipated, and he slipped back into an uncomfortable slumber.

Graduation day finally came. The long hours of work had been a challenge, but Rosy was being rewarded for her effort; she was graduating with high honors. A couple of years ago, she didn't think this would be possible.

Rosy nervously adjusted her graduation cap to sit neatly on her head. Stage fright slowly set in. *This'll be the first time I've stood before a crowd. I-I can do this.* She took a deep shaky breath. *I can do this.* she repeated over and over in her mind. Anxious, she stood tall, determined to show everyone how proud she was of her accomplishments.

The music, 'Pomp and Circumstance', began. She stepped off in a long line with her fellow graduates. They marched up the aisle and sat down in the rows of chairs in the front of the gym. After welcomes, speeches, and congratulations were made, the graduates lined up to get their diplomas. Waiting for her name to be announced, Rosy shifted eagerly from one foot to the other, ready to step off.

"Rose Pearse!" the announcer finally called. Rosy stepped out proudly, walking up the steps and across the high school stage. The principal presented her the diploma. "Rose, you're graduating with high honors! Congratulations!" She accepted the document, shook his hand, and thanked the administration for all of their help.

People in the audience began applauding, yelling her name, shouting, and cheering. Rosy turned and faced the audience. Thrilled and proud, suddenly her stage fright was gone. Throwing her arms up in the air and holding her diploma high in both hands, she grinned from ear-to-ear. At the same time, at the top of her voice, she let out a loud, "Yahoo! I did it!" She did a little tap dance across the rest of the stage, jumped down the steps, and ran over to her friends and family. She hugged them all. This was the biggest milestone in her life so far.

━━━━━⟫⟪━━━━━

The sun, newly awoken, was not too hot yet, and the breeze coming through the valley was still cool. Rosy enjoyed the warmth and strength of Coop's hand as it enveloped hers. She smiled to herself as they walked down the sidewalk. She loved the feel of the calluses that spoke of a man who was not afraid of hard work. Cutting her eyes to the side, she brushed away a strand of hair lifted by the light breeze as she stole a quick glance at Coop. All around them, silence seemed to hold the rose garden in its grasp. It felt as if they were the only people around, and that was just fine with her.

With high school behind her and nursing school completed, Rosy could enjoy her summer by spending more time with Coop. They followed the sidewalk as it wound in a lazy pattern around the building and eventually led through the heart of the rose garden. Originally created as a place for recuperating patients to find peace and solace, it served perfectly as a place for young lovers to steal away.

Rosy snuck another peak at Coop and smiled as hopeful thoughts snaked through her mind: *I wonder if Coop feels about me the same way I feel about him.*

Coop looked at her and smiled. "What?"

"Nothing, just thinking."

They walked in silence for the next few minutes, enjoying the sun and each other. The breeze picked up, teasing her hair again; the gusts of wind ruffled the varied bushes, raising a chorus of fragrances that tempted their senses. The day was full of promise.

Coop squeezed her hand, and a soft chuckle escaped his lips. "I love Sundays."

She looked at him and laughed. "I enjoy Sundays with you. The weekend is the only time we really have to spend together." He smiled, causing his cheek to dimple just the way she liked it. He was beautiful…he was kind…he was loving. *He is the man of my dreams, the love of my life. Love?* She gasped, surprised at what she was feeling.

Of course, she didn't say these things out loud, but only thought them as she enjoyed looking at him. She wondered where this relationship was headed.

She unexpectedly stiffened as memories of who—of what—she had been—came back to her. Like an unwelcomed guest who barged in and refused to leave, the images from her childhood returned with a vengeance.

Coop gave Rosy's hand a gentle squeeze. She looked up at him and forced a smile. He studied her profile, watching as she worked her jaw, imagining her chewing on a thought. *Gosh! Even when she is just thinking, she is beautiful.*

He loved the shape of her delicate hands as she fussed with errand strands of hair that were blown free by the wind. *Come on, Coop, you can face a German bunker, but you're afraid to talk to the woman you love?*

Where did that thought come from? He rubbed his chin with his free hand and wasn't surprised to find a sheen of sweat that had nothing to do with the sun. He swallowed and cleared his throat.

Reaching the center of the rose garden, Coop asked, "You wanna sit down, take a break?" They were the first words either of them had spoken in quite a while.

Rosy, startled from her thoughts, looked up at him, a soft smile pulling at the corners of her lips. "Sure, I'd love to." She returned the squeeze to his hand and in that moment she was back. For now, the memories had been safely tucked away.

They sat quietly as neither was comfortable admitting how strongly they cared for the other.

Rosy broke the silence. She tipped her head up and looked inquisitively at him. "Coop, you told me that when you tried to join the Navy, they wouldn't accept you because of your eyesight. What is wrong with your eyes?"

"Well, when I was a kid, I was hit in the left eye with a rock. It damaged my eye and left me almost blind on that side. A few years later when I wanted to join the Navy with my buddies, I couldn't pass the vision test and the Navy wouldn't accept me."

Coop shrugged. "So, I stayed home when they left for the Navy." He paused. "But...I guess I was lucky. My best buds were stationed at Pearl Harbor when the Japanese attacked. They all lost their lives during the bombing." He looked painfully out into nothingness and shuddered with the anguish of the memory.

Rosy could hear the sorrow in his voice.

Coop looked down at the sidewalk. "After the United States declared war, the Army wasn't as picky and started drafting anyone they could get. The Army accepted me after the war started but would not assign me to a combat unit. Instead, they sent me for police training at the Military Police School."

"Where were you stationed in the war?"

He turned and looked at Rosy as he spoke. "I was part of the 75th Infantry Division and was stationed in Europe."

Compassion filled Rosy's heart when she realized this was not an easy subject for Coop to talk about.

"The 75th Infantry Division was stationed in a number of places. My first and only battle was in Europe. We were part of The Battle of the Bulge and had never been in combat before. Since my rank was Private First Class in the Military Police, my job was law enforcement. I also got the clean-up jobs. I was assigned to help control the chaos and to clean up the towns and battle fields. I, uh…I still have nightmares about the death and destruction."

Coop swallowed hard, blinking to keep the liquid in his eyes from escaping. He cleared his throat. "I was one of the lucky ones. Someone must have been watching over me." He paused for a moment as if weighing his words. "Only forty percent of the soldiers came home from that battle alive. That's twice I could have been killed, Pearl Harbor and Battle of the Bulge."

"Coop, do you think it was luck, or could it be that God was protecting you?"

He contemplated for a bit. "I don't know. It could be luck. I suppose it could be God. Whatever or whoever it was, I'm glad I'm alive." He winked at her.

She looked at her feet, smiled shyly, and blushed.

Just as quickly, her eyes focused on him again. "Coop, when I went to church with Martha a number of weeks ago, one of the scriptures the preacher quoted was Jeremiah 29:11. It talks about God's plan for each of our lives. I memorized it when I was studying Martha's Bible. It says, '…*For I know the thoughts that I think toward you, saith the LORD, thoughts of peace, and not of evil, to give you an expected end.*' Is it possible God allows us to go through things so he can get our attention, so He can carry out His plans in our lives?"

"I don't know," replied Coop. "I was raised to believe in God, but after the things I saw over in Europe, I'm not convinced there even is a God. If there is, why does He let things like that happen? That's why I don't go to church anymore."

While she tried to listen to Coop, Rosy's own memories flooded her mind. As they barged in, her uncertainty overflowed with recollections of abuse and poverty. In her own mind, she asked the same question Coop asked: *If God really does exist and really does love us, wouldn't He want the best for us instead of putting us in situations that hurt us?*

Rosy looked up and smiled as Coop put his arm around her while he continued talking, but his voice faded away again as her own thoughts continued to clutter her head. Then a glimmer of hope flashed through her mind. *I want to believe in God. Like the verse said, I want to have peace in my life.* The confusing thoughts swirled in her mind. *But I can't forget the evil, the hunger, and the pain that I've been through.*

She glanced at Coop, and again spoke her thoughts. "In church I heard that God, the Creator, wants to be in our lives. The pastor says that God really cares for us and uses these things to teach us to depend on Him."

An anger filled Coop's eyes as silence permeated the air around them.

After hearing Coop tell of some of the hard times he had been through and seeing the anger in his eyes when she talked about God, Rosy grew quiet and sat silently beside him, not wanting to upset him more.

THIRTY-TWO

During the next few months as Coop and Rosy continued to see each other, their feelings for each other deepened.

One evening, Rose sauntered down the sidewalk to the rose garden, thinking of their relationship. She loved Coop deeply, but doubt of a future flooded her thoughts. Cruel whispers in her thoughts continually reminded her of her past: *Can I trust Coop, or are all men like Father? Coop's different than the other men...isn't he?*

She tried to squelch the doubts, but to no avail.

She stepped off the sidewalk, found a large rock, and sat down on it. Immediately, thoughts of Willie came back to her mind. She hugged herself and shivered against a chill that had nothing to do with the temperature.

From a nearby bush, she picked a rose, plucked the petals off one at a time, and placed them in her mouth as she gently bit down, releasing the delicate flavor. Besides, Coop knows nothing about my past. *If he finds out...I can never let him know. Is there even a possibility of a future for us?*

She brushed away tears and sat up straighter, but the heaviness of the memories remained with her.

Coop and Rosy sat at a table in the cafeteria at the hospital, each sipping on a bottle of Pepsi Cola during her afternoon break. The cafeteria was empty and quiet except for the clattering of pots and pans escaping from the kitchen door.

Coop picked up his bottle of cola and took a sip. His stomach felt uneasy.

He kept his voice soft and low, "Rosy, the weekdays are so busy that we aren't able to see much of each other during the week. The only time we get to see each other is every other Sunday and some Saturdays when you're not working. And even a lot of that time is filled with you doing homework. My work on the farm keeps me busy too."

Rosy fidgeted with her bottle and looked at him with puzzled eyes as she wondered where this conversation was going.

"Let's get together Friday night, even if it's just for a little while."

Rosy let out a small sigh and agreed. "I'd love to. Let's do it. I'll spend time with you anytime I can."

Coop hesitated, "Why don't we meet this Friday night, after work?"

Butterflies fluttered in her stomach as feelings of love tugged on her heart strings. She finally had admitted it to herself. *I've fallen in love with this man. I fell in love with him the first time I saw him. But I can't tell him…It's not proper for a woman to declare her love first. Besides, we've only been going out a few months.*

She bit her lip. *How does he feel about me? Could he love me? Her breath caught as another thought flitted through her mind; What if he doesn't feel the same way I do?*

She quickly glanced at him. "I'll plan on it, Coop, but I don't get off work until 10:00 p.m. I can meet you about 10:15.

"Oh no…" Rosy suddenly panicked as her eyes cut to the wall clock. She jumped up from the chair and took off. "I'm late, I have to get back to work right now." She looked back at him as she rushed off. "Bye, I'll see you Friday night."

Grabbing her hand as she hurried by, he stopped her. "Sounds great. Let's meet at the rose garden Friday night after work. And Rosy…Rosy, I love you."

Taken by surprise, Rosy gasped and froze, her hand still in his. She turned toward him, her eyes anxiously locking onto his. Her lips parted, "Oh, Coop, I…I love you too." Rosy smiled affectionately as they gazed at each other.

"Hey, Rosy!" Martha called from the hallway, bringing Rosy back to reality. "You're late for work!"

Rosy hesitated, gave Coop a quick peck on the cheek, and rushed out of the cafeteria.

Coop sat at the table for a while, thinking about what had just happened, and he couldn't help but smile. *I can't believe it.* He reran her words over and over in his mind. *She loves me too!*

The next morning, Coop sat on a large hay bale in the back field of his parents' farm. He pulled a stem of hay from the bale, put an end in his mouth, and started chewing on it. He crossed his arms and legs as he sat deep in thought, reflecting on the last few years. Gazing out over the green fields, painful memories of the war filled his mind. Agonizing memories of the conflicts plagued him constantly. No matter how hard he tried, he couldn't shake them.

What if I can't put the past behind me? I love Rosy; she's my whole life. I love her more than I ever thought possible. Can I be the kind of man she needs? Is there even a possibility of a future for us?

One Saturday evening, Coop and Rosy met at the rose garden again. It had become their own special place to steal away from everything and everyone. The evening was cool as the sun slowly descended toward the horizon. Roses of all kinds were in full bloom; their colors were vibrant and their fragrance enchanting. The sun's rays danced through the tall evergreens, casting long shadows, creating a perfect shaded area for a quiet evening meal.

Rose, as Coop had taken to calling her, unpacked a picnic basket for her and Coop. Sitting in the grass of the well-manicured grounds, the two enjoyed a peaceful dinner and each other's company.

After they finished eating, Coop stood up, walked over to a rosebush of small yellow roses, and picked a few for Rose. He handed her the flowers, smiled, and kissed her on the cheek. She blushed as she accepted them. "Thank you, Coop. You're so sweet to me." He sat down beside her, leaned against a tree, and put his arms around her waist as she leaned back and rested against him.

Reaching into his shirt pocket, Coop pulled out a small blue rectangle-shaped box. "Rose, I have something for you."

As he handed her the long, flat box, she lifted questioning eyes to his face. "You brought me a present?" She reached out a trembling hand to accept the gift. "Th-thank you Coop! It's not very often I get a gift."

"I brought this back from Germany. I can't play it, and since you love music, I thought maybe you might like it." Coop watched as Rose eagerly opened the small box.

With her thumb and forefinger, she carefully reached in and took out a harmonica made of brass and dark brown wood. She ran her fingers over the smooth, shiny instrument. "Oh, Coop, it's beautiful." She eagerly smiled.

He leaned forward and kissed her again. "I love to see you smile." She blew a series of discordant notes on the harmonica. They laughed. Rose continued to experiment with the harmonica for a bit while Coop put his hands over his ears and chuckled at her.

Still leaning back against the tree, he put his arms around Rosy's waist again. She snuggled up against him as he pulled her closer. "Thank you, Coop, for the harmonica. You're so thoughtful. I promise, I'm going to learn to play it." She carefully put the small instrument back into its box.

Coop and Rose fell into comfortable silence and relaxed for a short while. As Coop leaned his head against the tree trunk, his eyes seemed to stare into nothingness as his gaze slipped into a different time. For some reason, pictures of his childhood started to roll slowly through his mind's eye. Stories of his youth began to filter through his thoughts.

He sifted a strand of Rose's hair through his fingers, and she nestled back against him. "My parents," he began as if talking to himself, "struggled to feed us. I have memories of my mom lying on her bed crying because she had no food for us kids."

Surprised at his reminiscing out loud, Rose turned and looked at him. She could sense the heaviness he felt.

"My father and mother must have spent hours on their knees, praying for enough food for the next meal. When we moved here, Dad farmed a homestead and luckily, got a job at the feed mill." He laughed a self-depreciating laugh and didn't feel Rose stiffen.

Rose panicked; her heart started to race. *Martha told me about their dad working at the feed mill. What if their dad and mine knew each other?* Her face grew pale and her skin became clammy. *Emmett is such a small town; everyone knows everyone else.* As she tried to maintain her composure, Coop's words faded in and out. Rose remained silent and took deep, slow breaths to help settle her fears, refocusing on what Coop was saying.

"The Depression didn't help either, and Mom hadn't found work at the hospital yet. Business at the feed mill was very slow, and my family spent years barely scraping by. We only made it because Dad worked the two jobs, the feed mill and farming, and us boys worked the fields too. But many nights, our family still went to bed hungry."

Forcing herself to speak, Rose thought carefully about every word she said. "You know, Coop, we went through that too, and most families were in the same fix."

"Yeah, I know." He nodded his head slowly. "So early in my teens, I promised myself that when I had a family, they would never go hungry. It was then I decided not to be a farmer. I would look for a more secure and dependable job." While Rose leaned back against Coop, listening, the cool breeze tousled her hair. He paused to brush her hair away from his face.

"What kind of job do you want?" Rose was curious. "What do you like to do?"

"I love to build things with my hands." Coop kissed her on the cheek and then adjusted his shoulders to get more comfortable as he leaned back against the tree. "I decided that carpentry would be a profession I would enjoy, and it pays well.

"Since soldiers are starting to come home, the timing is perfect. The construction business is on the rise. Carpenters are in great demand right now. So, after some on-the-job training, I'm planning on a career as a carpenter. The work is hard, but the money is good. My family will never go hungry." Coop wrapped his large, callused hand around her smaller, dainty hand. His tender touch sent a wave of goosebumps up her arm, making her heart flutter.

"What about you, Rose? What was your life like?"

She didn't respond at first; her thoughts were still on his 'My family would never go hungry.' Was he thinking about her? About them having a family together?

"Rose? What about you?" he asked again.

"About me what?" She ran the conversation back through her mind. "Oh, me. Well, I'm training to be a nurse…" She fought down the sensations of panic that came with the thought of him asking about her past. She forced a smile and squeezed his hand. *If Coop ever found out about what I was, he wouldn't have anything to do with me.*

She changed the subject. " It's getting late, and I have a lot of homework tonight. I need to go."

"But it's only seven o'clock. You have lots of time," he countered.

"I have lots of homework," she repeated and quickly started packing up the picnic dinner.

Coop looked confused but complied. He helped her pack up and then walked her back to her room.

After Coop arrived home that evening, he sat out on the back porch in one of his folks' weathered wooden chairs. As he leaned back, the chair tipped onto its' two back legs. Gazing out over the family farm, Coop saw everything but noticed nothing, his mind focused on the strange events of the evening. *Rose acted strange tonight. I wonder why?*

He reran the evening in his mind, trying to figure out if he had said anything that upset her. As he thought about the evening, his focus quickly switched to their relationship. Coop closed his eyes, took a deep, slow breath, and gradually released it. His chest filled with a love he never knew was possible. *We have only been dating for a few months, but I know with my whole heart this is the woman I want to marry and spend the rest of my life with.*

The idea played over and over in his mind. It wasn't a new thought. *I can't imagine my life without Rose. The more I think about it, the more I want her to be my wife.* After a short time of reflection, Coop made up his mind. I'm going to do it! I'm going to ask her to marry me.

Determined to follow through with his decision, Coop stood and started pacing nervously back and forth. *So, now the big question is how should I ask her? Should I take her to dinner and pop the question? Or maybe a picnic?* He ran his fingers through his hair. *A drive in the hills?* Coop had no idea how to propose marriage, and it scared him.

Coop panicked. *What if she says no?* He ran his fingers through his hair again, trying to wipe the thought from his mind.

During the next few days, Coop thought of nothing else. Slowly a plan started forming in his mind as he reviewed their past relationship. Whispering his thoughts, he smiled as the plan came together. "What about the rose garden? That place is pretty special to us. I could set up a table in the garden, plan a dinner, maybe even have one of my buddies be the waiter. After we eat, we can go dancing right there in the garden."

He stood up and smiled. *This is gonna be great.*

THIRTY-THREE

The Japanese Emperor Hirohito announced the surrender of Japan on August 15, 1945 and formally signed on September 2nd, bringing hostilities to an end. A few weeks later, surprising the Grear family, a letter came saying that Coop's brothers had been discharged from the Navy and were on their way home.

Coop's mother had plans. With her sons coming home from the Navy, she was going to host a celebration for the entire family. On the other hand, Coop's plans for the special dinner with Rose were already in the works and he was determined that nothing short of a new world war was going to stop that.

The week flew by and Saturday was there before he knew it. Coop was ready. The table in the rose garden was set up, the food cooked, and the waiter ready to serve. Coop had rehearsed his proposal a hundred different ways and finally figured out exactly what he wanted to say and how he would say it, word for word.

I sure hope everything goes just right. Wearing his best clothes and a nice dinner jacket that he had borrowed from a friend, he walked up to Rose's door, slicked his hair back, and tucked in his shirt. With a quivering hand, he knocked on the door.

"Hi, Coop!" Rose greeted him with a hug and a quick kiss on the cheek. Seeing him all dressed up sent a small shiver throughout her body. She smiled admiringly at him.

"You look really nice this evening. Why are you all dressed up?"

Giving her a sly smile, Coop replied her, "I'm taking you to dinner, and I'm cooking."

She smirked. "You're cooking? I didn't know you could cook." Rose giggled as she teased him. "I bet you're quite a chef."

He chuckled. "Thank you, and I think you'll be pleasantly surprised at my cooking—at least I hope you'll be."

She took his arm and looked at him inquisitively. "Where are we going—to your parents?"

"No, it's just a short walk from here." He led her down the sidewalk to the rose garden.

"We're eating here...in the garden?" She looked surprised.

Coop smiled but never said a word. Following the sidewalk, he led her to a shady area, surrounded by trees and large rose bushes. As they turned and walked between two of the larger red rose bushes, Rose gasped and placed her hand over her mouth. There, sitting on the cool grass, in the midst of rose bushes and shade trees, was a small table that was covered with a green table cloth and set with china place settings...and right in the middle of the table, there was a small vase of yellow roses.

"Coop, this is gorgeous! I can't believe you went to all this work for me!"

He held out his arm to escort her to the table. She took his arm as she playfully stood with her shoulders back and her chin in the air, then strolled pompously over as he escorted her to the table.

Pulling out her chair, Coop bowed. "Have a seat, ma'am." Giggling, she sat down as Coop helped scoot in her chair. Rose's grin stretched from one ear to the other. She felt lightheaded just thinking about Coop doing all of this for her. He pulled a chair out and sat down across from her.

As they sat chatting, Coop's oldest brother, Dan, who had just come home from the Navy four days before, stepped out from behind the bushes and trees. Dressed in a suit, with a serving towel folded neatly over one arm and a tray of drinks in the other, he lifted his chin and walked haughtily over to the table, playing his part as a waiter well. Rose's mouth dropped open. "Coop, you even hired a waiter!" She giggled as Dan served them.

"Here you go, ma'am." Dan smiled at her as he set the drinks on the table, serving her and Coop each a glass of water and a glass of lemonade. Walking over to a phonograph that was sitting on a small bench by a large rose bush, Dan wound it up and put on a record. Frank Sinatra started singing. Dan turned, nodded politely, and exited through the bushes. He soon returned with dinner on his tray. After carefully setting the plates of hot food on the table in front of Rose and Coop, he nodded again and quietly turned and walked back into the bushes.

The aroma of grilled steak made Rose's mouth water. The fresh corn on the cob and butter, mashed potatoes with gravy, and the green beans with chunks of bacon made for the perfect meal. Dessert was served after they finished the main course, each receiving a large slice of warm cherry pie that was topped with homemade vanilla ice cream. Coop's brother wound up the phonograph one last time and left them to enjoy the rest of evening.

Sighing contentedly, Rose asked, "Coop, did you really prepare this feast?"

"I fixed everything except the pie. I asked Mom to make it. I think that's a little beyond my cooking skills right now."

Rose laughed. "Well, thank your mother for baking it. She's a great cook, and her skills must have rubbed off on you. Everything was delicious. Coop, I can't believe you cooked all of this. The whole meal was wonderful, and your brother…" She reached over and placed her hand on his. "Thank you for doing all of this for me."

Coop winked at her, pushed his chair back, and stood up. He walked over to Rose, took her hand, and pulled her chair out for her. As Frank Sinatra crooned, Coop put his arm around Rose's waist and started to waltz. Rose laid her head on his soft, strong shoulder, and they danced slowly in the quiet of the evening, not taking notice when the music stopped. The sun set slowly over the horizon, sending out brilliant golden rays and painting the violet clouds a fiery orange and crimson in the distant heavens.

Coop held Rose gently in his arms as they slowly waltzed. *Now is the time,* his heart told him. *This is the perfect time to propose.* As he worked to muster up his courage, his heart beat faster and his blood pressure shot up. He felt short of breath. While they continued their slow dance, Coop tried to speak, but his voice would not come…not a sound would come from his throat.

The tension rose in him until he simply froze in place. Pulling in a deep breath, Coop forced himself to speak, but the words seemed to make no sense. "This is—no, I mean…I enjoyed…um…dinner for you. I-I sure liked Mom's pie. Would you…?" The words sounded like they came from someone else. Everything he had planned to say had vanished from his mind. He struggled to retrieve the words. *It can't be this hard to say a few words! Confronting that German bunker seems easier than saying what I need to say right now.*

Coop tried to concentrate on the words he wanted to say as he started dancing again. Not paying attention to anything else, he took a step back, his foot catching on a chair leg causing him to lose his balance. He fell backwards onto the table, pulling Rose over on top of him. The table collapsed, and yellow roses flew from the vase and scattered everywhere. Dirty dishes, leftover food, and drinks soared into the air and splattered down on them as they lay sprawled on the grass.

It all happened so quickly. Coop was mortified; Rose lay atop of him, looking surprised, and a little worried. After a quick moment, their eyes found each other as they realized what had happened. As the shock quickly wore off, Rose smiled and started laughing. Coop's quiet chuckle gradually rose to a hearty laugh.

Coop's stress disappeared and his voice returned as he lay on the ground in the mess. Chuckling, he took Rose's hand and looked into her eyes. "Rose, I love you so much. I fell for you the first time I saw you, and now I've fallen for you again." He grinned. "I want to spend the rest of my life with you. Will you marry me?"

The surprise in Rose's eyes was obvious to Coop. He had really caught her off guard, but her response was quick in coming. "Oh, Cooper! Yes. Yes, I would love to marry you." She paused. Then softly added, "But...but—"

Disappointment and despair hit Coop like a concussive blast. He had never really believed she would say no.

Rose was quiet for moment, and then she spoke, "There's something I need to say...some things I need to tell you about my past."

Confused, Coop waited anxiously for Rose to continue.

She stared first into the darkening sky and then back at Coop, trying hard to look him in the face. She took a breath and it caught in her chest. Pressing a hand to her heart, she mumbled, "Can we go back to my room to talk?"

Silently, Coop took her hand and carefully helped her up as they brushed off the food as best as they could. Hesitantly, he put his arm around Rose's waist and quietly walked her back to her room.

As they walked, she cut her eyes at his stoic face as tears silently streaked her own. She knew she had to tell him everything, and then it would be up to him. *I love Coop so much, but nothing can change the past, and after I tell him, I don't know if he'll feel the same way about me as he does now.*

Tears spilled down her cheeks and dripped onto her bodice.

Coop noticed her crying, but rejection and confusion kept his mouth closed. He looked at her again. *I thought she felt the same way about me as I did her. I thought she loved me.*

He stopped her outside her door. "Rose, what's going on? I thought you loved me."

She turned her face away but stayed near him. "Please, Coop, come inside. Let's not talk out here. I promise, I'll tell you everything."

Frustrated, he slammed a palm against the door but said nothing. Reaching past her, he opened the door and stepped back so she could pass.

Not saying a word, he followed her into her room. She sat down on the edge of her bed. Coop pulled up a chair and sat down facing her.

"Now, Rose, tell me what's going on."

She swallowed hard. Bile burned the back of her throat. Struggling to find words, she shuddered. "Coop...I love you so much, and I would love to be your wife. But...when

I tell you this, you probably won't want anything to do with me, and I know you won't want to marry me." She brushed the tears from her eyes with her sleeve.

Total silence blanketed the room.

Coop could see the pain in her eyes and wondered what had hurt her so. He reached a hand toward her, wanting to build a barrier between her and whatever it was that haunted her. He said her name softly. "Rose…"

And when she looked up, he saw that she was afraid he would reject her. "Oh, Rose," he breathed, "there's nothing you could tell me, nothing that you could have done that would change the way I feel about you."

She reflected on his words. *Maybe there is hope.* She closed her eyes, she dared not trust in hope.

Rose sat unmoving, thinking about how she should tell him, about what she had to say. Thoughts swirled in her mind: *He has to know everything if he's really going to marry me. I have to tell him the whole truth, or it isn't fair to him. But if I tell him of my past life, I'll lose him. It's better that he knows now than later, after we're married.*

Coop watched as a whole battery of emotions washed across Rose's face. In pain, he clenched and relaxed his fist. Breathing deeply, he waited for her to decide what the next step would be.

She raised her head and looked into his face. Their eyes locked. "Coop, promise me you will listen to what I have to say before you say anything. Promise me you won't get angry at me or try to get even with anyone, just leave it in the past."

Coop was really confused now and reached to squeeze her hand.

She pulled her hand away. "Please, Coop, let me finish." She hugged herself and sat back, another shiver racking her body. "I-I've never told anyone this before. My past…nothing can change it, and I'm afraid it's marred me."

Coop had no choice. If he was to hear what she had to say, he had to promise. "Alright, I promise."

Tears continued to stream down her cheeks. Rose's heart raced. Her mouth opened and closed like a fish out of water. Stilling herself, she collected her thoughts. "W-when I was growing up, my father drank…a lot. Father was a mean alcoholic." Rose took a deep, shaky breath and continued. "When he drank, he beat and abused my mom the most, but he also molested and abused all of us kids."

Coop's eyes grew cold as Rose looked into them. She began to tremble, but she knew she had to continue; for Coop's sake, he had to know.

"W-when I was s-six-years old, he lost his job and couldn't make a living, so he went to California to look for work; we went with him. He couldn't find much work there, so he drank more and became even meaner. On that trip, he did many unspeakable things, including killing a lady and my younger brother."

Coop's eyes turned colder. "Your brother…?" He snapped his mouth shut and shifted in his seat when he saw her expression.

"He replaced him with the dead woman's son. I promise, Coop, I'll explain everything—at least I'll try." She sighed deeply. "When we g-got back to the farm, Father still struggled to feed and support us over the next few years. Since he couldn't make a living, after a while he started bringing men home and charged money to let them have sex with us. If we didn't do what Father said, he would beat us…or worse. That's how Father got money."

The muscles in Coop's jaw tightened and he clenched his fists.

Rose stopped and lowered her face. Her heart pounded even harder in her chest. *Okay, I said it. I've told him the hardest part, I think.*

Rose trembled; she was afraid that he would blame her and afraid that he might take revenge on her family. Rose took another deep breath, gathered her courage, and continued. "Father would beat my sisters and me and sometimes force himself on us. Then when my brothers got old enough, he taught *them* to do the same." She wrapped her arms around herself, closed her eyes, and hung her head, ashamed. She couldn't look at him.

From somewhere deep inside, she found the courage to go on; "Eventually times got a little better financially, but even when times were better and he quit bringing men home, Father continued his cruelty. Mom had to get us away from him. She was afraid that we would get pregnant. She finally got us out of the house by getting us this job and schooling at the hospital." Rose paused and chewed on her bottom lip as she thought about the next words that she would say.

"About six months before you came home, Father died of a brain tumor. I don't have to worry about him anymore. He's dead. I've tried so hard to put the past behind me and to move on." Rose took a deep breath and let out a slow sigh. She reached up and pushed the hair back out of her face. Nervously she fidgeted with the hem of her skirt. "But I had to tell you…"

Coop sat quietly, but Rose could see the anger growing in his face as it flushed red and shadows darkened his eyes. The muscles in his jaws and arms became taut.

She thought hard about the next words she would utter. "S-so, C-Coop, you see, I'm used, I'm damaged." Her voice broke. "I'm not the girl that you thought I was, but I didn't have a ch-choice. I'm sorry. I'm sorry that I didn't tell you sooner." She started weeping so hard that her body shook and trembled. Releasing the pent-up hurt and anger and fear of being found out that she had held for so long, she slumped back onto her bed.

Coop exploded from his seat and kicked the bed. He balled his fists and looked for something to punch, his arm muscles rippling with anger and the effort used to control himself. Losing the battle, he growled and slugged the wall, leaving the skin on his hand torn and bleeding.

Rose screamed and scooted away. "Coop, I-I only told you because you needed to know," Rose desperately pleaded. "Please don't be angry at me!"

He aimed his hot gaze directly at her, turned, and left, slamming the door behind him.

Cold fear slid down her spine. Sitting in silence on the bed, unable to move, her whole inner being ached, her body quivered, and her heart shattered into a million pieces. *What have I done? What have I done? Coop will never speak to me again now that he knows about me.*

Rose closed her eyes, pressed her fingertips to her temples, and rocked herself compulsively. Her breaths heaved as she curled beneath the weight of her sorrow. She pressed the heels of her hands into her eyes and screamed, collapsing back onto the bed. Overwhelmed by her fear— that Coop would abandon her—had come crushing down on her. She could not breathe.

She pulled her knees tightly to her chest trying to squeeze out the pain that had filled her gut. *Why did I say anything? I should have just kept quiet.*

"He will never want me now. I've lost him…I've lost him for good." She shivered as ice crept through her veins.

*Father's dead…*She closed her eyes tight. *But he continues to ruin my life.* She cried silent tears as sobs wrenched her body from the depths of her broken heart. She cried until she had no more tears to shed, her heart numb, her mind blank.

———————————≈———————————

Coop stalked down the steps. His anger seethed. *How could anyone treat people like that, especially their own children?*

He turned and slugged the brick wall of the hospital with his other fist. He was so angry that he didn't feel the pain in his hands as blood oozed from his scraped knuckles. His rage turned to thoughts of murder.

I'd kill him for what he's done if he was still alive. He'd never touch anyone again. Coop needed to release the fury that festered inside of him. He had to release it, but he didn't know how. Then he thought of the other men and of Rose's brothers that had abused her and her sisters. His anger and hatred boiled even more. He stalked out to the street. The lights from the buildings gave him a clear view of the street through the darkness. Without thinking, he started to run. He ran like he had never run before. He couldn't stop.

This is my Rose that's been mistreated.

His fury fed his body. He ran faster and harder until he could run no more, and then he kept running, his mind racing even faster.

How could a father do this to his own daughter? How could he? Why?

349

Coop ran until the only things he could see in the darkness were the light of the stars and moon and the shadows of darkness in his mind.

Finally, he slowed down and stopped. He had no idea how far he had gone. He trembled as he fell to his knees in the middle of the road and cried out to God, to the God he had once turned his back on; "God, help me! Take my anger and hatred away. Help me to be the man I need to be for Rose."

Coop's emotions started to recede as an unanswered question materialized in his mind.

"God, I don't understand. Why did You let this happen to her, to her family? Please help her…heal her heart." As darkness stained the sky, Coop looked upward. "Help me…"

He wept.

But suddenly the stars faded away, and the rage inside him arose worse than before, but this time it was aimed towards God.

"God, You let this happen! You could have stopped it! It's all Your fault! Why? Why didn't You protect Rose and her family? If You're such a good God…" Coop continued to spew his anger. Eventually, he was spent: his body stopped trembling, he felt weak, drained—powerless.

He stood shakily, walked to the side of the road, and sat down in the grass. His emotions changed from anger, to sorrow, to confusion, to love, to hatred again and again. After he was physically and emotionally drained, a gradual sense of resolve began to grow in his heart.

His mind suddenly cleared, and thoughts of Rose flooded in on him. Realizing that none of this had been her fault, he started sobbing again. This time, it was not out of anger, but out of compassion and love for her.

What must she be feeling now? What does she think about me?

"My Rose, the woman I love, abused, broken, and scarred. But no matter what happened, no matter what she was forced to do, I still love her."

Then he thought of the anguish Rose had gone through, the fear and mistreatment inflicted on her throughout her life as a child and young woman. He thought of how hard it had been for her to tell him about it.

She was a victim. It wasn't her fault, and I ran out on her.

As Coop sat in the grass, he questioned himself: *Am I strong enough for both of us? Do I have the strength and love for her that I need to help support her through all this? Am I a good enough man for her?*

His determination set in. Unwavering in his own mind, he knew he could; he knew he had to.

That's the past. We're going to look to our future, not only for Rose, but for me too. I need to show her that I love her, no matter what.

Suddenly, his arms ached to hold her, to comfort her, to be there for her. His heart melted as he realized how much he really did love her. He leaped up and started running, but this time running back to her.

He couldn't run fast enough. *I've got to hurry. She needs me more now than ever. We just started, and I've failed her already.*

Coop stopped just outside the door of Rose's room. Pushing the door open, he saw her lying, unmoving, curled up on her side on her bed. His heart broke for her again. He wanted to go to her but wondered if he had the right to do so after the way he'd acted.

Light from the small desk lamp caressed the side of her face, and he could see that she lay expressionless, unaware that he had even entered the room.

He sat down on the bed beside her, and still she didn't move. He said her name softly, "Rose…" When she didn't answer he laid his hand on her shoulder. "Rose, I'm so sorry."

Full of shame and fear, she flinched and shifted but didn't pull away.

"Rose, I was a fool. I was so angry. I felt like I needed to punch someone, but not you. Never you, Rose. I was half way across town before I remembered your father was already dead and I couldn't reach him."

She rolled over and looked up at Coop. He pulled her up close and put his arms around her. She turned into his shoulder, her tears wetting his shirt. Holding her tight, he cried with her as she sobbed. He held her for what seemed like eternity, never wanting to let go.

Then ever so gently, he placed his fingers under her chin and tilted her face up towards his. Holding her gaze with his, he whispered quietly, "Rose, I love you so much. Marry me. I'll never let anyone ever hurt you again."

Rose leaned against him and placed the side of her head on his chest. As she sat quietly, she could feel his heart beating. A tiny bud of hope opened in her heart while they sat and held each other. "Coop, after all I told you, are you sure you still want me?" she whispered as she wiped her tears away with her hand.

He brushed her hair back from her face, then gently lifted her chin with his fingers again and gazed into her eyes. "I still want you because I love you, Rose," he whispered back. "For now and forever, no matter what." He kissed her passionately. It set every nerve in her body on fire. "Rose, I love you more than I ever thought possible, more than life itself."

As she looked up and stared into his soft, tender eyes, she felt as if they would take her in and swallow her up. She whispered, "Yes, Coop. Yes, I'll marry you."

He kissed her again. "Rose, let's go to the jewelry store tomorrow and pick out our rings, your engagement ring and our wedding rings. I want to make our engagement official. You can choose any ring you want."

She was at a loss for words. It took a few heartbeats to really believe what he had just said. *He really does love me, past and all.*

As she grasped the meaning, her heart jumped, skipped a few beats, and started to race.

He still wants to marry me.

"Hmm…Mrs. Cooper Grear. I like the sound of it," she whispered. "Mrs. Cooper Grear." After a few seconds of silence, Rose added, "Coop, there's one thing I need you to promise me. Please let all this go. This is all in the past, and I want to leave it there."

Coop didn't answer.

THIRTY-FOUR

The next evening, while sitting on the floor in Rose's room, munching popcorn and drinking soda, the two lovers began planning for their future

Rose held her hand out and examined the engagement ring on her finger. She beamed. "Coop, it's beautiful. It's really beautiful! I love it."

Coop sat contentedly gazing at Rose, knowing that she would soon be his wife and they would be together the rest of their lives. He surprised himself when a question effortlessly slipped from his mouth. "Rose, when do you want to get married?"

Caught off guard, she considered the question for a few moments before she answered. "Coop, I love you, and I'm excited to be your wife. I know that everything is happening so fast, but what do you think about a short engagement?"

"I'll marry you whenever you want, whenever you decide." He leaned over and kissed her gently on the cheek. "You set the date. When would you like to get married?"

Rose stood up, walked over to the calendar on the wall, and studied it. "How about…the middle of October, next month? That'll give me time to adjust to my new job. It'll also give us time to prepare for the wedding and find a place to live. What do you think?"

"I like it. If you want to plan for the wedding, I'll start looking for a place to live. And since I have a carpenter job with on-the-job training, and you've started your new nursing job, by then we should have a decent income to live on. What day would be good?"

Rose studied the dates. "How about the 20th? That's on a Saturday. That would give us a few weeks to get everything organized and ready. Will that be long enough?"

Coop wrapped his arms around Rose and kissed her on the forehead. "Let's plan on it. It's a date!"

Rose smiled at her future husband. "The 20th, it is!" She circled the number on the calendar. "I think we need to do something special to announce our engagement too. What do you think about inviting everyone over to the rose garden for a potluck? We could announce our engagement then."

"Sounds great to me. I'll let my family know, and you can let yours know, and we can also invite anyone else we want. Mm...I hope my mom brings pies." Coop licked his lips and patted his stomach. Rose and Coop crunched on their popcorn, drank their soda, and continued making plans.

A week later, everyone showed up at the rose garden with their dishes of food, wondering what the occasion was, but in the back of their minds, they all knew.

Shortly after everyone arrived at the rose garden, Coop stepped up on a bench of a picnic table and called for silence. "Hey, everyone, may I have your attention please. I have an announcement to make." The chatter continued. No one heard him as his voice was shaky and quiet. Rose put two fingers to her lips and let out a loud sharp whistle. Silence ensued as the crowd turned toward her. As Rose turned her attention to Coop, so did everyone else.

Clearing his throat, Coop tried again, this time louder. "Thank you, everyone! Thank you for your attention." he said almost yelling.

"I have an announcement to make." Smiling, he reached out, took Rose's hand, and helped her up as she stepped onto the bench next to him. He put his arm around her as they looked into each other's eyes. Her face beamed. Coop turned to the crowd and grinned. "I asked Rose to marry me, and she did me the honor of saying YES. WE'RE GETTING MARRIED!"

Everyone started clapping and cheering, "CONGRATULATIONS!"

"We're planning on a wedding on the twentieth of next month." Rose yelled, "and you're all invited."

Martha screamed as she clapped her hands and jumped up and down. "I knew it! I knew it the first time he saw you, Rosy. I could see it in his eyes and in yours. Now you're going to be my sister!" She grabbed Rose and danced up and down as she gave her an enormous hug.

"Congratulations, brother!" Larry stepped up to Coop and gave him a gripping hug. "You're a blessed man."

Excited for her daughter, Doty ran up to Rosy, and hugged her as hard as she could. "Oh, Rosy, I'm so happy for you. Coop is a wonderful man, and he'll be good to you. I'm so glad you found each other."

Charles stepped up, reached out, and shook Coop's hand. "Congratulations. If Rosy is anything like her mother, she's a wonderful woman."

"You lucky dog, you." Dan slugged Coop in the arm, gave him a quick hug, and patted him on the back. "I must have done my job well as waiter a few days ago. Maybe this time you can manage to stay on your feet." He grinned.

Rose could hardly contain her excitement. Surprising everyone, she pulled out her harmonica and then tossed Coop his Jew's harp. "Come on Coop, let's play 'em a song!" Over the last few weeks Rose and Coop had been practicing a lot on their instruments.

Coop gave a cheerful laugh. "Alright, let's do it. Let's play 'You are my Sunshine'." Coop and Rose wailed on their instruments. Rose played like a mad woman, and then started tap dancing along with it. Everyone joined in with the music and the festivities. It was a hand clappin', foot stompin' time of celebration.

As Willie watched the celebration from a short distance, he chatted with a few people who were sitting at his table and drinking punch. He also kept a close eye on Rosy as she wandered around the rose garden, visiting with friends. When he finally saw her by herself, he got up from the table and approached her. Throwing his arms in the air, he scowled at her. "Hey, sis, what's this about you getting married? How come you never told me? I had to hear about it now. I'm your brother and you should've let me know." He pulled a flask from his belt and took a drink.

Rose glared at him. "You stink like Father. It's none of your business. Stay away from me." She turned to walk away, but Willie grabbed her arm.

"Let go of me," she yelled and tried to pull away. "Leave me alone. You're not my brother anymore. You're nothing to me." As she struggled to break his grip, his hand slipped off her arm, leaving large scratches. Willie stepped forward; his arm raised as if to strike her. She glared at him as blood oozed down her arm.

Suddenly, Coop's fist landed solidly on Willie's jaw, leaving Willie on the ground at Rose's feet. Coop stood over Willie. "If you ever touch her again, I swear I'll—"

"Coop," Rose said, wrapping an arm around his waist, "Come on, he's not worth it."

With his jaw taut, Coop allowed himself to be pulled away. He continued to glare at Willie, remembering that Rose had asked him to let the past go. Coop relaxed some, but stood his ground between Willie and Rose. The fierce look on his face told Willie to stay away from them.

After settling down some, Coop glanced at Rose. He suddenly noticed the scratches and the blood trickling down Rose's arm. "What the." A fury like Coop hadn't experienced since the war engulfed him. Without thinking, he dove atop Willie and began raining down blows onto his unprotected face.

Rose screamed again and wrapped both arms around Coop this time, and with all her strength began pulling him back.

Willie flailed on the ground as Coop poured blow after blow upon him. Coop roared, "If you ever touch Rose again, I'll kill you!"

The small crowd swarmed around the fight in disbelief.

"Coop! Stop! Stop! Let him go!" Rose screamed and grabbed his arm. "Somebody, help me!"

Both Dan and Larry grabbed Coop by his arms and dragged him up. With Willie lying unmoving on the ground, Coop finally calmed down. Pointing at Willie, he said, "You'll leave Rose alone if you know what's good for you."

Willie violently nodded. He managed to get to his feet on his own and slowly backed away. He wiped the blood from his face with his arm and limped off, glancing back to make sure Coop wasn't coming after him.

Rose walked over to Coop and put her arms around his waist, holding him tightly. Protectively, Coop wrapped his arms around her shoulders. "Rose, he'll never bother you again."

For the first time in her life, Rose felt loved and protected. She knew she would be safe with Coop. He was not like the other men that had abused her. She couldn't explain it, but she felt that no matter what, Coop would be there for her.

Coop knocked hard on Rose's door, hoping she was home. "Rose!" he hollered, knocking louder.

After a few seconds, Rose opened the door, looking worried. "Hi, Coop! Is everything okay?"

He rushed through the door of the small room, breathless. "Rose, guess what?" He gave her a quick hug. "I found the perfect place for us to live after we're married. Dad has this little one-bedroom house at the corner of town, and it's empty. My grandma used to live in it.

"It's not very big, but it'll do until we can afford something else. It's close to the hospital, and you wouldn't have far to go to work. It's perfect for us. When I asked Dad about us living there, he said we could and that I could fix it up however we wanted. It'll take a few weeks, but I can do it. What do you think?"

Rose's face brightened as she clasped her hands. "Coop, it sounds wonderful. A house of our own...our very first home. I love the idea. Let's go see it now"

They hurried out to Coop's car and drove the few blocks to the house. As Coop and Rose toured the small home, they saw many possibilities.

"Coop, I love the house. I can see it needs lots of work, but I'd love to help you fix it up. Let's do it."

He smiled at her and folded his arms across his chest. "Then it's ours. I'll tell Dad we'll take it and fix it up. We'll move in on our wedding day."

"I've good news, too." Rose reached into her pocket and pulled out her paycheck. "I've been paid just in time to help fix up the house and buy other things we'll need." She took his hand and squeezed it, and he pulled her close and kissed her. Standing together, she rested her head on his chest.

Every nerve in her body tingled as he held her. "Our own home, Coop. That sounds so perfect."

"No! Get down!" shrieked Coop. Mortars came screaming down around him, exploding in the already bombed-out town. Artillery was going off in the distance. "Stay down!" he screamed as bombs rained down from the sky. A frightened child ran from a nearby exploding building, followed by his mother, who was trying to save him. "No! Stay down!" Coop screamed again. "No!"

"Coop, wake up. Coop. You're having a nightmare." Dan shook his brother and then took a step backwards. "Wake up."

With adrenaline rushing through his veins, Coop grunted and sat up, his fists clinched and teeth bared. Looking around, he immediately realized he was home. His brother was standing beside him, a look of understanding in his face.

"No...not another..." Coop moaned. His body trembling, he dropped back onto the bed and dragged his covers over his face.

THIRTY-FIVE

This was the day that Rose had dreamed of ever since she met Cooper…October 20th, 1945, the day she and Coop were to get married.

Rose stood nervously in her wedding dress at the entrance of the sanctuary. She gazed up the long aisle that led to the front of the room. She could see Coop in his Army dress uniform standing on stage with the parson by his side. They were waiting anxiously for the wedding to start.

Just the sight of Coop took her breath away. She forced herself to inhale deeply as she watched him nervously straighten his tie and adjust his jacket. Letting his arms fall to his sides, he clasped his hands and then released them. She could tell Coop was just as nervous as she was. Her body gave a quick shiver.

Any doubt she had ever had about marrying Coop was gone. *Coop, you're the love of my life.* Her breath caught as she took a deep breath, then released a large sigh.

The sparkle in her eyes highlighted the happiness that radiated from her being. Rose was a beautiful bride, and she was happier than she had ever been in her whole life.

Coop in his Army uniform and his brothers, dressed in their best suits that were accented with boutonnieres of yellow roses, all stood in front of the sanctuary beside the parson. Rose's sisters, Annabel, Carolyn, and now Martha, dressed in sleeveless dresses in various shades of yellow, held bouquets of yellow roses as they stood waiting to march up the aisle. Doty stood beside Rose.

When the organ music started, everyone turned and watched as the bridesmaids strolled up the aisle to the front of the large room. Then after a short silence, the prelude of the "Wedding March" boomed out. The guests immediately stood in honor of the bride. As the organ music started, Rose's heart jumped and then skipped a few beats. It was time. Rose loved that her mother was giving her away. Reaching out, she took her mother's arm and together they slowly stepped off, gliding up the aisle of the sanctuary side by side.

Coop couldn't take his eyes off of Rose as she floated slowly down the aisle to the front of the sanctuary. He had never seen her look more beautiful. He loved her heart and spirit. He loved her for her kindness, for her compassion, for her love of life, and for her ability to move forward despite her past. His heart beat faster, and he felt chills ripple through his body just watching her walk towards him. *I can't believe that this wonderful woman is actually marrying me, that she loves me enough to commit the rest of her life to me.* As he watched her, he etched this moment permanently in his mind. *Rose is the love of my life. She is my life.*

When Doty and Rose reached the front of the church, the parson asked, "Who gives this woman to be wed to this man?"

Doty answered, "I do." She reached out and took Coop's hand, then placed Rose's hand in his.

There was a smile on Doty's face as she took her seat beside Charles. Thoughts of Rose's future raced through her mind. *Coop will be a good husband, and I can tell he really loves Rosy. She deserves happiness.*

Doty closed her eyes as she pushed thoughts of her past from her mind. *This marriage will be so much better than mine…It has to be. Coop is nothing like Fred.*

As she watched the ceremony, Doty's joy grew. *Even after all Rosy has been through, she still has a caring, gentle spirit…and she has a promising life ahead.*

She looked at Charles and then back at the bride and groom. *But now, Coop and Rose have their own lives, and I'll only be a small part of them. It's so hard.*

A tear trickled down Doty's cheek. *I'll miss her a great deal, but I wouldn't have it any other way. This is the way it's supposed to be.*

When the parson said, "You may kiss the bride," the congregation erupted in applause. It was a simple and beautiful ceremony.

Doty pressed her eyes closed and prayed softly, "Thank You, Lord. Thank You."

After the wedding and reception were over, the scheming started. The guests whispered and plotted; the shivaree began. The women snuck up behind Rose and kidnapped her. Dragging her into a waiting room in the church, the women laughed as they demanded, "Here, put this on."

Rose joined in on the fun, giggling. "No, stop, wait, what are you doing?" The women helped her take off her wedding gown and put on a long flannel nightgown.

The men kidnapped Coop and dragged him to another room. He wasn't having as much fun as Rose. The men were less gentle as they switched him from his uniform into red, woolen long-johns. He was objecting the whole time, but finally gave in to what his friends considered "fun".

When they saw each other, Coop and Rose laughed as hard as everyone else. Dan, standing between the two, took an arm of each and marched the newlyweds outside. Then without ceremony, he unloaded a wheelbarrow from the back of his truck and politely ushered the bride into her seat. "Rose, you get to ride. Make yourself comfortable in the barrow." She giggled as she climbed in.

Dan turned to face Coop. "You get to drive."

With mock hesitation, Coop walked over in his red long-johns and stood behind the wheelbarrow. Then he lifted the handles, careful not to dump out his bride. "Where am I supposed to go?"

Suddenly, numerous wedding guests crowded around the newlywed couple, shouting, laughing, and blowing noise makers, ready to accompany them on their trek. A large number of cars lined up behind them in a parade, ready to follow. Horns were honking and there was yelling, dancing, and singing, along with all kinds of other loud merriment.

Dan hollered over the noise as he continued the instructions. "You get to take your bride for a ride through town, and we get to follow!"

Coop groaned good-naturedly, not wanting to be the center of attention for any longer than necessary. "Alright, if I have to." As Coop stood behind the wheelbarrow, in his mind's eye he suddenly saw the comical picture of him and Rose. He chuckled quietly to himself as he stepped off, leading the parade. As Coop and Rose headed through town, the towns people whistled, shouted and waved. "Congratulations!" Everyone laughed and enjoyed the unusual spectacle.

The procession ended when Coop pushed the wheelbarrow into the front yard of their new house on the opposite side of town. The noisy crowd gave one more loud cheer and gradually dispersed.

Doty and Charles stood quietly at a distance and watched as Coop and Rose made their way to their new home. Charles took Doty's hand and walked her back to the church. He could tell she was deep in thought but knew she would share her thoughts when she was ready.

Without looking up at him, Doty spoke softly, "Charley, I'm sure Coop and Rosy will be happy."

He did not respond, but only held her hand as they walked.

"You know, Rosy deserves and needs someone to love her." She looked at him out of the corner of her eye. "Charles…" she began and then hesitated. "I don't know if I can ever bring myself to marry again." She left the thought hanging.

Charles smiled with understanding and squeezed her hand softly.

They continued in intermitted silence. Doty let her mind roll back over the past years of her life and then to Rosy's. "Ya know, Charles, even through all the struggles and hard times, Rosy survived. She's a fighter. Everything's made her stronger, courageous, and more compassionate towards others. I'm so proud of her." She sighed wistfully. "Now with a good career and a great husband, I can see a wonderful future for her."

Through all this, Charles hadn't spoken. Instead, he looked at this woman for whom he had begun to develop deep feelings. He thought about a possible future and what that would entail. Believing that they still had time to figure that out, he smiled and decided that, for now, he would simply wait. He squeezed her hand again and continued to listen as Doty talked on.

Doty looked again at Charles and wondered at his thoughts. His face was kind and he smiled as if he understood. She dropped her face as thoughts of her children broke in through the thin barrier she had erected.

What about my other kids? Will they have a chance at a good life too? Walking hand in hand with Charles, Doty's heart ached for them as she wondered about their futures.

Finally, alone, Coop and Rose stood just outside the front door of their new home. He looked at Rose and noted a look of worry on her face before she tried to hide it behind a smile. "Well, Mrs. Grear, here we go." He stepped toward her and scooped her up into his arms, kissing her soundly as he carried her across the threshold. "Rose, we can go as slow as you need. We have the rest of our lives to learn to love each other."

The next morning, Rose woke early and watched Coop as he slept peacefully beside her. She remembered the night before and thanked God that Coop had been patient with her. Then she prayed that she would be able to be all the woman her new husband needed.

I think I'll begin by making him a wonderful breakfast. She slipped quietly out of bed.

THIRTY-SIX

1951

June was a wonderful time of year. The semi-arid, grassy valley was full of life. Birds nested wherever they could find a safe place. Mother Nature seemed to be giving Rose and her family a renewed spirit of strength and love with the birth of their new baby.

Rose gave birth to a beautiful daughter. They named her Marissa and had decided to call her Missy for short.

Their son Tommy was born two years earlier, in 1949.

"Good morning, Rose." Coop greeted her as he and Tommy walked into the hospital room. "How're you feeling this morning?" Coop sat Tommy down in a chair and picked up Marissa. Keeping his hands around the baby, Coop squatted down by Tommy and held his daughter securely as he carefully helped Tommy hold her. "Say hi to your little sister."

Tommy smiled. "Hi, Mithy." He giggled and looked up at his parents.

Rose beamed. "I had a good night's rest, and I'm doing much better."

Tommy gently reached out, touched Missy's nose, and giggled. Excited to meet his baby sister, his hands were all over her. "Easy, Tommy. Be gentle. Remember, she's just a baby," Coop reminded him.

Coop, holding Missy with one arm, reached out and took Rose's hand with the other. "I'm glad to hear that you had a good night's sleep. The doctor said you could go home today if you felt like it. Do you feel well enough to go?"

Rose's face brightened even more as she grinned. "Boy, am I ready to go home—the sooner the better."

A few hours later Rose and Missy were checked out, and Coop had their belongings packed and in the car. As the nurse pushed Rose in the wheelchair with the baby snuggled firmly in her lap, Coop strutted proudly by Rose's side. Marching beside his dad, Tommy beamed with the glory of a big brother as the family made their way out the double glass doors.

After the short drive home, Rose walked into the house, astonished by the changes. "Coop, you and Tommy have really been working on cleaning the house. It looks wonderful! You didn't have to do all this."

"Now you don't have to worry about anything; just relax, rest, and take care of the baby and yourself. Tommy and I will take care of everything else. Right Tommy?"

"Yeth!" Tommy smiled.

Rose put Missy in her crib and sat down beside her. Suddenly, Tommy giggled as he ran up to his new sister. "Mithy's new wattle." Tommy shook the rattle and tried to force it into her hand.

"Oh, Tommy, thank you, but she's sleeping right now. I'm sure she'll love it when she wakes up." Resigned for the moment, Tommy laid his head against his mother's shoulder as she put her arm around him. Together, they gazed at Missy as she slept peacefully in her crib.

Later that afternoon, while her daughter lay napping, Rose made her way to the closet and dug out a small, tightly wrapped box. Sitting on the edge of her bed, she carefully opened the box and lifted out her old doll, Betsy. With tears,

Rose stared at the doll, and the memories and pain of the past came flooding back to her, hitting with the force of a blow. The long car rides, the stay with her mother's cousins, the camps, Willie and new Willie, the rock in the desert—they all came back, and with them a gripping fear.

Forcing her mind back to the present, Rose sucked in a breath and hugged Betsy to her breast. Rose smiled a sad smile, hugged the doll tight again, and ever so gently laid her down close to her baby daughter. "Missy, I hope you love her as much as I did," she whispered quietly. "Betsy and I have been through a lot together. She'll be there for you too."

1953

Coop walked into the kitchen and announced, "I have a surprise for you all. Let's go for a drive. I have something to show you." Happy to get out of the house for a while, Rose loaded Missy, now two years old, and Tommy, four, into the car, and they all headed out for a drive.

Rose sat back and enjoyed the passing spring landscape as the fresh cool morning air blew through the car windows, bringing with it the mild fragrance of the lush fields. The children giggled and played in the backseat. "Where're we going?" Rose asked.

Coop turned and smiled at her. "You'll see."

A recollection of Rose's childhood quickly flashed through her mind: a memory of when she was the child in the backseat riding down the road on a fresh cool morning, playing and giggling with her siblings. Pressing her lips together, her mouth formed a small crooked smile.

Eventually, Coop turned off the main highway onto a dirt road. After a while, he pulled the car over and parked. "We're here. Come on, I want you to see this. I'd like to know what you think."

A bit confused, Rose sat in the car, looking around at the open fields.

Coop quickly got out, walked around the car, and opened the door for her. "You know I've been saving money to buy our own place. Well, it's taken me a while, but I've saved up enough money to buy the land. I've been looking around and found this large lot. I think it would work great for us. What do you think?"

Rose stood next to him, her own excitement building. "Oh Coop..." She looked over the parcel of land, taking in its natural beauty. "This is ours?"

Coop grabbed her hand and led her into a large meadow with Missy on his hip and Tommy following after them.

"This is it. This is the place. It could be ours if you say so."

Rose gazed out over the open meadow. A gentle breeze stirred the grasses in the large field. Off in the distance, a long stand of deciduous trees stood swaying with the breeze. Rose shuffled toward the grove, Coop at her side.

Hearing the gurgling of water, she led the children through the trees to explore. A wide, shallow creek meandered through the grove of large trees and thick bushes. Clear water flowed lazily down the creek over smooth cobblestones. The gentle breeze wafted through the tall grass that grew along the banks, creating a small commotion in the foliage.

"The creek borders the back of the property," Coop told her, "and it flows into the river a quarter mile or so away."

Rose clasped her hands tightly and smiled. "It's beautiful. I love it."

"And Rose, look there"—he pointed to a house over two blocks away— "That's the closest neighbor. If you look around, you'll see very few houses and they're way off in the distance."

Rose raised her hand to shade her eyes from the sun as she surveyed the area.

Coop swung his arm in an arc. "And look around, this whole area is a farming community. We're surrounded by nothing but large farms and acres of Chinese gardens. They grow all kinds of crops around here. It's a beautiful, fertile area. The river's nearby and all the roads, irrigation canals, and ditches are already in place."

As Rose surveyed the land, a feeling of home started to settle in. It wasn't an old wooden shanty in the arid desert, but a place where they could build the home of their future. "Coop, it's gorgeous. I love the land, the creek, and the trees. I love all the openness."

Rose watched as Tommy stomped in the stream and Missy splashed along its banks. She inhaled the scent of wild clover and felt the breeze tousle her hair. Her mind started to race with all sorts of possibilities. "I think we should buy it!"

"I was hoping that you'd say that." Coop raised his hand above his eyes to block the sun from his face as he surveyed the area again. He smiled pleasantly. "This'll be a great place to raise our kids."

Eager to get the process started, he glanced at Rose. "I'll go talk with the owner this afternoon. Rose, you do know that this will take time. I need to save the money to buy materials before I can build the house, but I'll move a small trailer onto the property and build an outhouse. That way, we can still live on our own land while I slowly build our dream home, one section at a time."

"I know it'll take time, Coop. But I also know it'll be worth waiting for."

That day, Coop paid cash for the lot.

Coop got busy immediately. The next Monday after work, he loaded the bed of his pick-up with wood, then hauled it to the new lot. After unloading the planks and 2x4s, he stood and stretched his back. *It should only take me a few days to build an outhouse. When that's finished, I'll set up a small camper on the lot.*

Within a few days, the family moved into their temporary home.

In the evenings after Coop got home from work, he and Rose worked on drawing up the plans for their new home. Sitting at the table in their small trailer, Coop turned to her and sighed. "I think it'll be best to do this in two phases." He pulled out the rough sketch for phase one. "The first phase will have two rooms. One room will be the kitchen, dining room, and front room combined."

Rose shuddered as memories of the shanty ran through her mind. Seeing the excitement in Coop's face, she reminded herself that he was not Father.

Collecting herself, Rose forced a smile. "We'll even have running water!"

"The other room"—Coop pointed to the sketch— "will be a large bedroom where we can all sleep. We'll live in those two rooms until the second part is finished."

He pulled out the sketch for the second phase of the house; Rose studied his detailed drawings. "When I'm finished with this second part," Coop pointed to each room as he explained, "all together we'll have a kitchen, front room, living room, three bedrooms, a hall, a den, a bathroom," he grinned…"and hot water!"

Having set the memories aside, Rose allowed herself to fully enjoy the dream. "Oh, Coop, this is perfect." She rested her head on Coop's shoulder and comforted herself with his nearness.

A few months later as Coop was standing by Rose and they studied the house, he slipped her fingers into his.

"Rose…it's done. The first phase of the house is finished."

Rose grabbed Coop and kissed him. "Thank you, Coop, for doing this for us. Let's move in!"

Several months later, with them both juggling shifts, Coop began to think about Rose quitting her job and staying home with the kids. After putting the kids to bed one evening, he decided to bring up the subject.

Coop walked into the kitchen and sat down at the table with his wife. "Rose, I have a question for you." She looked up at him from a book that she was reading. Not sure how to ask the question, he hesitated. "Rose…I know that you have chosen to work evenings and weekends so you can take care of the kids during the week and I can watch them during the evenings and weekends. But what do you think about being a stay-at-home mom? The kids need…well, they really need their momma."

Rose froze.

From the panicked look on her face, Coop knew her thoughts had raced back to her own father and what her life had been like as a child. His heart softened. "Look, Rose, your mother helps out when she can, but we are both gone way too much. With me working days and you working weekends and nights, the kids need one of us to be there, they need some stability."

Coop let out his breath and pulled her into an embrace. "We've gotta do something. We can't continue at this pace."

It had not been an easy decision, but eventually Rose gave up her nursing job and became a stay-at-home mother. The fear of losing her sense of independence and depending on a man to take care of her had been the hardest part for Rose, but loving Coop had made the transition easier.

She hoped she wouldn't regret this decision.

THIRTY-SEVEN

1954

The family was sitting down for dinner when they heard a loud knock at the door. "Rosy! Rosy!" a young woman's voice yelled in panic. "Let me in! Please help me! Please!"

Rose jumped up from the dinner table. "Abigail?" She ran to the door and jerked it open. Coop followed right behind her.

Rose's 16-year-old younger sister, Abigail, fell into her arms, sobbing. "Oh, Rosy, you and Coop have to help me…"

Rose put her arms around her younger sister, quickly pulled her into the house, and shut the door.

Coop's military training immediately kicked in and his senses came into sharp focus. He slipped out the door and covertly scanned the area outside, making sure no one had followed Abigail. He backed against the outside wall, peering around the corners of the house. Seeing nothing, he made his way stealthily over to the stand of trees by the creek, making sure no one was there. Resolved that no one had followed Abigail, he went back into the house.

Rose grasped Abigail's arms, pulled them from around her neck, and looked into her eyes with concern. "Abigail, tell me what's going on. Are you in danger?"

Tears streamed from Abigail's eyes as she sobbed uncontrollably. "Rosy, you and Coop have to help me!"

"Abigail, what's wrong?" Rose repeated again as she put her arms around her sister's shoulders, trying to comfort her.

The children sat at the table, waiting to eat. They watched all that was going on with big eyes. "Tommy and Missy, I bet you two would like to have a picnic," Coop suggested. "Why don't you spread out a blanket on the bedroom floor and take your plates in there? You can sit on the blanket to eat your dinner."

"Yay!" yelled Missy. She grabbed her plate of food and glass of milk and took off into the bedroom. Tommy grabbed his dinner and drink and followed her. As Coop helped the children get set up in the bedroom, Rosy led her sister to the sofa and eased her down onto it.

"Now, Abigail, tell me what's going on," Rose softly instructed as Abigail's sobs subsided.

With Rose's arms still around her shoulders, Abigail looked up. "S-Sammy's in the hospital. H-he almost d-died. The doctors had to put in a feeding tube." Again, Abigail's sobs shook her body. "Th-they said he almost starved to death."

As Rose held Abigail, Coop walked up and sat next to Rose, taking Abigail's hand in his.

Rose recalled the events that Abigail had dealt with over the last few years. Even though Father was gone, his legacy lived on. At fourteen, Abigail had run away to avoid the abuse from her brothers and went to live with her boyfriend in another town. She was soon pregnant. She gave birth to a beautiful baby boy; she named him Samuel. A few months after she had the baby, her boyfriend had kicked her out of the house. At sixteen, Abigail was on her own, afraid, and too ashamed to go home.

"Rose," Abigail had confided at the time, "I thought he loved me." She had tried but couldn't provide for or take care of the child. That had been around two years ago.

Abigail's whole body trembled as she pleaded, "R-Rosy, I don't have enough milk to give him or any food to feed him. I can't even find a job to earn money." Abigail's sobs jerked her body as she took a deep breath. "I don't want Sammy to die…" She started weeping uncontrollably again. Rose kept her arms around her sister and held her tenderly as she waited for the weeping and trembling to subside.

Abigail rested her head on Rose's shoulder. After a short time, she raised her head, and her eyes questioningly glanced back and forth between Coop and Rose. She then seemed to gain control of her emotions and stood up straight, squared her shoulders, and held her head high.

With a deep breath and all the courage she could muster, Abigail asked, "Rose and Coop, will you take Sammy as your own son? I can't even take care of myself; how can I take care of him? I'm moving back in with Mom, but I can't put the extra burden on her, she can't afford to feed her own kids." Abigail tried to stifle her sniffles. "Coop has a good job and can afford to take care of him, and Sammy would have a good home and a brother and sister. Please? Will you take him in? I don't know what else to do."

Rose squeezed Coop's hand and then looked back at her sister. They were both stunned into silence. Their compassion for Abigail was overwhelming, but they had no plans for more children.

Abigail looked directly into Rose and Coop's faces, and said in a weak voice, "I know this is sudden, but would you at least think about it? Sammy will be in the hospital for a few more days. I'll let you know when he is ready to be released." Abigail turned and walked toward the door, then stopped and looked back toward Coop and Rose. Tears trickled down her cheeks again. "Please help him, I've nowhere else to turn."

When Abigail was gone, Coop and Rose just sat staring at each other, not sure what had just happened or what they should do.

"Coop, I don't understand it. I didn't know Abigail didn't have food." Rose looked overwhelmed. "She's so young to be a mother, but I thought she was doing okay, living with her boyfriend.

"The older boys are in the service, but Mom still has all the other kids at home to support. I know money's tight and that Sammy would be another mouth to feed. Mom's struggling to feed the kids she has."

Coop moved over to the kitchen table, leaned against the edge, and crossed his legs, and folded his arms. After considering the situation for a long moment, he asked, "What do you think about this, Rose? I know we decided to have only two kids, but would a third change things that much?"

Rose followed Coop to the kitchen. She wasn't hungry, her stomach felt like it was tied in a knot. Distracted, she began stacking the plates and removing their dinner from the table. "He's my nephew. He needs a home and food, and he needs love." Whispers of the past started to speak and gradually grew louder in her mind; voices of poverty, neglect, and abuse screamed to be heard. "We can't let him grow up like I did." She sat the dishes in the sink and then turned and looked at Coop. "What else can we do?"

Coop joined her at the sink, put his arm around her shoulders, and gently took her hand. "Before we make a decision, let's go to the hospital and talk to the doctor. There may be more to this than we know." Rose agreed.

The next morning, Coop and Rose put the children in the car and drove them to Coop's mother's house before continuing on to the hospital. They checked with the front desk and were directed to an office to wait for Sammy's doctor.

After a short wait, a middle-aged man entered the office and introduced himself as Dr. Smith. Coop stood and reached to shake his hand. "Hi, Doctor. My name is Cooper Grear, and this is my wife, Rose. We are Sammy's aunt and uncle."

Rose looked into Dr. Smith's face, her heartbeat increasing as the silence grew. She forced herself to swallow, trying to moisten her throat. "Abigail, Sammy's mother, is my little sister. She's asked my husband and me to help her out." Coop squeezed her hand and nodded, encouraging her. "She wants us to possibly have Sammy come live with us. Doctor, we need information. What can you tell us about Sammy's situation?"

He gestured toward a set of chairs in front of his desk. "Please, have a seat. I'll answer any question I can."

Coop and Rose each took a seat as Dr. Smith sat behind his desk.

"Yes, I heard. Abigail told me." Dr. Smith pulled out Sammy's file and opened it, then leaned back in his chair, fiddling with his pen. "I hope you're considering it. This child needs a lot of care." The doctor shook his head. "Sammy is not being fed or taken care of. Abigail can't take care of him, let alone feed him. She's little more than a child herself. I can't let Sammy go back into her care in good conscience…I'd have to report her to the authorities."

"What's wrong with him, doctor? What does he need?" Rose asked.

"Follow me. I'll show you." The doctor stood up and led them out the office door, down the hall, and into Sammy's room. Shocked by what they saw, Rose pressed her hand to her mouth as she looked down at her emaciated nephew. An IV dripped lifesaving nutrients to the child through a large vein at his ankle, which was wrapped and bandaged. His face was gaunt, and his body was thin and bony. His belly bulged.

"When Sammy was brought in," Doctor Smith stated, "he was filthy. It didn't look like he was being cared for at all." The doctor reached out and tenderly ran his hand over Sammy's head. "He's not yet two years old." The doctor raised the IV tube to show Coop and Rose. "This is how we're feeding him; he was slowly starving to death. We almost lost him."

The doctor looked at Sammy with compassion as he gently took the child's hand. "Abigail told me all she had to feed him was milk, and not much of that. He needs nutrition and a lot of loving care. You can see how thin he is. If he survives the next day or two, he'll have a chance. But it will take some time, and someone will have to make sure he eats often and gets plenty of liquids."

Coop turned to the doctor. "Are there any signs of abuse?"

"All we saw was neglect." The doctor gently patted the child's hand and tenderly brushed the boy's cheek with the back of his fingers. Looking directly at Coop, Dr. Smith said matter-of-factly, "This child wasn't fed, cleaned up or even changed for a long time. His physical development's been delayed due to a lack of proper interaction and nutrition."

Coop nodded. "Thank you, doctor." He looked back at the emaciated child. "We'll be in touch."

The doctor nodded once and left them standing at Sammy's bedside.

Rose's heart cried out for Sammy and for Abigail. She paced the hospital room, releasing her frustrations. "Coop, why didn't Abigail take care of Sammy…and how could she just let her own child starve? Was she just not feeding him, or did she really not have the food?" Rose stopped and faced Coop. "To have to give up her child…It's inconceivable." Sobered, they grasped each other's hand, turned, and walked out of the hospital room.

While walking down the hall, Rose spoke her thoughts. "I remember Mom telling me about my older brother and sister, about how they starved to death as toddlers. And how she miscarried one child because she was starving, and her body didn't have the nutrients that she and the unborn child needed. No matter how hard they tried, my parents couldn't provide the food needed; it was totally out of their control. And there were the years of hunger that my family and I went through when I was a child."

Rose leaned her head against Coop's shoulder as they walked. "I just don't understand how Abigail could let this happen." Rose sniffled and wiped at her tears. "Coop, how can we not take him? He's not being cared for; he's hungry and sick. He needs a home and a family to care for and love him."

Coop stopped her. "Wait a minute, Rose. Let's think about this before we make any hasty decisions. I know he needs a family and a home. Let's just slow down and think about what this would mean for us. We need to be sure we're making the right decision…" His voice trailed off as he opened the car door for her.

Rose felt downhearted but knew that Coop was right. "Okay. Sammy will be in the hospital for the next few days anyway. That'll give us a couple of days to think about it."

Neither Rose nor Coop could sleep that night. The visions in their minds of the starving little boy haunted them both. He had captured their hearts. They both knew what they wanted to do but didn't say anything until the next day.

The next evening when Coop came home from work, Rose met him at the door. "Have you thought any more about Samuel?"

He sighed. "That's all I've thought about. What about you?"

"Coop, I want him," Rose blurted out.

He smiled. "Me too."

"Let's do it," Rose whispered. "Let's adopt him and bring him home." Coop nodded his head in agreement. Throwing their arms around each other, they embraced, affirming their decision.

Coop grinned, "We're going to be parents again. But keep this in mind; we're going to make this all legal. I don't want Abigail changing her mind later. We need to adopt him."

Rose looked at Coop. "Let's talk to Abigail about Sammy tonight," she suggested. "I'm sure she'll be relieved." That evening, Coop and Rose dropped their children off at Coop's parent's' house on the way to Doty's to see Abigail.

Coop and Rose stepped just inside the door of the house as they greeted the family. After clearing his throat, Coop hesitated, then said softly, "Abigail, we'd like to speak to you about Sammy?"

A look of apprehension darkened Abigail's face. "Sure." She glanced at Doty before saying, "Alright." She leaned against the wall, her legs growing suddenly weak. Doty took the rest of the kids into another room.

"Abigail," Coop gazed compassionately at his sister in-law. "Rose and I have decided that we would like to help out with Sammy. But we don't want this to be one of those back-and-forth things…So what we'd like to do is adopt Sammy as part of our family. If you're okay with that, we can get the process started."

"We'll take care of him and love him…and give him the best home we possibly can," Rose promised. "Abigail, I'll never replace you, but I promise to be the best mother that I can be for him."

Coop echoed the sentiment, "And I'll be the best father that I can be."

Relief and sadness both flooded Abigail's eyes. She reached over and gave both Rose and Coop a hug. "Oh, thank you," she choked up. "I know that you'll be good parents for him, or I wouldn't have asked you." Heartbroken but relieved, she said, "I'll tell Doctor Smith, and we can have the paperwork and everything else done by the time Sammy leaves the hospital."

Rose took Abigail's hands and looked her directly in the eyes. "Abigail, we know that this is hard for you, but just know that we'll love him and raise him as our own child."

Having said that, Rose could see that she and Coop being there right then was hard for the young mother. She had just given her child away. It was time for Abigail to come to terms with what she had done. She needed time to emotionally deal with her decision.

"We'll pick him up from the hospital when it's time." Rose released her hands.

The door opened and Doty came into the room. Seeing them, she knew what had been decided and slipped a supporting arm around Abigail. "Thank you," she mouthed over Abigail's head and closed her eyes, holding her daughter.

Rose followed the doctor's orders as close as possible. She made sure Sammy was fed small amounts often and received lots of liquids. She cuddled him and rocked him. Tommy and Missy couldn't keep their hands off their new brother. They played with him the best they could by giving him toys, talking with him, and just loving on him. Coop would hold Sammy in the evenings after work and dinner, telling him about his day.

The legal papers were signed, and Sammy officially became part of their family. With the love and care he was receiving, Sammy started to gain weight. Soon he was tromping around with his new brother and sister.

THIRTY-EIGHT

1956

The three children splashed and played in the rippling water of the shallow stream. Rose relaxed and watched them while she sat in the shade on a rock by the stream and kicked her feet in the cool water. *I love staying home to raise my children.* She sighed a deep, contented sigh. *They're growing up so fast. It's hard to believe that Missy's already five years old now and going into kindergarten, Tommy's seven and going into second grade, and Sammy's four and thriving.* She smiled at the thought as her mind continued to wander.

However, she couldn't help but compare her own childhood to those of her children's. Just as quickly as the smile had come, it disappeared as the buried memories of her abusive childhood followed and started to writhe their way to the surface of her mind, crowding her head with confusing thoughts and sickening feelings. She tried to bury them again. She closed her eyes and slowly rubbed her temples, attempting to wipe away the recollections.

I don't understand why I can't leave the past behind. She stood up in the stream and waded in the water with the children, hoping to get her mind focused on something else.

Over the next couple of years, Coop's job continued with long days and hard hours. The money was good, but it meant more time spent away from home.

After arriving home from a tedious day, Coop snuck up behind Rose, shushing the children, as he put his finger to his lips. Wiping the drops of moisture from her face with the back of her hand, she stood in the large kitchen area, doing laundry in the wringer washing machine, her dress damp with sweat.

Coop watched as Rose busied herself. He loved the way the light lit up the natural highlights in her hair, and the way she bit the tip her tongue when she concentrated. He felt a flush of heat warm his face and neck as he slipped his arms around Rose's waist. "Guess what?" He pulled her back against his chest as he deeply inhaled the sweet scent of her shampoo.

Startled, she jumped and then relaxed as he snuggled her neck. "Coop, you scared me." She smiled up at him and he pressed his lips to her neck. This time it was Rose who blushed. "Coop…the kids are watching." She turned and put her hands on his chest before looking at her children, who stood by giggling.

"Rose, it's taken me a couple of years, but we finally have enough money to finish the house. I need to finish a few odds and ends and put up the siding; then it will be done. I should have it completed within the next few weeks."

Rose's eyes widened as her mouth dropped open in surprise. "Really?" she squealed. "That's wonderful." She grabbed him and hugged him tight. As she stepped back, she kept her arms clasped around his neck and grinned. "It's really going to happen."

She beamed as she turned to the washer and pulled a shirt out of the machine's tub and fed it through the wringer. "It'll be great to have an indoor bathroom and a new washing machine."

After nailing the last panel of siding on the house, Coop stood back and admired his work. Crossing his arms, his chest swelled with satisfaction and pride at a job well done.

Coop didn't stop there. The next year, they expanded their property and bought the lot next door. He planted a large vegetable garden, a small fruit orchard, and for Rose he planted some yellow rose bushes in the yard. They purchased a milk cow and a few chickens, and before long were producing and supplying most of their family's food. Although they had started from scratch, soon the Grear's house was the nicest place for miles around.

Rose's face beamed as she stood with Coop in their front yard and watched Doty and Charles wave as they drove away. Her mother and Charles had surprised everyone with the announcement of their elopement. They had slipped away the day before and got married. Rose could see that the newlyweds were happy and she was thrilled for them.

But as Rose rested her head on Coop's shoulder, familiar feelings of heaviness settled over her heart. She frowned and closed her eyes. *Good for you, Mom. You've put the past behind you. I'm still trying…*

THIRTY-NINE

1957

The lazy days of summer were finally here. The children spent most of their time playing outside, splashing in the stream and running in the nearby fields. Rose loved the warm, relaxing days too, especially when the children were home and played well together. Even Coop enjoyed the warm afternoons under the shade trees.

Rose stood watching out the large window that faced the back yard, double checking on the boys' whereabouts. Keeping a close eye on the children, she watched them play, never letting more than a few minutes pass without checking to make sure they were safe.

Rose continued her housework as the boys ran around the back yard playing cowboys. She looked back at Missy, who was playing quietly with her doll, Betsy. As Rose set aside a pile of clothing, she shifted her gaze to the yard again.

After a moment, Rose suddenly realized that Sammy was nowhere to be seen. She ran to the window, continuing to scan the yard looking for him, but no Sammy. She panicked.

Sammy's gone! He was just here. I just saw him—but—he's gone.

She burst out through the kitchen door to the backyard. "Tommy, where's your brother? Sammy?" she hollered, not giving Tommy a chance to answer. "Sammy! Where are you?" Her voice broke into a screech.

"I'm right here, Mom," Sammy answered fearfully, reacting to his mother's panic.

Rose turned in the direction of his voice. Seeing Sammy step out from behind a tree, she ran to him, dropped to her knees, and hugged him to herself. "Just wondering where you were." Rose took a deep breath and released it, chuckling dryly. After a moment's hesitation, she turned and went back in the house.

As Rose reentered the kitchen, Missy looked up into her mother's face, alarmed by her mom's outburst. She relaxed again once she saw that her mother was no longer concerned. Rose walked past her daughter, touching her cheek with a comforting hand, before continuing with her usual daily tasks.

As Rose finished up her ironing, the phone rang. She answered, "Hello?"

"Is this Rose Grear?" asked a voice on the phone.

"Yes, it is. May I help you?"

There was a slight pause. "Rose, this is Nurse Lori at St. Luke's hospital. Your husband, Cooper, has just been admitted to the emergency room. Today at work, he fell from a two-story scaffolding. We don't know the extent of his injuries yet. You'll need to come down to the emergency room. We'll direct you from there."

Rose couldn't breathe. Her mind tried to make sense of the woman's words; having just dealt with the fear for her child, this just didn't seem to make sense to her.

"Mrs. Grear…are you there?"

Rose forced her mind back to the conversation. "Yes—yes, I'm here."

"Mrs. Grear, we need you to come down to the emergency room, immediately."

Images from her days working in the hospital flooded her mind. Rose pressed a hand to her forehead and closed her eyes. "Oh, God…" Her voice caught on the two-word prayer.

"I'll be there as soon as I can." Rose slammed the phone down, and then with trembling hands, immediately picked it up again and dialed her neighbor. "Beth, I just received a call from the hospital!" Rose's tongue felt tangled, her mouth couldn't speak fast enough. "Coop's been in an accident at work! He's in the emergency room. Would you watch the kids for me? I need to get to the hospital now!"

"Yes! I'll be right over!" Beth came immediately.

A neighbor and widow, Beth lived by herself and had become a sort of second grandmother to Rose's children. Rose knew her kids would be safe with her.

She quickly gathered her children. "Kids, Daddy's been hurt. I've got to go to the hospital to see how he's doing. Beth's coming here to stay with you"

Beth raced in the door. "Go Rose—go now! I'll watch the kids!"

Rose's fingers turned white as she gripped the steering wheel and raced to the hospital, her mind conjuring up the worse possible scenarios. The fear of losing Coop, of raising the kids alone, of losing her only love, filled her heart and mind with dread.

God, please help Coop be okay. Without realizing it, her heart reached out to the God she rarely even spoke to.

When she arrived at the hospital, Coop was still in the emergency room. Rose rushed up to the registration desk. "I'm Rose Grear. I'm here to see my husband, Coop Grear. He was just admitted to emergency."

The two nurses on duty glanced at each other with eyes full of uncertainty and sympathy. The head nurse, the one sitting at the desk, looked at Rose. "He's still with the doctors. You'll need to wait until they're finished with their examination. No one is allowed in the examining room during this time. Right now, we'll need you to register…"

Rose pushed the clipboard back at the head nurse. "No! You've got to let me in, now." Spinning away from the nurses, Rose raced toward the hallway that led to the examining rooms. Slamming against the double doors with her body, she barged into the corridor, frantically calling Coop's name.

The nurse standing closest to the door quickly ran after her. "I'm sorry, ma'am, but the doctors are with him right now. We can't let you go back there. You'll just be in the way." She gently took Rose's arm to lead her back into the waiting room.

Rose jerked her arm away. "Let me see my husband!" she insisted. "I'm his wife and I'm a nurse! I need to see him! I just need to see him."

She tried to push past the nurse, but to no avail.

"I'm sorry," the nurse repeated again as she stepped in front of Rose. "Mrs. Grear, since you're a nurse, you know I can't let you go back there. I know it's hard, but you're gonna have to wait, you need to settle down."

The head nurse came up behind Rose and together the two nurses, one on each arm, guided Rose back to the waiting area. "Now, please, sit here Mrs. Grear, and when we hear anything, we'll let you know. The doctors are taking care of your husband. There's nothing you can do to help him right now."

Rose gave in. She stopped fighting, settled down, and then crumpled onto the couch, her entire body trembling.

She looked up when someone called her name. Bella and Martha were both rushing over to her. The women sank down beside Rose and hugged her. Martha and Rose cried together while Bella checked with the head nurse.

Bella, bringing all her years of experience into play, stood, turned, and faced the head nurse at the desk. "I'm Bella Grear. I'm Cooper Grear's mother and the charge nurse at Mary Secor Hospital. Bring me up to speed."

The two senior nurses spoke quietly together while Rose filled Martha in on what she knew. After a few minutes, the head nurse cleared her throat and turned her attention back to Rose. "Mrs. Grear, I'll go back and check with the doctors, but I'll need you to wait out here while they are helping your husband. I've spoken with your mother-in-law and explained that we're doing all we can. Since you're a nurse, you already know the policies and the reasons that hospitals have to follow them."

Rose exchanged a look with Bella and dipped her chin in agreement. The nurse handed her the registration forms on a clipboard with a pen. "Here are the forms. You can fill them out while you're waiting."

Rose tried to fill out the forms, but the adrenaline pulsing through her body, made it impossible to concentrate. After struggling to write with a shaking hand for a few minutes, she finally gave up and slapped the clipboard down on the chair beside her. The pen shot off the board and landed on the floor. Unable to stay seated, she stood up, kicked the pen, and paced around the waiting room. Bella and Martha waited with her.

Adrenaline raced through her veins as fear and anguish ran through her mind: *I can't lose him. He's my life. Oh, please, God, don't let him die.* She walked over and stared out the waiting room window, and then, like a frightened wild animal in a cage, she started to pace quickly back and forth between the window and the emergency room door. *Please, God! Show the doctors what to do. Please!*

The next three hours were emotionally draining. The waiting and not knowing, the fear and anxiety, were completely overwhelming. Exhausted from sitting and waiting, Rose, Bella, and Martha had become stiff with nervous tension.

Finally, the doctor came through the double doors, and the nurse at the counter pointed him toward Rose. Rose jumped up and rushed over to meet him. She stopped halfway between the couch and the doctor and looked back to where her mother- and sister-in-law stood waiting. Rose nodded at them and waved them over. "Please come with me. I really need your support," Rose softly begged Bella and Martha."

"Ladies, let's go to a more private place. This may take a while." The doctor led them into a consultation room. Fear filled their being. The three women sat across the table from him.

The doctor cleared his throat, glanced at Bella and Martha, and then looked straight at Rose. "There's no easy way to say this, Mrs. Grear."

At those words, Rose collapsed in the seat as a shriek built in her throat. "No, God, no. Please let him be alive," she whispered hoarsely.

The doctor reached out and touched her forearm. "Mrs. Grear, your husband is alive. He's gonna have a hard time, but there's no reason why he can't make a full recovery in time."

Rose pushed away the panic growing in her chest and sat up again. "Please, doctor, tell me what happened."

"Your husband fell from a two-story building he was working on. We have spent the last three hours ensuring he was not in any immediate danger and making him comfortable. He's sedated for now and resting."

After stetting her mind into nursing mode, Rose had sobered and was concentrating on what the doctor was saying. *Coop's alive—the rest I can deal with.*

"Your husband fell from a two-story building and landed on his feet. Both legs are broken, one ankle is crushed, and he suffered multiple fractures in both feet." He looked up at Rose to see how she was handling the news. When she nodded, he continued. "We're not sure of the damage to his back yet. We won't be able to access that until some of the swelling has gone down. He may or may not be able to walk again. We'll just have to wait and see what the examinations tell us. He is in a body cast right now and will be for some time."

The doctor set his folder on the table and leaned back; fatigue etched in the lines of his face. "Mrs. Grear, your husband has a hard road ahead of him. When he can handle it, we need to do surgery on his left foot and ankle. We'll keep him here in the hospital until we know he is doing okay and is able to function at home. I'm sure you have questions. I'll answer any that I can." Clasping his fingers together, he rested his forearms on the tabletop.

Rose had dozens of questions, but the only one that came out of her mouth was, "Can I see him now?"

The doctor gave her a warm smile. "You can see him, but realize he is sedated and sleeping. Don't be surprised when you see the IVs in his arms."

Rose raised a hand, cutting him off. "I know I was acting a bit crazy earlier, but I'm a trained nurse. I won't be bothered by seeing him."

The doctor nodded. "We'll do regular checks on his respirations. Of course, he's casted from his chest down, and his legs are suspended in a functional form to decrease the loss of joint mobility. But of course, you know all that. We'll keep him that way for a while. He needs all the rest he can get right now. I know you'll have more questions, and your training will go a long way in helping your husband recover. But if any of you do have questions, let me know." He stood, nodded at the women, and walked out of the room quietly. Martha and Bella followed him out, wanting more information.

Rose sat in silence, trying to process the information she had just received. The details whirled inside her head. *The doctors don't even know if Coop will ever walk again.* Her body trembled at the thought. *What if he doesn't?*

Rose fought to compose herself. After a few tears had escaped from her eyes, she sat up straight and held her head up, determined to help her husband get through this. *I have to be strong for Coop.* Rose stood up, pulled her shoulders back, and walked with determination to the reception desk, where she was directed to his room.

The doctor had warned her, but seeing Coop like this hit her harder than she expected. His eyes were closed and his face pale. Rose felt lightheaded and her body started to tremble. *How can this be? I just saw him this morning, and he was fine.*

Tears welled up in her eyes. She couldn't grasp all that she saw; IVs, monitors, body cast, sedation, paleness, brokenness, helplessness. *This is my husband, and there's nothing I can do to help him.*

Rose sat in a chair by Coop's bed, watching him sleep. Then, slowly, it dawned on her. *Maybe there is something I can do...I can pray. I can pray hard. If there is a God, He'll surely hear me*. With trembling hands, she reached out and took one of Coop's and held it tenderly. Her voice shaking, she spoke quietly in desperation. "God, if You are real, please heal Coop, make him whole again. Don't take him away from me. Touch his body with Your healing, and give me the wisdom, strength, and courage to help Coop get through this."

She continued to sit by his side, praying in her heart for her husband's healing.

Shortly, Bella and Martha quietly walked into Coop's room. Rose jumped up and fell into her mother-in-law's embrace. Martha reached up and brushed back loose strands of tear-wetted hair from Rose's face. After a few minutes and some relaxing breaths, Rose pulled herself together.

With fearful eyes, Bella and Martha looked anxiously at Coop and then back at Rose. The three women sat down, held hands, and prayed for Coop's healing.

After a short while, Bella and Martha left the room, giving Rose time alone with her husband.

That evening, the two ladies returned. "Rose," Martha said. "I called Beth and the children are fine. Why don't you go on home? The children will need to know their father's okay."

When Rose looked toward Coop, Bella laid her hand on Rose's forearm. "Rose, Martha and I will stay here with Coop tonight. You're no good to him all worn out. Besides, your children will need you. You go on home, try and get some rest, and come back tomorrow."

Rose knew she had to tell the children when she went home that evening. She continued to call on God. "God, are You listening? Can You hear me? Please give me Your words to say to the children." She prayed all the way home.

It was late evening when Rose arrived home, the children were still up. They all gathered around her at the door. She looked first at Beth and then at the children. "Your dad will be in the hospital for a while before he can come back home. He has a cast on so he can heal."

It took a moment for the children to process the information, then Tommy's questions started coming: "Mom? Will Dad be okay? When will he come home? When can we see him?" At eight years old, Tommy was old enough to realize the seriousness of the accident. His bottom lip stuck out and started quivering as tears began streaming down his cheeks.

Rose moved over to her oldest son and put her arm around him. She answered as honestly and simply as she could: "Tommy, the doctors think he will be okay, but it will be a while before he can walk. He's in a cast to hold his legs still so they can heal, but I don't know how long he'll be in the hospital. He'll be there until the doctors say he can come home."

Missy and Sammy understood that Dad was in the hospital, but they did not realize how seriously he was hurt. However, when Tommy started crying, it scared them, and they started crying too. It didn't take much for Rose to join in.

Beth hugged the four of them as they cried together. "Rose, let me pray for you all." Rose nodded, and after a heart felt prayer, Beth said good-bye to Rose. "I'll be back in the morning to watch the kids again so you can go see Coop," she whispered as she walked out the door.

After the children settled down, Rose gently instructed them, "Listen, kids, it won't do us any good to worry. So far, Daddy's doing well, and I'm going to see him every day. I'll let you know how he's feeling. Right now, we all need to get to bed. It's going to be a long day tomorrow, and we'll need our rest. Now scat—it's bedtime." The children reluctantly shuffled off to their beds.

Rose laid in bed alone, tossing and turning. Sleep evaded her. The events of the day rolled over and over through her mind. The image of Coop lying in bed in a body cast with IV's in both arms flashed through her mind. The doctor's words echoed in her ears, and before her, the unknown future stretched out, bleak and hopeless. Rose's heart ached as she lay helplessly in bed while her husband, the man she loved more than life itself, lay broken in the hospital on the far side of the valley.

Rose's muscles were taut with tension and her body filled with anxiety. Unable to sleep, she got up and went outside. *Maybe some fresh air will help me relax and breathe.*

She walked into the backyard and sat down in Coop's chair, gazing out into the darkness. Chilled, she rubbed her arms with her hands and then started to tremble. Her emotions were spent.

Trying to wrap her mind around all that was happening, she felt the fear, hopelessness, and pain slowly churn in her gut and begin to swell. Suddenly, it turned into anger. The anger quickly rose, filled her chest, and then started to simmer. She had no one to blame, no one to release her emotions on…no one except God.

Without warning, Rose looked up to Heaven and exploded. She started spewing words: "God, if You're real and in control of everything, why did You let this happen to Coop?" Angrily she yelled, "You're supposed to be a *good*

God! He's a good man. You could have stopped this! It's all Your fault!" Uncontrolled tears streamed down her cheeks, ran down her neck, and dampened the neckline of her nightgown. Her trembling intensified.

She released all her wrath at God, all her pent-up rage, bitterness, hatred, anger, hurt, and fear that she had been burying deep down over all the years. "And God, if You've been with me all my life, why didn't You help me and my family?" Her fury at God continued as she spat out all the things that she hadn't been able to talk about or deal with, memories that haunted her, the bitter emotions she couldn't shake. "Why did You allow Father to use me, and what about all the men Father tracked through our house…the hunger and death in my family?" She screamed. "If You're really the Almighty God, You could've stopped all of it if You'd wanted to!"

She hugged herself and groaned as if she'd been punched in the gut, toppling to her knees. Her wails had become bitter moans. "If You do exist, You're not a good God. You're mean and cruel, and You don't care!"

Laying in the moist grass, Rose wiped at her tears with the sleeve of her nightgown. She laid that way for some time before the quaking finally came to an end. She took a deep breath and stood shakily. Looking around at the darkness, her shoulders slumped, and she headed back toward the house. Suddenly, she stopped, turned around, and looked up to the sky. "And if You are real, I hate You, and I don't want anything else to do with You. Ever!"

Rose knew they would need an income while Coop was recovering in the hospital, so she applied for a job; nurses were in great demand, and she was hired immediately. She would be able to support the family and see Coop every day.

Rose worked a midday shift from 11:00 A.M. until 7:00 P.M., which left her mornings free to spend a little time with Tommy and Missy before school, and allow her part of the morning with Sammy. She arranged with Beth to watch Sammy during the day, along with the older children when they came home from school. Rose needed the help and knew Beth needed the money; Rose insisted on paying.

Rose didn't make much money. At a dollar an hour, she made less than a third of what Coop had earned. *How can I pay the bills and buy food, let alone pay any medical bills? Coop doesn't even qualify for Workman's Compensation since he's a subcontractor.* Rose could feel her anxiety grow along with her responsibilities. It seemed that the whole world was starting to weigh down on her—first Coop, then the kids, and now the finances.

A few days later, the doctors scheduled the surgery for Coop's crushed ankle and foot.

The surgeon called Rose in after the surgery. He placed the x-rays of Coop's ankle on the light panel. "Look here, Rose"—he pointed to the pins in Coop's foot and ankle—"most of the bones were broken, and some were crushed. The pins will hold the bones in place so they can heal correctly."

Rose examined the pictures.

"The surgery went well, and there is the possibility that Coop will be able to walk again if his back is okay." The doctor placed the x-ray of Coop's back on the panel. "We're still not sure what damage has been done to his back. It wasn't broken, but the x-rays show numerous collapsed discs and misaligned vertebrae." He pointed to clusters on the film where whitish-gray masses seemed pressed together. "We're concerned about the pinched and damaged nerves. Time will tell."

Over the next few weeks as Coop laid in bed, he had plenty of time to think about all the things he could do absolutely nothing about. Thoughts of his family and his current situation overwhelmed him.

I know that Rose is trying, but I'm supposed to be the breadwinner. I'm supposed to be taking care of her. Now she's working, taking care of me, the kids, and the household, all at the same time.

Worried, stressed, and in pain, Coop constantly fretted about the finances and his family. He pressed his eyes closed as tears of desperation and helplessness spilled down the sides of his face. He whispered to himself, "I'm sorry, Rose. I'm sorry that I've put you through all this."

Rose visited Coop numerous times every day. She came in on her breaks, during her lunch hour, and every other chance possible. Even though she didn't always feel it, she kept up a positive attitude. Coop already knew they were struggling without him and didn't need to be reminded. Right now, she just needed him to get better.

Coop's recovery was slow. He was young and healthy, but healing would be a long process. He lay imprisoned in his cast, unable to move any part of his body but his arms and his head. From the early hours of the morning on through the rest of the day, his eyes desperately drifted around the hospital room, looking for possibilities of escape that he knew didn't exist.

Disillusion and depression were setting in. Every time he closed his eyes, he was plagued by images that flashed through his mind: images of him falling from the building and hitting the ground, images of him being put into an ambulance, images of nurses and doctors hovering over him.

Glimpses of the war were also mixed with his tormented memories: bombs dropping, artillery firing, men falling, all that came along with war and death. The recollections replayed every time he closed his eyes. It was too much for him to handle.

It would've been better if I'd been killed in the war or when I fell. I probably won't even be able to walk, and I'll be nothing but a burden on my family.

Day after day, Coop lay in bed reliving the past, fretting about the future, and worrying about his family. There was nothing he could do about it.

The realization that he could not keep the promise he made to himself and Rose, the promise that his family would lack for nothing, hit hard. As a husband, father, and as a man, he felt like a failure.

After three long weeks of lying in a hospital bed, Coop could stand it no longer. "Doctor! Doctor!" he yelled as loudly as possible. Grabbing his breakfast tray from the bedside table with shaking hands, he picked it up and heaved it at the closed door. The dishes fell to the floor and shattered. "I need to get up! I have to get out of here!" he yelled. "Get me out of this bed, out of this room!"

His determination then melted in his eyes. "Please… please…" his voice turned to a whisper as what was left of his resolve trickled down his face. "I can't stand it any longer…" Deep sobs jerked his chest.

Rose rushed in. "Coop, settle down. It's okay, Coop… it's okay." Taking one of his trembling hands, she held it tightly. "The doctor says you're doing well. It won't be much longer before you can go home—"

Rose looked up when the doctor walked into Coop's room.

The doctor stepped carefully over the shattered mess and smiled. "Good morning, Mr. Grear, I have some good news for you. We were going to remove the body cast from your upper body on Monday, but"—looking around the room, he smiled again at Coop—"I think we'll do it today instead. It's a few days early, so keep in mind that even though your back isn't broken, the vertebrae are severely out of alignment. Your back will probably bother you for quite a while, but it seems to be doing okay. However, we'll have to leave the casts on your legs and foot for quite a while yet.

"Since we're removing your body cast, we'll have you try a wheelchair in a couple days. I'm not sure when you can be released from the hospital, but if you're doing better these next few days, it's a possibility. As soon as you're strong enough to steer the wheelchair around, I'll let you go home. You might even be able to go home as early as next week depending on whether or not you can manipulate the chair."

Coop closed his eyes and took a deep breath. *Freedom at last. I'll be able to get around instead of just lying in bed.* The tears of relief trickled down his face as a nurse wheeled in a cart and they began to remove his body cast.

Two days later, the nurses and doctor helped Coop into his wheelchair. He sat in his chair, took a deep breath, and smiled for the first time in weeks.

At first, it was difficult to manipulate the wheelchair because it put pressure on his back when he used his arms. But as Coop's back got stronger, he became very skilled at maneuvering around the hospital. He couldn't get out of the chair without help, but he could wheel wherever he wanted to go.

FORTY

Excited to be home, Coop started watching the children when Rose was at work. He was glad he could do something to help. This also meant they didn't have to pay for a sitter anymore. Since he was wheelchair-bound, the chores went to the children. They took turns doing different jobs every day after school.

Rose leaned back and tried to relax in Coop's wooden chair as she sat in the shade of a black walnut tree. The sun slowly descended over the distant mountains, coloring the evening sky. A gentle breeze cooled the warm summer evening as it tousled the loose strands of hair that tickled Rose's face, but she did not see the spectacular view or feel the breeze. Instead, the weight of what she was dealing with hung heavy on her mind. She sat in a trance, eyes looking but not seeing.

Her body was exhausted, but her mind raced.

Over the past weeks, the hospital bills have continued to pile up; what little money I earn is just not enough. There's always another bill. No matter how many hours I work, there's just not enough money.

She closed her eyes and took a deep breath, trying to relax, but to no avail.

I struggle just to provide enough for my family. Our supply of canned foods is gone, and there's no garden. Even with help from our families, we still just barely get by. I can't remember the last time we had a decent meal.

A sparrow flew by and caught her attention. It landed in the tree beside her, singing its song. She stared at it for a moment, and then a Bible verse she had learned when she went to church with Martha came to mind:

How does that go? "Behold the fowls of the air: for they sow not, neither do they reap, nor gather into barns; yet your Heavenly Father feedeth them. Are ye not much better than they?"

Rose's anger and bitterness flared. *Yeah, God. You'll feed the birds of the air, but not my family.* She pushed the thought from her mind.

Her concern turned to her children. *My kids need me now more than ever. They handle my absence as best they can, but I know they miss me…and I miss them. I've always been there for my kids, but now we hardly see each other.*

Rose was overwhelmed, her emotions spent. *There isn't enough of me to go around. How can I provide the support that my family needs? She leaned forward and placed her face in her hands. I can't even afford to feed them.*

In the darkening evening, deep-rooted memories of her childhood started seeping into her mind. She remembered how her father struggled for many years with the same thing; he couldn't feed his own family. As she reflected on the past, she could recall the poverty and hunger she had suffered as a child.

I remember having no food and struggling to make it through the day while hungry. I watched as Father did everything he could to provide for us. I saw how he released his anger and frustration on others and turned to the bottle.

Rose stood up and started wandering around the unkempt yard in the twilight of the evening.

Father did everything he knew to feed us and keep us alive. But the time came when he reached his breaking point. He went bad and we went hungry.

She realized that her father must have felt all the things she was feeling now: helpless, scared, and completely devastated with nowhere to turn. She released a slow breath. But turning against his own family…that was one thing she would never understand. Armed with at least a measure of new understanding, Rose felt she could begin to see what had driven father to the darkness.

The pressure he felt must have been overwhelming. He had turned to alcohol, and in the end, even that failed him.

A humorless smile tugged at her lips, but no light brightened her eyes.

As the twilight faded, Rose wandered toward the house. Only one dim light remained on, telling her that her family was sound asleep in bed. She quietly opened the back door and tip-toed in to check on her children. Going from bedroom to bedroom, she gave each child a gentle kiss on the cheek. As she gazed at her children, her thoughts circled back to the present. She had a foreboding feeling that the past was repeating itself. Rose went back outside and sunk down in the wooden chair, releasing a disheartened sigh.

My kids are hungry.

Despondent, Rose hung her head and closed her eyes as she considered the impending possibilities of the future. *If my children were dying of hunger, how far would I go to save their lives? Would I sell myself like father made me do? Would the guilt and anger cause me to strike out at everyone? What would I turn to in order to forget the pain, to put certain deeds out of my mind?*

And what about Coop? He has to continue his medical treatments; we have no choice. Since we have no money, what would I do to make sure he gets medical care?

Coop lay wide awake in bed as Rose sat in the back yard. He felt helpless as he faced the harsh reality. He couldn't even get out of his chair without help, let alone walk or work. He was a proud man, and yet he was powerless to control his own little world.

Look at me. After everything I've done for my family, I'm failing them.

———————≈———————

The next morning before work, even though she didn't want to, Rose felt she should talk to Coop about the finances; he needed to know. She waited until after breakfast. Coop sat in his wheelchair in the living room, and she sat down on the couch beside him. Staring at his broken feet for a moment, then down at the floor, she quietly told her husband, "Coop, I'm doing everything I know how to do to help our family. I'm paying the bills when I can and I'm taking overtime hours, but there's still not enough money to go around. And the time...I can't spend any time with you and the kids, and I know that all of you need my help. I don't know what to do."

Coop could give no response. He sat quietly in his wheelchair, feeling useless and angry. He could think of nothing to say that would help. As their eyes made contact, each could read the fear in the other. They were scared and had nowhere to turn.

That evening, Rose was outside, sitting in the backyard in the night again. Disheartened, she gazed up to the heavens: the sky was clear, the moon was full, and the stars were bright.

Finally, she turned her thoughts toward God. Her anger and bitterness rose up against Him again. Trying to control her feelings, she spoke out loud. "God, I'm so angry. I'm angry and scared. You could have stopped this…" She hid her face in her hands. The words were hard to say, but she forced them from her mouth. "God, why? Why did You let this happen?" She dissolved into tears.

Gradually, memories of her times at church with Martha came flooding back into her mind. She remembered the feelings of warmth and acceptance as she had prayed and felt God's presence. She remembered sitting on the rock in the desert.

New sobs rocked her body, but this time the sorrow was different. "God, I'm sorry for the things I said. You're my only hope." She sat quietly, letting her feelings subside.

A gentle peace started to slowly settle in her heart.

Oh, God, she pleaded silently, please help me provide for my family. Don't let them go hungry. I also pray for Coop's complete healing. God…help me. I can't do this alone.

~

Late the next Saturday afternoon, there was a knock on the front door. Rose was working, so Coop rolled his wheelchair to the door and answered it. Standing in the doorway was a tall, slender man about Coop's age with a huge box of groceries in his arms. "Hello, Mr. Grear? My name is Brad, and I'm a member of Community Christian Church down the road a ways."

When Coop didn't invite him in, Brad smiled and set the box down on the porch. "Your neighbor Beth goes to our church and she told us about your accident. The congregation decided to get together to see if we could help you guys out."

It didn't take much to remind Coop of his feelings of failure. Looking at the box of food, bitterness and self-loathing piqued, and his feelings of uselessness rose. "We don't need help from your blasted church. I can take care of my own family!"

Brad stepped back but continued to smile uncomfortably. "Ah…Mr. Grear, I assure you, umm…that we had no intention of offending you—"

Coop shook his fist in the man's face, cutting him off. "Get out of here." He swore at the man. "And don't you ever come back onto my property!"

Brad swallowed, tipped his hat, turned, and walked away. He got into his car, waved and sped off.

Coop left the box of groceries on the porch and slammed the door. "Those uppity church-folk—who does he think he is?" Coop was fuming. "I can take care of my own family. I don't need any help, especially from that stupid church, and I won't take charity. Who do they think they are anyway?" He was still cursing when he turned to see his children staring into his face.

A few hours later, Rose came home from work. "Hey…Coop, what's in the box sitting out on the front porch? Where did it come from?"

Coop turned in his chair to face her. He was still feeling a bit chagrined about being caught cursing by the kids. "Oh, some church guy dropped it off. I think it's groceries. He doesn't think I can feed my own family," Coop growled angrily.

Rose looked at him for a long moment, then quietly said, "Coop, right now you can't." He glowered at her.

She went out to the porch and dragged the large box into the house. She gasped. "Coop, there's milk. The kids haven't had milk for over two weeks," she said excitedly, hoping the milk had not spoiled and the food was still good. "There's bread, meat, canned vegetables, and…and so much more. We can finally have a decent meal."

After carrying the food into the kitchen, Rose started dinner. She began to hum one of her favorite songs as she cooked. It was the happiest Coop had seen her since his accident. *Maybe I was a little hasty toward that guy. After all, he was just trying to help.* Coop knew his family needed help, but it was hard for him to admit or accept it.

The next Saturday, there was another knock on the door. By the time Coop had wheeled over to answer the door, Brad was chuckling as he walked back across the yard towards his car. He smiled back at Coop, waved as he jumped in his car, and drove away. There was another box of food sitting on the porch. And the Saturday after that, another was left, and the next Saturday, and the next…

Tommy stood, watching out the front window as he did every Saturday afternoon, waiting for their weekly delivery. "Mom, who's giving us all the food?" he asked. Before Rose could answer, there was that familiar knock. Tommy ran to the door to answer it, curious to see what they would have for dinner. He saw Brad wave, walk quickly to his car, and drive off. Tommy grinned and waved back.

Rose watched Brad drive off as well and then looked over at Tommy as she answered his question. "The people from the Community Christian Church down the road is bringing us food." Rose dragged the box of food off the porch, carried the items to the kitchen, and started putting the groceries away.

"Why would they do that?" Tommy asked as he helped his mother unload the box.

"Somehow, they know we need food to eat and that we can't afford it." Rose's thoughts floated back to her prayer in the backyard, and she wondered if the two things were somehow connected. "They seem to be very generous people and are helping us out." Rose's face radiated thankfulness.

Tommy reached to hand her a can of tomato sauce, but stopped. "Why don't we go to church?"

Tommy's question caused Rose to stop and think. It slowly dawned on her that she had never taught her children about God. She gave her son the best answer she could. "Well, we just never found one we liked, and we never had time." She turned and continued to put groceries away.

"Mom, why don't we go to church? Grandma Doty and Grandma Bella go to church, and so does Aunt Martha. Why don't we just go with them?"

Rose was flustered. "I don't know, Tommy. Why don't you talk to your dad about all this? Oh, never mind, go outside and play." She lifted the near-empty box from the floor and placed it on the table. "Go outside and find your brother and sister. Keep an eye on them until I call you for dinner."

Tommy looked questioningly at his mother but made his way out the backdoor. Rose leaned against the table and pondered the question.

Why don't we go to church?

Coop slowly healed and recuperated over the next few months. His back hurt some, but as the doctors examined it, they felt it was going to be okay. Soon the casts on his legs were removed. For a while, he used a walker, then a cane. It took a year for Coop to heal and start walking on his own again, but the doctors were amazed at his progress.

He still walked with a limp, and the left ankle that had the pins in it had not regained full strength or mobility. Coop, however, was not going to let that stop him.

Even though he was healing well, he was still in a lot of pain. He spent many hours per day in his shop, sharpening his carpentry skills, looking forward to the day he could go back to work.

One day right before Coop headed out to the shop, the phone rang. "Hello," he answered.

"Hi, Coop, this is Brad. How are ya doing?"

"I'm okay, doing fine," Coop answered unenthusiastically, and a mutually accepted pause grew between them.

"Good, I'm glad. Hey, um…I need to replace the cabinets in my kitchen. Would you be interested in the job? I'm not in a hurry. You can take your time and work when possible."

Coop couldn't believe it. *Work?* "Yes, I'd love—" Coop's voice broke with disbelief. "Y-yes, I'd love to have the work. When do you want me to start?"

"Anytime. Just let me know and I'll have the materials ready for you."

Coop hobbled as quickly as he could from the front room into the kitchen. "Rose? Hey, Rose, guess what!" he shouted, rushing as quickly as his bad leg would let him. "I just got an offer for a job to do some small cabinet work."

Rose finished putting some laundry into the washing machine. With a concerned look on her face, she turned and watched Coop as he quickly limped into the kitchen. "Are you sure that's a good idea right now? You're still recuperating, and your legs still need to get stronger."

Coop's mind was made up. Determined, he firmly placed his hands on his hips. "I'm going to take the job. If I start slowly, maybe I can build up the strength in my legs and feet. Then eventually, I can work fulltime. I can go back into construction and finally take care of my family again." Coop felt hope rise inside himself for the first time in over a year.

"Are you sure, Coop? I don't want to see you hurt again."

He crossed the final space between them and took her hands into his. "When I married you, I made you a promise. Rose, I'm gonna keep that promise; I'm gonna take care of you and our children." He studied her face for a moment, looking for something. When she smiled, he had his answer. Pulling her into his arms, he pressed his lips against hers.

She smiled reservedly up at him. "Okay, if you're sure. But please don't hurt yourself trying to go too fast. Promise me you'll take your time. It's a miracle that you're even walking."

"I'll be careful," he said, grinning. "Once I get back to work, maybe you could stay home with the kids again if you want to."

Rose sighed. "That would be great, but I think we'll need the extra income for a while to get the bills paid off. Then I'll think about it."

Accepting cabinet work and small jobs, it took Coop months to gradually build up his strength. He knew he would always have some residual pain, and limping just became a part of life, but he would have to learn to tolerate the pain and inconvenience to get back to work. Soon, he was working fulltime to support his family.

As soon as Coop was back to work, the food donations stopped and a few months after that, Rose quit her job and became a stay-at-home mom again.

FORTY-ONE

1958

Rose loved the quiet fall mornings. She would often get up before everyone else on the weekends and sit on the back porch, drinking coffee. This particular morning was warm and bright. She relaxed and leaned back in her chair, just letting her thoughts wander as she reflected over the recent past.

Eventually, Coop meandered outside with a cup of coffee and gave her a kiss on the cheek. He joined her at the table. "Morning, Rose. You're up early."

"Hm," she moaned noncommittedly. She smiled at him, reached over, and took his hand. "Just sitting out here, enjoying the warm sun and cool breeze. It's a beautiful morning, don't you think?" She took a sip of coffee and set the cup down on the table.

Coop smiled and gently squeezed her hand. "Yeah, it really is."

Looking at him thoughtfully, she hesitated a moment before speaking. "I've been thinking about you, Coop."

He raised an eyebrow. "Yeah?"

"Do you realize that there have been three times now that you could have been killed: in Pearl Harbor, in the Battle of the Bulge, and when you fell off the scaffolding?"

"Yes, I'm very aware of that. I've been pretty lucky," Coop agreed as one corner of his mouth formed a lopsided grin.

Rose looked out into the distance for a moment and let out a shallow breath, wondering if she should bring up the subject of God. She lingered over her coffee for a short moment and then took a sip. "Coop. Think about it. It can't be all luck. I feel that God has a lot to do with it. God's been looking out for us. When I was going to church with Martha, I read in the Bible that He loves us and has plans for us."

"What kind a crazy talk is that? I'm just plain lucky." He chuckled.

"Well, Coop, you and I have survived all these years in both of our different circumstances. I survived the poverty and abuse, and you've survived the war and a broken body. God's provided for us when times were hard and protected us through everything. I feel that He's taking care of us."

The two silently exchanged looks. Peering into her empty cup, Rose stood. "I'm getting more coffee. Want some?"

Coop didn't answer as he swirled the dark liquid in his cup and then took a sip. Rose rested a hand on his shoulder before she turned and went in the house. After a few moments, she returned, bringing the coffee pot with her. She filled both their cups and sat down. He still didn't respond.

"Look what the church did, Coop. They fed us for over a year and they didn't even know us." She fidgeted with the handle of her coffee cup. "Maybe-maybe we should go to church and thank the people one of these Sundays. We should thank them for feeding us, for helping us through one of the hardest times in our lives."

Coop remained silent.

Rose glanced over at him. "When I went to church with your sister, I really enjoyed it. I'd like to go again. Besides,

Tommy's nine years old now and has a lot of questions about God that neither you nor I can answer. When I was a child, I had no one to answer my questions. I spent much of my time wondering and never knowing. He needs answers. And…" she paused, "I don't know why, but deep down I feel pulled, led to go to church. Would you be willing to come with me?"

Coop's thoughts turned to the people of the Community Christian Church and how they had provided food for his family during their time of need. His gratitude was strong. "I guess if you really want to go, I'll go with you so we can thank them. We should at least do that much."

Rose's eyes brightened. "How about next week? Beth said there's even a Sunday school. The kids would love it."

He smiled at her. "It's a date. Next Sunday, we're on." He gave her a kiss. "I'm hungry; I'm going in to find something to eat." Glancing into her eyes, Coop smiled and headed back into the house.

The next Sunday morning, Rose was up early and had the children's clothes laid out and breakfast on the table by the time everyone was up. She sat down with the children while they ate. "Kids, remember, we're going to church today. You'll need to be on your best behavior. Will you do that for me? Will you be polite and sit quietly and listen?"

"Yes, Mom," came the choir of voices.

"Mom, what do you do at church? Why're we going?" asked Missy.

Rose looked across the table at Coop, who suddenly found himself engrossed in the sports' page of the morning paper. "Lot of help you are," Rose said and was rewarded with a chuckle from behind the paper.

She looked back to her children. "Well," Rose organized her thoughts, "you go to meet people, socialize, and sing, but most of all, you go to learn about and worship God. You'll find out when we get there. Now hurry and get dressed or we'll be late. I want to be there before the service starts to meet and thank the kind people that helped us when Dad was hurt." As soon as everyone had eaten and was ready to go, Rose hustled them all out the door.

The church building was an old Army barrack donated by the Army base. It had been fixed up nicely, with light green siding on the outside and hardwood floors on the inside. A stage had been built in the front of the long room. Ten rows of folding chairs were set up facing the stage, seating about eighty people. Horizontal to the church building, sat another restored barrack. It was fixed up for classrooms.

When the Grears entered the church building, the people welcomed them with open arms and kind words; even Coop warmed up and seemed to relax. The pianist started playing, and the people of the congregation moved to their seats. The Grear family sat towards the back of the room, not wanting to draw any more attention.

Rose looked at her children, reminding them of their promised behavior. "Now, kids, please sit quietly and listen," she whispered. "We want to hear everything they say. Okay?" The kids weren't paying attention to Rose. "Hey, guys, please sit quietly." Rose whispered a little louder. People in the row in front of them glanced back and smiled.

A short lady with curly, graying hair had been sitting on a folding chair on the front corner of the stage. She stood and introduced herself. "Good morning, I'm Reverend Estie Tasher. Welcome to our service today."

A warm, grandmotherly woman, Estie was the widow of the church's first reverend and a reverend herself. Since her husband passed-away, she had been acting as the covering elder until a suitable replacement could be found.

After giving a short welcome, Revered Estie sat down. Then the song leader stood, turned to the small choir behind her on the stage, and motioned for them to stand. Turning to the congregation, she announced, "Please turn to page 127 in your hymnal." The piano started playing, and everyone stood and joined in the singing.

The songs were familiar to Coop. They were songs he had heard when he was younger and went to church with his family, so he joined in the singing. But Rose had not heard these particular songs. She marveled at the words and felt joy in the music, and tried to sing as she followed along. *I love this! I love singing with my own congregation. Whoa!* The thought startled her. She stopped singing. *My own congregation?* She looked around and slowly surveyed the people and the sanctuary. *I already love this place and these people. And this is my first time here.* The thought made her smile.

The children sat spellbound, watching and listening to everything around them.

When the singing was over, the congregation sat down. Then the choir leader signaled to the children in the junior choir to stand and come forward. The children in the front two rows stood, walked up to the front of the church, and formed a mostly straight line across the front of the stage. The piano started playing, and the children sang an action filled, Christian, children's song. They grinned and wiggled as they sang. They did the actions, sang out of key, and had a wonderful time doing their best. During the performance, the congregation grinned and chuckled. An enthusiastic applause burst out after the children had finished singing.

Reverend Estie stood again, this time to make the announcements. "Tonight, there will be junior choir practice at 6:30. All kids, grades first through sixth, are welcome…"

Rose looked at her children and wondered if they would like to join the choir. *They could get involved. I bet they would love to sing with the other kids.*

"Our Bible study tonight at 7:30 will be on God's Heart. It'll be a great topic and discussion time," Estie continued.

That sounds good too. Rose considered going. *I wonder if Coop would go with me.*

"Wednesday night, the teens will meet at 7:00 and make plans for their upcoming get-together this weekend." After the reverend finished the announcements, she remained standing.

Smiling at the congregation, she asked. "If you have had a birthday this week, would you please come join me up front?" Two adults and one child came up and put pennies in a small white church-shaped bank, one penny for each year of age. She had them introduce themselves and give their age if they wanted to, along with any other information they wanted to tell the congregation. Then everyone sang 'Happy Birthday'.

Reverend Estie then asked, "Does anyone have a memory verse they would like to share?" One by one, five people stood up in the congregation and recited verses from the Bible that they had memorized that week. Rose and Coop were both impressed. These people were actually taking the time to study and remember God's word. After this, the reverend took her seat again in the chair at the corner of the stage.

The preacher, a young man that had been sitting in the center chair, stood and stepped up to the pulpit. "Good morning! Welcome to our worship service today. For those of you that don't know me, my name is Jim Bennett. I'm the lay preacher here at the Community Christian Church until we find a minister to replace our dear departed Reverend Mr. Tasher. Welcome to all of you. Welcome to the House of God!

"Would you please stand and turn with me in your Bibles to the Scripture for today's sermon, Romans 8:28." Jim read the scripture out loud as the congregation followed along. Neither Coop nor Rose had a Bible, so they listened closely. "The scripture for today is, *'And we know that all things work together for good to them that love God, to them who are the called according to His purpose.'* " He paused. "You may be seated."

Jim began his sermon. "Today, we're going to talk about the question Why? Why did God allow this to happen in my life? Or maybe at some time you've been in this quandary: Why does God allow bad things to happen to good people? Have you ever been in a situation that you've reflected on one of these questions? I'm sure most of us have been there.

"I think back to the time when my daughter was four years old. She was hit by a car. At the time, the doctors didn't think she would survive, but she did. While she was in the hospital for three weeks, she had two surgeries and then physical therapy. It took many months for her to recover, but God restored her to full health. I still wonder why God allowed that to happen. I have no answers; only God knows.

"It's hard to deal with the difficult situations in our lives. You're probably dealing with one now: a difficult relationship, financial issues, sickness, career concerns."

Coop stirred in his seat. It felt like the preacher was talking directly to him. The accident, the injury, the pain of recovery, and the mounting bills had all been a constant source of worry for him over the last months. He swallowed and turned his attention back to the preacher.

"And then there're choices. Maybe you or someone else has made a poor choice that has affected your life. Or sometimes things just seem to happen for no reason, like a sickness or an injury. We may blame ourselves, others, or even God. However, my friends, God has His reasons for allowing these circumstances in our lives. We don't know why, and we may never know." Jim flipped some pages in his Bible.

"When God created the heavens and the earth, He made everything good and perfect. Genesis 1:31 says; *'And God saw everything that He had made, and behold, it was very good…'* The word 'everything' includes mankind. We are part of His perfect creation.

"When He created us, God chose to give us free will. He wanted us to follow Him willingly, so He gave us that choice. But because of our humanness and our own desires, sometimes we choose to sin and follow our own path. We choose to disobey God."

Rose sat forward with her hands clenched in her lap. She glanced sideways at her husband, and it seemed to her that he was similarly affected. The words of the preacher pierced her heart, bringing up memories and feelings just like the first sermon had as she sat beside Martha over ten years ago. These words made her feel both warm and distant at the same time. The hope they represented warmed her heart, while at the same time, it revealed a separation, a gulf that existed between her and God.

As the pastor continued, Rose tried to focus on his message. "But even though we make poor choices, God still loves us and lets us choose to do what we want. We can choose to do what is right or choose to do what is wrong. The Bible says in Luke 18:19, '…*none is good, save one, that is, God.*' There are no good people; we are all infected with sin. Romans 3:23 says '*For all have sinned, and come short of the glory of God…*'

"Our choices affect ourselves and other people. As human beings, sometimes we make poor choices. Let's say you rob a bank, so you have to spend time in prison for your crime. Or maybe you change jobs and have to move. Your choices affect you, those around you, your family, and your friends. Choice never affects just one person alone. It reaches out into life with a ripple effect; its effects go on and on. Every choice you make has a consequence in this life that you and others have to live with, good or bad. You and your choices become a part of history.

"Other people's choices affect us also. We've all been under the authority of others in our lives or in situations where things others say or do, directly or indirectly, affect or change our lives. An example is gossip. Your life can be ruined by what someone says about you. Or maybe there's been some sort of abuse in your life, or a lost job for some unjust reason. Someone else's choices may determine the direction of your life.

"But the hardest reason to understand is that bad things just seem to happen, sometimes for no reason, things such as sickness, accidents, or death."

Coop rested his hands on his legs and closed his eyes as memories flitted through his mind.

"As you think back, I'm sure that you see examples of all of these situations throughout your life. You wonder, Why? You did nothing to deserve it." Jim paused and scanned the congregation.

"In all these circumstances God *has* allowed it or decreed it."

As Rose sat in her chair and listened, she thought back to her youth and the abuse inflicted by her father and others. *I had no control over my situation, and my painful memories still resurface often. Father's actions affected and hurt not only me but many other people. If God was there, why did He let this happen?*

As Coop heard the message, the memories of war casualties, of the loss of his friends, of his accident at work filled his mind. The pain—physical, mental, and emotional—was still there. *How can this be good? I lost my friends, my health, my ability to take care of my family. If God is a good God, why did He allow this?*

"God is in complete control." Jim's statement brought Coop and Rose back to the present.

"In Isaiah 45:12, God says, '*I have made the earth, and created man upon it: I, even My hands, have stretched out the heavens, and all their host have I commanded.*' This simply means that God created the universe and all that is in it. He is in command of all things, including us!

"Nothing happens in our lives that God doesn't allow or decree. But God has given mankind free will and control of its own actions, this allows us to make our own choices. Man is the one that chooses to exercise his own free will, not God. But God also allows sickness and physical ailments. He allows these things to happen. But evil, sickness, and pain are not of God, even though He does allow them to exist…for now.

"But why?" Jim cleared his throat and walked out in front of the podium with his Bible in hand.

"God allows and uses all these circumstances to bring us closer to Him, to teach us to depend on Him and to trust Him. His comfort, strength, assurance, and sustaining love are always available to us. You might call our trials 'mercies in disguise'. If we didn't have hard times, we wouldn't need to call on God. He uses them for our good, to help us accomplish His will for our lives, to become more like Christ. In Romans 5:3-4 the Bible states, *'And not only so, but we glory in tribulations also: knowing that tribulation worketh patience; and patience, experience; and experience, hope: And hope maketh us not ashamed; because the love of God is shed abroad in our hearts by the Holy Ghost which is given unto us.'* In plain English, this means there is joy in troubles because troubles produce patience, and patience produces character, and character produces hope. Through this hope, God has poured out His love to fill our hearts through the Holy Spirit.

"The hard times in our lives are what build God's strength in us. They aren't meant to destroy us; they're meant to refine us. Trials bring us into relationship with God because they force us to look to and depend on Him. He walks with us through these difficult times. He draws us closer to Him and grows our faith. God never said life would be easy, but He did promise that He would be there with us and for us. Besides, if we didn't have crises and hard times in our lives, how would we even know when we were having good times? And if we only had good times, why would we need God?

"We are all undeserving of His love. But because of God's love, He allows us to go through these hard situations. I know that it is difficult to understand. It sounds backwards. We think that if He really loved us, He wouldn't let bad things happen. However, God's ways are not our ways. God, in His infinite wisdom, knows what it takes for each of us to turn to and trust in Him.

"Again, Romans 8:28 says, *'And we know that all things work together for the good to them that love God, to them who are the called according to His purpose.'* God uses the good and bad to grow each of us spiritually to accomplish His purpose in our lives."

Rose and Coop sat, a little confused, and tried to comprehend all that they were hearing.

"Friends," Jim continued, "God loves each and every one of you, and He *longs* for a relationship with you. He loves you so much that He sent His only Son to die on the cross for your sins, so that you might have forgiveness and develop that relationship with Him. If you ask for forgiveness of your sins, believe in your heart that Jesus died and rose for your sins, and confess that Jesus is Lord, you will have that life, that relationship, now and forever. You will have the comfort and peace in knowing that God is with you at all times, that He is walking with you in all situations, and that He is growing you to be more like Christ.

"He will use your past to teach you in the present, to prepare you for the future. He uses everything in your life to accomplish His will in you. So, friends, give Him the past, walk with Him in the present, and trust Him for the future. It's your choice."

Jim left the pulpit and sat down. The congregation sat quietly and contemplated on what they had just heard.

Coop's heart stirred. He had heard the plan of salvation many times, but this was the first time he had heard it in a way that actually made sense to him. He took it to heart. As he sat in the silence following the sermon, he experienced a tug in his spirit that he had never felt before. There seemed to come over him a sense that, through Christ, everything would be okay. *Is this God? Why haven't I listened before?*

Sitting next to Coop, Rose dropped her chin and stared at the floor. The feelings in her heart swirled around like dust motes captured in a shaft of sunlight. A part of her wanted what the preacher was talking about, but another part was afraid. She was afraid that God, like Father, might hurt her, might disappoint her and leave her wanting. Tears dripped from her chin and pooled on the backs of her hands before she knew she was crying. Brushing them away, she quickly hid her face. This was the same message, this plan of salvation, she'd heard sitting beside Martha when she attended Martha's church. Her heart had been stirred then too. Both times, she had felt His presence. Martha had explained it as having been the Holy Spirit.

Does God really want to be in my heart, in my life? Rose pondered on the idea. *I need and want Him in my life, and I know He wants to be in it. He's just waiting for me to ask Him.*

When the service was over, the congregation was dismissed for Sunday school. At first, the children were hesitant to go, not knowing anyone there or what to expect. But it didn't take long for them to get acquainted with the other children in class. Soon, they were laughing, playing, and learning. The children loved the Bible stories, crafts, and games. They learned of God and His creation from Genesis. They learned of a God who loved them and wanted the best for them.

Sunday school was also a time for Coop and Rose to get acquainted with other people, and it was a perfect time for discussion and questions. Rose asked the questions she had thought about for a long time and, through discussion, received answers to many of them. Even Coop asked about his concerns. The answers gave rise to more questions for each of them. They felt encouraged to come back the next week to learn more.

A few times during the Sunday school class, Rose excused herself and went to check on the children, ensuring they were safe and enjoying their class.

Coop and Rose had planned to thank the people of the church for the help and support provided during their difficult times. However, Coop had a hard time speaking his heart, especially in a group. But as the session drew to a close, Coop nervously stood and addressed the class. "Before Sunday school ends today, Rose and I have something we would like to say." He glanced around at the people uneasily, then cleared his throat. "When I was laid up during this last year and couldn't work, you came to our house and left much-needed food for us and our children."

Rose joined in. "We don't know how we'd have fed the kids if you hadn't supported us in our desperate time of need. Thank you so much for your help. It's something we'll never forget."

Then Coop looked straight at Brad, the man who had delivered the boxes of food. Coop walked over to him and stopped directly in front of him. "I sincerely apologize for yelling and swearing at you. I hope you'll forgive me."

Brad stood, put his arms around Coop, and gave him a big hug. Smiling, he replied, "Not a problem: apology accepted. I probably would have done the same thing if I had been in your shoes." He patted Coop on the back. They smiled at each other and sat down. It was the beginning of a long friendship.

When the children got in the car to go home, they chattered excitedly about the Sunday School class. "Look,

Mom and Dad! Look what we made in Sunday school." Each child shared his or her picture that they had colored and a craft they had made of clay. Their pictures were colored on Sunday school papers with the story of creation and the verse that they learned. Each clay figure represented one thing that God had created. Coop and Rose were fascinated as they listened to the children's chatter about the fun they had in class.

"God made animals, so I made a monkey." Tommy grinned as he presented his clay animal to his parents. "See its tail. Next time I'm going to make a tree it can hang from."

"And I made a bird, but the wings won't stay up." Missy showed her blue clay bird with sagging wings.

"I made the moon, but it works for a ball too." Sammy threw the clay ball, and it stuck to the car window.

"Sammy, please don't throw that in the car," Coop instructed. "Save it for outside."

"Okay." Sammy pulled the clay from the window and stuffed it in his back pocket, then sat down in the backseat.

Rose sighed and shook her head. *Great, now that clay is smooshed in his pocket. I'll never be able to wash it out.*

During the drive home, Coop and Rose sat in the front seat, each quietly reflecting on the message of the sermon. The children giggled and continued to play with their clay toys.

Coop was the first to speak. "Rose, I enjoyed church today. It was a good time for me to revisit what I was taught as a child and to look at what I really believe. The kids enjoyed it too. I think we should start attending regularly. What do you think?"

Rose's eyes brightened as a smile spread across her face. "I'd love to go every week. It would be good for all of us."

Anticipation immediately sprung up inside her. "The kids could get involved in the children's programs like the junior choir and Sunday school. I'd really love to sing in the church choir. Coop, it would be a chance to get to know other people and to learn more about God too."

Coop grinned. "It's settled then. From now on, every Sunday morning, we'll all go to church." He smiled to himself, knowing in his heart of hearts that he had made the right decision.

Rose's mind raced. *God, I finally get to learn more about You, and I want to know more about this special 'Gift of Life' that You're offering.* As she sat gazing out the car window, she looked up at the clouds. *And the kids, they can grow up learning about the God I never knew existed as a child. There is hope for them, for our family, hope in a God that loves and cares for us.*

Rose took a deep, relaxing breath. She leaned her head back on the seat and rode the rest of the way home in silence, knowing she had made the right choice too.

The next Sunday, the Grear family was in church again. This time at the end of the service, the preacher opened the altar to those who wanted to ask Christ into their lives. Rose hesitated. She wanted to make this commitment, but she was still afraid that God, like Father, might disappoint her and leave her wanting. She was also very hesitant to make the commitment itself, to get up in front of the church and to let others know that she believed in Christ and accepted Him as her personal Savior. Uncertainty encompassed her.

Trying to put the fears out of her mind, she became steadfast. *I've been waiting for this moment most of my life.* She thought about the rock she had sat on in the desert at six years old. She remembered the presence that had protected her, given her peace, and taken away her fear. She wanted to give everything to God. Afraid or not, this was it. It was time she said, "Yes, God."

Rose determinedly stood up, took a deep, shaky breath, and stepped out. As she walked down the aisle, her fear dissipated as joy filled her being.

Kneeling at the altar, she bowed her head. Rose prayed and asked God to forgive her for the wrong that she had done. She gave her life to Christ and asked Christ to come into hers. She gave Him everything: her bitterness, her hatred, and her past, present, and future. As she prayed, Rose felt a peace fill her heart and soul, a peace that only God could give. She felt His presence and knew He had always been with her, even on the rock in the desert. It was as if she could feel His arms around her, holding her tight.

After a short time, she felt someone come and kneel beside her. Her eyes cut quickly to the side to see who it was. *It's Coop. He came to the altar too.*

Coop prayed for Christ to be in his life, that God would take his fear, his nightmares, his past, and fill him with God's Spirit. He also committed his life completely to Christ.

As they were praying, a number of other people from the congregation quietly knelt beside them. The people prayed along with and for Coop and Rose. Everyone in the church could feel the presence of the Spirit of God.

Having made their commitment to Christ, Coop and Rose took their promise seriously. They had been victims in their lives, but now they chose victory. They chose victory over their past, victory over their sin, and victory in Christ.

FORTY-TWO

A few weeks later, eight-year-old Missy raced as fast as she could out to the car after church. "Mom! Dad! Today in Sunday School, my teacher told us about Recreation. Since school's out for the summer, Recreation starts tomorrow, and it lasts all summer. It sounds like fun, and it doesn't cost anything. Can we go?"

Rose looked confused. "I've never heard of it before. What is Recreation? What do you do there?"

"My teacher told us that we can make crafts, have swimming lessons, check out books from the bookmobile, lots of stuff." Missy's eyes grew big with excitement. "It lasts all day, and they provide milk for us at lunchtime, but we need to bring a lunch."

Missy had her mother's undivided attention. "That sounds fantastic." *Hmm…these are things my kids normally wouldn't get to do.* "We'll check it out tomorrow morning. It sounds like great fun."

On Monday, the first day of Recreation, Missy and her brothers were ready to go at 8:30 in the morning. Rose walked them the mile to the church to see what was going on. When they arrived, a large group of children from the community were already there, waiting for instructions.

There were boxes of tools and materials sitting out on tables under the shade of the tall locus trees. All that was needed were little hands to get busy.

The Recreation teacher began her explanations and demonstrations on how to create each project. After the demonstrations were finished, the children crowded around, choosing which craft they wanted to make.

Rose watched and marveled as the children worked. *This is a chance for my kids to learn something new; plus, they can make new friends.* Rose wandered around the tables and inspected the crafts. *I wished I could've done these types of things when I was a kid.*

Finally, she informed ten-year-old Tommy, "I'm going home now. You kids have a great time. When the activities are over, you can walk home. Please, make sure all three of you walk home together, and watch for traffic. I'll tell the other kids I'm leaving. I love you. Have fun."

It was all Rose could do to walk away from the church and leave the children there. She knew in her heart that although unlikely, the possibility of danger was real, even in a supposedly safe place. *I have to start giving them a little bit of freedom.* With every step she took away from the children, Rose could feel the pull to go back.

At home, Rose pulled out her ironing board and iron and started to work, but it was hard for her to concentrate. Fretting about the children, she muttered to herself, "I think I'll just walk back down to the church and check on them, make sure everything is okay." So, later in the morning and once in the afternoon, she walked back to the church and peeked in on the children to make sure they were safe and having fun.

When the children got home that afternoon, they could not contain their eagerness as they crowded around Rose to show her their handmade creations. Missy showed her mother a small, crooked wooden box that she had nailed together, Tommy presented his wood-burned picture, and Sammy proudly held up his pirate ship.

"Wow! You kids did a wonderful job on your crafts," Rose exclaimed.

"And, Mom," Tommy cheerfully announced, "on Wednesday the bookmobile is coming, and we can check out books."

Sammy added, "And on Friday, we start swimming lessons."

"My goodness, that all sounds wonderful." Rose was as excited as they were.

As the children ran off to play with their prize projects, Rose's gratitude grew. She reveled in the fact that her children had these wonderful opportunities.

The next day, Rose hugged each of her children and watched nervously as they headed out of the house to go to Recreation.

"Bye, Mom, we're leaving. See you later!" Missy's voice rang out as she and her brothers raced out the door and headed down the road.

"Make sure you walk together!" called Rose. "Bye!" She stood, frozen in the doorway, trying to shake the memory of the first Willie, of how he had walked away and she had never seen him again. Willing herself to give her children some freedom and resist the fear, she grasped the doorframe and clung tight so she wouldn't follow them.

However, she couldn't do it. She couldn't let them leave her protection, not even for a little while. Unknown to the children, Rose followed at a distance, making sure they made it safely down the road and to their destination. Rose walked to the church and back two more times that day, checking on the children without them knowing.

On the last short trek to church, one of the women waved her over, and Rose stopped to talk. "What are you ladies doing, working with Recreation?"

The lady smiled. "Some of us are. Some help with sorting items for the secondhand store, while some others help clean the buildings."

Rose looked around at the various women working and made a decision. "I'd like to help. How can I join in?"

The woman laughed and handed Rose a bag of used clothing. "Just start sorting and folding."

Smiling to herself, Rose started separating and folding the clothing, feeling very satisfied with her choice. *I can walk with the kids in the mornings and stay and help with the work here at the church. That way, I can keep my eye on the kids at the same time.*

Rose loved working in the churches' second-hand store. Seeing the people in need, she often thought back to her impoverished childhood and wished that someone had come along and helped her family the way the church was helping these people now. She knew how these people felt and was glad she could do something to show God's love to others.

However, it seemed like no matter what she did, nothing would take away her emotional pain and trauma of the past. It festered in her heart continually. The quiet whispers and stirring shadows hid in the corners of her mind, waiting for an inopportune time to rise up and rage through like a thunderstorm. Even after trying to give it all to God, the emotional pain and accompanying fears always returned.

Rose stood at the kitchen sink, cleaning tomatoes that Coop had grown in his garden. She worked without saying a word. Coop brought in another bushelful for her to can, set it down, and picked up an empty basket. He headed out to pick more, but then stopped, concerned about Rose.

She had been chatty at lunch, and Coop noticed a change in her attitude. "Rose, are you okay?"

She turned and looked helplessly into his face. "Coop," she could barely speak. "I need to do something about my childhood memories. I'm so tired of constantly fighting the bitterness, anger, and the hurt. I try to give everything to God, but it keeps coming back." As tears filled her eyes, Coop stepped up and put his arms around her. She laid her head on his shoulder and began to sob as he held her.

Relaxing some, Rose whispered, "I think I need to talk to someone, but I can't bring myself to do it. Maybe if I called Rev. Estie, I could talk to her. Would you come with me?"

Coop answered in a quiet, low voice, "I know how you feel, Rose. I struggle with things too. If you really want me to, I'll go. But just to support you," he added. He was not ready to bare his soul to anyone—not yet.

Rose made the appointment, and Coop drove her to see the minister that afternoon. When she got out of the car, Rose had second thoughts. She stopped, shut the car door, and stood by the vehicle.

Coop could tell Rose was struggling, so he walked over to her and took her hand. He could feel her tenseness as she grabbed his tightly. After leading her gently to the office door, he knocked. Reverend Estie opened the door and greeted them with a smile on her face. "Hi, Rose. Hi, Coop. Come in, come in." The couple stepped through the door. "Please, have a seat." Estie pointed to three chairs sitting in a small circle.

Coop nodded his head once towards the woman. "Thank you for seeing us on such short notice." The three of them walked over to the chairs and sat down.

"It's my pleasure. So, what can I help you with today?"

Rose looked at Coop, giving him silent permission to speak. "Rev. Es—"

"Please, call me Estie."

"Okay…Estie, Rose is trying to deal with her past, and it's very hard for her." He turned to Rose to give her control over the conversation.

After a few moments of silence, Rose looked up across the small circle at Estie. "Reverend Tasher—I mean Estie…" Rose paused and swallowed. She looked at Coop for help, but then back to Estie. "I-I need to talk to someone…I'm struggling with my past. Thoughts of my childhood keep coming back and haunting me, memories of abuse and of things I've done," Rose confessed.

Suddenly, the words wouldn't come; Rose couldn't speak of her past or verbalize her feelings. She closed her eyes and sat silently for a moment as her body began to tremble. *Maybe I'm not ready to open up to anyone yet.*

Clearing her throat, she opened her eyes and looked up at Estie. "I can't do this right now," she said, her voice breaking. "I-I'm not ready."

Rose stood to go and reached for her purse, and then stopped and looked at the reverend. Coop started to stand but stopped when Rose sat back down. "But I would appreciate it if you would answer one question for me. I've become a Christian and given my life to God. If I've given my life to God, why does my past still haunt me?"

Not knowing anything about Rose's past, Estie answered as best she could. "Rose, if you were a victim, you will not forget the past, but you can learn from it. Satan has a way of throwing things back in your face. When he does that, just give it right back to God, over and over, as many times as it takes. God will take it back as many times as you give it to Him. And Rose, do not trust your feelings; they change. Trust in God's promises and the facts. They don't change."

"I have tried so many times," Rose whispered as tears welled up in her eyes.

Estie could see it was hard for Rose to speak. Leaning forward and gently taking Rose's hands, she said in a motherly tone, "Rose, God has forgiven you, and He wants to heal you. The question might be, do you *really believe* that God can and has forgiven you for the sins you did commit? And do you believe that He can take all this brokenness and hurt away? That requires a strong trust and faith in God."

Rose looked helplessly at Coop as he sat with his head down, and then back at the minister. "Rose" —Estie looked compassionately at her— "when you actually believe that God can and has forgiven you, then you will forgive yourself. And when you feel the horrid memories of the past float effortlessly through your mind, you'll know that you have forgiven yourself and others."

Coop sat listening as he leaned forward on his elbows, hands grasped together tightly. He still struggled with his own haunting memories. He wouldn't speak out, but his thoughts were stirred up. Seeing in his mind scenes of destruction and death, he shivered.

Rose and Estie's discussion faded into the background as Coop questioned his own demons. *Can God heal me from all the brokenness, hate, and devastation?* He did not join the conversation.

Estie could tell Coop was struggling. She spoke to both of them. "We're not skilled enough to always understand why things happen. Only God knows why He allows things to take place. He has His reasons, and it will take faith and trust in Him to deal with your past. It may also take some help from others. But God is the greatest healer. Give it to Him, and He will provide a way."

Coop stood abruptly. "Thank you, Reverend. You've given us a lot to think about."

Seeing that Coop was ready to go, Rose stood quickly too. In a shaky, forced voice, Rose spoke. "Thank you. I-I a-appreciate you making time to talk to us." She followed Coop out the door.

Dusk was falling the next evening, and the gentle breeze cooled the warm air, rustling the leaves and playfully teasing Coop's short brown hair. The sun was gradually setting over the distant purple mountains as shafts of soft maroon light radiated up into the sky.

Rose watched Coop intently from the large window as he sat in the backyard in his wooden folding chair, leaning back in the shade of the walnut tree. He sat in a trance and stared into the distance, his eyes glazed over, his expression blank.

Coop did this quite often, but Rose wasn't sure what was going on. She would watch him sit for long periods of time with a vacant look on his face, and sometimes his eyes were red and swollen afterwards. He refused to talk about it.

This evening as he sat in the shade, she took a chair out and sat down beside him. She waited silently, hoping he would speak. He didn't, so she finally started the conversation.

"Coop," she whispered, "talk to me..." He slowly turned and looked at her, and the helplessness in his eyes brought compassion to her heart. She suspected he was reliving memories of the war, but he would never voice it.

"Rose, please just go away and leave me alone. I want to be by myself."

"I can't do that anymore, Coop. You sit here by yourself and spend hours staring out at nothing. There's something wrong, and I want to help."

"Just go away, leave me alone..."

Refusing to leave, Rose sat by his side and waited patiently. She watched as different emotions slowly rolled across his face and through his eyes as he stared into the distance.

Eventually, Coop spoke quietly, "I've so many bad memories trapped in my head. They're always there, in the back of my mind, playing over and over like a bad record, never ending."

Rose held his hand and resisted the urge to slip into the darkness of her own past. Forcing herself to focus on him, she stilled herself. "Can you tell me about them?"

He sat in silence; the only sounds to be heard were the rustling of the leaves as a gentle breeze drifted through the foliage and the quiet babbling of the nearby creek. Gradually, his tears started to flow freely. He spoke his thoughts inaudibly a first. "I was in the 75th Infantry Division. After a short training..." Coop turned and looked at Rose. He spoke a little louder so she could hear. "After a short training we were rushed to the battle-front in the Ardennes Forest in Belgium, and on December 23, 1944, we moved in. On January 8th we relieved the 82nd Airborne Division when they pulled out. We were new and had never seen combat or any action before, but we were dropped right in the middle of battle."

As Rose held his hand tightly, she could feel it trembling.

"As the 75th stepped into battle, we could hear the rifle shots and machine guns in the distance. The storms of explosions destroyed everything in their path, everything from houses and towns to civilians and soldiers.

"Bombs exploded all around us in the darkness. Artillery was going off everywhere. I could hear the rat-a-tat of rifles close by. There were men hollering, screaming. They were crying and begging for help. No matter how hard we fought, there were just too many of us being wounded and killed. Then there would be minutes or hours of total silence…Then suddenly the fighting would erupt again."

Rose had never heard these stories, and the weight of them fell hard against her. She could see in her mind the horrors Coop described that he'd lived through. Tears washed her face as she watched the man who she loved hurt over things he could not change and would probably never forget.

Coop shifted uneasily in his chair. "Eventually, the Germans pulled back as a result of lack of supplies and manpower…" His voice trailed off.

Rose waited for him to continue.

"Since my primary specialty was military police, I was assigned to make sure people didn't lose control of themselves and take vengeance on enemy soldiers or loot property. I was also assigned to look for snipers that may have held back to pickoff our troops.

"The weather was so bad…below zero at night. As I patrolled, I saw scattered bodies, ripped and torn and then frozen where they lay. There were pools of blood and red icicles hanging from the arms and faces of the dead." Coop shivered. "Some soldiers didn't die from wounds; they just didn't have warm clothes or boots, so they froze to death."

He stopped and took a deep breath. "I found fox holes lined with ice, red with frozen blood. The bodies in them were frozen solid, expressions of pain and fear fixed on their faces." Coop pressed his face into his palms as his shoulders quaked. Deep sobs erupted from his gut. He cried, "I found bodies blown to pieces, some missing limbs, some frozen with eyes or mouths open. Some didn't even look like men, just frozen pieces of raw meat and bone. There was a leg here, an arm there, and guts over there."

Coop stopped talking. He was silent for so long that Rose squeezed his hand and then reached out to touch his face. He didn't respond. It was as if he was not aware that she was even there.

Coop finally took a deep breath and continued. "I-I…" A sob shook his body. "I found a woman's severed hand." His face puckered. He was unable to breathe. "I didn't know what to do with it. There was a bombed-out church up the road and there was a priest there, so I gave it to him. He looked as bad as the rest of us, but he took the hand, and I left." Coop gulped a breath of air.

He stopped talking for a moment to gain control. "When the fighting was over, one of my jobs was to help clean up the battlefield and the towns. We used flatbed trucks to collect the dead bodies. We would drive around and pick up bodies and body parts and load them onto the truck. I recognized some of them." Coop's chest jerked with deep sobs as he slowly continued. "They—they were my friends. I p-picked up my buddies' b-bodies along with civilians and even dead Germans." Memories of the horror erupted in Coop's eyes again as tears overran his eyelids, spilling down his face.

"Some of the bodies weren't frozen yet. When I threw them on top of the pile, their blood flowed down and dripped onto the other dead bodies and ran down the sides of the truck. I was covered in their blood; I can still feel it. And the stench is still on my skin...I can smell it." Coop's eyes went blank, his mind seeing only the distant past. Rose looked at him sympathetically, reached out, and placed her hand on his tremoring leg.

"Every once in a while, I would find someone alive. I'd call for the medics, but they didn't always come. I tried to help the wounded, but I didn't know how or what to do. I watched as several soldiers died..." Coop's body jerked with another sob. Rose cried with him as she held his hand and listened silently.

"There were too many bodies, too many wounded, and not enough help." He tried to continue speaking, but the words became harder to voice. "M-more men d-died than survived...and I c-could do nothing. I was covered in their blood...and sometimes in my mind, I'm s-still covered with it. I-I try to wash it off, but it's like it stained my skin. It always seems to be there.

"The dreams—nightmares that I have are full of the horrors of the war. And the images are just as vivid now as they were then."

He finally gave up speaking and sat quietly, waiting for his body to stop trembling. He couldn't talk about it anymore.

Rose loved him so much and hated that he relived that horrifying part of his life over and over. "I don't know, Coop…I don't know, but maybe this is the type of thing, I mean, for both of us, that we just need to try and give to God."

He was silent for a bit longer, then answered in a pained voice, "I did give it to God, but I took it back. Every time I give it to Him, I take it back and relive it."

"Coop, neither one of us can change our past, and we don't know the future, but maybe we can do this together. We can give this to God right now." She took both his hands in hers, and his tears wet the backs of her knuckles. "Coop, can we pray?"

He sighed, his face still down cast, he nodded but did not speak.

Rose took a shaky breath, and when he still didn't answer, she began, "Lord, we need help. Both Coop and I need to leave our past in the past. Help us to give it to You and leave it there. We know You love us and that You're walking with us every day. We may never forget, but please take the pain away…and teach us how to walk with and trust You as You teach us to deal with the memories. Please give us peace." Rose was crying in earnest. "Help us realize that we are still here…with each other and our kids because You are not finished with us yet. And God…thank You."

Coop's eyes finally met hers, and they sat together in a comfortable silence.

FORTY-THREE

The Christmas season was here. This was the first Christmas since Coop and Rose had accepted Christ, and this would be the first Christmas that the Grear family had ever attended church as believers.

As a child, Coop and his family had celebrated Christ's birth every year. He regretted the fact that he hadn't taught his kids about Christmas as a celebration of Christ's birth, as Jesus' birthday. He pulled the Bible off the bookshelf and flipped through the pages, looking for the Christmas story.

This year is going to be different. I'm going to make sure the kids know the real meaning of Christmas.

Rose looked at Coop and saw their previous agreement reflected in his eyes. This was going to be the best Christmas ever, and their children were going to learn the importance that Christ played in their lives. The whole family looked forward to going to church and celebrating the true meaning of Christmas.

Early in the morning, two Saturdays before Christmas, Missy ran into her parents' bedroom and jumped up on their bed, waking them up. "Hey, Dad? Today's the day! Today you said that we get to decorate the tree!"

Rose lay in silence as memories of her own childhood Christmases threatened to overtake her. Closing her eyes, she called to mind her prayer with Coop in the backyard and focused instead on the cheerful sounds of her husband's and children's voices.

Coop answered sleepily, "Yes, it is. I'll get the decorations out." He dragged himself out of bed and the children followed him around as he dug the artificial Christmas tree and the decorations out of the closet. They hovered around him as he set up the tree in the living room. They paced, wanting to help as Coop strung the lights on the tree while Rose made popcorn for the garland. The children jumped and danced, stimulated by the rhythm of the popping corn.

The smell of the freshly popped popcorn filled the house and the children's noses. The aroma made their mouths water. The sight of Rose filling the bowls sent the children running in circles.

"Hey, kids, the popcorn's ready. Come sit down so we can string it," Rose called. They ran into the front room and sat down on the couch, waiting for their own bowl of popcorn. Rose gave each a bowlful, and Coop handed each one of them a needle and string.

"Now don't eat it all; we need it for the tree," Rose chided playfully.

Giggling, the children promised, "We won't eat all of it." They happily munched as they strung the popcorn.

Rose always enjoyed watching the children create their Christmas tree masterpiece. Whatever it looked like when they were finished, the tree was always beautiful to her.

After all the decorations were on the tree, Coop announced, "Sammy, it's your turn this year to put the finishing touch on the tree: the star on the very top."

"No," Missy complained, "he did it last year."

"No, he didn't, Missy. You did it last year," Tommy corrected.

Coop laughed. The children had the same 'who did it last' argument every year. "I said it was Sammy's turn," Coop announced officially ending the dispute.

"It's my turn?" Sammy eagerly grabbed the star and ran over to his dad. As the young boy reached his arms up to his father, Coop picked up Sammy and placed him on his broad shoulders. Sammy stretched up as high as he could, grabbing the very top branch of the Christmas tree. Placing the star on top, he positioned the decoration just right. The light on the very top branch of the tree shone through the star and made it sparkle. "Look, the star shines like it did on the first Christmas," Sammy announced.

The family sat and gazed at the tree, the lights reflecting brightly on their excited faces. In his out-of-tune voice, Sammy quietly started singing "Silent Night". The whole family quickly joined him in the song.

That evening after dinner, Coop brought out his special Christmas hard ribbon candy, and Rose brought out a special treat: chocolate cream drops. The children sat in a circle, munching on the sweet treats, listening quietly as their father read the Christmas story from the Bible.

Then Rose brought out a small Nativity scene and set it on the table. Playing with the nativity characters, the children took turns telling the story of Christ's birth and setting up the nativity scene.

"Hey, guys," suggested Missy, "let's all sing 'Away in The Manger.' " She started, and her brothers joined in.

As Rose saw her children's excitement, she contrasted this against her own memories of childhood Christmases that were haunted by anger and pain. Tears crested on her eyelids. *I wish someone had told me about Jesus and His birth when I was a child. I wish I could have had Him to lean on through all the heartache.*

Rose quickly grabbed a handkerchief and wiped her tears, hiding her emotions behind a quick series of coughs.

She leaned against the wall, folding her arms and crossing her feet as she watched Coop and the children make memories. Then, slowly, a gentle smile formed on Rose's face as the Spirit's Christmas joy and peace gradually filled her.

I'll treasure these times in my heart as long as I live. I pray that the kids will look back on their childhood Christmases with fondness.

Coop and Rose sat in church. Sunday worship services were pretty routine: music, worship time, announcements of weekly activities, and the message. This particular week however, Rev. Estie included something new in her announcements.

"Two weeks from today, at seven o'clock in the evening, we are going to have a baptism service. Since we don't have a place here to perform the baptisms, we'll be using the First Baptist Church's facilities. If there is anyone here that wants to be baptized, please let me know."

Rose tugged on Coop's sleeve and looked questioningly at him. She whispered, "What's the meaning of baptism?"

Coop whispered back, "I know what it is, but I'm not sure what it means. I think it's a way of saying you believe in God and have accepted Jesus as your Savior. If that's so, maybe we should be baptized. We can leave the children in their Sunday school class a little longer and go ask Estie about it after church."

Rose agreed and once the service was over, Coop and Rose hunted down Estie. They found her at the door saying goodbye to people as they left. Coop approached her after the crowd was gone. "Rev. Estie?" She turned and smiled at them. "Could we talk to you for a little bit? We would like to know more about baptism."

"Certainly, I would love to talk to you about it."

"Coop and I would like to know what baptism is and why a person should be baptized," Rose continued. "What does it mean?"

Estie smiled at Rose. "That's a good question. Let's all go into my office to discuss it."

"We'd like that." Coop nodded in agreement.

The three of them went into the office and sat down. "Thank you for meeting with us," said Coop.

Estie opened her Bible. "I'll make it as short as I can and then answer any questions you have. Tell me what you believe, and I'll start from there."

"Well, we believe in our hearts that Jesus is God's Son and that He died for our sins." Rose interlocked her fingers in her lap, then glanced at Coop. "We've asked for God's forgiveness and have accepted Christ as Lord of our lives. We did this when we went to the altar in church a year ago and confessed Jesus as Lord and Savior."

"What else do we need to do?" Coop inquired.

"Nothing for salvation," the reverend answered with another smile. "Jesus already did the rest."

"We would like to know more about baptism and what it means," Rose said eagerly.

Estie couldn't help but smile at their excitement. "Baptism is your public testimony of your faith in Christ. It's how we show everyone that we are identifying with Christ's dying, being buried, and His coming out of the grave alive. It's our outward sign of the work God has done in our hearts. Ultimately, it's an act of obedience to the command of the Lord for all Christians to be baptized.

"When a person is baptized, he or she is physically laid back in the water and then raised up out of it. As we are laid in the water, it signifies being buried with Christ, and when raised from the water, it represents our rebirth, a new life in Him. Baptism is part of your testimony. It does not save you, but it is a public testimony of your faith in Christ. You should be baptized in obedience to the Lord Jesus Christ as a testimony of your salvation. Romans 6:4 says, *'Therefore we are buried with Him by baptism into death: that like as Christ was raised up from the dead by the glory of the Father, even so we also should walk in newness of life.'*"

They discussed the issue of baptism for a bit longer. Finally, the couple made their decision.

"Rev. Estie, I'd like to be baptized on Sunday night," Rose stated.

"That makes two of us," Coop added.

"Great! I'll plan on it." Estie reached across the desk and took their hands, happy for their decision. "Jim Bennett will do the baptizing. You'll need to bring a set of dry clothes to change into after you're baptized. I'm excited for you."

Estie prayed with them, hugged them, and said, "I'll see you next Sunday."

The next Sunday came faster than expected. Rose and Coop were nervous. Coop had seen baptisms before, but Rose had never seen one and was not sure what to expect. Four other people were also being baptized that evening. The church was full of people who came to watch and celebrate this special occasion. Tommy, Missy, and Sammy sat in a pew with wide eyes, taking in the stained-glass windows and the high vaulted ceiling. It was their first time inside the Baptist Church.

The service started as the choir leader stepped to the front, welcomed the congregation, and led them in congregational singing. The kids wiggled and giggled through the singing, but when the curtains on the baptistery were pulled back, the children settled down and watched with interest. Looking through the large baptistery window, they saw a small room, waist-deep with water. Jim Bennett descended the steps into the water.

After welcoming the congregation, Jim explained why Christ commanded us to be baptized. "Matthew 10:32 says, *'Whosoever therefore shall confess Me before men, him will I confess also before My Father which is in Heaven.'* Tonight, these people have come here to be baptized and to give public testimony of their belief in Jesus Christ as their own personal Savior."

Jim called the name of the first person into the water to be baptized: "Cooper Grear." Nervously, Coop took a deep breath, said a silent prayer praising God, and stepped down the steps into the water. The preacher stood beside Coop and asked, "Coop, have you accepted Jesus Christ as your personal Lord and Savior?"

"Yes, I have," Coop answered in a confident voice.

"And is it your choice to live for and follow Him?"

"Yes, it is."

Jim asked one more question. "Have you chosen to be baptized of your own free will?"

"Yes, I have."

"Then I baptize you in the name of the Father, the Son, and the Holy Ghost."

Putting one hand behind Coop's neck and holding his hands with the other, the preacher laid Coop back in the water, immersed him, and then raised him up out of the water. As Coop rose up, he grinned, made a fist, and punched the air, shouting, "Yes!"

The congregation applauded and cheered. Coop had just made his public testimony for Christ. He was so excited that he grinned from ear to ear. His joy in Christ was evident on his face.

When Coop stepped out of the water, Jim called Rose's name. Coop stopped and hugged her as she stepped down into the water. The joy on her face radiated as she, too, was baptized and gave testimony of her love for Christ.

That evening, Coop and Rose were baptized with four others. Six people professed their love for Christ that evening. It was an evening that they would treasure in their hearts forever.

FORTY-FOUR

1961

On the first Sunday of September, right before the church service was dismissed, Reverend Estle stood and walked to the middle of the stage. She stood quietly for a moment, pondering, finding it hard to say what she needed to say. She addressed the congregation with obvious hesitation. "Over the past years, I have loved serving with you." She paused. Taking a deep breath, she looked directly out into the faces of the worshipers. "You and I, working together, have watched this church grow and be a blessing to many people while we proclaimed the Word of God." Tears welled in her eyes.

"God has finally answered our prayers. Your new pastor will be taking over next month."

Surprised, the congregation sat quietly for a brief moment, digesting the information. Then after a short outburst of applause and amens, Estie raised her hand for quiet. Smiling through her tears, she continued, "At sixty-five years old and with a few aches and pains of my own, it's time for me to step down. I'm confident that you can and will continue to do God's work in this community." She dabbed her eyes with her handkerchief.

"This is hard…" She stopped again, and the congregation began applauding and encouraging her along. "Oh, stop it." She laughed, waving the handkerchief at them. "This is hard enough without all you making a scene."

The congregation began laughing, and Estie laughed along with them.

"I feel I've done what God has asked me to do," she continued again, "but don't worry, I'm not going anywhere for a while. I'll be here until the end of the month to help the new pastor get settled in." She paused and sobbed, trying to calm her emotions and organize her thoughts.

"Your new pastor is the Reverend Dave Phillips. He's twenty-six years old and just two weeks out of seminary, so this will be his first pastorate. He and his wife, Ginny, are expecting their first child." She took a moment and made eye contact across the congregation. "But most importantly, he has a true heart for God and for God's people. He will be a fantastic pastor for you, and you will be a blessing to him and his family.

"I pray that you'll welcome them with open arms and help them to feel at home here. Thank you for your friendship and years of devotion to God and this community."

Estie stepped off the stage, and the congregation surrounded her with hugs and words of affirmation and thanks.

Rose and Coop were sad to see her leave. She was very loved and had been instrumental in their first year of life as believers. It was hard for them to say good-bye, but they believed it was time to let her go. It was time for the church to move on to the next chapter in its story.

Everyone was excited to meet the new pastor—everyone except Rose. It was hard for Rose to see Estie go. Rose needed someone to talk to, and the new pastor was a man. She wondered if she would be able to tell any man other than Coop about what had been done to her.

A few months into his ministry, Pastor Dave requested that everyone remain after the service for a brief business meeting.

"Thank you all for staying afterwards. I promise I won't keep you long. The board and I have been meeting for a while and we have assessed where we are and what it is we feel the Lord wants us to do.

"First, we're going to need a new and larger facility. We're starting a building fund to that end."

There was a rumble of discussion that ran through the congregation, but no one spoke out against the idea.

Pastor Dave continued, "It may take us a while to raise the money, but if we don't start now, it will take even longer and we'll never get there."

This was met with laughter.

"We have skilled people here at the church that may be willing to volunteer a lot of the labor, and we will be seeking donations of materials and money. If this is God's will, He will provide."

Soon, the program was under way. It wasn't long before the money and materials started pouring in and the blueprints were designed. Members of the congregation started volunteering their time and skills.

Being a skilled carpenter, Coop was excited to help. One Sunday, he approached Dave at church. "Hey, Pastor?" Coop grinned. "I'd like to volunteer to help with the church building. I can work some evenings and most weekends. Since I'm a carpenter and work on commercial buildings for a living, I can supervise a lot of the work on the building."

Knowing of Coop's outstanding reputation around town in carpentry, Pastor Dave eagerly took Coop's hand, shaking it vigorously. "I'd love to have you on the team. Thank you for your willingness to help."

"You know, Dave, I want to do this to help others. Rose and I struggled to feed our family for over a year, and other people stepped in to help us. I don't know how we would have made it through the hard times without help. I thank God every day for the people of this church being there for us. Now I want to be there to help others."

"Well, then." Dave grinned as he patted Coop on the shoulder. "Let's get started and go take a look at those blueprints."

After studying the plans, Coop helped head up the project. He became a key part of the construction team, volunteering his evenings and weekends along with the other volunteers.

Rose helped provide food for the workers on the weekends. She also helped paint, decorate, and clean the building.

Coop and Pastor Dave worked together on the building, becoming good friends through the process. The more they worked together, the deeper their friendship became. Slowly, Coop began sharing with Dave about his war experiences, his nightmares, and about how his work accident affected him.

While the two men worked, talked, and prayed together through the months, Coop gained a new understanding from Dave. "Coop, God's ways are not our ways. We don't know why God allows these trials in our lives. Our troubles help us to realize just how much we need God, and if we didn't need God, we wouldn't call on Him. He wants to walk with us hand in hand throughout our lives."

This new realization shifted slowly from Coop's head down to his heart. He gradually gave all the pain and anger that he harbored in his mind and heart to God. As he turned them over to God again and again, the memories lost their power over him and floated painlessly through his mind, gradually fading away into times past. He would always remember, but the pain of the memories was gone. His agony slowly faded away as his new life in Christ began to flourish.

Rose watched as the congregation dedicated themselves, not only to building the church, but also to loving and helping those in need.

She quietly wondered at the relationship Pastor Dave and Coop had developed. Over the past few months, Coop had become a different man; his eyes had lost that haunted look, and he hadn't had a nightmare in weeks.

FORTY-FIVE

1963

The house creaked in the summer heat. A small air conditioner in the kitchen window groaned as it worked hard trying to cool the stifling air. Heavy drapes were drawn together against the glare of the sun.

Rose found herself sitting alone in her front room while Coop was at work and the kids were off swimming with the church's youth group. She closed her eyes, hung her head, and released a pent-up breath as she again fought off the vile memories and accusing whispers that still tormented her. *How many years has it been? Tommy is fourteen now, Missy is twelve, and Sammy's eleven. Even after all these years, my past still festers and haunts me. Why can't I forgive and let go of the awful memories of my youth?*

Rose's volunteering at the church helped keep her busy during the week and was a good distraction while the children were in school during the school year or off playing in the summer. But she needed to keep her mind busy to stop the dark shadows of her past from storming through her consciousness. The memories were still buried in the dark recesses of her mind, writhing their way through her thoughts at their own discretion.

Working at the church seemed to help her put them out of her mind—for a time. But as hard as she tried to forget, the past still haunted her, and no matter how many times she gave it to God, the memories and feelings continued to resurface. Sitting motionless in her dark blue armchair, Rose tried to shake off the recollections.

I can't live like this anymore. *My whole life, I've been full of bitterness, hatred, and guilt.*

She silently gazed into the dark shadows of the past. Her eyes glazed over as she stared into the shadowy room. Her hands started to tremble, and the battle inside her intensified. Perspiration beaded on her forehead and ran down her face and neck, her cotton dress sticking to her back and chest. Taking a deep breath, Rose tried to force herself to relax.

She took another breath and exhaled. Determination slowly set in. It was time. She had to deal with this once and for all. The telephone sat on the end table beside her chair, daring her to make the call. As she glared at the phone, her breathing grew shallow and quick, and her heart rate increased. The walls seemed to be pressing in around her, and the muggy air was hard to breathe. Rose opened and closed her hand as she reached for the telephone hand-piece.

Lifting the receiver from the cradle of the black rotary phone, she fought the trembling in her arms and hands. Suddenly, the handpiece slipped from her fingers, bounced on the floor, and then dangled by its coiled black cord.

Rose's doubts started to return as she watched the receiver swing back and forth just above the floor. *Who am I to tell someone—anyone—about what had happened? After all, am I not the one to blame? Isn't some of this my fault?*

Staring at the phone's handpiece, she spoke into the still, hot air, "I don't need to do this. I've survived all these years without talking about it. Why should I now?"

She turned her face away from the phone, its receiver still dangling from the end of the coiled cord, the dial tone sounding an angry buzz into the room.

As she turned away, a picture on the wall caught her attention. Above the couch hung her family's portrait. The bright eyes and smiling faces of her husband and children looked back at her. But even in the photograph, there was the familiar shadow of darkness in her eyes. Seeing the picture of herself with her family brought back her resolve.

After all these years, I'm tired of battling my emotions. I need to deal with this. I have to face the issues and talk to someone.

She looked down, refusing to meet the accusing gazes of her family. She closed her eyes and let her shoulders droop. *I want to live a normal life.*

Gradually releasing her breath, Rose slowly raised her head, pulled her shoulders back, and once more found her resolve. Reaching out, she grasped the dangling handpiece and put it up to her ear. *I have to make the call! Now!*

She dialed the phone number and watched as the wheel clicked noisily after each number.

A male voice answered: "Hello, this is Pastor Dave speaking."

She glanced back up at the family photo for reassurance.

With a quivering voice she addressed him, "Hi, Pastor? This is R-Rose. I need to make an appointment to talk with you."

"Of course, Rose. "When would be a good time?" he asked.

She knew she needed to do it now or she would change her mind. "Would right now work? If this isn't a good time, as soon as possible."

"Now would be fine." Pastor Dave immediately sensed the tension, the near panic in her voice. "Come on over to my office. I'll be expecting you."

"I'm on my way now." Slamming the phone down, Rose paused, not believing she had made the call. She grabbed her purse and rushed out the door before she could change her mind.

Ten minutes later, she stood motionless at the open door of Pastor Dave's office. She could see him working at his desk, but no words of greeting would come from her mouth. Paralyzing fear gripped her, leaving her unable to move or speak.

The moderately sized office was situated in the northwest corner of the building with a small secretary's office and a street access for business and counseling. It also had an alternative exit, which led across a short hall back to the sanctuary.

Realizing someone was there, Dave glanced up from his desk and saw Rose standing in his doorway. He stood and closed the door behind him that led to the sanctuary. Motioning her to come in, he walked over to greet her. "Rose, come on in." He smiled reassuringly at her. "I'm glad to see you."

She took a small step, stopping just across the threshold.

Dave walked up and welcomed her as he took her hand in both of his. However, he looked up as he felt a slight tremble in her arm. Immediately, Dave realized something was disturbing Rose. He cleared his throat as he looked at her, compassion coloring his face. "I hope I can be of some help. Come on in and have a seat."

With slow, careful steps, Rose walked over and perched herself on the edge of the light green couch. Reaching into her purse, she pulled out her handkerchief and began to fidget with it, pulling the worn cloth between her fingers. Looking everywhere but at Pastor Dave, she surveyed the small office, her eyes darting between the two doors, wondering which of the two would be the quickest exit.

She could feel him looking at her and immediately her face flushed; heat crept up her neck. She stared at her feet, refusing to meet his gaze. After several moments of heavy silence had passed, she glanced up. When she did, she saw the compassion and understanding in his eyes that she had known would be there, and she began to relax.

This is Pastor Dave, my friend.

Her desire to flee began to fade. Rose scooted back on the couch, struggling to make herself comfortable as Pastor Dave walked behind his desk and rolled his chair over to sit across from her.

He sat down facing her. "Rose, what can I do for you?"

Taking a deep, cleansing breath, she lifted her head and looked directly at him; she was not going to lose her resolve.

Tears started streaming down her cheeks as she confessed, "Pastor, I can't do this anymore. I-I need help." Rose wept. "I'm t-tired of reliving the past." She began to shake as the sobs worked their way from her gut up through her body. Fear to speak of the past and worry of judgment and rejection filled her being. Gripping the edge of the couch, her knuckles whitened as she concentrated on breathing—just breathing. She dropped her eyes to the floor. "You're the only person I could think of to call, the only one I felt I could trust." Her body shook with every sob. She wiped her tears from her cheeks with her handkerchief, then clasped it tightly with one hand as she brushed a loose strand of hair behind her ear with the other.

Pastor Dave leaned forward, putting his elbows on his knees and clasping his hands. "Rose, you're safe here. Take your time. I'll be here when you're ready to talk." He sat quietly, waiting for her to signal she was ready to continue.

Looking into her eyes, he could see her pain and turmoil. His heart ached for her. Before he said anything, Pastor Dave sent up a silent prayer. *Lord, please give me Your wisdom and Your words to help Rose. Make Your presence known to her, and give her a peace only You can give.*

Dave sat silently for a few minutes longer, waiting for Rose to calm down. Then quietly and gently he said, "Rose, I can see that you're hurting; you're heartbroken. How can I help you?"

Rose tried to suppress her sobs. Her eyes dropped back to the floor. "Pastor, I-I need to talk to someone. I c-can't let go of the past." She paused, choking back another sob. "It keeps haunting me even though I give it to God over and over again. Instead of getting better, it keeps festering inside of me. I have tried to talk about it with Coop. He knows all about it, but he gets angry when I try to discuss it with him. He doesn't want to hear it, and I can't blame him."

Forcing herself to look up, Rose saw that Pastor Dave was silhouetted by the bright sunlight streaming through the window behind him. The sunlight created a gentle aura around this man, and through it, she sensed a love that seemed to hold them both in its embrace. It reminded her of the first time she felt the presence of God, when she had been in the desert on the big rock alongside the road.

The image struck like a blast of warm air. She closed her eyes and opened them again to make sure she had seen what she thought she had. But the aura was gone, leaving only the feeling of warmth and safety behind. For a moment she thought it had been an angel, but after looking again, she saw it was only Pastor Dave.

Closing her eyes, she silently spoke to the unseen One, the one she knew was always with her. *God, are You trying to tell me something?* As she looked to God for answers, deep down in her heart, she knew that He was with her as she took this step of faith. *Thank You, God, for answering my prayer, for providing someone whom I can trust and confide in, and for giving me courage to speak to him.*

When the realization began to sink in, her shoulders gradually relaxed and she leaned calmly back on the couch. The tension she had felt started to melt away as a peace slowly filled her being. She could feel the presence of God's Spirit fill the room.

Rose silently watched Pastor Dave. His 5'10" frame didn't seem large enough to contain the immense measure of God's love and compassion that emanated out of him.

Dave continued to sit silently for a few more minutes, giving Rose a little more time. Then, quietly and gently, he spoke again. "Rose, I can see that your heart is broken. You are hurting. What can I do for you?"

"Pastor Dave, I need to face the past and deal with it once and forever. Would you help me, listen to me, council me? All this hatred, guilt, and bitterness from the past is tearing me up inside." Rose's eyes were pleading with him, fear of rejection and condemnation lingering near.

Pastor Dave leaned toward Rose; his eyes focused on her face. A look of compassionate understanding softened his features as he smiled reassuringly. "Rose, this sounds like it won't be easy. While I'm sure God will bring you the healing you need, this may take some time," he cautioned. He gave her a moment to think about what he'd said.

When she didn't respond, he continued. "But it looks to me like you might be ready, and you being here suggests you're willing. I'm here for you."

He laid one of his hands on the back of hers. Rose's eyes darted to where their hands met; she stiffened but she didn't remove her hand.

She released a breath. "Thank you, Pastor. You have no idea how much this means to me."

"Rose, I don't know what happened, but we can confront the issue together. Are you ready yet to talk about it?"

Rose pulled at the handkerchief with her fingers and nodded her head, tears still wetting her face.

Pastor Dave sat quietly and gave her a gentle smile. "Shall we begin?"

Rose paused to think. Using her handkerchief, she wiped her eyes, blew her nose, and stuffed the cloth back into her purse.

She had pictured herself in this moment, sitting and talking to Dave. She had planned everything she would tell him, how she would tell him. But now…now the words simply disappeared from her mind. Doubts rose again.

Her voice quaking, she managed to speak, her words were little more than a whisper. "Pastor, I'm struggling with what happened to me…the things that were done to me and that I've done as a child and as a young woman.

"I'm a Christian now; I accepted Jesus, and I know He loves me. I can feel that I'm growing in Him and I've learned so much since I've started going to church. But how I feel about myself and the pain of my past…it just keeps haunting me, and it won't go away." She dissolved into tears, again.

Pastor Dave interlaced his fingers and rested his elbows on his knees. He resisted the urge to reach out and take ahold of Rose's hand, opting instead to allow her the comfort of him just being with her. He nodded his head to show her he was listening.

Rose kept her face downcast. "From my earliest memory, I was abused. I had to watch my father beat my mother and us kids as well. Times were hard for everybody, but my father…it made him mean.

"He drank all the time, and when he did, he hurt us. When we got older, he began touching us." She looked up quickly, checking Pastor Dave's response.

Dave nodded again and said, "Go on, Rose; you're doing good."

Rose swallowed. "My father, Fred, was not a good man. He did things to us that no father should do to his child. He made us do things to each other. I never knew all the details, but while we were traveling to California, he did something to one of my cousins, something bad; he abused him and hurt him bad. We had to leave before everyone could find out what he'd done.

"Father drank all the time, and then he would hurt us…my mother mostly…in the beginning, at least. But then, like I said, the older we got, the more things he did to us…my sisters and I mostly."

As Rose continued to talk, the words began to pour out of her like a spicket that had been broken open. The words flowed unhindered. Pulling the handkerchief back out of her purse, she ran it through her fingers absentmindedly, pulling it over and over around her digits.

"Then, when driving back to Idaho, we saw a woman and her son whose car had broken down on the side of the road. Father stopped to help them, but then something bad happened to the woman. He dragged her behind a rock. We could hear her screaming and then everything went silent. My little brother Willie ran back to check…and he screamed and never came back either."

She looked up at Pastor Dave. "Do you understand what I'm saying, Pastor?" He nodded, but Rose wasn't convinced he understood. She took a breath and forged ahead. "Pastor Dave, when my brother went to see what my father was doing, we never saw him again…ever."

As what she was saying dawned on Dave, he sucked in his breath before he could catch himself. "Are you saying…"

"Yes, my father killed my little brother and left his body lying behind a rock in the forest with the woman that he murdered."

Dave regained his composure. "What did your mother do?"

"She did what we always did: we did what Father told us. When he came back to the car, he brought the woman's son with him. He told us that this was the new Willie and that he was now our brother. We were never allowed to talk about it after that.

"When we finally made it back to the farm, we all hoped it meant things would get better for us. They didn't. Not only did Father continue to force himself on my sisters and me, he began to sell us to other men for sex. He told us that he was doing it for us…to feed and take care of the family…but most of the money went to pay for his liquor."

This time, Dave did take hold of Rose's hand and squeezed it reassuringly. He had tears in his eyes.

Rose took comfort from Pastor Dave's contact. Instead of shutting her down, she felt strengthened by it. "That still wasn't the worst, Pastor." She checked his face for permission to continue. When he nodded again, she dared. "My new brother…the one we called the new Willie; he and I began to be good friends. For whatever reason, this angered Father, so one day, he brought Willie into my room and made him watch as father raped me. When he was done, he made Willie rape me as well. The hardest part about it was that I knew Father did it just to hurt me. It wasn't for pleasure or need or to help the family; he just wanted to show me that he had all the power and that I was nothing, and nothing at all to him.

"When Father finally died, I was happy. I felt like I had finally been set free…but I hadn't. Father still haunts me; he still has me locked in that prison."

Rose couldn't say anymore and instead broke down and cried. When Pastor Dave moved closer to her, opening his arms to her, she collapsed against him and sobbed out the years of pain and self-loathing that had made up the walls of the cell where she'd been trapped.

There was a long silence where the only sounds were the creaks of the walls and the hum of the air conditioner as it struggled against the heat. The two sat in companionable silence for some time before either of them spoke.

"Rose, I can't imagine a child having to live through that—any of it. What you described was horrible, but it was not your fault. You were a child, and the adults in your life were supposed to protect you."

"But I-I…there were so many men that I…" She couldn't finish.

"Rose," Pastor Dave said gently, "Rose, look at me." He waited. "None of that was your fault. You were a child, and those things were done to you…by people who should have known better."

Rose wanted to believe him. Her heart fought desperately to hold his words as truth.

Dave continued. "Your heart and spirit have been bruised, but you're not defeated."

Rose looked at him, a burgeoning hope filling her eyes and heart.

"You say you can't forget what happened. To be honest, you probably never will, but you can be free of the pain."

Dave paused, allowing himself a moment to process all that he'd heard before continuing. *God, give me your words to share with her.*

After a few minutes, Pastor Dave said quietly, "We don't know why God allowed all this to happen, and we may never know. However, I can see that God has used this in your life."

Rose's eyes snapped up.

Pastor Dave lifted a hand in a 'give me a chance to explain' gesture. "God has brought you to the end of your resources so you can find His." Leaning forward with his hands clasped and his elbows still resting on his knees, he paused again as he glanced past her and looked up at the cross hanging on the wall. Drawing strength and wisdom from God, Dave continued: "God is using your past experiences and that difficult time in your life to help point the way to Him, to draw you closer, and to teach you how to trust Him.

"When you accepted Christ, you became whole, and you have a new truth and meaning in your life. God is now your Heavenly Father who desires the best for you. He knows about everything that happened and has been with you every step of the way. And to God, your past no longer exists. He loves you. You're His child."

"But why did God let all of this happen?" she interrupted, her anger at God erupting. "I was a child! I had no control over what happened to me." Rose started sobbing.

"Rose…" Dave paused to make sure she was listening, "We don't know why God allows things to happen. God's ways are not our ways. But God has given all people a freewill. When people sin, it's not God's doing; it's Satan's. People can choose whom they follow; Satan will use anything he can to turn people away from God."

"Your earthly father, Fred, had freewill and chose to exercise it over others. His evil actions hurt those around him, including you. Your earthly father failed you, but your Heavenly Father loves you. He will always be there for you and *never* forsake you.

Rose looked up at Dave, her eyes red-rimmed and swollen. "Sometimes, I feel like it's all my fault, but I know it's not. Why can't I get past it? I carry it with me all the time. Why can't I let it go? After all these years, I still feel guilty even though I was the victim." Rose continued to sob.

"You have to realize that Satan is in the business of lies," Pastor Dave continued. "Jesus said Satan was the father of lies. It's what he does best. He takes a tiny bit of truth and twists it into a huge lie that we believe. Because we see that tiny bit of truth, we think it must all be true." Dave paused to give Rose time to process what he was saying.

"Rose, I know you must feel hatred and bitterness and even guilt, but I think your real problem is that you don't believe that God can forgive or heal you. Only He can set someone free, bind a broken heart, and heal a broken spirit…"

"I've been told that before," Rose recalled. "Rev. Estie and I talked about it. Maybe I just needed to hear it again. I do struggle with not believing that God can or will forgive me. My guilt and anger are so strong, I can't even forgive myself. I know I need to give it to God and put it behind me. I'm really trying, but it's not easy to do."

"Rose, your pain has been shutting you off from the light of God's love. Its only God's love that can heal your heart and take away all that pain you've been carrying around inside you. The secrets we try to hide from God can split off and develop lives of their own. Given time they will grow and can take control of your life without your even realizing it. I know what you're feeling is strong, but that's not sin; that's you hurting. It's what you do about it that makes all the difference."

Dave stood, walked over to the window, and then gazed up into the sky. He put his hands in his pockets, contemplating what he should say next.

He spoke without turning. "Rose, do you know how special you are to God? He is your true Father, and He will never fail you. God walks with you constantly, guiding and protecting you. He loves you like you love your own children. When your children hurt, struggle, or do something wrong, that doesn't mean you love them any less. You have even more compassion for them."

He turned to face her, leaned back on the windowsill, and rested the heels of his hands beside him on the sill. "You take your children's hands, walk with them, and teach them. Just as your love for your children overrules any situation they're in, God's love overrules any situation you're in.

"You're special to Him, Rose, not because of anything you have or haven't done but because you're His daughter.

You accepted God's invitation when He invited you to be His child. He did the rest. He sent His only Son to die for your sins. He forgave you, and He accepted you into His family. Now, as a child of God, you have the 'right' to enjoy a special relationship with Him. He's your Father; you're His child. The past doesn't exist anymore. You're whole in Him.

"Once you understand and believe that He has already forgiven you and that He has provided your healing, then you can accept that forgiveness and healing for yourself. The pain from your past will lessen over time, and healing will begin. Even though the memories will always be there, the bitterness, anger, and pain will eventually disappear. God will continue to renew your mind and heart. You'll grow in Christ as you walk with Him. It's a process that will take your whole lifetime as you learn to become more like Him."

Pastor Dave walked back to his chair and sat down. He took Rose's hands and looked directly into her eyes. "Rose, do you realize who you are in Christ?"

She looked confused, "What do you mean?"

"Rose, you are more than what people see on the outside and what you feel on the inside. You are the daughter of the one and only true God. Through Christ, you are God's child. You are born of God, part of His family. You are God's workmanship, Christ's sister, a child of the one true King, and an heir with Jesus. I could go on and on about who you are in Christ. *Nothing* can separate you from the love of God."

Still somewhat confused, her pain was beginning to lessen as the words managed to penetrate through to her heart. Rose asked, "So, what do I do? How do I deal with my past and my feelings?"

"First, you need to believe that He has forgiven you and that He can heal you. Pray about it. Seek Him and study His word. Praying is our way of talking to Him; the Bible is His words to us."

He paused and gave her hands a gentle squeeze. "And forgive. I know it's hard to forgive those who have wronged you. But not forgiving creates bitterness and hatred in your own heart. If you don't forgive them, it will slowly eat you up from the inside out. Not forgiving someone is like swallowing poison, then waiting for the other person to die. It doesn't harm the other person; it only hurts you. Don't let the wrongs these people have done maintain their hold over you any longer, ruining the rest of your life. Give it to God, over and over, as many times as you have to. And, Rose, you may have to many, many times. It's a process."

She closed her eyes as she tried to take it all in. Deep down, Rose knew Pastor Dave was right. Dave released her hands and sat back. For a long while, they sat in comfortable silence.

When she looked up, Dave could see a measure of peace in her eyes. "Rose, before you leave, let's pray together." They both bowed their heads. "Why don't you start?"

As Rose opened her mouth to pray, words wouldn't come; the only thing she could do was sob.

"I-I…" She began but could go no further. Lowering her face, she pressed the handkerchief to her eyes.

So, Pastor Dave prayed, and as he did, Rose found that he prayed the very words that were heavy in her heart:

"Dear Father God, thank You for Rose and her heart for You and for the new life You've given her. Thank You for using her past life to point her to You. We know that

You have forgiven and forgotten her past. You are the Great Physician. We ask that You begin to heal her heart and spirit. Help her to know in her heart that You have begun and will continue to heal her. Take away any guilt, bitterness, and hatred of the past and replace it with a freedom in You. Set her free of this bondage and fill her with a peace and joy that only You can give."

As the pastor prayed, Rose stopped sobbing and a peace settled in her soul. She felt the presence of God within her and all around her.

She slowly realized that she hadn't accepted God's forgiveness because she didn't feel He could forgive her, so she hadn't forgiven herself. She also recognized that the abuse wasn't her fault and she had to let go of the destructive emotions that she harbored deep in her heart.

She sat for a long moment with her head bowed, silently meditating on all that she had just heard and on how it applied to her life.

Gradually, in her mind and her heart, it became real to her. She realized that God had already forgiven her; she finally accepted His forgiveness. As she looked to God, the bitterness and hatred started to fade. A sense of forgiveness quietly started growing in her heart, a forgiveness for herself and for others that had wronged her.

She whispered, "Amen."

The two raised their heads and smiled at each other. They both knew they were in the presence of the Holy Spirit.

"Now, Rose, there's something that you need to know," Pastor Dave continued. "Remember, Satan is a liar and a trickster. He's going to tell you this is all a lie, that God can't heal, forgive, or forget. He'll try to get you to doubt and take back your past. When this happens, remember

Marsha Hood

what happened here today; remember what God did for you, and give all that ugly back to God. Give it back every time it comes to mind. Healing can be a slow process. I'll give you some scripture to memorize." He smiled. "Satan can't stand against God's Word.

"And, Rose, call me if you have any problems or when you need to talk again. We can talk whenever you want. That would give you a chance to deal with these problems and work through them, one at a time. Think about it. Maybe we could set an appointment every two weeks or so. Just let me know."

Rose stood to leave. "Thank you, Pastor. Thank you for everything." She smiled at him, gave him a hug, and walked out the door with a lighter heart and a new understanding of God and His love.

When she arrived home, Rose sat down in her armchair and took time to think and meditate on what Pastor Dave had said. As she pondered, memories of her childhood started rolling through her mind; thoughts of Father and his abuse filled her consciousness.

Then, slowly, an understanding and forgiveness started to grow in her being. *I'm here today despite, and even because of, what Father did. Father chose his own actions, and his choices hurt me and other people.*

Whispering quietly to herself, she began to think more on what Father had done. Seeing Father through the brokenness of sin made it easier. It made it possible for her to consider forgiveness. As Rose thought about all the things God had forgiven her for, she made the decision to forgive her father.

God, there's no way anyone can justify what Father did, but, God, I choose to forgive him. Give me forgiveness in my mind and my heart for Father and all those that abused me.

The more she prayed, the more she realized how God was using her past situations to teach her to trust Him and to look to Him for everything.

Then a scripture that she had memorized resurfaced in her mind, Romans 8:28; '*And we know that all things work together for good to them that love God, to them who are the called according to His purpose.*'

As she reflected on God's word, she rose from her chair and slowly paced back and forth in the room. Understanding slowly dawned on her as God's Spirit settled in her being. She realized what He had actually done for her.

Rose walked to the window, looked out toward heaven, and spoke to her heart, "Thank You, God, for allowing the bad in my life to direct me to You, for helping me to see through Your eyes, and for calling me into a relationship of trust and love with You." Grateful tears perched on the edge of her eyelids.

As the bitterness and anger slowly dissipated and the memories of her past floated effortlessly through her mind, she suddenly realized she had forgiven Father. She knew God had forgiven her. A peace that only God could give settled in her heart as tears of joy flooded her eyes. She rejoiced in God's victory! *My heart is free!*

"I'm free!"

Epilogue

It took over two years, but the congregation finished the new church. The sanctuary was large enough to hold four times as many people as the older one, and it had a large stage and choir loft in front. The carpet matched the cushions on the pews and the curtains on the baptistery, which were all a striking blue velvet. The fellowship hall had folding doors that would close to make three large separate rooms or open to create a huge hall. The kitchen and fellowship hall were large enough to serve as a soup kitchen. There were also numerous classrooms, a nursery, bathrooms, a foyer, and offices. All of this had taken many months of hard work and precious donations to complete. It was a beautiful building, built out of love.

Coop had done a lot of work on the building, more than most. His evenings and weekends for many months had been spent working on the church. He had helped with the foundation, framing, walls, doors, and many other carpentry jobs.

But Coop had taken extra special care in finishing the front wall of the sanctuary. He had handpicked each redwood board and placed it vertically, fitting it together with other boards to produce a beautiful wood-grain-patterned wall across the front of the sanctuary. In the middle of the wall was the baptistery window.

But Coop wasn't done yet. He stood back and evaluated his work on the front wall of the sanctuary. *Lord, this is the wall that everyone will see during the church services as they worship You. It'll be the background to whatever happens in the sanctuary:*

the choirs, sermons, programs, and meetings. I want this to be my masterpiece to You and to my fellow brothers and sisters.

Coop spoke out loud to God. "I have one last thing to finish, one last final touch for You, God, before this building is complete."

He went home and started working in his shop. As he laid wood out on a counter to work with, he looked up and spoke out loud to God again. "Lord, this is my gift to You."

Coop spent the next few days in his shop cutting, shaping, sanding, staining and finishing a large, wooden cross. He took his time and special skills to make the most beautiful cross he could. When he finished it, he center-mounted the large, handmade cross on the wall high above the baptistery so everyone in the sanctuary could see it.

Coop walked to the back of the sanctuary, sat on the floor, and leaned his back against the brick wall. Sitting quietly, he gazed up at the cross and the redwood-paneled wall. He was pleased with how it had all turned out. He took a deep breath and gave a huge, relaxing sigh. *My masterpiece, the cross and the front wall of the sanctuary, is complete, it's finished.*

As he sat in the back examining his work, the last few years rolled through his mind. He thought about all that he and Rose had gone through and how far they had come. He thought about the good friends they had made, the time and talent used to work for God, and the future use of the building. Over the past years as both he and Rose learned to walk with and trust God, the pain of their pasts had faded. They were learning to give everything to God. The joy and peace he felt inside as he sat enjoying the presence of God's Spirit was indescribable.

A sudden rush of excitement to share this experience washed over him, so he hurried to the church's office and called Rose. "Rose, I just finished the front wall in the sanctuary. The cross is hung on the wall above the baptistery. I'm finished! The building is completed. I would like you to be the first one to see the finished work. Would you come down and celebrate with me?"

Rose's excitement ran deep. She was eager to rejoice and celebrate with him.

"Coop, I would love to. I'll get the kids and we'll be there in a few minutes!"

She quickly grabbed her purse and hollered at her children, "Hey, kids, come on, let's get in the car and run down to the church to see your dad. The church is finished, and he wants us to see it."

Tommy complained, "I've already seen the church. I don't want to go."

"I don't want to go either," Sammy chimed in. "I'm watching TV right now."

"I'll go," Missy agreed, "but I need to walk to Julie's house from there to get my schoolbooks."

Rose and Missy jumped into the Chevy and drove to the church.

Deep down, Rose was glad the kids weren't going to be there. She wanted this time alone with Coop. His work was finished, and he wanted to share this special time with her. She had never seen him more dedicated to anything else as he was to his work for Christ. This was a big deal for him.

When Rose entered the church building, she found Coop in the back of the empty sanctuary, sitting on the floor and leaning back against the wall. She could see the satisfaction in his face as he evaluated his finished work. Rose sat down beside him and kissed his cheek. He took her hand and smiled as she sat beside him and studied his masterpiece with him.

"Coop, the wall is stunning. The deep, rich colors of the redwood and the wood grain patterns are gorgeous." She marveled as she studied his work. "And the cross above the baptistery is the most beautiful cross I've ever seen. It's a breathtaking final touch." Rose nestled her hand in his. "Coop, it's beautiful. You did an amazing job."

Coop smiled. "Thanks, Rose." There was a peaceful stillness around them. "I want this room, this sanctuary, to be God's special dwelling place where people can come and worship in His presence. Rose, will you pray with me to dedicate my work on this building to God for His glory, that He will use my work for the furthering of His?" Tears of joy glistened in his eyes.

Rose took his hand, and they walked to the front of the sanctuary and knelt at the foot of the cross. Coop faced her, bowed his head, and spoke his heart, "Dear Lord, thank You for the opportunity to work for You, to use the skills You have given me for Your glory. I dedicate my work on this building to You. Use it according to Your plans.

And, Lord, I give You everything: my past, my present, and my future. I dedicate myself and my family to You. I plan to raise my children in this church. Please help me to be a godly husband, father, and friend to others. I pray Your Spirit will fill this church and touch the lives of all who come to seek You. Amen."

As Rose silently knelt beside Coop, she felt God's Spirit surround her and a restful peace settle over her. In her heart, she knew that the pain of the past was gone, and their future was in God's hands.

Rose gazed up at the cross for a moment. Then she clasped her hands together, bowed her head, and whispered, "God, thank You for being with us and bringing us through the past, and thank You for Your presence with us now. I pray that you will walk with us into the future, and show us how to love others. Give us Your wisdom as we raise our children and teach them about You and Your love." She paused and glanced up at Coop and then closed her eyes again. "And God, thank You for my husband, his skills, and for his willingness to use them to further Your kingdom. Please bless his work. Amen."

Missy stood quietly in the shadows at the sanctuary's entrance. She watched as her parents knelt before the cross praying. She listened carefully as they poured their hearts out to God, but she also remembered the pain and hurt her parents had fought to hide for so many years. Although she didn't know the details, she could still remember how both of her parents at times had dealt with dark secrets concerning their past, and fear tickled the edges of her mind. As her parents prayed and dedicated their family to God, Missy hoped that the troubles were indeed all behind them. She took comfort in seeing her parents the way they were now.

Missy sighed, shaking off the dark feeling. She thanked God for her mother and father, and for walking with them through their difficulties.

Deep in her heart, Missy knew God loved her too, and would always be there for her.

Acknowledgements

A heart-felt thank you goes to all those who have given their time and effort to help with the story development, research, editing, and publishing of this book.

First and foremost, thank you to my husband, Bob Hood, for being my shoulder to lean on, and my question and answer man. Special thanks go to my granddaughter, Aurora Keene, for her help editing and for modeling for the cover, to my daughter, Jennifer Keene, for editing and suggestions, to my son, Bobby, for his tech support, and to my son, Joshua, for the artwork.

Thank you to all the people at NCC Publishing; Ray Ellis, Debbie Sloane, and Mike Sloane, for all of their support and hard work to help me write and publish my first novel.

And thanks to Bud Campbell…for the use of his cabin where I could work in peace.